PANTHERA

My Tiger's Eyes

BY

BRIAN PAUL MILLER

ISBN: 978-0-615-83936-3 paperback edition
ISBN: 978-0-615-93024-4 e-book edition

In development: www.mytigerseyesbook.com

ACKNOWLEDGEMENTS:

Stephanie R— Thank you for all of the encouragement, thoughts, suggestions, and support. Thanks for taking me seriously when I said I was writing a book. Most of all, thanks for not laughing when you listened to my idea.
Patty R— Special thanks to you for the wonderful insight on your worldly travels.
Deb C— Extra special thanks for the attention to detail, grazie!
To all of my beta readers -I thank you for any and all of your input.

Most importantly— to everyone who works hard for their money and chooses to buy this book, and then takes time out of their busy lives to read it, I thank you. Namaste!

About myself— I have worked in the health care field for over twenty years as both a paramedic and a nurse. When not working or writing, I enjoy traveling. I am a native of Pennsylvania. This is my first novel.

"For every one book you read for entertainment…read two for knowledge." BPM

"Save the Tiger and all things endangered, especially peace!" BPM

This book is dedicated to
Abdulrahman al Aulaqi (Awlaki)
He never got to read it.
"Gone but not forgotten"

CHAPTER I

The tiger stops and crouches just inches above the grassy jungle floor. I do the same. I look around in the darkness trying to see what the tiger has spotted. The voices of two men arguing break the silence. Nocturnal insects of the jungle join in like an accompanying orchestra, but are probably discussing the developing situation that they too are watching. I follow the tiger's gaze and spot the men on the trail in front of us. One of the men looks angry and is pointing and hollering in a muffled yell at the other guy. I don't know what they are saying because I can't understand the language they are speaking. The tiger waits patiently watching the two men as do I. The animal is frozen still; I can't even see a twitch from the tiger's oversized muscles. Its ears are locked forward like radar dishes homed in on an unaware target. The angry man turns around and begins walking down the trail. I stay quiet on the jungle's edge. My heart should be pounding, but I feel as calm as the tiger. The angry one disappears from sight. The tiger creeps forward like a sloth and stops ten yards from the lone man on the trail. I can see a rifle slung over the unsuspecting man's right shoulder. I look at the tiger again. It has never taken its eyes off of the man. The man takes a few steps to his left unknowingly passing by the tiger. Suddenly, he stops and turns facing the tiger probably sensing something. He struggles to see in the thick black night, but the tiger has blended into the dark. Slowly, he slides the rifle off of his shoulder. He grips the weapon tightly and moves his head from side to side. In a blur, the tiger jumps up on its hind legs. The massive front paws come crashing down on the man's shoulders. He drops the rifle as the tiger buries its dagger like fangs into the side of his neck. The majestic creature lowers the lifeless body and begins to drag it off of the trail and into the jungle...

"Lily, it is time to wake up darlin'!"

I struggle to open my eyes in response to my mama's voice. It is good to snap out of another one of those dreams. They seem all too real. I thank my mama silently.

"Five more minutes, I beg you Abby!"

"I am your mama, not Abby, and in five more minutes we will have to walk to India."

And swim. That's a lot of water to fly over to get to India. What time is it? Slowly, the big green numbers on my alarm clock come into focus; it reads 3:30am. Either the alarm is broken, or like me, is not awake yet. I never heard it. I'm seventeen and this is summertime. I am thinking noon is always a good time to sleep to when there isn't any school.

"Lily!"

Mama again with a different tone. That means I should make an effort to roll out of my cozy bed.

"I'm gettin' up mama." I look at my dog lying next to me. "Mornin' Jax," I say rubbing Jackson's belly as he lets out an approving moan as I am trying to coax him out of bed. My Jack Russell is no dummy. He ain't movin'. Jax is thinking what I'm thinking: way too early to wake up for the day. Can't blame him for not wanting to get up. Smart dog. Time to get my last shower for two weeks. "I'm up and heading to the shower mama."

My mama, Abby Morgan, RN, part perfectionist, part worry-wart. I guess you have to be in that type of career. She thought it would be a good experience for me to go with her and my daddy to India on a medical mission. My daddy, James, or Dr. Jim, as his patients like to call him, agreed. Since I am considering a career in the medical field after high school, I figured why not? Most kids my age don't get to travel out of the country, and besides; it would be a great vacation. Definitely beats going to Panama City Beach again, not that there is anything wrong with PCB.

After a quick shower, I get dressed, say goodbye to my bed, and drag my luggage down to the car.

"Mama I am done with the shower, but you are joking about washing in a river for a month, right?" I hope she was kidding about that.

"Yes honey darlin' we are staying in a five-star luxury hotel." Judging by the amount of laughing coming from my mama and daddy in the kitchen, I'm thinking they're teasing me.

"Lily you will be fine. We have been there before and it wasn't bad at all."

Mama is still laughing so I am not so sure. I enter the kitchen. My mama is looking beautiful as ever with her shoulder length dirty blonde hair and blue green eyes. She still has her slender figure, but I grew an inch taller than her since last year.

"Thanks mama. I feel much better now, not."

Mp3 player, gum, makeup, nail polish, and mosquito repellent. I wonder if I should bring some tiger repellent also. Mama said there aren't any tigers where we will be. She said they didn't see any big animals last time except for the elephants. Oh, and extra batteries in case I can't recharge my mp3 player. I don't think mama will mind me bringing my DVD player and a few movies to past the time away. What else do I need? My daddy's list is pretty small. More gum. Fifteen days in India should require about four suitcases, I would think.

"Hey mama where are my sunglasses?" I just saw them. Now they're gone.

"Look up darlin', your glasses are on your head."

"Oh, yeah, duh, thanks."

Mama still grinning ear to ear at my expense. I'm laughing. Understandable, 'cause I ain't awake yet. No teenager in their right mind ought to be up this early unless they are just now going to sleep! Jackson is still thinking we are nuts as I drag my duffel bag to the kitchen door. I guess I should'a used the handle and wheels, but I am still half asleep.

Time to get my daily hug.

"Good morning daddy," as I brace for the coffee breath. Yuk! Daddy drinks three cups at home every day before he goes to his office. I don't get it. Maybe when you get my folk's ages you need coffee to wake up. Sounds 'bout right to me.

"Good morning darlin'," he responds in his usual cheery voice. His brown crew cut hair is just starting to recede by his temples with just a bit of gray by his ears. His dark brown eyes can sometimes pierce right through you making him look more serious when he needs to be. He is still as fit from his army days and is almost a foot taller than my mama.

We play soccer together when he is not busy with his medical practice. I am going to miss the first week of practice this summer. I think he is good enough to turn pro, but he is pretty humble and content to coach me while on our trip. Yesterday was the last summer league game for me until I get back from the trip. I am a midfielder on the Barbour County High soccer team. We placed third in the state AAA tournament last year and I think we can win states this year.

"Daddy, how much coffee do ya drink at work?" He always says just one cup, but I don't believe him one bit.

"One cup darlin'." Mama laughing again in the kitchen tells me she knows better.

I know I am going to miss Eufaula when we leave. The only other times I was out of Alabama was when I was little and my dad was stationed at Fort Bragg in North Carolina. He did some of his medical training there after becoming a doctor. He then was assigned to Fort Rucker near Enterprise Alabama. I remember his stories when he was a flight surgeon. Flying in helicopters sounds like a lot of fun. On occasion we fly in his single engine airplane. Dad calls it a tail-dragger 'cause of the little wheel at the back of the airplane instead of the front. I like it when I get to fly it, well, actually I am steering the plane, he flies it. We don't tell mama though. Too many questions.

We all usually go down to the beach at Panama City in Florida every summer too. Most of the time my best friend Ally Stephano comes down from Columbus Georgia with her mama, nurse Carilyn, and daddy, Doctor Nick, and we all go together. Our only concern is trying to stay out of trouble. Ally and I almost always find a way to attract too much attention to ourselves. Going to see Ally is the usual extent of my travel.

"Mama, can I bring Jax with us?" trying my luck one more time.

"Now honey darlin', I told you Jackson will probably not get along well enough with the elephants to bring him," smiling at my fool hearty last request, "that and I think there is quite a bit of paperwork to get him a passport."

Daddy is shaking his head as he pours his third cup of coffee. Jackson is now in the kitchen wondering why we're all awake and it's still dark out.

"Lily, there's some muffins I picked up from the store yesterday." Sounds like a good idea. I wonder if they have muffins in India. Mama says all the food is really spicy. Spicy muffins? Guess you wouldn't need coffee to wake up. Couple of spicy muffins to set your tongue on fire would do the trick.

"Thank ya mama." Ummm blueberry muffins this early in the morning isn't as bad as I thought. As I am giving mama a hug and kiss her cheek, Jax is jumping on my leg requesting to go outside. I grab Jackson and then head out to the front porch to eat.

It is already warm and the humidity thick. Welcome to Alabama. The porch swing invites me over and I accept as I admire the sky above Lake Eufaula which I can just make out above the trees. It looks like the sun is just starting to come up somewhere over Georgia. I think the lake has a different name, but I always refer to it as Lake Eufaula. It is a very big lake, though not as big as the Atlantic Ocean, which by the way, I am not looking forward to flying over. There is over three hundred miles of shoreline around the lake. The coolest part about it, is that it's not very wide which means you can see the state of Georgia on the other side. Our place is just off of highway 30. Dad bought five acres here off of his uncle after he got out of the army. Jackson approves of it also because he has a huge fenced in play area. He is now at my feet wanting to get up on the swing, but his little legs are too short. So I lift him up and sneak him a piece of muffin. Jax's tail is still wagging at me saying I better give him the rest of the muffin. As usual I give in and he wins.

Here comes my dad carrying my bag heading to the mini-van looking excited.

"Lily, ya bout' ready?"

Jax jumps down off my lap with his little tail going a hundred miles an hour.

"Yes'm daddy, all ready."

Dad heads to the mini-van and Jax follows, tail still wagging. I swear it never stops. His tail is so short that his butt shakes more than his tail does.

"Morning y'all," I hear coming from a familiar voice walking up the driveway in front of the house.

"Good morning Uncle Jake."

I am always happy to see my aunt and uncle; well they are actually my dad's aunt and uncle, who have come over to see us off. It's convenient to have them live next door about an acre away. It was part of Uncle Jake's land that he sold off to my dad at a good price of course. Uncle Jake is my grandfather's only living brother. I lost all of my grandparents when I was really young. It is something my folks have in common that I think has given them an unbreakable relationship over the years since. Aunt Bess and Uncle Jake have always been like my surrogate grandparents to me. Uncle Jake has the bushiest white mustache that I don't think has been trimmed in quite some time. He is just a bit pudgy around the waistline from Aunt Bess' home cookin'. A little extra cornbread at each meal I suppose.

"Good morning Aunt Bess," I say as I greet her while taking note of her gazing at my sunglasses. She is somewhat thinner than Uncle Jake, but her hair is about the same color as his mustache. Less cornbread in her diet, for sure.

"Bit dark out for them shades there honey, ain't it?" Sensing the sarcasm I pull the glasses down onto my face and give her a big kiss.

"The view is much better now," I respond trying not to laugh too hard. I have to be nice to them. They are taking care of Jackson while we are away.

"Wish I could slip Jax in to my carry-on bag."

After taking a sip of his coffee, my uncle hands me a rolled up wad of cash.

"Lily honey, here is some spending money for ya," he says while taking another sip from his oversized Roll Tide mug. "You will have to exchange it for the local currency and then ya can buy one of them pretty and really bright dresses they wear in India."

"Thank you so much Uncle Jake. I think they are called a sari. I'll be sure to get ya one too." I give him a big hug. Aunt Bess and Uncle Jake are two of the nicest people I have ever met. Real sweethearts that would do anything for you. I hate it when they give me money 'cause they ain't rich by no means, Uncle Jake inherited his land. They even used to drive down to Enterprise and watch my games when I played for the Wildcats. We've been up here in Eufaula for almost two years now and my aunt and uncle still come to all my games. I love having them there even though Aunt Bess can get a little bit loud at times. Kind'a fun to have an enthusiastic number one fan. I am really going to miss them even though we won't be gone that long.

"Morning. Y'all all here to help us pack?" mama says as she hands her suitcase to Uncle Jake knowing he is going to have to part with his coffee.

I was wrong. Carrying a giant mug of coffee and suitcase, Uncle Jake heads for the mini-van. Didn't spill one drop. My dad and Uncle Jake finish loading the luggage in to the mini-van and head back to the porch.

"Abby, ya dint know I was that talented, huh?"

He shows the mug to mama and she realizes she'd been had, 'cause he drank it all.

"Oh, very funny wise guy." Mama shakes her head. "Hey'a Aunt Bess, tell me once more, where did ya find this sweetheart of a jokester?"

Jax and Aunt Bess are looking amused sitting on the porch swing.

"Well Abby darling, I found him at wise guys-r-us, but wouldn't trade him for nothing, now that he's housebroken."

We all enjoy a good laugh at Uncle Jake's expense. Even he's laughing.

Dad looks at his watch and shakes Uncle Jake's hand. I realize it must be time to get going.

"Jim y'all be careful and have a safe trip. Don't be getn' too drunk on them there coconuts."

Daddy's turning red with laughter.

"Naw, Uncle Jake, I think you got coconuts confused with some other kind of fruit." He lets go of Uncle Jake's hand and gives Aunt Bess a great big hug. "Thank ya for watching the place and taking care of Jackson. Don't let him tell ya what to do. Remember no snacks after eight and in bed by nine." Jax is looking attentive after hearing his name.

"Jim ya know them's my rules for your uncle. Me and Jackson will go to bed after some late night television and late night snacking." We all enjoy another laugh at Uncle Jakes expense and then hugs all 'round.

"Abby, y'all heading straight to Columbus?" Uncle Jake is now finishing up Aunt Bess' coffee.

"Nope. We have to stop by the hospital and pick up the medical supplies that were donated for the trip. After that we'll head up to Columbus and then onto Atlanta."

Mama is starting to look depressed because she hates to leave Aunt Bess and Uncle Jake. They are such good people. The kind you only meet every now and then.

All my things are in the mini-van so I pick Jax up and give him a big squeeze and kiss on the top of his head. He ain't looking too pleased right now because he knows we are going away for a little while. I've seen his look before. I head into the house and give him some of his favorite treats. He perks up a bit. One more big hug and I tell Jax to behave for Aunt Bess and Uncle Jake.

"Jackson, you are in charge now. Make sure Uncle Jake behaves, ok?" Everyone is laughing and we say are good-bye's and jump in the mini-van. "Oh, and Uncle Jake I am going to bring you back some sandals from India, so that you don't have to wear them brown and tan cowboy boots all the time."

"But Lily darling, you know I am on a monthly allowance and Miss Bessy here won't increase it."

"Aunt Bess, are ya sure you and Uncle Jake don't want to come with us?" my dad asks as he starts up the mini-van.

"Jimmy, that sounds like a good idea. Your Uncle Jake can stay here and do the dog sittin', house sittin', and whatever other kind of sittin' needs to be done because you know that is his specialty, sittin'."

We keep laughing.

"Now get out of here and y'all have some fun. Bye," says Aunt Bess.

"Bye. See y'all in a couple of weeks," mama replies.

"Bye bye," I shout as I blow kisses to the both of them.

CHAPTER II

The hospital is not that far from our house. We drive down our long drive way and make a right turn on to highway 30. A couple of miles down the road my dad turns on to highway 431. There's hardly any other traffic out this early in the morning. Mama is checking her packing list and looking around the car trying to see if we forgot anything.

"I'm here mama, what more do ya need?" She sends a big smile my way and keeps checking her list. I am already missing Jax. It's still dark out, but I can tell that the sun is trying to make its daily appearance. The day must be over by now in India. The time zone thing always confuses me. Mama said it is like a ten hour difference. India is ahead of us here in the USA, so I guess the sun is probably still up at the place we are going to.

Dad starts to slow down as we head in to Eufaula. There's a light on at the Waffle House and a car in the parking lot, but most of the other stores are still closed. The van is going even slower now as highway 431 becomes Main Street Eufaula. No need to get a speeding ticket from Eufaula PD, although dad knows all the officers and they would probably just say good morning and have a nice day Doctor Morgan.

Eufaula ,which is pronounced u-fall-la, has a very historic main street that is lit up at night. This gives you a chance to take in the scenery of the beautiful historic mansions. In fact, the whole town has hundreds of registered historic buildings. The most popular is the Shorter Mansion with its huge white columns across the front of the mansion. Dad said it is over one hundred years old. Every year there is a pilgrimage through Eufaula to tour the historic homes. My mama, Aunt Bess, Uncle Jake, and I went this past April. It was my second time and I enjoy seeing people dressed up in period clothing from the past. Ally is going to come down this year at Christmas time and we are going to dress up and attend the old fashioned historic Christmas tour. I can't wait; it should be fun. Aunt Bess is helping us make our own gowns.

A lot of people attend these events, but there is always something going on in Eufaula. Dad and Doctor Nick always take part in the fishing tournaments since they say Lake Eufaula is the "Bass Fishing Capital of the World." The town, whose name comes from one of the Creek Indian tribes, the "Eufaula's," has come a long way since the lake was created from building a dam on the Chattahoochee River. I love that name: Chat-ta-hoo-chee. We continue to drive down past the historic homes and turn on to Washington Street and pull up to the hospital emergency room.

"G'mornin nurse Shay, we've come to pillage for supplies for our trip." Daddy is joking with some of the staff he gets to work with when he is moonlighting in the ER.

"Doc ya know we are going to have to inventory that stuff when ya leave to make sure you don't steal too much, but don't worry yourself none, we'll send ya the bill." Shay teasing with her usual southern charm. She is one of my favorite nurses in the ER. "Hey there Miss Lily, ya better keep an eye on your daddy there and make sure he doesn't take more than what he can fit in his pockets."

"Well Miss Shay, I'll do my best, but daddy says he has some boxes sitting 'round here already packed." Miss Shay leads us down the hall to the doctor's room. There are four boxes with a list of the contents taped to the outside of the box. The box closest to me has MEDICATIONS and IV FLUIDS written on it. I go to lift it, but just as I get to it, nurse Wayland steps in and volunteers. Since he is stronger than me, and I don't want to be rude by arguing who will lift the heavy stuff, I oblige him.

"Thank you sooo much Wayland. I dint wanna break a nail." Mama throws me a look that says be nice to Wayland or I will have to carry the heavy box, though I could tell she wants to laugh.

"Not a problem Miss Lily. Wish I was going with y'all." Feeling bad 'cause Wayland is grunting while lifting the box; I grab another box that is labeled BANDAGES-DRESSINGS-TAPE-KLING. Below that it has BP CUFFS-STETHOSCOPES-GLUCOMETER-STERILE INSTRUMENTS. Just as I guessed, much lighter. Dad follows carrying the box with SYRINGES and NEEDLES written on the side. Mama grabs the last box with the TRAUMA KITS-PULSE OX-SUTURE KITS and heads with us to the mini-van. I think she is waiting to get outside then laugh. She is probably going to get embarrassed by me a few more times on this trip. Mama gets flustered when I embarrass her.

Dad lifts open the tailgate by pressing the button on his key ring and we put the boxes in next to the suitcases. Mama said Dr. Nick has some hard boxes we can transfer all the supplies in to so they will not get damaged during the trip to India.

"You guys need a hand?"

"Hey there Doc Lacefield," mama says excitedly as she gives him a good morning hug. "Not unless ya wanna pay for our flight."

"Well I would, but my wife wouldn't let me take my wallet to work," as Doc Lacefield pretends to search for his wallet in his light blue scrub pants. "You guys want some coffee instead?" Doctor Lacefield talks funny 'cause he's from the north, but moved here for our fine weather. Dr. Lacefield is about fifty with balding black hair and a well-trimmed black mustache. I must be two inches taller than him. My daddy ain't never turned down a cup, so I know what's coming next.

"Elliot, you're speaking our language." Now daddy is grinning cheek to cheek. "How's bout one for the road?"

I am right again. Still never turned down a cup of coffee. Hum. Mama gets to work with Doctor Lacefield and his wife, Janelle, in the hospital a few times a month. Janelle, who is from Alabama, met Doc Lacefield at medical school. She is one of the obstetricians in town.

"You guys going up to Atlanta now?" Doc Lacefield is sipping his coffee and admiring all of our luggage and boxes sitting in the back of our mini-van.

"Naw Elliot. We'll be stopping in Columbus first to pick up Nick and Carilyn and the donated supplies from their hospital." Daddy takes a drink of his fresh cup of coffee.

"You guys are going as part of Doctors Helping the World, right?"

Doc Lacefield takes another drink of his coffee while I'm thinking about barfing. It's not that I don't like coffee; I just usually stop at one cup. My dad is done with his sip and explains that Doc Nick and Carilyn are actually founding members of Doctors Helping the World. DHW is a non-profit one hundred percent volunteer medical organization that provides free medical care around the world and here at home. The Indian couple that we will be staying with in India, are the other founding members. The organization currently has three-hundred and thirty-five physicians, nurses, and other medical personnel from all over the world. There have been DHW volunteers that are not trained in anything and just provide an extra set of hands to help out which is always appreciated. There have been college students, retired people, and everyone in between.

"Elliot thanks for the brew. I'll finish this mug on the road. Tell Miss Janelle we'll see her when we get back in a couple of weeks." Dad climbs behind the wheel in the van as he takes another drink of coffee before buckling up his seatbelt. Mama gives Doc Lacefield a hug goodbye. He is her favorite doctor at the hospital.

"Y'all take care now, ya hear," Shay says speaking in her lovely southern twang. "And don't be bringing back any elephants, monkeys, Duengue Fever, or anything else to Eufaula that you ain't supposed to. Keep an eye on her Miss Abby."

"Oh, now that's not a problem. I'll keep Miss Lily in line. You just have some of your apple pie and biscuits ready for us when we get back Miss Shay. Bye y'all." Mama waves as she walks toward the van.

"Nurse Shay gimme some lovin." I throw my arms around her and kiss her cheek making her blush in front of everyone who has come outside from the emergency room to see us off. "Now I wouldn't dream of it." Laughing my way over to the van. "Bye bye Doc Lacefield. Bye Wayland. Bye Miss Shay."

The door on the van is open and I jump in and start searching for my mp3 player. My backpack is like a black hole, but after some digging around, the mp3 player is finally in my ears playing some music for the short ride to Columbus. After a few more waves goodbye, the door shuts after dad pushes a couple of buttons and we pull out of the hospital parking lot and turn left onto Main Street. Dream land is calling me and I can feel myself starting to doze off. I hope it's not the same dream. We aren't even past the doughnut shop yet. I can't wait to see Ally. She is probably still in bed. Lucky girl. Jax is probably still in bed too. Lucky boy.

CHAPTER III

"Watch out Jim!"

I wake up hearing my mama screaming. Daddy is slamming on the brakes and swerves the mini-van off the road and onto the grass. We are bouncing up and down roughly. Out through the windshield I see a car's brake lights going end over end down the road and then disappearing in to the trees. I catch a glimpse of a deer running the opposite way to the other side of the highway and off in to the woods. Its white tail up in the air, feeling pretty lucky, I am sure. There is a violent deafening crunching metal sound coming from where the car entered the trees. The van's headlights catch what looks like a person flying through the air in to the brush. This has to be a dream, but then I realize I am gripping the back of my mama's seat headrest. My hands hurt from trying to brace myself. Dad is still trying to get control of the van, but is skidding in the wet early morning grass. He finally gets the van to stop about ten feet from the torn up chunks of grass and brush left behind by the car we were following. There is a strong smell of burning rubber and gasoline in the air. A small cloud of dust is settling around the car. Mama asks if everyone is ok and myself and daddy say we are. My mp3 player flew off my lap and into the front of the van. Dad grabs his flashlight from the glove box and tells mama to call 9-1-1 to report the accident and that he his checking for injuries. I keep thinking this is a heck of a dream and reach around for Jax, realizing I am not in bed; I ask mama what I should do. My heart is pounding like it will blow up any given minute. I see my dad shine his flashlight into the rear window of the wrecked car, which is lying on its passenger side looking for victims.

"Lily baby, I will open the hatch up. I want you to grab the box marked trauma kits and open it, ok?" There is a sense of urgency in her voice. She is in emergency nurse mode. She dials 9-1-1 and the operator answers.

"9-1-1. What is your emergency?"

Mama replies, trying to slow her voice, but is calm enough to relay what just happened to the operator.

"There is a one vehicle accident, rollover, my husband is Doctor Morgan. He is checking for injuries."

"What is your location Abby? How many victims?" There is a look of surprise, and relief, on her face as I get out of the van and run to the back to get the box.

"Hey Darbie! We are about three miles north of Pittsview on highway 431 in the wooded area south of Seale. Jim is checking for victims." Mama gets out of the van and comes around back to help me. We locate the box marked "trauma kits" and open it. Darbie our neighbor who lives across the street from us is still on the phone. She has worked at the county comm center for ten years. Always a professional.

"Ok Abby, advise when you find out how many victims and injuries. My partner is on the line with Alabama Highway Patrol. They have units responding. I am dispatching EMS, fire, and rescue from Pittsview and Seale." Mama keeps the phone in her hand. I am wide awake now and shaking a little bit not knowing what to expect. This, I think, is a bit beyond my first aid training at the high school, but I hope I can recall some of my prep for the trip to India.

"Abby!" My dad is shouting. It sounds bad. "The car is empty. There are two victims. One ejected from the vehicle. Possible femur and tib-fib fractures, conscious. Second victim, also ejected, is unconscious, pinned between trees and the vehicle. We'll need a helicopter!" Now I am shaking even more. I wish I was back home in bed, but I know these people need my help.

"Ok Jim!" Mama puts the cell phone to her ear even though the speaker phone is on. Not a good sign. "Darbie?" Mama points to the box marked trauma kits and signals for me to take one to my dad.

"Abby I overheard what Jim said. We are dispatching aeromedical and we'll advise responding units of the victims and situation."

"Thanks Darbie. I am going to help Jim. I will call you back if there are any changes in their conditions." Mama grabs the other trauma kit and follows me down to the car. There are pieces of the car thrown all over. A crunching noise is coming from under my feet. Looking down, I realize I am walking on shattered glass. It looks like most of the windows in the car are broken. Someone's tennis shoe is lying on the highway. One of the victims is moaning loudly. It's the one that was thrown out of the car when it was rolling over. She is about thirty feet away from the vehicle lying between some small trees and high grass.

"Lily. Drop that trauma kit here. You and your mama go help that patient that was thrown from the car." Dad is all doctor now. I know these people are in good hands.

"Ok Dad!" He takes the trauma kit from me.

I run up to the other person. Her right leg is twisted a way that it shouldn't be twisted. There is just enough daylight now to make out what looks like blood soaking through the bottom of her pants. I can also see cuts and scrapes on her face and arms. Her shirt is torn across the belly.

"Hi. My name is Lily. What's yours? We are going to help you. My mama is a nurse and my dad is a doctor. He's helping your friend by the car."

"Deeeeeerrrrrrr...." She's still moaning.

"What? I don't understand. What is your name?" I ask again.

"Deer. We swerved to miss a deeerrrrr.....where am I? Who are you?" My mama arrives and kneels down on the other side of the patient. She starts asking questions and is shining a mini-flashlight over the patient's face.

"Mama, I think she is confused. She doesn't know her name or where she is." I stare at her hair which looks like it has red hair gel caked in it. Who uses red hair gel?

"I know Lily. She probably has bumped her head. Go ahead and kneel behind her head." Mama starts to do an exam. "Lily, I want you to place a hand on each side of her head to keep her from turning her head and injuring her neck."

There are sirens approaching in the distance. I keep looking at her hair which seems to be covered everywhere with the thick crimson hair gel glistening from the flashlight. I think that is odd and then realize it is blood not hair gel. I get a chill despite the heat of the early morning air. I try to avoid touching it. Mama is talking to the patient and feeling about her head, face, and neck. Working her way down the patient's body, she stops at the belly, the patient moans loudly. Then continues to her hips and both legs. She then feels way under both sides of her ribs trying to feel the patient's back.

"Jim! We have a rigid abdomen, positive right femur fracture, and bilateral tib-fib fractures. Looks like she was knocked out too. She is confused and slow to respond."

Mama then shines the flashlight into the patient's eyes and says to herself that the pupils are equal and reacting. I'm not sure what that means, but I nod and say ok. There are flashing lights coming from just down the highway. The sirens are getting louder. A highway patrol car pulls up just behind and to the side of the mini-van and turns on a spotlight on the patrol car, shinning it on the wrecked car and my dad. The sky is filled with the emergency lights turning it and the trees red and blue. The trooper yells out that fire and EMS are two minutes away. He starts to light flares placing them on the ground, working his way back from the crash scene. The driving lane is blocked off from any other traffic that might come down the highway. I can hear the trooper talking into his radio microphone clipped to his shirt. There are more flashing lights and sirens coming down the highway. My dad is yelling for me.

"Lily!" my dad yells. "Abby take care of that patient." I am starting to sweat, but I realize I'm not shaking as bad as I was. "Lily I need your help!" my dad yells again as I run to him.

A fire truck pulls up behind the wrecked car. Several fire fighters jump out and start pulling gear off the truck. The reflective stripes on their helmets and coats are bright white with all the lights shining on them. It looks like they are plugged in to a receptacle. One of them is reaching for a small firehose attached to the side of the firetruck. ENGINE 3 is written across the back of his coat in big letters. In the middle it says PITTSVIEW. Below that it has RICKERT in smaller letters. Another fireman comes over to me and my dad. He has a white helmet on. It says ASSISTANT CHIEF across the front. EDMONDS is written on the bottom. A "star-of-life" with the letters E-M-T is on the left chest of his coat. The star-of-life looks like a blue "X" with a line down the middle of the "X" that has a snake on it. I have seen those before. It means he has some medical training.

"Lily, grab some Latex gloves out of the trauma kit and put them on so you don't get any blood on your hands." Looking down, I can see that my dad already has gloves on and is holding the patient's head the way my mama had me hold the other patient.

"Lily, take over holding his head for me." We switch our hands so that I am holding the head, concentrating, trying not to turn his head and injure his neck. This patient is a guy who doesn't seem too much older than me. He is not talking. In fact, he is breathing funny. His legs are under the car which is on its side. The roof of the car is contorted lying against a large green pine tree. There are broken branches lying all over, including on top of the patient. His left side is up against the pine tree. He is stuck between the tree and the car. There is enough of his head sticking out to hold his neck. Blood mixed with pine needles is running down the left side of his face.

"Daddy, he looks pretty bad."

"He is in bad shape Lily, but we'll do the best we can for him." Daddy looks up to talk to the fireman. "Hey Chief. I'm Doctor Morgan from Eufaula. We have two victims. Victim one: male, early twenties, ejected and pinned by the vehicle, head injury, blown right pupil, agonal respirations, fractured left ribs. We're going to need air bags to lift the car. Victim two: female, eighteen to twenty, ejected from vehicle about thirty feet, head injury, internal abdominal injury, leg fractures. What is the E-T-A on the helicopter?"

The fire chief says something that sounds like "sheeeet" and starts talking in to his radio. "Engine 3 chief to Aeromedical One...." He waves to some of his firemen and asks them to get the airbags from the rescue truck which just pulled up behind the other fire truck. "Aeromedical One to Engine 3 chief, go ahead." The chief grabs his radio again. "Aeromedical One, what is your ETA and can ya take two critical patients?" The chief lets go of the button on the side of his microphone. "Engine 3 we are seven minutes out. We only have room for one critical patient." I can swear the chief says something that sounds like "sheeeet" and then replies ok. Daddy cracks a little bit of a smile after hearing the chief's extra vocabulary. Chief Edmonds turns to one of the other firemen and tells him to notify the Trooper that we will be landing Aeromedical One on the highway in front of the crash scene and gives him the ETA.

There are more fire trucks here now. Some of the fire fighters are wearing different color fire coats. SFD is written on the back of some of them. They are probably from the Seale Fire Department. One coat has Engine 1 on it. Another has Truck 1 on the back. I have no clue what it all means, but I'm glad they are all here. A fire fighter wearing a tan coat with yellow stripes, reflecting from the lights, comes over to us.

"Taylor...Rescue 5...I'll take over c-spine for ya."

He reaches for the patient's neck and puts his hands on top of mine. Dad says it's ok and explains c-spine is short for cervical spine stabilization and I slowly pull my hands out. I glance over toward mama. There are about eight or nine fire fighters kneeling and standing by her and the other patient. One of them has a blue coat on with the word PARAMEDIC written on the back. Someone is holding an orange backboard. There is a green oxygen tank lying next to the patient. Mama is putting an oxygen mask, with a clear inflated bag attached to it, on the patient's face. Looking the other way, I can see that there are three ambulances here now. One of them, white with blue and red stripes, slowly drives past our van and stops next to the other patient. I can still hear her cry out occasionally. Someone has placed a hard collar around her neck, I guess to protect it from getting injured. They slowly roll her on to her side and place the backboard behind her and lower it back to the grass being careful not to hurt her. One of the paramedics is fastening straps around her. I can see a fireman standing next to her holding an IV bag.

"What's your name?" I look back the other way. It's the fireman in the tan coat.

"It's Lily...Taylor from Rescue 5."

He smiles at me.

"Well Miss Lily we have to ask y'all to step back a bit so we don't drop the car on your pretty toes."

My daddy replies before I get a chance to, probably thinking Taylor was going to ask me out.

"Thank ya Mr. Taylor from Rescue 5. We'll be right over here getting some equipment ready for when y'all have him free from under the vehicle."

My dad grabs the trauma kit and we move back away from the vehicle. We start pulling out stuff from the kit. Daddy grabs a small rolled up case that says INTUBATION on the side. He then grabs another package that has CHEST DECOMPRESSION KIT labeled on it. Lastly he reaches in the kit and pulls out another case that says RAPID TRACHEOTOMY KIT on the top of it. He sets these items aside and turns to watch the rescue.

"Hey there Doc, what ya got?" It's a female wearing a blue paramedic coat and blue helmet.

"Well hello Annabelle. I can't get at his airway to bag him effectively. Partial obstruction, I think. I tried the bag valve mask, but couldn't get any air in to him. We're going to have to trach him as soon as we get him free from under the car. It sounds like he has pneumothorax or hemothorax too and we'll have to pop that chest."

"Ok Doc. I'll be set'n up my equipment. Who's this young lady?" The paramedic hands me two IV bags to hold.

"I'm Lily. Doc's my dad. I can spike these for ya. I know how. We're heading to India today on a medical mission."

"Sounds great Lily."

The paramedic hands me some IV tubing. I take one of the packages and tear it open. Holding one of the bags of IV fluid upside down, I remove the cap from the spike on the tubing and slowly insert it into the bag. I then turn the bag over, squeeze the clear plastic chamber on the tubing, and then slowly open up the roller clamp. The IV fluid starts to run down the tubing and I wait until I see a few drops come out of the end, then turn off the fluid by rolling the clamp the other way. I check the tubing; there's no air bubbles. I am surprised I remembered and happy to help. Another person in a blue helmet and coat takes the IV from me and I spike the second bag.

"Nice job Lily."

Annabelle takes the second IV from me. The car is starting to move up in the air. The noise all around us is deafening. Generators are running. Fire trucks are running. Flashing lights are everywhere. I can smell the pungent sulfur from the flares burning on the road. One of the vehicles has the PA system on. Someone is calling Aeromedical One.

"Engine 3 incident command Aeromedical One ETA four minutes."

Another Fire Chief in a white helmet grabs his radio and announces, "roger Aeromedical One. Landing zone is thirty meters north of crash scene. Forty meters by forty meters. You will be landing on highway 431, paved, marked with flares and orange panels, winds from the west at three knots." The chief puts the radio back in his coat pocket.

"Aeromedical One, roger, we have the scene in site."

My dad is back over by the patient. They have the patient freed from under the vehicle and he is lying on top of a yellow back board.

Annabelle is down by his chest and I can see a long needle in her hand. She has his shirt cut completely off and is counting down the ribs on his left side. She then pushes the needle into his chest. There is the sound of what sounds like blowing air coming from the needle Annabelle just pushed into the chest. It lasts for a second or two. I cringe a little bit having never seen that done before. Annabelle then asks for a one way valve. The other paramedic hands it to her and they tape it to the patient's chest. There is a massive whoosh of air as the helicopter flies over the top of us, goes about another fifty yards, stops, turns to the left and then settles down on to the highway.

"Aeromedical One on the ground."

The comm center replies, "10-4 Aeromedical One, on the ground, 0545."

I look over to see how my mama is doing with the other patient. They have the patient up on a litter and are pushing it over to one of the ambulances. Mama is walking along side of the litter carrying two IV bags. The paramedics and EMT's line up the head end of the litter and start to push it inside the ambulance. One of the fire fighters bends down and lifts up the wheels on the litter as it starts to slide inside the back of the ambulance. A paramedic at the foot end of the litter struggles a bit with the weight of the patient and litter. Two fire fighters are helping to lift from the sides of the litter. Mama hands the IV bags to someone in the ambulance and she climbs up inside.

I look back at my dad again. He is bending down by the patient's head, but off to the side. Taylor from Rescue 5 is continuing to hold the patient's head and neck. Dad takes something from the rapid tracheotomy kit. It looks like a syringe with some kind of blade attached to the end of it. Annabelle scrubs the neck with some solution to clean the area. My dad is feeling around on the patient's neck. He stops his left hand and with his right hand inserts the blade into the patient's neck. After pulling back on the syringe, he slides a plastic piece off the syringe and in to the front of the patient's neck. Annabelle disconnects the syringe and attaches a bag valve mask to the round plastic piece left in the neck. Dad looks down at the chest and seems pleased for the moment. The fire fighters and paramedics finish securing straps around the patient so he doesn't fall off the backboard. Taylor applies a cervical collar around the patient's neck. Annabelle is still squeezing the bag valve mask to give the patient oxygen. Taylor and an EMT put rigid orange blocks on both sides of the patient's head and strap them in place. The head and neck are stable now and Taylor is no longer holding them with his hands.

The flight crew from Aeromedical One, wearing burgundy flight suits with white reflective stripes down the side, walk past me over to the patient. One of them is carrying a small metal litter and throws me a look as to say, "why are you standing here wearing shorts and Crimson Tide flip flops?" I kind of nod back at him saying, "yep I know." My dad tells them who he is and what injuries he has found so far. Then relays the treatments to the flight nurse. I know she is the flight nurse 'cause it's on her leather name badge on her left chest. The flight nurse kneels down beside the patient and does a quick head-to-toe exam. She tells my dad that if the patient has a blood pressure then she will take both patients in the helicopter to the trauma center. Dad is nodding ok. Taylor from Rescue 5 squats down by the patient's head and grabs the back board on both sides while another fire fighter squats down by the patient's feet and grabs the back board at that end. Together they lift up the patient and one of the flight crew slides their litter under the back board. More straps are applied around the patient. The other flight crew member, who I can now read his name tag and it says Flight Medic, attaches an EKG to the patient's chest. Done with that, he hands Annabelle a blood pressure cuff and she puts it around the patient's arm.

The flight medic presses a button on the blood pressure machine and after a few seconds calls out, "92 over 64."

The flight nurse tells dad that they will take both patients. He says great. Some of the fire fighters bring over the bigger ambulance litter with the wheels on it. Taylor, who I am starting to admire his strength, once again, with help, lifts the patient up on to the other litter. Even more straps are put around the patient. Four fire fighters, Annabelle, and Taylor head toward the helicopter pushing the litter carefully, so as not to trip over the brush or car parts. The helicopter's rotor blades are still turning and the smell of aviation fuel catches my nose reminding me of being at the county airport with my dad.

"You did good Lily." I turn to see my dad standing next to me.

"Thanks daddy. I didn't do too much. Ya think he'll make it?" He grabs my hand and we start to walk over to the ambulance mama is in.

"You did good. You never panicked. Sometimes remaining calm is as important as anything else we do." Dad is shaking his head. "It's hard to say. He has some serious injuries, but we did everything for him here that we could. Let's go see how mom is doing."

We watch the other patient being loaded in to the helicopter. Dad leans in to the other ambulance and tells my mama that the helicopter will be taking this patient in a minute. I can hear the girl talking more clearly now. Both of the patients are not much older than me. I start to wonder about their parents and the fact that they don't know they have kids who were in a very bad accident. It wasn't their fault. It just happened.

"Lily honey, you ok? Mama climbs out of the ambulance and gives me a hug.

"Yeah mama, I'm fine. Just didn't expect any of this. We should have been eating breakfast with Ally, Carilyn, and Doctor Nick by now."

The girl patient is loaded in to the helicopter and the doors are shut. The flight crew is moving around in the back of the helicopter connecting more EKG wires to the girl patient and hanging up IV bags.

"Aeromedical One en route to trauma center, five souls onboard," blasts over the firetruck's speakers.

The helicopter engine starts to get louder and the rotor blades are spinning faster. The wind from the blades turning, start to push me backward. I have to squint my eyes and turn away as small pieces of dust and dirt pelt my face and legs, stinging a bit. Wearing shorts seemed like a good idea when I put them on this morning. Who knew? The helicopter lifts off from the ground and turns to the left once more facing the way it came from. Aeromedical One flies over us again increasing in altitude. I watch as it becomes smaller in the distance hoping the patients onboard will be ok. There is a sense of calmness as now just the fire truck's engines running are the only sound. Some of the fire fighters and EMT's have their heavy protective coats off and are gathering up equipment. The car is back on its wheels. They must have done that when the helicopter took off. Annabelle comes over to us and we follow her over to her ambulance. Dad tells her what supplies we used from our trauma kit and she graciously replaces them for us.

"Miss Lily, do ya wanna come work for me when ya get back from your trip? We could use another pair of steady hands?"

Caught off guard a bit. I wasn't expecting that. Now I'm sure I am blushing, "well Miss Annabelle, I would love to, but I think some prince charming is going to sweep me off my feet in India."

"The offer still stands anytime you want it." Annabelle shakes my dad's hand and tells mama thanks for their help. "Y'all be careful on your trip now, ya hear?"

"We will. Thanks for the quick response to the crash." Dad grabs our trauma kits and puts them in the mini-van.

Taylor walks over and gets a quick 'goodbye, nice to meet ya' in before dad and mama notices.

"Bye Taylor, nice to meet you too." I head to the van and climb in to the back seat. "Hey mama, I hope the rest of the trip isn't going to be like this."

"Oh Lily honey, no I don't think so. We'll have a good time. It will be a wonderful experience for you."

CHAPTER IV

As, we drive away from the crash scene, I can't help thinking about the two patients and their families. There is still quite a bit of sweat on my face and forehead and my heart is still beating fast. My parents are used to that kind of stuff, I guess, as much as someone can be. They have the training and education along with years of experience. At times I wanted to go hide in the van until it was over. I really felt like I didn't know what I was supposed to do. Almost like a bystander watching from a distance. I was there, but I wasn't there. This trip is not going to be a vacation, but at least I now know I can help out if needed. Dad said they didn't have any emergencies last time they went to India. He hoped I wouldn't be bored once we got over there and started doing routine treatments. The adrenaline is keeping me awake for the time being. Still feeling a bit jittery I reach for my mp3 player, but then I remember what happened the last time I put on some music and tried to sleep. I decide to leave it where it is and just try to relax for the rest of the short ride to Columbus.

It's not much longer before we arrive in Phenix City and turn right to go over the bridge in to Columbus Georgia. My dad and Doctor Nick first met while attending the Army's Airborne school at Fort Benning next to Columbus. It was after that that they both went to Fort Bragg which is where I first met Ally. She is a year older than me and a sweetheart. Doc Nick and Carilyn would like her to go to medical school, but like me our first love is art history. Our parents said we can take art history classes in college, but it would be difficult to make a career out of it because the art history jobs are hard to find. Ally and I dream of working in one of the major museums in Europe and possibly teaching at some university. I don't know what to do yet, possibly major in nursing or pre-med and take some art history classes as a minor, or just go for it all and major in art. Ally will be starting college when we get back from India. Going to school in Europe would be awesome too. Wait until Ally hears what happened on the way up to their house.

Dad pulls in to Doc Nick's driveway and Ally comes running out of the house causing her long blonde hair to swing side to side. She is almost out of breath when she reaches me. Her ocean blue eyes are open wide.

"What happen to y'all? My mama said y'all was in an accident. Everyone all right? Your van looks ok."

I give Ally a hug and begin to explain, "Yes we're all fine. It was a car in front of us that daddy was following. It flipped over trying to miss a deer. I was sleeping. It was a guy and a girl a little bit older than us. They was hurt pretty bad. Daddy and mama took good care of them 'till the ambulance got there. I got to prep some IV's for the paramedics. There was this really cute fire fighter named Taylor who I think was hitting on me. I think I got some glass stuck in my flip flops."

"Wow, what a start to your vacation! Taylor? Did ya get his number?" Ally is giving me all her attention now since she and her boyfriend just broke up.

"Y'all two need to concentrate on school, not boys, and Lily took care of the patients along with us. She did real good."

"Thank ya mama, and yes mama, we know, school is first." We start to laugh and go inside to see Miss Carilyn and Doc Nick. The house smells like freshly made coffee. They have even more luggage than we do and next to them are hard plastic blue containers filled with medical supplies. "Good mornin' Miss Carilyn and Doctor Nick." They both give me a big hug and offer some cappuccino for the drive up to Atlanta. I gladly accept. Doctor Nick's full beard tickles the side of my face. It matches his dark hair which is in a ponytail hanging about half way down his back. Just as fit as my daddy, but more of a free spirit, I guess. Carilyn is as radiant as ever. Brown shoulder length hair and as tall as Ally. She was a model before she became a nurse. Both are in their mid-forty's.

"Now tell us about your adventure on the way up to see us. Your mama told a bit of the story when she called on her cell to say y'all be running late."

Sipping my freshly poured French vanilla cappuccino; I start to explain what had happened.

"I have never been part of anything like that before Doc Nick. There were fire trucks everywhere. Ambulances. Highway Patrol. I even talked to the flight crew from Aeromedical One. It was exciting, but I just hope the guy and girl are going to be ok." Half of my cappuccino is gone already, but the doughnut shop aroma of the house has me wide awake.

"Your mama and daddy said you did a very good job and they were proud to have you with them." Doc Nick hands me a pink stethoscope, with a matching blood pressure cuff, and pink scissors, the big ones that you see around the hospital or on the hips of EMT's. Carilyn comes over to me and hands me a pink mini flashlight.

"Congratulations on your introduction to medicine. We were going to surprise you with these when we got to India, however, due to the circumstances of your trip up here we think ya should have them now."

Speechless once again, first money from my uncle now gifts from Carilyn and Doc Nick.

"I don't know what to say, but thank you. I will put them to good use."

Each deserving of a big thank you hug, I wrap my arms around them both, and offer to carry some bags out to the van. Ally and I take the blue containers out to the van and open them. Mama asked us to take the things in the boxes that we brought up from Eufaula and put them in the blue containers so that they will be protected during the trip overseas. We start to empty the boxes and when I get to the one with trauma kits, I stop and show Ally the stuff my dad used.

"Wow Lily. I don't know if I could have handled seeing all that. Didn't you freak out? Come here darling let me give ya hug"

"Thanks Ally. I need to go change in to some travel clothes and put my flip flops in my luggage." I follow Ally in to her bedroom. "Ally, I did not want to say anything in front of my mama and dad, but I was pretty scared at that accident. The patients were maybe just a little older than us. My folks gave me training for this trip, but that was basic stuff like taking blood pressures and giving medicine, among some other things. I wasn't prepared for bodies lying around squished by a car." I grab my long pants and shoes and change quickly.

"I can only imagine what you went through. Our parents are in medicine so we hear a lot about that kind of stuff, but until you have been trained and have experience, it can be scary." Ally follows me to the bathroom, so I can freshen up a bit.

"I was so nervous, but it's kind of like at the same time my training kicked in. Even though I don't have the knowledge or experience, and even though I felt like running away, I knew these people needed my help. I was just glad my dad and mama were there, my teachers. If I was on my own, it would have done me in."

Ally nods in agreement, "me too honey."

The back of the van is just about full and Doctor Nick and my dad come out with the rest of the luggage and place it on the rack on the roof of the van. They tie everything down with straps and tell us it's time to go or we'll have to swim to India. I heard that somewhere already today. Mama and Carilyn come out, lock up the house, and we all pile in to the van. Dad says it will be about an hour and a half to get to the Atlanta airport.

"Everybody ready? Ok then, let's go." Dad backs the van out of the driveway and we head down the road to get on Interstate 185 then to Interstate 85. Jokingly, dad says to wake him up when he gets to exit 72, so that he doesn't drive past it making us even more behind schedule than what we already are. I don't know how he and my mama can be so calm after just saving two lives. Hope I can be that relaxed one day. I sit back and talk to Ally.

"Where in India are we going?" Smiling now, she explains it to me again.

"Lily we are going to Southern India to the state of Kerala. To get there we have to fly from Atlanta to Paris where we will have a short lay over. Then from Paris we go to Cochin, India which is the main airport in Kerala. The locals refer to it as Kochi. We'll be staying near Marayoor about fifty miles from Cochin. There are some wildlife sanctuaries and national parks nearby. If we have time, we might get to take a trip down to Trivandrum which the local name is T-H-I-R-U-V-A-N-A-N-T-H-A-P-U-R-A-M," Ally spells the city and then continues. "Thiruvananthapuram. We can possibly even make it to a beach for a day. It all depends on how many other volunteers show up and how many people need to be seen at the clinics we set up."

"I remember now. I'm excited to go somewhere new and help out. I'm looking forward to meeting the people and learning their culture. My Uncle Jake gave me money to buy a sari, so that should be interesting. Is it still safe where we will be? Your mama and dad went last year and said there was nothing to worry about, right?" The sun has finally come up and my cappuccino is finally empty. Doctor Nick turns around before Ally can answer my question, probably sensing some concerns in my voice.

"Hey there Lily honey, you'll be fine. Bad guys did several attacks in Mumbai back in 2008. It was said that the attackers came from Pakistan somehow and attacked different places in Mumbai. There were a lot of people killed using bombs and gun fire, but Lily we are not even going to be close to Mumbai. In fact, when we went last year we were very safe. Besides, the Indian authorities captured one of the attackers alive. He gave away all of the details of the attacks. The authorities know how it was done and now they have intelligence and security in place so that it can never happen again. They even found out the name of the attacker's group responsible for the attacks. So, you and Ally will be just fine although, it would be nice if everyone in the world could just get along. Enjoy the experience."

Doctor Nick turns back around in his seat and I feel a little better about going to India. He went on to say that the attackers used small boats to carry out the attacks, and that there was no way they could reach us in a place as far away as south India. I thought he was done; now I have more concern. Doctor Nick then went on to tell us about some other issues closer, but still pretty far, to where we will be, but not done by the same bad guys.

"There were some kinds of disturbances around the state of Orissa. There have been problems there since the 1990's, but we won't be bothered with." Doctor Nick said it's because we help everyone who needs or wants medical treatment. "It doesn't matter if you are Hindu, Muslim, Christian, Sikh, Jain, Parsi, or nothing. We are going to India to do good, not harm." Doctor Nick and Carilyn learned about all the history of some of the different religions last time they were in India.

"Thank you Doctor Nick. I feel much better now."

There still are some concerns of mine that I don't want to share. It's better if everyone tries to relax and concentrate on providing the medical care that we are trained to do. That's the main reason for the trip, so why get everybody nervous. I am probably just anxious because it's all new to me and I'm not as experienced as everyone else is. I decide to change to a different subject while the cappuccino is still working its magic.

"Hey mama, Ally said the family we are staying with has a son our age, is that true? Is he good looking? What's his name? What's he do? Does he live in a big house? Does he have a girlfriend?" Giggling back at Ally who is also laughing. Mama gives me the routine no-boys-until-you're-done-with-school look.

"Yes Lily. The Karup's do have a son. His name is Brandon."

"Brandon?" I sit forward a bit in case I miss heard what she said. She pronounces the last name like ka-roop, but I have trouble understanding the non-Indian first name "Brandon doesn't sound like an Indian name mama."

"Well that's because his dad is Indian, however, his mama is American. He is around seventeen or eighteen. I don't know what he is doing these days. He might have a girlfriend or he might not. You can ask him when you see him. The house they live in is large by local standards, but that is because they have a lot of guests that come to stay with them." Mama turns back around looking for the next exit sign.

"Oh, I see. There is hot water and a shower right? Ally and I are a couple of divas, you know that." Ally is poking me in the side and laughing.

"Hey wait a minute, don't get me in trouble Lily." I poke her back.

Carilyn turns around and explains. "Yes they have hot water, but it's not like here when you turn the faucet on and you have instant water coming from the water heater. Over there they have large tanks on the roof of their house. They're filled with water and the sun heats it up. It's kinda like a solar hot water system which is slowly catching on here in the states." Carilyn finishes her coffee and continues to explain. "There is a shower and a toilet; however, we are bringing our own toilet paper because it's not common in some locations."

"What?" Now she has mine and Ally's attention. "Wait a minute, no toilet paper. What do they use?"

"Well girls, it is a different culture with different customs, but it's not uncommon to use the left hand to wipe after they go to the bathroom and then clean it off in a bucket of water sitting in one of the bathrooms that, how do you say, is not so modern."

"Hey mama, you and dad never mentioned that about your trip to India last year." Ally has a look of concern on her face that I am sure looks exactly like mine. What do we do if we run out of toilet paper among other things? Doing as the locals do doesn't sound too appealing at this point. This must have been my folk's evil plan to get Ally and I in the car and on the way to the airport. We surely can't jump out and head home; although, it would be good to see Jax. Then again he doesn't use TP. Wait a minute! Mama better have a plan.

"Hey mama, what happens if we run out of TP? Can me and Ally go stay in that five star hotel?" You know the one I am talking about. It has air conditioning, a bed, no mosquitoes, oh yeah, and TP!" Everyone starts to laugh as my daddy just about misses the exit for the airport.

"Nice one Lily! Hey, I know. We can swipe extra from the airport bathrooms, and if that is not enough, we can swipe it from the airplane's bathrooms. That would be funny! Over the middle of the Atlantic ocean with no TP, well except for us of course. Then we could sell it to the other passengers to make some extra travel money- to buy more TP!" Ally is roaring and both of our parents are giving us two, looks that say you better not, but still they laugh. Hey I am sure they are probably planning on how to get a few extra just-in-case rolls of TP on board the airplane. Maybe I'll grab one extra roll.

Daddy slows the van down as we exit the highway. "Ok y'all, I will drop everyone off at the South terminal. We can off load all the luggage there. Then I will go find economy parking and catch the airport shuttle back over to here. Check in, and check in all the luggage and gear and head up to the security screening. Jump on the plane train and get off at E concourse. Our gate is 37, so it's like the furthest dang gate away. Tell the pilot not to leave without me!"

My dad gets lucky and pulls up behind a white limousine in front of the International departures sign on the South terminal. We all get out and go to the rear of the van. Every one of us is stretching and there are a few yawns thrown in for the sake of it. It's my first time here. I look up to see a large jet airplane flying overhead climbing higher after I guess just taking off. That will soon be us. I cannot wait. We have been out of the car for only twenty seconds and another jet flies over the top of us. Busy airport. This is a first time for me, but I am sure there will be a lot of firsts for me on this trip.

"Hey daddy what kind of airplane was that?"

"Honey, that looked like a 7-6-7. Probably heading overseas, or maybe across the country. Do you and Ally want to grab a couple of those carts over there for the luggage?"

"Yes Doctor Jim, we can do that for ya." Ally answers my dad before I get a chance, so we go over to one of the airport workers and ask for two luggage carts while everyone else continues to unload the mini-van. We are only gone for a couple of seconds when we get back to the van, about ten feet away, and it is already unloaded. It appears that we might still be a little bit behind schedule. My dad is already back in the driver's seat. Mama goes over and gives him a peck on the cheek.

"Ok dear, hurry back. I will tell the pilot not to leave until you get back." Dad gives us all a wave and heads to the economy parking lot; I think that's the cheap one, but they say nothing is cheap at an airport.

"You ladies ready?" Doctor Nick is already pushing one of the carts through the automatic doors. Thankfully he has grabbed the heavier one.

"Right behind you Doc."

Carilyn walks past us with a small pack on her back and her carry-on bag in tow behind her with its handle extended. Mama walks by us, also pulling a carry-on bag. Ally and I put our bags on the second cart and together push it inside the terminal.

The terminal is already filling up with people. We follow Doctor Nick and Carilyn to the International departures. That line isn't so bad. There is only about four people in line ahead of us and not as much luggage as us. We each have a large rolling duffel bag plus carry-on bags. There are four medium sized containers with the donated medical gear. Doctor Nick goes first followed by Carilyn and my mama. Then it is Ally's turn and finally me.

"Ticket and passport please."

I hand them over to the nice lady behind the check-in counter and put my duffel bag on the scale. It's forty pounds exactly. She grabs the duffel, wraps a tag around the handle straps, and puts it on the conveyor belt disappearing behind a plastic curtain. I wonder if I will ever see it again. Oh well, not much I can do about it now. My bag is going somewhere; I just hope it happens to be India. I don't plan on using banana leaves as toilet paper. The nice lady prints out a boarding pass and hands it to me. She smiles at us, but the look on her face says we made her lift too much luggage.

"Have a nice trip."

I nod at her. "Thank you."

We all head toward the security screening area. I wonder if dad has found parking yet and is on the way back to the terminal. According to my boarding pass, we should be getting on the plane in thirty minutes.

"Lily, do you and Ally want to go first and then we'll follow?"

"Sure mama. I am happy not to be in my Crimson Tide flip flops. This floor looks like it has been stepped on a million times and not cleaned once!" I toss my shoes in to the basket and then put my carry-on in next and slide them toward the x-ray machine.

"Lily, that's what your socks are for. You know. To clean the floor for them." Ally does the same as me and puts her carry-on in the basket next to mine followed by her shoes.

"No way Ally. My Crimson Tide socks are not for cleaning the floor in an airport located in Bulldog territory. Eww!"

Everyone else follows us. My baskets get to the other side of the x-ray machine and I step through the metal detector. Nothing beeps. That's good or so I thought because the nice large gentleman in the uniform signals for me to follow the not so friendly looking lady in uniform over to the next table for a bag search. Oh this is great. I turn to see mama shaking her head. Reading her mind I can tell what she is thinking, me too, why did I wear these socks in Bulldog country? That's got to be it.

"Hey mama, go ahead without me. When dad comes, we'll just take our private jet and catch up with y'all." The security lady is biting down hard on her bottom lip. She probably wants to respond, but decides to take it out on my bag instead. One by one, she pulls every item out. I bet she is a fan of the Yellow-Jackets or the Bulldogs. That must be it. Note to self- wear Crimson Tide shirt, pants, coat, hair tie, hat, and earrings next time I go through this lady's security screening line. Dang, hope her lip don't start to bleed. She must be reading my mind.

Everyone else makes it through and are standing off to the side waiting for me. Ally disappears in to the first bathroom. I finally get to pack my carry-on back up again, tell the nice security lady "thank ya," and catch up with mama.

"Well, that was not fun. Are we going to make this flight?" My shoes are back on and Ally comes out of the bathroom with a smirk on her face. Carilyn is shaking her head. Ally's bag looks a little fuller.

"No Lily, that was not fun. I guess she ain't a fan of that team you like sooo much." Mama is looking worried. There is no sign of daddy, so we head to the plane train which is some kind of automatic people carrier that takes us to the airport gates. This thing better be able to find its way and not deliver us in hot-lanta. Ally and I follow behind the others.

"Hey honey, how many rolls did you get?"

I reach toward her bag to check and she pulls it away from me and whispers, "Three silly, get your own, or use the banana leaves."

There is one more bathroom off to my right just before the plane train. I run in and look for an open stall. Bingo! Two rolls. I rip them out and put them in my carry-on. Didn't lose any time. Mama didn't know I ducked in to the bathroom. Must be all my soccer training keeping me quick on my feet.

"How many did you get Lily?" I tell her four so that she thinks she is going to lose this friendly competition. I can barely contain my laughter, but I'll see how long we can keep this up.

"What are you two up to?" Ally replies before I get a chance to.

"We ain't doing a thing Mrs. Morgan."

Once again, we can't control our giggles and once again mama shakes her head and bites her lip. Carilyn joins sides with mama and shakes her head. They both probably realize I'm breathing a bit faster. Gave it away. We arrive at the automatic people carrier, yet there are no signs of my dad.

"Mama, shouldn't we wait here for daddy?" Mama is still biting her lip. Suddenly I realize it's not over me and Ally, but daddy missing the flight.

"No Lily dear, your father will make the flight. I am sure he is going through security as we speak." Mama ain't sounding too reassuring.

"Mama, can I have dads TP if he misses the flight?" Ally grabs my arm trying to not remind mama and Carilyn of our present mission.

"Honey I think you two have enough 'extra' TP in your carry-ons, right?" Busted. The plane train stops in front of us and we all get in. A few others join us and soon we are headed to the last gate. I think everyone is starting to wonder if dad is going to make this flight or catch up with us in Paris. After not a very long ride, the automatic people carrier comes to a stop at the E concourse. We get off and start to head to gate 37. This is a big airport and I'm getting tired again. Still a bit sore from yesterday's soccer game, and just basically lack of sleep, is kicking my butt. Oh wow!

"Ally, it looks like they are already boarding the flight." Before she can answer. The nice friendly airline worker makes an announcement: "We will continue boarding the rest of First Class passengers and now, will passengers sitting in rows 30 to 37 please board next." I check my boarding pass and it looks like we are in row 15, so we should have a little time before we get on the plane.

"Attention passengers going to Paris on Flight 3020, we are now boarding rows 25 to 29." Like the fire fighter said-sheeet!

"Attention passengers please have your boarding pass ready and ID check for final screening." Oh, that's good. I thought she was going......"Attention passengers for Flight 3020 to Paris, we are now boarding rows 20 to 24."

Well, ok then. Never mind. "Mama, how much time before we leave?"

"Lily, I think the airplane will close its doors in about fifteen minutes. Plenty of time. Don't you worry." That's not a lot of time.

"Attention passengers Flight 3020 to Paris is now boarding rows 15 to 19." Sheeet! That is us now. We all get up and get in line which seems to be moving pretty fast. The line is moving quicker than I would like it to. Maybe if I create some kind of diversion to make the plane not take off until my dad gets here. Ally and I can go and toilet paper the airplane's front windshield. That should buy us some time. Probably extra ten minutes before they scrape that off and the pilots can see. I can tell them I misplaced my baby once I get on board. Surely they would not leave if I can't find my baby. Right? That might take an extra fifteen minutes to find a misplaced baby. They would have to look in the over-head compartments, under the seats, and maybe the cockpit before the airplane would leave. Then when dad shows up, I can just say oops, left the baby home, sorry. Nope, not good ideas. I will just cross my fingers.

Doctor Nick, and Carilyn are next to be boarding. They each hand over their boarding passes, the passes are scanned and they head off down the tunnel disappearing from view. Ally goes next. She has no issues and follows her mama and dad. It is my turn. I hand over my boarding pass and passport. The gentlemen scans the boarding pass, the machine beeps, and he hands them both back to me. I step toward the tunnel and turn and wait for mama. She does the same and we start down the tunnel with no daddy in sight.

"Mama, can you tell them to wait?"

"Absolutely Lily. We can tell them, but don't know if they will. Your daddy will just catch the next flight. No big deal." She is worried, yet won't show it. Kind of like that nurse training.

"Attention passengers for Flight 2030 to Paris we are now boarding rows five through nine."

Wait a minute! I missed the whole rows ten to fifteen then I turn and realize the large group of people following us must be them. Lost in my thoughts I guess. Some of them are speaking what sounds like, I think, French. Oh, that makes sense now. Another 'duh' moment. This plane is going to France.

"Attention: will all remaining passengers traveling on Flight 2030 to Paris, please board now."

We catch up to Ally and her folks. "Hey Ally, fake a knee injury when you are about to get on board so they can't close the airplane door."

"Lily honey I would love to, but my mama says that she wants some of our extra TP or she will tell the airline on us. Sounds like blackmail to me." I nod at her and decide I want the extra TP. The line slows up a little bit now while everyone starts to board the airplane single file. There are two very sharply dressed flight attendants welcoming everyone on board. One female and one male, but both in navy blue uniforms with gold trim. More makeup on the woman than the man. That's good. Very friendly and cordial. They greet Ally and her folks and then Doc Nick and Carilyn turn right and disappear from sight again. Ally is next. She looks back at me, reaches down at her knee, and throws a smile my way. I return the smile. Mama goes next.

"No drama Lily."

I tell mama that I won't do anything crazy and then she makes the right turn and heads down the aisle.

"Hello there young lady. Welcome aboard."

I say hello back to the female flight attendant, "Hello my dad is running a little late. Can you give him an extra five minutes please?" Hoping my plea sounded desperate enough.

"What is his name dear?" The male attendant grabs his papers in his hand and holds them up to read.

"It is James Morgan. Please, five more minutes. He'll be here. I promise." The attendant looks down at his list and then back at me.

"He didn't make it to the gate yet, but I will let the Captain know, ok?" He turns and walks toward the front of the plane. There is some relief coming over me now that I know they will at least talk to the Captain. I take a quick look at the other attendant's name tag.

"Thank you Miss Danielle." After I make the right turn, I realize mama was standing there the whole time stuck in 'traffic' created by all the passengers trying to put their luggage in the compartments above them. Ally is stuck in front of mama. We slowly make our way to the seats.

The airplane is big inside. We get to row fifteen. There are three seats by the window which are ours and we have another three seats in the middle section to our left, but all in a row so that we can sit together. Carilyn hands her carry-on to Doc Nick who then puts it in the compartment over the center seats to our left. He then grabs mama's carry-on and puts that in the compartment above us to the right. Ally jumps in the window seat. I make my way over and side step into the middle seat. Mama sits down next to me. Carilyn is in the aisle seat across from her, next to Doc Nick. A few more passengers move past us down the aisle and there are some more in front of us putting their luggage away.

"Hey mama, I did ask them to wait five more minutes for daddy and they went and told the Captain."

"I know Lily. Thank you. He'll be here. No worries." She has her eyes fixed on everyone coming down the aisle. I can still see out the window which is cool. There are TV screens in the back of all of our seats and I can see larger ones mounted in front of us in different locations in the plane. The TV has a picture of a map of what looks like Georgia and a tiny airplane is in the middle of it. Down in front of me are some magazines stuffed in the back of the seat and a fold down table as well.

Suddenly, I hear what sounds like the airplane starting up. That's not good. There is a tiny smell of aviation fuel. I recognize that from our county airport.

"Ladies and gentlemen, welcome aboard Flight 2030 with non-stop service to Paris. In just a few moments we will be closing the cabin door. At this time we ask you to please turn off all cell phones and electronic devices. Please direct your attention to the nearest video monitor for an aircraft safety briefing. Thank you."

I look over at mama who is checking her cell phone one last time when I hear the phone 'ding' letting her know it is a text message. It reads "HERE" as we both look up to see my dad making his way down the aisle dripping in sweat.

CHAPTER V

"Were y'all starting to worry? I had some parking issues and then missed the first courtesy shuttle." Dad looks at his black and purple watch on his left wrist. "See, plenty of time to spare."

The airplane starts to move backward. I guess we are going. Too late to change my mind. The friendly female flight attendant comes down the aisle checking the overhead bins and looking under our seats to see that all the carry-on stuff is stored. Dad sits in the aisle seat across from mama as Carilyn and Doc Nick slide over one seat to make room for him.

"Dad, I knew you would make it, but mama had some concerns. Please be more punctual next time." Ally and I start to giggle. Actually, I am relieved that he made this flight.

Doc Nick looks over at my dad. "Hey Jim, did you stop for another coffee or what? We were beginning to think you hired your own plane for the trip."

"No way Nick. I wouldn't want to travel with anyone else but you. Shhh, don't tell our wives. You know that you are my favorite doctor." Dad flags down the flight attendant as the aircraft starts to move forward away from the terminal.

"Miss what time will the coffee be served?"

She smiles at him, "What time sir? Oh, at about 10,000 feet. I will make it special for you. The pilot only waited for you because you have a very sweet daughter and she asked us to wait. I will see you in a bit." She heads off down the aisle and disappears.

"Lily, did you ask the pilot to wait for me?" Still sweating, dad grabs the airplane safety brochure from behind the seat in front of him.

"Absolutely Dad, mama was worried, so I intervened."

"Good job Lily and thank you. You're going to do fine on this trip." Dad glances over the brochure and then the video monitor.

The video monitor is now saying something in French and a flight attendant is pointing at the exits in the plane. Shouldn't need them for a while. I turn my attention back to the inside of the plane, not only is it big inside, but it is very blue. Blue everywhere. The interior decorator must have been on vacation when they made this plane. Blue is calming and soothing, but I think after five more hours I will lose my mind. Ally is already admiring the entertainment system in the back of the seat as I feel the plane roll over a few bumps in the pavement. I think I will see what they have for movies. No. I'll wait a few minutes. Too early for that.

I look out the window next to Ally and see a jet taking off on the runway. Looks like we are getting ready soon. This is pretty cool. The captain makes another announcement: "Flight attendants please take your seats. We are aircraft number three for departure."

There goes another jet rumbling down the runway. I can hear the roar of its engines as it goes by. Ok that means one more. Our plane starts to slow down as it makes a turn. I can't see the next jet, but I hear more rumbling and then it disappears. We start to move forward again and then turn once more. The engines start to rumble and we slowly move forward. The plane starts to gain speed and I am pinned back against my seat. Ally and I look at each other and start to giggle some more. Mama reaches down and grabs my hand.

"It's ok Lily, this is the fun part." Mama is looking out the window the best she can as she leans over me. I can tell she is a little worried and I try to reassure her.

"Thanks mama. This is cool. Just like a roller coaster." I feel the plane lift off of the ground and it feels like we are kind of floating. There is a little rumble under the plane and I realize it is the landing gear coming up. Then there is a whining noise and guess that must be the flaps coming back up. Wow it's like dad's little plane, but bigger! The plane banks as we start a turn. Cool. It banks to our side and I have a nice view of the ground below us. I catch a glimpse of the airport for about a second and we level off. The sun is now shining directly through our side of the plane. I don't want to pull down the window shade, so I put my sunglasses on and try to see Atlanta from the air. The plane banks again and I lose my view of the city. So much for that.

The video screen in the back of the seat in front of me is showing the little airplane moving along with a red line behind it. The altitude in the corner of the screen says three thousand feet and is climbing quickly. There is a speed indicator in the opposite corner of the screen and it is reading 239 mph. Wow! We're moving now. Five thousand. Five thousand two-hundred. Three-hundred. I look out the window again. The house and buildings are getting smaller. Back to the screen. Six thousand feet. Looks like dad is going to get his coffee soon. The plane banks to the left and it looks like we are heading north up the coast. "Ally, should we look at the safety brochure?"

"That's a good idea Lily, but I watched the movie." Instead she hits a couple of buttons on the video screen monitor and soon has a list of things to choose from. "Lily darlin' I think a real movie or some music is on the menu. What ya think?"

"Sounds good to me. Mama already had the adapter for my ear buds and I have an extra one for ya baby." I reach down and pull out my carry-on from beneath my seat. The top is open slightly, I guess from the take-off. I grab my buds and adapters and I hand the other adapter to Ally who already has her ear buds out. My video screen now has the little airplane at 12,000 feet and zipping along at 280 mph.

"Hey mama, tell daddy it is coffee time." I look around to see if the flight attendant is coming up the aisle. Nothing yet.

"Lily darlin', I am sure your dad is already lookin' for her. Mama smiles and goes back to reading her book which she must have pulled from her bag when I wasn't looking.

"Ally, what movie do you want to watch? I am feeling like a comedy, no wait, a love story." She turns and looks at me slightly deterred, but not serious, and reaches for my buds. I lean away from her buzzing laughter. I knew that would get her. "Sorry. Sorry. Ok, comedy."

"Love story? No chick flicks. Not for this chick. Where are the snacks and drinks? We couldn't grab any in the airport since we were running late. How do you think those people are doing, the ones from the car crash?" She scrolls down the list of movies and settles on an episode of *House, MD*. Good choice and appropriate.

"Dad said he would call back home to find out about the car crash victims when we land. Ok Ally darling, let's get some popcorn. This party has got to start sometime." I look back over the seat and see the flight attendants coming up the aisle like she said she would. My dad already has his tray down in front of him waiting for the coffee no doubt. The monitor in front of my mama's seat is showing an altitude of 18,000 feet and a speed of 305 miles per hour. Wow! Cruising now. I look back at our screens and notice Ally has changed the movie to a chick flick.

"Hey there sweetie pie, why did you pick that one?" Knowing I could never be mad at her for anything she does, I just smile.

"Well, silly, they all have happy endings. Where are the snacks? I am starving. Stealing...I mean borrowing bathroom products from the airport made me miss the outrageously priced airport snacks and drinks store." One of the flight attendants reaches our seats. She is beautiful with dark hair and amazing makeup. She must be French, once again realizing the crew must be half American and half French due to this being an international flight. I'm starting to figure this out. Glancing at her shiny gold name tag, I see the name Genevieve.

"Hello girls, may I get you some beverages?" There is a faint hint of a French accent in the flight attendant's voice and a large hint, yet not overwhelming, of a pleasant perfume in the air around her.

"Bonjour mademoiselle Genevieve, comment allez-vous? J'adore ta tenue. Cuisses de grenouilles elle, mademoiselle Lily?" Ally says something in French to her and they both look at me. Ally is laughing pretty hard and Genevieve is trying to remain professional, but cracks a little bit of a smile.

"A couple of iced teas would be great." The flight attendant pours each of us a glass of tea over a cup of ice. Hoping it is extra sweet, Alabama style, I take one glass and pass it to Ally. "Merci." Yep, my French needs a lot of work.

"Je vous en prie." She then looks at mama. "And for you mademoiselle?"

"Je voudrais un verre de vin rouge, s'il vous plait."

Mama's French is pretty good, I think. Genevieve pours her a glass of what looks like red wine and sets it on the little table in front of her. She then turns toward my dad and asks him the same question.

Before he can answer I hear Ally, "cuisses de grenouilles!"

Genevieve tries to remain professional, but finally gives in. "Sorry, I don't think we have any frog legs on the flight, but I can check with the captain to make sure."

Everyone is now looking at Ally including some passengers in front of us. Dad points to my mom's glass and tells Genevieve he will have the same as her. Now I know dad is not feeling well or something.

"Dad, no coffee?"

"Naw Lily, I think it's time to relax a bit. Lots to do when we get there. When the heck did Ally learn French?" Shaking his head, he takes the glass of wine from Genevieve and takes a sip. Looks like Carilyn gets a coffee and so does Doc Nick. I turn back to the movie which has already started, and notice we are now at 36,000 feet and crawling along at 400 mph. When did that happen? We are over the Atlantic Ocean now. Back to the movie. It's one of my favorites and most of it is based in Italy. Someday I will get there, maybe after college.

About another hour goes by and I see the flight attendants are serving a full meal which is good because I am starving. Mama and Carilyn did pass out some snacks for us, which got me to this point. "They better not be serving frog legs Ally."

"Only if they are dipped in chocolate, right?" Ally takes her tray from a different flight attendant this time. He then hands me mine and I set it down on the itty bitty table tray in front of me. The plane bounces over a small amount of turbulence; otherwise, it has been a smooth flight thus far. I glance at mama's map on her video screen and can see we are well over the ocean now. The food looks good, even if everything is tiny. Ally, mama, and I are eating and it looks like Carilyn, Doc Nick, and dad got their dinners too.

Looking out the window, I can see lots of water and even make out some white caps on the tops of some waves as they swim together like an uncoordinated dance. There are some puffy clouds, but not too many of them. Can't remember what they are called. Cumulus? Nimbus maybe? Actually, when I look again, they are a little flatter like a blanket, might be called cirrostratus clouds. Our altitude is around 36,000 feet, so they would be in the high cloud family. Dad would know, as would all pilots. We always talk about the weather when flying.

The movie is almost over, along with my mass produced airline dinner. It's the part where the girl is standing on the balcony and her man is down below telling her he loves her. Ahh! Why can't that happen in real life? Someday. Maybe.

"How was your dinner girls?" Ally, still chewing hungrily, beats me to the reply.

"Exactly the same as yours Mrs. Morgan. We all had the same thing. And so did the other couple of hundred people on board." She takes another bite of desert. "I thought I asked for pizza?"

"Not bad though. When we get to India, we will eat local foods, not pizza, not for a while anyway." Mama hands her tray to the flight attendant who is now picking up the meal trays.

"Miss Abby, how much Hindi do you speak?" Ally grabs her phrase book out of her backpack.

"Well Miss Ally, I speak a little bit of Hindi, just some basics, however, darlin' they don't speak Hindi where we will be. Well, a lot of the people will understand Hindi." Mama takes Ally's phrase book and flips through the pages.

"What do they speak there Miss Abby?" Ally orders another ice tea.

"In the state of Kerala, where we will be, the language spoken there is called Malayalam. I know enough to get by, but the complicated medical translations I leave up to Mr. and Mrs. Karup and some of the others that will be with us." The flight attendant has collected all of our trays now.

"Interesting. So, for Lily's sake, how would you say I love you will you go out with me?" Ally puts both her hands up so I can't pretend to strangle her.

"No way mama. Don't listen to her. I am on this trip to learn. Ally needs a boyfriend."

"I'll tell ya what, when we get there I will ask and write it down for both of you, sound good?" Mama hands the phrase book back to Ally with the page turned open to Malayalam.

I settle back into my seat and start to feel my eyes getting heavier. It looks like it is starting to get darker outside.

Oh no! Leave her alone. Tiger. Where did it come from...? I awake from another one of my unexplainable dreams to hear an announcement:

"Attention passengers, will anyone on board with medical training please identify yourself."

I wake up to see Doc Nick pressing the attendant light. I must have been asleep for a good amount of time because it is dark outside and the little airplane on the map is closer to Europe than the U.S. Then Genevieve, the flight attendant, comes over to Doc Nick.

"Sir, do you have medical training?"

"Yes, I am a doctor. What can I do for you?"

"We have a passenger that has a history of asthma and thinks she might be having an attack now. Can you help us?" She points to the back of the plane.

"Absolutely, show me where." He undoes his seatbelt. Dad gets up and follows. Hey Nick, this one is all yours. I am tipsy after that glass of wine."

"I had a taste of Carilyn's wine and it was weaker than cranberry juice. Be back in a minute honey."

They both follow Genevieve down the aisle. "Mama, do ya think they need help?"

"Your dad is in capable hands. Nick will keep an eye on him. No, I am sure they will be fine. Try to get some more sleep. You were out for a while." Ally turns around to take a look.

"What can you see?"

"They stopped by a lady and my dad is listening to her chest with a stethoscope. I think your dad is taking her blood pressure. That's about it." Ally does not look too concerned.

Several minutes pass and my dad and Doc Nick come back to their seats. Carilyn beats us to the question.

"What happened?"

"De l'asthme. The lady has a past medical history of asthma, but she forgot her inhaler. She is moving good air and I can't make out any wheezes when I listened to her despite the aircraft noise. So, her vital signs are ok. Genevieve said the captain wants to know if we need to declare a medical emergency. I told her that we would keep an eye on her, but at this point she is pretty stable and not having an asthma attack."

I fall asleep again. When I wake up, Ally is nudging me and pointing out the window. It's night time now and I can see lights from small towns and villages below. I glance over at the map and can see that we are over land. Good timing because Genevieve is back and serving a snack tray with fresh fruit and croissants.

"Ladies and gentlemen, this is the First Officer speaking. We are now beginning our decent in to Charles de Gaulle International Airport Paris France."

The feet are starting to tick off of the altitude reading in front of me. I can feel some butterflies buzzing in my chest. This is my first stop in a foreign country. The message is repeated in French, and from what I can make out- nothing about frogs. The fruit and croissants on my tray are all gone now, as are Ally's. Time for another mission before we land. "Mama, excuse me for a minute; I have to use the salle de bain." She gives me one of those utt-oh looks.

"No funny business, behave." Mama unbuckles and stands up in the aisle to let me pass.

"Wouldn't dream of it mama. Ally you coming?"

Ally follows me down the aisle. My legs are a little stiff and we hit a couple of more bounces in the clouds. The bathroom is unoccupied. Inside is barely enough room for a troll and toilet. The TP is jumping in to my pocket. It is tricky with the airplane swaying left and right and up and down, but I manage. As refreshing as banana leaves sound, this is an important mission as ever. I pull off a few more feet, wash up, and smile at Ally as I exit the bathroom and return toward my seat. Mama inspects me and I show her my two empty hands. Ally returns a minute later and shows her hands to Carilyn. We sit back in our seats that we have called home for the past hours and buckle up.

Our trays were collected when we were gone. There is a warm moist towel there instead. I pick it up and wipe my face trying to freshen up. The air is a little bit stale by now. Can't wait to land. We are at 25,000 feet now and continue to make our way down to the ground. I can make out more lights spurting through the broken cloud cover. Moon light on top of us; electric lights below us. The airplane is slowing down as we descend. Everyone in the cabin is packing up all their things and returning them to the overhead bins and carry-ons under the seats. Now we are at 18,000 feet. The male flight attendant comes by and collects our towels. I find that the TP in my front pockets is pressing on my hips and is making it difficult to sit. Landing can't come soon enough. Down to 12,000 feet now. We are at 300 mph. Paris, here we come!

"Ladies and gentlemen, this is the First Officer, we will be landing in approximately ten minutes, eleven p.m. local time. The temperature is sixty-four degrees. Flight attendants please take your seats."

There are lights everywhere I look outside the window now. The sky is lit up almost like day time. We must be passing over Paris. I can feel the landing gear come down and hear the whine of the flaps on the wings being lowered. Soon, real soon. Mama grabs my hand.

"Lily, I don't like this landing part."

"It is ok mama. This is the greatest thrill known to mankind. Flying is second." That's what dad says anyway. I look around the airplane one more time and can see passengers taking pictures out the windows. Looking back out my window I see the edge of the runway. A second later we touch down. There is a thud as the wheels make their first contact with the runway. The reverse thrust and brakes cause all of us to bend forward in our seats. It ends in seconds and soon we are taxiing to the terminal. Viva la France!

"Ladies and gentlemen, we are pulling up to Terminal 2E. On behalf of the crew, I would like to thank you for flying with us and hope you enjoy your stay in Paris, or if connecting to another destination, have a safe journey."

The plane comes to a stop and people are up getting their things from the overhead bins. We do the same.

"Hey Doctor Nick, how did that lady make out with the asthma?" I pull my backpack out from under the seat and swing it over my shoulder. My hips feel a little better, now that I am standing. I can see Ally rubbing at her pockets also.

"Lily, she made out ok. I checked on her several times when you were sleeping. Probably a food reaction."

He grabs his bag and follows Carilyn down the aisle to the exit. Ally jumps in front of me and we slowly follow the crowd. One of the flight attendants is heading to the back of the plane against the crowd. She looks like a salmon swimming up stream. I step aside for her to get past me.

Ally turns around, "might be going to re-stock the toilet paper in the bathroom."

"Hey, do you think the captain will check our pockets to see if we have any bits of his plane?" Ally shakes her head as we approach the flight attendants gathered at the exit. Genevieve is one of them and so is the one who asked the captain to wait for my dad.

"Bye bye," says Genevieve.

"Au revoir, bonne unit, merci beacoup."

Ally's French is pretty good.

"Je vous en prie. Comment vous appelez-vous?"

I think Ally said bye, goodnight, and thank you very much, but all I could make out was something 'name' from Genevieve.

"Je m'appelle Ally." Genevieve turns toward me.

"Comment vous appelez-vous?" I heard 'name' again so I respond like Ally.

"Je m'appelle Miss Lily."

"Very good Miss Lily. Will you be staying in France?"

"No. We have a short layover and then off to India." Realizing we are holding up the line, I shake her hand and thank the rest of the attendants for the flight and turn toward the exit.

"Au revoir Miss Lily." They respond one at a time.

CHAPTER VI

It is hard to believe that I am in France. I have never been in a different country before. As I look around the inside of the terminal, I notice people from all over the world, or at least it looks that way, looking at the way they are dressed. Definitely in an International airport now. We all kind of gather together loosely. Everyone is stretching. My body is trying to remind me I was just cooped up on the plane for what seemed like a day. Overall, I don't think it was a bad flight except for the fact my tired skin is trying to crawl off my stiff body. It is still dark outside except for the airport lights. I can see them taking the luggage off the airplane we were just on. There goes our blue containers with our medical supplies, so that's a good sign. I can't see my bag anywhere. I guess I will have to hope it made it.

"Hey mama, what time is the next flight?" I ask to see if we get some kind of break before leaving for India. Mama pulls her ticket out of her bag.

"Lily, it looks like we board in about two and a half hours." She goes back to looking at her ticket and then up at the gate signs in the terminal. My dad and Doc Nick follow her lead and do the same.

"Thanks mama. Is it ok if I grab Ally and go for a walk to stretch our legs? We won't be gone long." I pout my lips and hope for approval. Ally hears her name mentioned and comes over and stands by me— pouting.

"Carilyn, do you mind if the girls go for a walk to stretch their legs?" Mama glances at her ticket one more time.

"Abby, it's ok with me." Carilyn then ok's it with our dads. "Girls the plane leaves from this terminal, Gate E-73, so don't be too long."

"Not a problem mama. We will take a walk to the stores and see what's open." Ally gives her mom a tight hug. "We'll be quick, au revoir!"

We leave our carry-ons with them and turn right heading through the terminal. "Be back in a few mama."

"Ok, but be careful and watch for strangers trying to pick your pockets." Mama says with some concern in her voice. I understand her reasoning, because we are not in Alabama anymore.

"We will. Stop worrying." Already a ways from them, we keep walking.

Ally checks her airport map. "It looks like there are some shops down toward Gate 35 and that area."

"Sounds good to me." We continue to walk until we come to the first bathroom and head inside to freshen up. Once inside we realize that we forgot our carry-ons, so no TP this time. After washing my face and hands we head back out and keep walking toward the shops. I contemplate on whether or not to tell Ally about the dreams I have been having. We walk a little farther. I feel almost compelled at this point, so I figure I would go for it. She is my best friend after all and would be the last person to think that I am crazy.

"Ally baby, I need to tell you something that you might find a little bit weird." We keep walking looking for the stores at the same time.

"What is that sugar?" Ally looks at me with some interest now. "You can tell me anything. You know that."

"I know. Thanks. Anyway, I keep having these dreams over and over again. Well, actually it seems more like visions."

"Go on."

"They keep happening more often, almost like a continuing story. Each one seems to reveal a little more than the previous one. I can't explain it. I keep dreaming about a tiger and the last dream on the plane had a beautiful woman in it dressed in red and gold..."

"Aw darlin' that was just me coming to tell ya I love you."

"You're sweet, but I am serious. I can't figure any of it out or what it means." We start to pass some stores, but most are closed.

"Well tell me more. Does the lady say anything to you? What is the tiger doing?"

"It's hard to explain. The tiger appears out of nowhere, and the lady and I are talking, but I don't know what we're talking about."

"I think the dreams or visions are just something caused by all the excitement of this trip and I wouldn't worry, but let me know if you can see any good looking guys for me, ok?" Ally responds in a rather serious reassuring voice.

"I will let you know darling. Thanks for listening and don't tell anyone, please."

"I won't. Hey there is a Printemp store. Too bad they are closed. They are in Paris also. Wow, Prada and Dior too. Closed. We should open one up in Eufaula." Ally sounds off with some more seriousness.

"What is Printemps?" I ask trying to look through the glass window in front of the store.

"Fashions, clothes, shoes, and stuff." Ally's eyeballs are opened wide taking it all in as we both try to catch a glimpse of the things in the store.

"I guess we have to come back after we get our prince and can afford it."

"Might need a King, Lily baby." Ally and I keep walking past the shops: Salvatore Ferragamo, Cecile & Jeanne, Cartier. Even better: La Maison Du Chocolat. Don't need to speak French to know what that means, besides we can smell it. We both look at the chocolate through the glass, and also closed, sheeet! At Gate 36 there is a Miyou, Noura, Fusion Wok, and Piatto Del Gusto. My stomach is rattling like a bag full of marbles. Still smells like they are cooking, but closed. This walk might all be for exercise, which is fine, but a snack would be good right about now. We continue to walk in hopes of finding some place that is open and then I realize that all we have is American money.

"Hey Ally baby, do ya have any Euro's,?" I ask hoping that she says yes.

"Mama said just to use the credit card until we can exchange some money in India." Ally then points to another store up ahead of us and we walk toward it. The airport crowd is somewhat thinned out a bit now. There are people sitting in the seats by the different gates. A lot are sleeping. We stop to look into the window of another closed store. As we are doing so, I notice a guy in the reflection in the window that is standing a couple of feet behind us. It looks like he is staring at the two of us. I turn around.

He is gorgeous! Better looking than his reflection. About six foot tall with black hair, beautiful brown eyes, and light complexion. Well built, but not overly muscular, maybe a soccer player? Ally doesn't notice him. She is looking at something in the store, so I tap her on the shoulder and she turns around. The look on her face says it all.

"Bonjour mademoiselle. On s'est deja recontre? Comment vous appelez-vous?" he says while extending his hand out.

"Je m'appelle Lil..." Ally cuts my reply off in mid-sentence. Her face changes to one more of concern than one of checking out this good looking guy. Now I am confused.

Ally snaps at him in a stern voice, "Allez-vous-en!"

He has a look of surprise on his face and is not smiling anymore.

"Toutes mes excuses," he says, then turns and walks away.

"Ally what's wrong?" Hoping to find out what just happened I grab her arm and we start walking the opposite direction of Mr. Handsome.

"Lily, he was trying to pick you up. He was hitting on you. First he wanted to know your name and then he asked if you two had ever met before."

"Really? I think he was just trying to be friendly. I saw the way you looked at him." I squeeze her arm jokingly.

"Well yeah, at first glance, but like your mama said be careful who we talk to."

"Ally baby, we can't help the fact that we are the two best looking chicks in the airport and some guys will be attracted to us. It might be the long blonde hair."

"Hey, no chances. We ain't in Alabama anymore sugar." Ally points up ahead to a store that looks like is open, finally.

"Bout' time."

We search for some food for now and snacks for the next flight. I don't recognize much, but I know a cola when I see one. I grab one and read the label: made in France, I think, cool! I get a few extra for my mom and dad. What next? Oh, I see potato chips. A couple of bags of chips. Some candy is good, couple of chocolate bars will do. Here are some things that I can't read the label. Can't read it, don't eat it. Sounds good.

"Ally, what are these?" I hand it to her.

"La malbouffe." She hands the package back to me.

"Well?"

"It is junk food, get two."

I take her word for it and grab a couple of them. We both get extra for our moms and dads and head to a checkout. Near the checkout, I spot some souvenirs. I grab some magnets of Paris for my Aunt Bess and a coffee cup with the Eiffel Tower on it for my Uncle Jake. There are some nice hats in pink, for me, and light yellow, for Ally, with Paris Rocks on the front in white, so I grab them too. We pay for our things and head out of the store. I reach in my bag, take out the yellow hat, and put it on Ally's head. Then I put the pink one on.

"Thank you Miss Lily." Ally spins all the way around with her hands up modeling her new hat.

"You are very welcome Miss Ally, now find us a bathroom." Ally turns and points to a sign.

"Toilettes Femmes." She says out loud.

"I guess Hommes is for men?" Ally raises her eyebrows and laughs at my deductive reasoning through the process of elimination; we head to the bathroom. Time to fill up my bag with a little extra TP. We should have enough for the whole trip now. Great.

"What was our gate number Ally?"

"Pretty sure it was 72 or 73. We should see everyone sitting there. We turn back toward the way we had just come from and start walking. There are more people coming toward us. It looks like a plane just landed and unloaded all of its passengers. Another international flight by the looks of it.

As we get closer to our gate, I notice quite a few people wearing sari's. Very pretty and in many colors. Ally stops for a minute and I stop with her. She turns to face me.

"Lily, don't say anything about that guy to your mom or dad, or mine." I know her serious voice.

"Why not? He was good looking and friendly. He probably just wanted to make conversation."

"Lily we don't know that. He could of have been a pick-pocket. Besides, if you say something, then our parents might not let us have that much freedom for the rest of the trip. That means no sightseeing if we have some time off."

"That's a good point. I didn't think of it that way." Walking again, I notice a large group gathered by Gate 73. Our parents are sitting by the window looking out at an airplane, ours.

"Hi everyone." Carilyn and my mama look over at us.

"Hey y'all been gone a while." Mama taps my dad on his arm.

"We thought we would have to report y'all to the lost in found." Dad turns back to admire the pilots doing some kind of pre-flight check in the cock pit. I know he wishes he could fly it just once.

"Don't know if you heard it, but they already boarded the first class passengers and the last couple rows." Mama and Carilyn start to gather up their bags and stuff.

"Sorry mama, we forgot the flight number and our tickets are in the carry-ons." Ally grabs her carry-on and I get mine.

My dad stops giving his flight lesson to Doctor Nick for a minute and waves me over to where he is sitting. "Lily I called the trauma center back home for an update on our two trauma victims. They both had surgery and are now in the intensive care unit, but stable. By the way, nice hats."

"Wow dad, it is great to hear that. Thanks for checking on them. Couldn't resist the hats and we bought some extra snacks for y'all." Relieved to know that they will probably be ok; I search for my ticket.

We go through the rest of the boarding process, like in Atlanta, and enter the plane. I follow my mama and Ally is behind me. This time our seats are about half way down the aisle of the plane.

"Oh no, it's him" I say aloud without thinking.

"Who is him?" Mama looks at me demanding to know.

CHAPTER VII

"Hey Miss Abby, Lily just saw one of the many cute guys I pointed out while walking through the airport. I guess one of them is going to India with us." Ally climbs in to her seat and settles in for the flight. I sit down next to her.

"Oh, I see. No boys. We won't have time." Mama puts her carry-on away and sits in the aisle seat like before. She starts talking to my dad for a minute.

Ally leans over and cups her hand around my ear and begins to whisper, "hey that was close. Don't say anything about him."

I check to see if mama is looking. She is not. I whisper back to Ally. "Sorry, I won't. Just surprised to see him and all."

Can't believe I almost ruined the trip for Ally and I. Mr. Handsome didn't notice us, at least I don't think he did. I hope he is not mad at us. It would be awkward if he came over and talked to us while on the flight.

"Hey dad, how long is this flight going to be?"

"This one will be around ten hours. Little bit longer than the last one." He sits down in the aisle seat across from mama.

This time Carilyn is sitting between Doctor Nick and my dad. The flight attendants are making their final checks like before. Seems to be going quicker now because I know what they are doing. Next there are some announcements in several different languages. The engines are running already and we start to taxi to the runway. I look out the window next to Ally. It is still dark. This airplane is a little bigger than the last one. Maybe my home for the next ten hours will be a little better; doubt it. One of the pilots makes the final announcement for the flight attendants to take their seats. We turn onto the runway and the engines begin to roar. Off we go! Within seconds we are in the air again. I lean over Ally once more and take in the night time scenery. Lights, airplanes, lights, airplanes, and more lights. Better than a movie.

"Lily baby, you want to watch a movie?" Ally is already flipping through the selections.

"I think I am going to read for a while and then maybe pass out. There are a few things I want to brush up on before we land in Cochin."

I grab my carry-on and pull out my ear buds. Next I put on some music. Then I get out a handbook my dad gave me about tropical medicine. Flipping through the pages I find a section on medicine specific to southern India and begin to read.

Malaria sounds interesting. I decide to read up on that. All of us are already taking Doxycycline, an antibiotic, as a prophylactic in case we get bit by an infected mosquito. It won't be the rainy season when we get to India, so maybe the mosquitoes won't be real bad. Though I am sure some other things will gladly take their place and try to bite me. What are the symptoms of malaria? Fever, headache, cough, diarrhea, or chills. Not a party I want to attend. I know dad and Doctor Nick have brought some malaria quick test kits and if we don't have to use them then that will be fine by me. D-E-N-G-U-E fever. Sounds bad. Passing on that fever will also be on my list of things to avoid. Not just a fever, but a high grade fever along with a very bad headache. One might also have the pleasure of diarrhea and a rash. Comes from the bite of the mosquito. Man, pesky little critters. Don't like the humans much I guess. What else is there? Let's see. Avian flu, um, from mosquito? Nope. It's from birds. Probably bit by dang mosquitoes. High grade fever and flu like symptoms. No thank you. Japanese B encephalitis, yep transmitted by mosquitoes. I wonder if there are any mosquitoes in Antarctica? The magazine holder in the seat in front of me is telling me to stuff this handbook in there and read it later. Sounds good to me.

I put the handbook away and look out the window. Still dark and not many lights on the ground. The moving map with the little airplane on it says we are almost over the Mediterranean sea going toward Italy. Another dream destination of Ally's and mine. She is still watching a movie. A flight attendant stops by our seats with a food cart. I tap Ally to get her attention.

"Hey Miss Ally, let's eat."

She takes out one of the ear buds. "What are they serving?" she asks while laughing. "That's not steak."

The flight attendant hands me a tray and I pass it over to Ally.

"Hello, what can I get you to drink?" She hands me a tray.

"Hello. I think we will all have ice tea with extra sugar."

"Yes miss. The sweeter the better," Ally replies as she grabs the first glass of tea from the flight attendant. Mama gets her tray and tea and I look over and see that dad Carilyn and Doc Nick are already eating. This seat cushion is already worn out and it's my home for about eight more hours. Wow! Maybe a walk around the airplane after dinner. Sounds good. Chewing the airline food is giving my jaw a work out. It's even harder to swallow, but I manage. Out of the corner of my eye I see Mr. Handsome walking up the other aisle toward the front of the plane. I try not to look. I can't help it. Oh no he turns to his left and is coming down the aisle toward us. Ally gives me a nudge on my leg. I look at her and nod. She already spotted him. I reach up and pull my hat down over my face a bit. I am sure he is a nice guy, but I am still embarrassed over the way Ally treated him even though she was looking out for me. I look down at my tray and notice his khaki colored pants as he makes his way past us. His eyes are burning a hole in my head. At least that is what it feels like.

I expect him to keep moving, but soon realize he is stopped and not continuing down the aisle. Then I hear the flight attendant and notice that Mr. Handsome is stuck behind the beverage cart. I keep looking down and toward Ally. Suddenly the plane hits some turbulence and I see him put his hand on my mama's seat back to keep his balance. I wasn't expecting that. He is almost leaning on my mama. This is so awkward. Ally reaches down in to her carry-on bag and pulls out her camera. What is she doing? This ain't the time for pictures.

"Smile for me sugar." She points the camera at me and I give my best fake smile.

"What was that for?" She takes another picture.

"Hey just trying to capture some memories of the trip." Ally turns and takes a picture of the people and inside of the plane in front of us. Well, I guess we haven't taken many pictures on the trip so far. Makes sense to me. Off to my right I see the khaki pant legs move away. Thank goodness. Ally turns to the right and strains to look up over the seat. She shows me the pictures she just took. My smile looks ok considering I just ate then just above my face and hat is a pretty good picture of Mr. Handsome from the side. She pretended to take my picture to get one of him. Now I follow. Flipping to the next picture I see Mr. Handsome turn his head. It's mostly the back of his head and somewhat out of focus. Maybe he knew what she was doing. No, that doesn't make sense.

"Good ones Ally. You should turn pro." My ice tea is empty so I pull out one the colas we bought at the airport.

"Hey sugar, a couple for the scrap book, you know. When we get home we can tell everyone how you got hit on by a French guy at the airport." She gives me a big smile and finishes her last bite of dinner.

"Everyone done eating?" Mama asks us as the flight attendants return to collect our trays.

"Yes'm. Another fantastic airline meal fit for a queen." The attendant gives me a little smirk out the side of her lipstick covered mouth. I smirk back.

"Mama, excuse me for a minute while I check out the bathroom."

"Sure thing honey." She moves her legs to the side and I get up and slide past her heading to the restroom in front of us.

"Miss Carilyn y'all enjoy that dinner?"

"Wonderful Lily."

"Ally and I have some extra colas and snacks for y'all."

"Sounds good. I'll let you know when we get hungry again."

"Ok."

I make my way up to the restroom and it's vacant. Good. Inside I help myself to a few more wads of toilet paper and stuff them in my already over stuffed pockets. I open the door and almost walk in to Ally.

"Good luck. I got it all. There ain't no more." I tease and hold the door open for her.

"I don't believe you honey." She goes inside.

Before sitting down, I decide to take a small tour of the plane near our seats to stretch my legs. I make a loop around the front of the plane. Ally comes out of the restroom and I follow her down the aisle. Mama gets up and lets us back in to our seats.

"There better be some toilet paper in the bathroom when I get there." We smile and mama heads to the bathroom.

I settle back in the seat trying to get comfortable. I adjust the pillow behind my head, pull out the blanket, and cover up.

"Who are you? What is your name? Where am I? What is this place?" It's her again. Beautiful. Slightly older than me. Twenty something? She is wearing a bright red-orange sari with a matching shawl draped across her left shoulder angling across her body to the right side. They are vividly decorated with gold and silver embroidery and interlaced with what looks like pearls. The sari wraps around her in pleats and returns to her front with an excess amount of it perfectly layered on the ground in front of her covering her feet. Her left midriff is exposed and there is a white gem covering her navel. Around her chest and underneath the sari is a band of gold silk. Upon her head is a gold crown covered with different jewels and gems. Some appear to be diamonds glistening in the bright sun light. Some look like emeralds. Others look like rubies. All shining brilliantly. She has many gold bracelets on both wrists and rings on all fingers. There are long swinging gold earrings on each side of her perfect face. Just below her crown is a ruby encircled by diamonds attached to her skin. There is a diamond piercing on the left side of her nose. Her hair is a light red-brown flowing with a small breeze in the air. Her skin is almost the same shade as her hair. There are many butterflies of many colors flying around her like they were trained to be there. She is holding a gold and red striped staff in her left hand. A smell of some kind of spices mixed with flowers fills the air. I try not to stare at her, but I am in a trance I think caused by her glacier blue eyes.

"Soon Lily...soon." She speaks for the first time and then fades away. Another dream. I awake to hear an announcement.

"Ladies and gentlemen this is the captain speaking. The flight attendants will be making their final rounds prior to landing. Please secure all personal belongings."

The little airplane on the map in front of me is next to the coast of India. Wow, I was asleep for a while.

"Well hey there sunshine, you're awake. We didn't want to wake you knowing how much you need your beauty sleep." Mama says with a sarcastic tone in her voice.

"Thanks mama. I appreciate that. Did I miss anything?" I reach down and slide my carry-on back under the seat.

"They served some fresh fruit and croissants while you were away in dream world." Ally reaches up and adjusts my hat.

"Dream world is right."

"Another one?" Ally asks.

"Yes. Too real for me."

"That's because we are almost there sweetie. You'll be fine." She reassures me.

"Ladies and gentlemen this is the captain, we will be landing in ten minutes. They are reporting clear skies and 98 degrees in Kochi. I want to thank you for flying with us and enjoy your stay in India."

Outside the window I can finally see some green land instead of water. The ground is getting closer now and I can see the flaps on the wings are deployed. Once more I feel the landing gear coming down as the plane bounces a bit with the new drag. There's the bump as the plane touches the runway and then slows rapidly. We turn onto a taxiway and I catch a glimpse of the terminal. Cool, made it to India.

CHAPTER VIII

The plane comes to a stop and the passengers start to get up and gather their things. We slowly begin to file off the plane. We all thank the flight crew and attendants standing at the exit as they welcome us to Kochi. People are everywhere inside the terminal; yet the airport doesn't seem too big. We re-group as Doc Nick points to a sign that says Customs. We head that way.

"Hey Ally, do you have anything to declare?" I ask teasing her back.

"Just you and my TP silly. Hope they don't confiscate all of it." She grabs my hand and pulls me along. Mama dad Carilyn and Doc Nick make it through without any problems. I step up to the window.

"What is your purpose for your trip to India?" the nice lady behind the glass asks me.

"I am here on holiday." She stamps my passport and slides it back to me. Wow my first stamp!

"Welcome to India. Enjoy your stay," she replies with a straight face. Can't smile while on duty I guess. Ally follows and does the same without any issues. We head over to baggage claim to retrieve our luggage. Hope it all made the flight with us.

We arrive at the baggage claim and I notice a man standing there with a big grin on his face. He is staring at us and holding a big sign in front of him that reads: "Clampett's party of 6." Doc Nick spots him too and begins to crack up. I realize from the pictures back home that this is Doctor Karup. His wife, Jillian, and daughter Pareet, are standing beside him. I don't see their son anywhere.

"Hi Doctor, how are you? How was your flight?" My dad shakes Doctor Karup's hand.

"I am fine Doctor. The flight was good." He shakes Doctor Nicks hand.

"Doctor good to see you again."

"Thanks Doctor."

"Doctor."

"Ok ok ok. Enough wise guys." Carilyn intervenes.

"Hello Jillian. Hello Pareet. Great to see y'all again." She gives them each a hug and kiss on the cheek. Mama does the same.

"I would like you to meet Ally and Lily, our daughters." Mama points to Ally and then me.

"Boy is Brandon going to be happy," Pareet blurts out. Her mom looks at her.

"Whoops. Sorry mom." Pareet blushes.

"Hello. Very nice to meet you and Lily."

"Nice to meet you too Pareet." We give her and Jillian a hug. Jillian is very pretty. Mid forty's with light brown eyes. An American doctor by training exhibiting beautiful dark features. Pareet is also as stunningly pretty as her mother. She is about my height with black hair and a perfect smile. I believe she is the same age as me. She and her mother can pass for sisters. Both are wearing sarees.

"Looks like our bags made it." Dad points to the revolving baggage carousel.

Doctor Karup already has a cart for us, so we pile all our luggage on it and follow him, Jillian, and Pareet to the terminal exit. Outside I walk into a wall of heat that feels like Alabama, but thicker and with a few more people. Doc Karup stops in front of a silver Land Rover. Not realizing it, I find myself watching Mr. Handsome get in to a small blue car across from us. He only has a single brown bag with him. It looks like some woman is picking him up, no wait, maybe a man. Can't tell, but whoever it is does have long black hair. The car is a TATA. What the heck is that? Back home that is something entirely different. Oh well, hope he enjoys his stay in India. Won't be seeing him again.

"Nice car Doc. New since last time we were here?" dad asks.

"Yes Jim. Not typical, but we needed something bigger to transport all of our guests in and needed the four-wheel-drive because of where we go. You know that much."

"Yep, that is very true," dad replies as he starts to pile our stuff into the back. The blue containers get fastened to the roof. Once all the bags and luggage is loaded, we pile ourselves in. A bit snug, however, we manage.

"How long is the drive again?" Mama looks cramped already.

"It's about two hours. Our highway system is only one lane with four lanes of traffic in it," Jillian reminds us while laughing. As we turn out of the airport, I realize that despite the laugh, she was serious. Cars, trucks, scooters, bikes, people, and more people everywhere. I take in the scenery around us. Neat. A three wheel car. A bunch of them everywhere like an epidemic.

"What are those things called?" I ask.

"They are rickshaws. They are like mosquitoes," Pareet yells out.

"Thanks I'll remember that. I like your sari. I hope there is time to buy one before we go home."

"Oh. Thank you. I like your hats. This is actually called a mundum neriyathum." She reaches down and touches the mundum." It is similar to a sari, but like two pieces instead of one. Very common dress of the woman of Kerala. I am sure you will have time to buy one, besides you just got here." Pareet who is sitting on the luggage behind us tries to adjust herself, but doesn't have much room to work with.

"Pareet, are you sure you don't want me to switch seats with you?" I ask seeing her discomfort.

"No no. I am fine. You are the guests." She shifts her body around some more. "We can take you shopping for a handmade sari in Balaramapuran. It is near Thiruvananthapuram."

"Thank you Pareet. That sounds good to me," Ally replies.

We are on a paved road moving with the traffic. There are trucks, buses, cars, rickshaws, motorcycles, scooters, and it seems like they are all blowing their horn. Every vehicle, or form of transportation, are wildly decorated. Guess it's the Indian way. Customize their ride. Lots of people walking too. Buildings of all sizes and colors. Not big and not like back home. More bunched together and covered with signs. One reads: Medicals Chemists & Druggists. That's a pharmacy I guess. A Honda Activa scooter zips by us in traffic. We pass a gas station with a big blue and orange sign that says Indian Oil. They have prices listed for petrol, Xtra mile, and Xtra premium, and diesel. Some of the other signs look like they are written backwards. That will take some getting used to. Seems like everything is a different color. I sit back, try to adjust, and continue to take it all in. Ally is doing the same. The Doc's are having their own conversation and so are the moms.

About an hour in to the drive we make a turn down a road and slow down for a paving crew. Just beyond them we turn again and I can't believe my eyes!

"What the heck? Mama look an elephant!" She stops talking and looks out the front of the Land Rover.

"You are not in Alabama anymore Miss Lily." Mama doesn't seem too alarmed having been here before, but it's my first real up close elephant and lucky for us, it did not run out in front of the car.

"Hey the only other elephant I have seen up close lives in Tuscaloosa Alabama" Ally shouts out loud.

"You have elephants in Alabama?" asks Pareet with some hesitation in her voice.

"No Miss Pareet, Ally is teasing. She is talking about the mascot for the university in Tuscaloosa." Carilyn jumps in to clarify the confusion.

We continue driving. The sun is going down, but it seems the temperature ain't. It is a little bit more green away from the towns we have been going through. We pass by a couple of more elephants, each with a chain around the bottom of its back leg like some kind of leash, as if? Still pretty neat to see.

Eventually it turns dark as day becomes night. We turn off the paved road and drive a short distance alongside of what looks like a concrete wall and stop at an iron gate. Doctor Nick jumps out and pushes the gate open. Doctor Karup drives through. The Land Rover's headlights light up a light sand colored concrete two story house. The top is smaller than the bottom almost looking like a two tier wedding cake which produces an upper wrap around balcony. The house is trimmed in white around the doors and windows along with the edge of the balcony. Two windows on the front of the house on the ground floor and two windows on the second floor on either side of glass patio doors. Off to the right is a carport and we drive under it and park.

"Great drive Doc," dad says as he gets out of the car.

"It was not a bad drive James, isn't it?" Doctor Karup replies as we all pile out of the car.

Jillian goes to the rear of the Land Rover and lets Pareet climb out. She stretches and shakes out her legs a bit as we follow her lead and do the same.

"Ok ok. Let's get the car unloaded." Dad starts grabbing luggage as Doc Nick begins to undo the blue containers on the car's roof.

Jillian turns to Pareet. "Please show Lily and Ally where they will be sleeping and can store their things."

"Ok mom. Follow me please and I will take you to your room."

Pareet takes one of Ally's bags and carries it for her. We follow behind. Inside the house, we pass through one room with no furniture in it and then another before reaching a set of stairs. Pareet opens a door to a room and she waves us inside. There are two twin size beds and a big window on the outside wall. I head over to the bed closest to the window.

"This is a nice big room Pareet. Ally do you mind if I take this bed?"

"Not at all Lily baby." She puts her carry-on bag by the other bed and Pareet puts the wheeled duffel by the same bed.

"Pareet, does this window close or have a screen?" I put my things on the bed by the window.

"No you don't need them, but you do need the big bars there to keep out the big animals." She laughs and points out the door. "Follow me and we will go downstairs to get some drinks and food. The bathroom is down the end of the hallway. You will find clean towels and wash cloths in there."

We follow Pareet down the stairs to another room that has one large table in the middle of it surrounded by simple chairs. Jillian is pouring tea and I think my dad is drinking a coffee, I can smell it. He'll be up all night. There are several bowls of fresh fruit on the table. Mama points at them.

"Help yourselves to some tea and fruit. Jillian has also made some rice cakes which are called idlis, and vegetables called pallya," mama explains as she hands us a paper mat for a plate and puts some food on it for us.

"Thanks mama." I look around and don't see anyone using forks so I do what everyone else is doing and dig in with my hand.

"Doctor Karup, what time will we be starting the clinic tomorrow?" I bite in to the idlis.

"Please please call me Singh while you are my guests. We should be heading out early in the morning. We will set some things up in an old school not too far from here. Maybe an hour toward the Ghats, the mountains." He goes back to eating.

"Thank you Singh. Will there be a lot of people to see?" I take a drink of tea, very good. Must be local from one of the tea plantations I have heard about.

"We will probably see anywhere from a couple of hundred to over five-hundred people a day. The word has already been put out that a free clinic will be operating this week and the word travels quickly around here and for quite some miles." Jillian, who is pouring more drinks, replies.

Ally leans over to me and whispers in my ear. "No I am not going to ask that." I gently push her away.

"Lily...."

"Don't you dare!" I try to put my hand over Ally's mouth but to no avail.

"Lily wants to know where Brandon is?"

Jillian and Singh look curiously at each other.

"He is not home yet but is looking forward to meeting both of you," Pareet answers enthusiastically.

I can feel my face burning with blush, so I think now is a good time to head up to bed.

"Jillian, Singh, and Pareet I thank you for everything, but I think I will turn in now. Goodnight everybody." I excuse myself from the table, give mama a kiss on her cheek, and try to fight the urge of wanting to run up the stairs and away from my embarrassment.

"Goodnight Lily," everybody replies in harmony.

CHAPTER IX

I wake up to see the most amazing red and gold butterfly sitting on the edge of my pillow. It seems to just be watching me. I think it realizes my eyes are open now and begins to gently flap its wings. Not wanting to scare it, I cautiously look back over my shoulder to see if Ally is awake. She is not. I turn back to the butterfly, which is now hovering in front of my face.

"Well hello there little butterfly," I say softly, again not wanting to scare it off. The butterfly flies a couple of feet toward the window and hovers again looking at me. I sit up slowly. It flies another couple of feet toward the window and stops again. I put my feet on the floor and sit fully up. If I didn't know any better, I would have to say that it wants me to follow it to the window. The butterfly flaps its wings faster.

"Are you reading my mind?" I whisper. Its wings flap harder still almost creating a buzz. It flies to the left and then to the right and turns toward the window as if excited now. I look back at Ally once more, still sleeping. I stand up and walk slowly toward the window. The butterfly flies to the window, lands on the edge, and appears to be looking outside. I reach the window and look outside.

"Oh my wow..." I blurt out a bit louder than I wanted to. I look back at Ally. She turns over to her other side after letting out a sigh. "Now I see why you wanted me to follow you." I look down at the butterfly and it is flapping its wings about, but not flying. Outside is a gift from the gods. "Thank you little butterfly." It must be Brandon. It has to be Brandon. The most perfect male specimen of the human race. My folks didn't tell me that. Incredible! Short wavy raven black hair resting just above his ears. Deeply tanned skin. His muscles glistening with a touch of sweat from beneath his black tank-top which is resting over black baggy long pants. Maybe four percent body fat, no, three percent. He is moving around on the grass almost like a gymnast, but he is throwing punches and kicks and such. I never saw anything like it before. There is rock music playing in the background, but not loud enough to wake anyone. WOW! I look down and the butterfly is gone. I run to Ally almost tripping over our luggage.

"Ally Ally Ally, wake up. You gotta see this. It's Brandon!" I turn and head back to the window. Ally gets up moaning and follows me.

"What is it baby?" She looks out the window. "Wow! Is that Brandon? Isn't he dreamy? Mom and dad didn't mention that. What's he doing? It's five-thirty in the morning. The sun isn't fully awake yet."

"Yep I think it is him."

"Well sister, put your shoes on and go say hello."

"No way. Are you crazy?"

"No time like now. Go on."

"Come with me?"

"Ok ok."

We both turn and find our sneakers, stop in the bathroom and quickly use the mirror, and then quietly head downstairs. We go out the door by the carport turn and walk around to the back of the house. He comes into view as we round the edge of the house. His back is toward us and he doesn't see Ally or me. Now he has a sword in his hand and is still doing whatever he is doing. Kung fu maybe. Definitely not yoga. Don't know. There is a soccer ball lying next to the house. I use the tip of my sneaker to grab it and line it up behind my foot. I kick the ball toward him putting all five foot three and a half inches of me into the kick. The ball flies past him. He turns our way, realizes we are watching him, stumbles, and the sword goes flying out of his hand toward us. Ally and I scatter to get out of the way. The sword lands sticking up out of the ground a foot away from where we were just standing.

"Namaste!" I shout out.

"Sorry I didn't know anyone was watching. Nice kick. Namaste."

"Is that kung fu?" I ask.

"No it is something older called kalarippayat." Brandon walks over and pulls the sword out of the ground.

"Where did you learn k..kalipat?" I struggle to pronounce the word.

Brandon smiles. "Kalarippayat." He turns and sets the sword down on the patio wall. "It was taught to me by my father. Hello I am Brandon." He reaches out to shake my hand.

I touch his hand and expect to feel his intense grip judging by what I have just seen, but it's soft and gentle. He reaches up and sweeps his long straight bangs to the side of his face revealing a better view of his golden brown eyes in the dim morning light. I guess him to be about five foot eight or ten inches tall. I feel like I am in some kind of fantasy and am yet to awake.

"My name is Lily and this here is Ally." I point over my shoulder. Brandon gives me a look like I am crazy.

"Who is?" he asks and moves his head to look around me.

Puzzled, I turn and Ally is nowhere to be found. Great. Nice one Ally. She bailed on me.

"Oh, sorry. I thought my friend Ally was with me." Starting to blush and now wanting to bail on Brandon; I don't know what else to say.

"Do you want to learn?" Brandon looks down and I realize I still have his hand, but seemed to have stopped the hand shake a while ago. Quickly I let go.

"What, the kalipatat?" I trip over the pronunciation once more.

"Yes kalarippayat. I will show you. Follow me."

I follow Brandon over to the middle of the yard. He stands next to me.

"Do what I do. First we stretch out," he says.

He steps out with his right leg and I do the same. He then squats down until he is almost touching the grass. He keeps his right leg straight and his left is bent at the knee. I follow his lead. Suddenly he is upright again and swings his right leg up over my head and spins in a circle. I try to follow, but end up with my leg spinning into his shoulder. He catches it and laughs just a little bit, but not to tease me. I am stuck there wondering what to do. His smile disappears and is replaced by a stare. We seem to check each other out while we lock our gazes. It's like an animal magnetism. Almost hypnotic. He hypnotizing me, and I him. I feel the temperature rise, I think. Neither of us making a sound, except for our breathing, which has become heavier.

"Love birds!" Saved. That was intense. He lets go of my leg gently. I try to catch my breath. We both look up to see Ally on the terrace.

"Brandon, I would like you to meet my disappearing friend Miss Ally the Magician." I try to give her a thanks-a lot-look, but it doesn't work.

"Nice to meet you Brandon. If you two are done we have to start getting ready for the clinic."

"The pleasure is all mine Miss Ally. If you happen not to vanish next time; I can show you and Lily some Kalarippayat." Brandon and I start to walk to the house.

"Sounds good Brandon. Namaste. There is some cold juice and tea for y'all in the kitchen." Ally folds both of her hands together palm to palm. Then takes her drink off the white decorative concrete railing and heads back into the bedroom.

It is almost completely day light out now. We walk back into the house and stop in the kitchen.

"Good morning you two." Pareet is standing there holding a glass of juice in each hand. "It is pineapple." She hands me a glass.

"Thank you. I like pineapple." I take a drink. It's good. Not from any can; that's for sure.

Brandon walks over to Pareet, takes the other glass of juice and gives her a kiss on the cheek. "Thanks Pareet."

"You know Lily, Brandon is one of the best practitioners of kalarippayat in Kerala. He could teach you how."

"Thanks Pareet. I believe I just had my first lesson." I finish my juice and put the glass down.

"Yes Pareet is too kind, but maybe you can teach me how to kick that soccer ball like that and we will call it even. I have to get washed up. See you in a little while."

"That's a deal Brandon," I tell him and head up stairs.

Passing through the middle room, I notice several people sleeping. Some are on cots and some are on mats on the floor. They must have arrived last night after I went to bed. Quietly, I seek out Ally.

I walk into our room and Ally is already showered and dressed lying on the bed.

"I am going to strangle you Miss Ally." I run over and jump on her. At least I try to. She moves and I hit the empty bed.

"Hey you found your prince. I gave you two some quality time."

"Thanks for the rescue. We were stuck there. I didn't know what to do. He is so hot I think he is on fire. I am on fire! Do you think he likes me?"

"From what I saw, yeah I think he likes ya."

"Hope so. Wow! On fire!"

"I know, right?" Ally seconds my opinion. "They don't make too many like that, do they?"

"Nope. Wow! I need a shower. A cold one, maybe," I say as I head off to the bathroom.

I finish with my shower and get dress. Ally is not in the room, but I hear people moving about the house, so I guess everyone is getting ready. Out in the hall I run into a pretty woman.

"Ciao. I am Valentina. I am a paramedic from Italy. Is the bathroom empty?" she says. I guess her to be about thirty, around my height, and with brunette shoulder length hair. She speaks with an almost unnoticeable Italian accent.

"Yes it is. I am Lily from Alabama USA. My dad and mama are in the medical field. I am here to help out."

"Yes. I met them last night," she responds.

"Where are you from in Italy?"

"Firenze. You might call it Florence."

"Yes Florence. Art museums. The Uffizi. Michelangelo's David. Leonardo da Vinci," I blurt out remembering my art history.

"That is very good. Have you been there?"

"No. Maybe someday."

"Never stop dreaming. See you later Lily." She heads to the bathroom.

"Nice to meet you." I head down to the kitchen.

It seems most everyone is awake and grabbing a quick bite with a sense of purpose. Mama and dad, along with Carilyn and Doc nick are here eating. Ally is standing next to Pareet. Jillian is putting out more idlis and fruit. Singh is already carrying stuff out to the car. Brandon is not here though. There are several people I don't recognize.

"Good morning Lily. How did you sleep?" mama asks me.

"Pretty well. I don't think the jet lag is as bad as I thought it would be. I'm ready to get out to the clinic."

"That's good. Singh has told us that some people from the medical clinics are already out there and quite a few more arrived here last night." Mama signals to dad to help Singh and start carrying things to the car. He obeys while still chewing his breakfast.

"Yes dear," he replies and picks up one of the blue medical boxes in the corner and follows Singh. In walks Brandon from outside.

"Hello Miss Lily did you enjoy the work out?" he says as he walks up to me.

I nearly choke on my food. Mama and Carilyn look at each other then, at Ally. Ally shrugs her shoulders. "Don't look at me," she responds as she heads out the door with a box of stuff.

I gather myself. "Oh, yes I did. We will have to do it again sometime. Mama, Carilyn; this is Brandon."

"Yes we know. We have been here before. We've met." Mama grabs a bag and heads toward the door.

"Good morning Brandon."

"Good morning Miss Abby."

"What kind of workout were you two doing?"

"Well Miss Lily gave me a soccer lesson," Brandon says looking at me. I look away.

"Oh, I see." Mama heads to the car. I am sure she is thinking there is more to the story than just a lesson.

"So Miss Carilyn. Who else came last night?"

"Well Lily a couple of paramedics came from Italy. There is a nurse from Greece, named Petra. Another couple from France, who I think are doctors, are already at the clinic. There is a nurse from Ireland and one from Australia. And several others, including a German who helps out with the shortwave radios because the cell phones don't always work where we are going. There is about sixteen, maybe nineteen, of us all together that came on this medical mission."

"Sounds like a pretty good turnout. We should be able to help a lot of people on this trip," I say while still chewing. The last of my fruit is gone. I grab my pack and sling it over my shoulder by one strap.

"Ok everyone. Introductions later. We will be leaving in five minutes. Double check to see if you have everything and let's head out to the cars," Jillian says.

"Allow me," Brandon says as he takes the pack off my shoulder and heads out the door. I follow. There are three cars here now. All four by fours like the Land Rover. Brandon puts my pack in the back of the second car. "You, me, Ally, and my sister are riding in this one. So is Valentina and Marco, the Italians, and Ludwik from Germany," Brandon informs us.

Ally and I get into the back seat. There is already a gentleman sitting there. Attractive. Not too old. Maybe late twenties with blond-brown hair cut in a flat top style.

"Welcome. I am Ludwik from Germany," he introduces himself.

"I am Lily and this is Ally. Very nice to meet you." We slide in next to him. Ally is in the middle of us. Pareet jumps into the front passenger seat. Valentina and a thin guy with long brown hair tied in a ponytail and a well-trimmed goatee for a beard climb in behind us into the third row. Also, a cute girl, a little bit older than us with short red hair and a touch of light brown freckles high on her cheeks gets in and sits next to Valentina. I love her green eyes.

"Hello everyone. I am Marco and this is Valentina." He reaches forward to shake hands as we turn around. I turn and shake his hand.

"I am Lily and this is Ally," I repeat as I also introduce our new friend. "And this is Ludwik from Germany."

"Please to meet you all," Marco responds with a thick Italian accent and we continue shaking hands with everyone in the car.

"Hello I am Moira. I am a nurse from Ireland."

"Nice to meet you Moira."

I turn back around. Brandon jumps into the driver's seat and starts the car. Looks like all the cars are loaded up and we back up and head out up the driveway and turn left opposite the way we came in last night.

"Hey Brandon play this," Marco says as he passes a music CD to Brandon.

"Which band is this Marco?" Brandon pops in the CD and adjusts the volume on the car stereo.

"It's the new one from the metal band Lacuna Coil out of Milano, Italy."

"Great, I saw them play live in England." Brandon cranks up the stereo a bit louder hoping to drown out the horns, I'm sure.

This should be about the most interesting thing I have ever done. It has been so far. A different country on the other side of the planet. Meeting new people from around the world. Cool stuff.

CHAPTER X

We drive down a narrow dirt road and turn onto a narrow paved road. It isn't long before we pass some more elephants going the other way. Chains clanging along the road. They still have a chain attached to their back legs and some Indian people are holding it walking behind the elephant. I guess it really is supposed to be some kind of leash. Maybe it is the elephant walking the humans. Looks like it to me. Still, I get a kick out of seeing them.

There seems like an endless line of cars and trucks going each way. All trying to get around one another. All vividly personalized with their own decorations. In Alabama, all you either see is an Auburn University sticker in the back window and an Auburn University license plate on the front of the car, or a University of Alabama sticker in the back window and a University of Alabama license plate on the front of the car. That be about it. The vehicle customizing is taken to a whole new level here. It is still pretty early and not so hot yet. Looks like it's going to be a clear day with just a couple of small clouds in the sky.

"Hey Brandon. How far we going?" Ally asks.

Brandon turns down the music just a bit. "Let's see. It will probably take about one hour to the turn off and then maybe twenty or thirty minutes from there. Most of the people who will be coming are very poor and live far enough away from the hospitals and doctors that it is impossible for them to get any medical care. We come out here about six to eight times a year. We also come out here for some special house calls to check up on some of the more needy of the people." Brandon continues to drive steering around the cars, trucks, people, and animals.

"Sounds good to me. It's more toward the mountains though, right?" Ally ponders.

Pareet turns around and looks at Ally. "Yes. We are heading to the Ghats. It's a pretty big mountain range. It runs from the north all the way down to the south of India. Not the tallest peaks in the world, but a little more remote than most other areas around here. There are some wildlife preserves out that way and some tea plantations near where we are headed."

"That's good news. Sweet tea and tigers. Good combination." Pareet faces me. "I like the tea but I have never seen a tiger here in all of my seventeen years."

"Lily will just have to settle for the tea then." Ally chimes in.

"Tea will be just fine with me. Brandon, every now and then I detect a bit of a British accent, am I right?" I ask him to see if I am losing my mind or imagining things.

"Yes you are right. I have gone to school in England for several years. Every once and a while my British accent slips through. I guess you would call it proper English, right?"

"We are from Alabama, so any English is proper to us. If I went to the Northern United States, they would say I talk funny. I think your accent is charming." Can't believe I just said that. Oh well.

"Thank you. Maybe I should use it more often around you then," Brandon responds with a bit more enthusiasm.

"Brandon, that won't be necessary. I think Lily has already been charmed." Ally gives me a light slap on my shoulder.

"Thanks Ally!" I try not to act to embarrassed.

"Are we missing something here. I don't understand," Marco asks curiously.

"Marco, I think there is a thing going on between the two of them. We should probably mind our own business," Valentina explains.

"Oh I get it now," says Marco sheepishly.

"I think that they would make a cute couple. Look about the same age. Perfect for each other," says Moira from behind me in a strong Irish accent.

I can see Brandon grin in the rearview mirror. I slouch down in the seat and try to change the subject. "Valentina, what is Florence like?"

"It is a great city. Home to many great masterpieces. Some are in the museums like the Uffizi and the Academia. Others are out in the open like the famous Ponte Vecchio bridge and the Duomo which had its dome designed by Brunelleschi. Most of the streets are narrow like the one we are on now. The people are polite. The river Arno runs through the city. You can walk to most places because everything is close together. There are many palazzos, or town squares, where you have many cafes, indoors and outdoors, to choose from. It is a good place to shop for gold and leather goods like handbags. Cobbled streets. You would enjoy it."

"Is this where you work as a Paramedic?" I inquire.

"Yes. Marco and I both work in Florence for Misericordia di Firenze, a hospital near the Duomo."

"Thanks for the information. I have great respect for the job Paramedics do."

"You are very welcome," says Marco. "Someday maybe you can come to Firenze and do a ride along on the ambulance with us."

"That would be awesome. I would love that. I will bring Ally," I say happily volunteering her.

"Ok. I will bring Pareet *and* Brandon." Ally throws it out there for some payback.

"How much further Brandon?"

"Moira, we are almost at the turn off," Ludwik answers before Brandon can.

Looking out of the windows, I don't see a lot of what we would call houses. More like simple huts. Some have a thatched roof. The forest, or in this case more like the jungle, is much thicker now. Still, cars and trucks are going both ways, but maybe not as many. We soon turn off the paved road onto a dirt one. Singh and my parents are in front of us. We travel about five miles and slow to a stop. Brandon puts the Land Rover into four-wheel-drive and we turn onto another dirt road and immediately I can see why we need the Land Rover. The vehicle is bouncing up and down and using all of its traction to get up this road if it ever was one. Off-roading Alabama style minus the red clay that you can never wash off your tires. We are not going fast; only about the speed that the terrain will let us.

We go about another mile and a half and pull into a clearing with two old small concrete buildings in the middle. They are rectangular with what looks like several windows on each of the sides. The white paint is peeling badly as if screaming loudly for a touch-up job. There is a small covered area in the front with a thatched awning. In between the buildings lies a fireplace that looks like it is used for cooking and some seats made from stone or concrete. There is smoke coming from the top of the fire place and an Indian woman appears to be smothered in smoke yet still cooking something. That is really impressive considering the temperature. It is already hot and it is going to get hotter, yet she is standing next to the fire and doesn't seem to be complaining. There are several other vehicles here. A large group of people in Indian dress are already here too. Patients I assume. A couple of people head toward us wearing more western style clothes. The French doctors I suppose and a few others. We all get out of our vehicles and start unloading gear from the back and the roof. My dad goes to meet the people coming over to our cars.

"Good morning. I am Jim from Alabama." He extends his hand.

"Bonjour Jim. I am François and this is Noella. We are physicians from France. I received your emails. Nice to finally meet you in person." He shakes hands with dad. François seems cordial; about five foot eight with thinning brown hair. Noella follows suit. She is pretty. Dark auburn colored long hair tied behind her head in a loose ponytail. A couple of years older than my mama.

"Looks like a good turn out so far. How many did you treat yesterday," dad asks politely.

"Well I think we saw about one hundred patients. The word is out and so I think it will get busier," Noella, an attractive forty-something years old responds. She takes a box and heads back to one of the buildings. François grabs a box.

"Jim follow me and I'll show you the set up."

"Ok. Right behind you." Dad takes a box from the back of their Land Rover and follows François into the same building as Noella.

We all grab something and follow. Inside the building there are tables set up along the length of the back wall loaded with medical equipment. There is a single door off to the far right, but doesn't seem to go outside. Maybe a second room, otherwise we are standing in one large open area. There are straw mats on the floor and a couple of chairs near the medical stuff. I don't see electric lights or ceiling fans.

"Hello. I am Doctor Hiro from Japan. Sakurako, my wife, is in the building next door with some patients," a thin, maybe fifty something year old, oriental man tells us.

"Hi Doctor Hiro. I am Lily. This is my father Doctor Jim, my best friend Ally, and that coming through the door over there is my mother Abby. Right behind her is Doctor Nick and his wife Carilyn, Ally's folks. Following her are Valentina and Marco, paramedics from Italy." I run out of breath introducing everyone.

"You can call me Hiro, it is my first name. Hello everyone." Hiro offers greetings to all of us and then introduces the Indian fellow sitting next to him. "This is Tushar our translator and druggist."

"Hello everyone," Tushar responds while counting medication bottles.

François shows us where to set the boxes and I head back outside with Ally. Brandon and Ludwik are pulling out what looks like a large antenna and the container next to them is open with a large radio in it, the shortwave I assume. Brandon picks up the radio and heads inside the building we just came out of.

"You need some help there Brandon," I offer.

"Thanks. I got this, but if you can catch Ludwik when he falls off the roof, that would be great."

"Ok."

I turn to see Ludwik heading up what looks like a homemade wooden ladder resting on the side of the building.

"Hey Ludwik. We are here to help you."

"Good. Please hand me the antenna when I get up on the roof," he heads up the ladder with a rolled up set of cables over his shoulder.

"Ready?" Ally asks.

"Ready," Ludwik puts down the cables.

Ally and I pick up the antenna and lean it toward Ludwik. He grabs the end and pulls it up to the roof placing the bottom end into a rusty metal bracket near the edge, takes a wrench from his pocket and tightens it into place. He then unrolls the cable, connects it to the antenna, and then lowers the rest of it to us.

"If you can please pass that through the window to Brandon."

"Sure thing Ludwik." I grab the end and hand it through to Brandon who was waiting for Ludwik to fall off the roof.

"Here you go Brandon."

"Thanks. That should be enough." He pulls it through the window. Ludwik climbs down luckily without falling.

"Nice job Ludwik," Ally tells him and we head back to the Land Rovers to see if there is anything left to be unloaded. There are some more people who we have not met yet, so we head over and introduce ourselves.

"Hi I am Lily and this is Ally. We are here with our parents from Alabama USA." We take turns shaking hands.

"It is nice to meet you Lily and Ally. I am Petra, a nurse from Greece. This is Gala, a nurse from Sweden, and Jia Li, a doctor from Hong Kong." She points to each of them on her left side. "And this here is Laney, a nurse from Australia." She turns and points to Laney on her right side.

Gala looks to be about forty, slim, short blonde hair, with a heavy Scandinavian accent. Jai Li is friendly, about five feet tall, with black hair resting slightly lower than her cheek bones. I think she is around thirty five.

"Well thank goodness for girl power. Nice to meet y'all." Ally continues shaking hands. "What's left to unload?" she asks.

"There are some more boxes left in the last Land Rover," Laney tells us in her Aussie accent. She is another young nurse, seems social and likable, around my height with brown hair resting just above her shoulders. We follow her to the car and grab some boxes.

"Where we putting these ones?" I ask.

"Let's put them in the same building as the other supplies. We can unpack them and take what we need for the other building and leave the rest for these patients." Petra informs us. She is taller than me with long black hair pulled back into a ponytail restrained by a colorful hair tie. Pleasant with leadership qualities. You can tell she has been a nurse for some time.

We all take our boxes back into the same building. Inside I see Brandon and Ludwik in the far corner sitting at a table that has the shortwave radio set up on it. Ludwik is speaking into the microphone. "Read you loud and clear, out." He adjusts a few knobs and stands up.

"Singh, the radio is up and working," Ludwik tells him.

"Ok that is great," Singh answers.

"I will help sort out the supplies." Ludwik comes over to us and so does Brandon. Just then, another person who I have not seen yet comes out of the back room.

"Someone mention supplies? Good morning I am Kenneth. Kenneth Hammersmith. I handle most of the supplies, or at least try to keep track of what we are using and what we need." A very good looking male of the human species says to us. He looks like he is around twenty, short sandy colored hair and an unshaven face like he has been out here a couple of days. He appears to be in shape, but not overly muscled. Might be about six foot two.

"Hello Kenneth Hammersmith. I am Ally Stephano and this is Lily Morgan. We are from Alabama. I hear an accent. Where might you be from? I detect an English gentleman, Correct?" Ally jumps in.

"That is very good. I am a paramedic from London. It is a pleasure to meet you both." He takes a box from Ally and sets it on top of another table. "Thanks, I'll start inventorying these right away." Kenneth nods to Ally and gets to work.

"I will help you," Ally responds.

"Do you want me to show you around?" Brandon offers to me.

"Yes. Show me."

I follow Brandon outside. For the first time, I realize there are some more roads leading into the clearing. More like dirt paths leading off in several directions. I take out my digital camera and snap some pics of the clearing, clinics, people, and of course Brandon.

"Brandon, where do these other roads go?" I ask.

"Most lead to other roads, more like the main road we came in on, and some go to small villages. We are somewhat hidden out here because of the differences between some of the people in the past. The clinics are also used for church and schooling. It's not that much of a secret that we are out here anymore though."

"I see. How about that small pathway over there?" I point to the far corner of the clearing where the grass is gently sloping up hill.

"That one heads to a tea plantation."

"Really? How far away is that?"

"Wow. You are pretty excited. It is about a quarter of a mile."

"I've never seen a tea plantation, or a live tea plant for that matter. Will you take me there if we have time?" I ask him hoping he will say yes.

"I am sure we will have time and yes I will take you; and don't go without me," he puts his arm on my shoulder and turns me around the other way. It kind of catches me by surprise, yet I feel secure by his touch.

"Why not?" I say being a little confused.

"Snakes. Cobras, Russell's vipers, and a few others. Giant spiders too. Now Let's go see what is going on in the other building. We will call it clinic two," he says cheerfully.

"Snakes? Spiders? Ok Brandon, I won't go without you. Let's check out the other clinic. Maybe they can use some help." I am liking him more and more every minute I am near him.

We walk over to clinic two, walk past some Indian folks standing outside the doorway, and go inside. There are more tables set up. A few more chairs and some mats on the floor. It looks like Sakurako, Doctor Hiro's wife, is tending to some patients. She might be forty five with short dyed brown hair parted in the middle with a few dark roots showing.

"There is Sakurako. Come on I will introduce you," says Brandon.

"Hello Sakurako. This is Lily from USA. She is here with her mom and dad, Abby and Doctor Jim."

"Thanks Brandon. Nice to meet you Sakurako. Can I help you?" I offer. She shakes my hand.

"It is nice to meet you. Yes you can," she says in a soft voice. "We are to triage the patients as they come to us to find out what their needs are. Do you want to take their vital signs and test their blood sugar if needed?"

"Yes Sakurako. I can do that. I will be right back. I am going to get my things from next door." I walk rapidly out of clinic two I guess because I am excited and head for the other building to retrieve my things. I don't realize it immediately, but I totally blew Brandon off as I left. I run into the other clinic and locate my pack. I pull out my pink Paris hat, tuck my hair behind my ears, and put the hat on. Next I grab my pink EMT scissors, pink stethoscope, and pink blood pressure cuff. I dig in the bag a bit and find my pink pen-light and put that in the cargo pocket of my pants.

"Hey, where ya going?" asks mama.

"Next door to help out Sakurako with triage. Ally, come on?"

"No, I am going to stay here and help out." Ally gives me a wink and nods over her shoulder toward Kenneth who has his back to her.

"Oh. Ok. Gotcha. See ya in a bit." I run back over to clinic two. Brandon is standing in the doorway. He has that beautiful smile on his face of his.

"Thought you might need this." He hands me a bottle of water.

"Sorry about that. I didn't mean to take off on you. Sometimes I can get excited when things are new to me." I take a big un-girlish like gulp of the water. Surprisingly, it is cold.

"Hey this is cold," I say wondering where the cold water came from.

"Yes it is. There is a refrigerator in the back room powered by a small generator out back. It is very quiet. We have some medicines and drinks in there. I am going to see what my dad wants me to do now. I will see you a little later on, ok?"

"Yes Brandon, thank you," I say, already missing him for some unknown reason. What is wrong with me? Focus Lily, focus.

CHAPTER XI

In the front of the clinic that we now call clinic two, are Jia Li, Laney, Gala, and Sakurako. There is a main table set up to the left which now has a bit of a line of patients forming up in front of it. Laney seems to be doing triage. I go to her and see what she needs.

"Hi Laney. Where do you want me?"

"Do you want to sit next to me and take vital signs?" Laney says in her cute Aussie accent.

"You got it. I can do that."

There is an empty chair next to her, so I take that one and sit down. I put my things on the table: stethoscope, blood pressure cuff, scissors, and pen light.

"You came prepared," Laney says checking out my array of pink kit.

"They were gifts. I am sure they will get broken in real soon. Who is the next patient?" I ask getting ready to do some actual work for the first time.

"This nice lady here is next. I have been told through Mandara, our translator, that she is complaining of itching and has a rash. She also says she has diarrhea and abdominal pain. We can get her vital signs and let's take her temperature. I am leaning toward a pinworm type infection."

Laney glances down at the patient's feet. I do the same. She is barefoot.

"Oh. I see. I read something about getting infections through the soles of someone's feet. Without shoes it is common to step on to an infected area and then have the worms enter the body through the skin, especially broken skin, right?"

"Lily you get to run the clinic now. Where did you go to school?"

"I am still in high school, senior, my last year starts when we get back home. My dad is a doctor and my mom is a nurse. Jim and Abby," I explain to Laney.

"Right. From next door. I couldn't remember if you were with Nick and Carilyn or Abby and Jim," says Laney.

"Temperature is 99.9 degrees. BP is 126 over 72. Pulse rate is 68 and her respirations are 14. I'm sorry, but I don't recall the treatment," I say feeling a bit stupid for not knowing. It was something I read on the airplane.

"No need to apologize. Let me run it by Jia Li to get official orders."

Laney turns to Jia Li and gives a report on the patient. Jia Li checks the patient's feet, listens to her lung sounds, looks inside her mouth with a flashlight, and inspects her rash on her arms and legs.

"Let's give her Mebendazole 100 milligrams by mouth for three days. A dose now and two to take with her," Jia Li orders.

"Thanks Doc." Laney turns to a large green square container to her right with many small white plastic drawers labeled with the names of medications. It looks like a four foot tall medicine chest. She takes out three pills and grabs a small brown paper pouch on the table and puts two of the pills in it.

"Mandara, can you ask this nice lady if she would take this one pill now and then one tomorrow and one the next day. Tell her she should feel better in about a week. Here is some Acetaminophen for her fever, take two now and then two every six hours as she needs them."

Laney puts some Acetaminophen in the small pouch as Mandara translates. The patient is all smiles. I smile back at her as I admire the bright colorful designs on her sari. I look at the doorway to see Moira and Doctor Nick come walking in. They are carrying a couple of boxes which they proceed to set down next to our supply table.

"Hey y'all. We thought you might need some extra stuff. You also got me and Moira to help. Also François will be over shortly."

Doc Nick and Moira set up on the table next to mine.

"Hi Moira. You just missed a good case of pinworms," I say teasing her just a little.

"Maybe next time. I am sure we will see more. Is this your first time seeing patients? You don't look much younger than Laney and I and we just finished nursing school last year," Moira asks me.

"Well sort of. It's my first time in the clinic setting, but I had a crash course in emergencies on the way to India."

"Really? What happened?" Laney inquires while digging through the new boxes of supplies.

"There was a bad car crash right in front of us soon after we left the house. We weren't even at the airport yet and we were treating people. It was real-world experience. I'm just glad my mom and dad were with me." I finish explaining the details to everyone and they are all a little surprised.

"You had no training except first aid and what your parents taught you? You handled it very well," Moira chimes in.

"I know Moira. I think I would have coughed up my breakfast on the patients. We are not that prepared for stuff like that even after several years of nursing school. Thank goodness you were not alone," Laney replies after organizing the new supplies.

"She can handle it. She is a Morgan. Tough like her father, Doctor Jim. Who is the next case?" Doc Nick looks around eager to treat somebody.

"Laney, I thought you did cough up your breakfast all over a patient once," Moira looks at Laney wanting I am sure, to share a story with us.

"Yeah I did, but that was my first bedpan! That's all I am saying. I got better since then."

Laney starts to triage the next patient and gives Doc Nick a report. This is a male patient in his fifties. I take his vital signs. His blood pressure is 190 over 110!

"Hey Doc Nick, his blood pressure is off the charts!" I relay the vital signs.

Mandara explains that he was taking a medicine for his blood pressure, but has since run out of it. She also tells us he has a throbbing in his head. He describes the pill to her.

"Yep I bet he does. Let us give him a two month supply of Metoprolol. Tell him to take one a day and someone can re-check him at the clinic in two days. Let's give him some Acetaminophen now for his headache."

Doctor Nick gives the patient a quick exam checking his pupils with a pen light, his pulse in each wrist, and listens to his heart with the stethoscope.

"Yep, sounds good."

Mandara takes the medicine from Laney and translates Doctor Nick's instructions to the patient. Laney hands him a paper cup of water and he takes two pills and thanks us in all smiles as he leaves. Such appreciative people unlike some of the stories I have been told about the people dad treats in the emergency room back home. I can already feel the heat of the day and these patients are standing outside, under the blazing sun, without chairs, or air conditioning, yet they smile when we can finally see them. Puts a whole new perspective on things when some patient back home who has been sitting in the air-conditioned waiting room of an 'Emergency Room' for two hours and starts to complain because their Emergency of a cough hasn't been attended to. Wow! Let us see who is next.

A lady sits down in front of Laney and is saying something to Mandara. She has gold hoop earrings hanging from her nose. Her head is partially covered by an orange-red shawl somewhat clashing with her blue sari. I think she is thirty something with dark brown weathered skin. She points down to her leg which has a cloth wrapped around the calf area just above her ankle. There is a small cranberry colored area that looks like dried blood which has apparently soaked through her homemade bandage.

"This nice lady cut her leg this morning and says the cut is deep and keeps bleeding," Mandara informs us as Laney begins to remove the bandage.

"Hey love. How about taking your pretty scissors and let's cut the bandage off her leg and we can see what we got," Laney instructs me.

I grab my pink scissors and grab the edge of the bandage and I am about to cut when the patient says something a bit louder to Mandara.

"Wait. She will un-wrap the bandage. She still has uses for the cloth after she washes the blood off of it," says Mandara.

"Tell her I am sorry. I did not know."

I try to explain to the patient. Mandara translates. Laney taps Doctor Nick on the shoulder.

"Doc would you like a suture tray? This nice lady has a 4cm LAC on the outside of her left lower leg," she says meaning a four centimeter laceration. "She cut it on a broken tree branch about three hours ago," Laney tells Doctor Nick. He takes a look at the patient's laceration.

"Yep. That sounds like a good idea. Can you please get me a suture tray, some Betadine, Lidocaine 1%, some sterile normal saline, 8.0 gloves, and 4.0 silk."

Doctor Nick washes his hands thoroughly with hand cleaner since we don't have a sink with running water while I try to figure out what the heck he just said. I decide to ask Laney.

"What did he just say? I haven't got a clue."

"Come on follow me and I will show you how to set up for this procedure." Laney stands up and heads to one of the tables behind us with supplies stacked up on it. "You will need one of these suture kits. That's an easy one because it is written on top of the package." She hands me a small white rectangular plastic container about six inches by seven inches. "You also need a bottle of Betadine and a bottle of sterile saline. Hopefully they are not opened then you know they are not contaminated since this procedure is as sterile as it can be to help prevent the wound from getting infected. The worst thing you can do is sew somebody up that still has bacteria in the wound." I grab the brown plastic bottle and a clear plastic bottle from Laney. "Nick's glove size is 8.0, nice size hands for a man by the way, and 4.0 is the size sutures he is asking for. So, we grab a pair of sterile surgeon's gloves. Here is the size on the packaging."

I never thought about my best friend's dads hands, but I catch her drift. She points to the large number 8 on the package and flips them around to make sure they are not open.

"In this box are various sizes and types of sutures."

She reaches in and takes out a small green package, maybe two inches by three inches, very flat with silver foil on one side, points to the 4.0 on the label and then points to the picture of the needle on the front of it, which happens to be curved.

"I will show you what to do next."

We head back to our seats and place our gathered up supplies on the table. I watch Laney open the suture kit. She explains how to unfold the wrapping inside in a special way in order to lessen the chance of contaminating what she refers to as the 'sterile field' which is everything except the outside one inch border. Next she pours Betadine into a small section of the plastic white tray which I can now see has different sections in it. Next, Laney pours sterile saline into a different area of the tray.

"We next open the packaging that contains the needle and thread so to speak. You can open it just enough to allow the contents to be dropped onto the sterile field. Once Doc has his sterile latex gloves on, he will use the instruments included in the suture kit to actually do the suturing. These include the two pairs of Kelly forceps, the scissors, and syringes with needles to do some irrigating and numbing of the wound."

Laney points to each item as she explains what is what, but doesn't touch them.

"Doc Nick, everything is ready," Laney says as Mandara helps the patient put her leg up on the chair.

Mandara then explains to the patient, in Malayalam, that the doctor is going to numb her laceration, so that the sutures will not hurt her.

Doctor Nick opens up the paper packaging that the gloves are in. He carefully grabs the inside of the right glove with his left hand and spreads the opening wide with his fingers to let his right hand slide into the glove. Next he takes the other glove with the now sterile gloved right hand and grabs the left glove, opens it from the outside under the rolled down wrist portion, and inserts his left hand into it. He joins both hands by interlocking his fingers and works both gloves snug onto each hand a bit further. Laney then holds up the bottle of Lidocaine and flips off the blue plastic top. She then holds the bottle toward Doc Nick. He takes a syringe from the instruments on the sterile field, uncaps the needle, and inserts it into the bottle of Lidocaine. Laney inverts the bottle upside down and Doc withdraws a syringe full of the numbing medicine. He sets that syringe down and takes another syringe and draws up some Betadine and then some sterile saline. He then irrigates the patient's wound with the saline and then the Betadine. After that he drapes a blue paper cloth over her leg. There is a large circular hole in the middle which he centers over the laceration.

"Mandara, if you can please inform this nice patient that I have to give her the numbing medicine and she will feel a couple of small pokes with the needle until the medicine starts to numb her leg and then I will put in the sutures. Thank you."

He turns and takes the syringe full of Lidocaine and removes the cap from the needle. Mandara says something that sounds like abcdefghijklmnopqrs and so on. All I hear is the alphabet. I try to mimic the syllables in my head, but have no clue. So I ask her.

"Mandara what did you tell her?"

"Charmam owshad'am keytupaatuteerkuka kaal. Oh, I just told her that the doctor is going to give her some skin medicine to repair her leg." Mandara explains.

"Does the patient have any allergies?" Doctor Nick asks. "No known allergies Doc," replies Mandara who is holding the patient's leg on the chair so she does not move it.

"She has good distal pulses and the foot is nice and warm, so I don't think there is any damage to the nerves or blood vessels. I think a few interrupted sutures should do the trick."

Before I can ask Doctor Nick, he explains what an interrupted suture is.

"Lily, I am just going to do one stitch at a time, cut the thread, tie it off, and then do another one instead of doing a whole bunch in a row like you are sewing a dress for the Eufaula Pilgrimage. I will start in the middle of the laceration, or wound, and then divide each section into halves and place a stitch in the middle of each one of those until I am done. She will probably get about seven or eight sutures total."

"Oh, I understand. One stitch at a time. Got it." Laney hands me a flashlight.

"Here you go. Try to hold this over the laceration, so that the doctor can see what he is doing. Not much for lighting in here," Laney instructs me.

Doc inserts the needle of the Lidocaine filled syringe into the skin next to the laceration. He moves the syringe around by twisting it and pointing it in different directions while the tip is still under the skin and depressing the plunger on the syringe with his thumb. He pulls out the tip of the syringe and picks out another spot and repeats the same method of injecting the skin as before. Doc Nick pokes the skin around the wound a few times. There is no response from the patient. Not even a flinch. The Lidocaine is working and the area around the laceration is numb. He then takes the syringe filled with the clear sterile saline and irrigates the laceration until the syringe is empty. Next he squirts Betadine into the laceration, irrigating some more. Laney had already washed the outside of the wound with a Betadine surgical scrub brush.

Doctor Nick takes one of the Kelly forceps and clamps the needle, with the suture already attached to it, on the end of the forceps. The Kelly forceps have a section about half way up the forceps that clamps together with what almost looks like teeth on a saw blade. This way you don't have to hold and squeeze them at the same time as trying to do a procedure such as suturing. There are two loops on the end of the handle portion that lets you put a finger in each one making it less likely to drop them. My dad showed me how to use them before we left home. I have not seen suturing done up close like this before and definitely never assisted with sutures. This is interesting.

"Here I go. You want to insert the needle at a ninety degree angle to the wound and go as deep as about the wound is wide."

I watch as the needle goes into the skin and feel my stomach go queasy for a second. I don't feel bothered seeing this. Maybe just because I have not eaten in a while.

"Next disconnect the Kelly's as the needle comes up through the skin on the other side, and reconnect them so that you can pull the needle all the way through the skin. You may be able to go through both sides at the same time catching both edges of the laceration, or you might have to do each edge separately. The key is to bring both edges together at the same height. You don't want one edge of the laceration higher than the other and you don't want to curl the edges either. If that happens you will stop blood flow in the capillaries and end up with dead tissue on the wound edges and a crappy looking scar. Then just bring the edges together so that they are touching. Not too tight and not too loose. If it's still open then you will have a bacteria pool of infection. Not good. And a couple of square knots should do it."

Doc Nick then takes scissors and cuts the thread leaving enough for the knots. He uses Kelly forceps and fingers to tie the knots. He grabs the end of one thread with fingers and the other end with the pair of Kelly's. In a blur, Doc Nick wraps the thread around one finger of his left hand and then pulls the ends of the thread together until there is a small visible knot on top of the wound. He then takes the pair of sterile scissors from the suture kit and trims the edge about a quarter inch from the laceration.

"That's one. Surgeon's knot or square knot. They'll both hold. A few more and we can break for lunch."

I glance at my watch and realize it is almost noon. Looking around I see many different patients have been coming in and have been treated while we were taking care of this nice lady. The morning has passed by quickly.

"You learning anything from this quack?" A voice says from behind me. I turn around.

"That's a funny one. At least some of us came here to work and not slack off," Doc Nick responds to the comment and then laughs. "Can't you see I am in surgery?"

"My daughter could have had those stitches in quicker than you. As a matter of fact, Jackson our jack russell, would have been done and on to the next case by now."

I hear lots of snickering after that one.

"Hey did you hear the one about the elephant and the American doctor?"

Louder snickering. Jia Li and François look over to see who is making the comments.

"Dad, when did you get here? I didn't see you come in."

"Just a minute ago. We have some food next door, so when you are done here with Doctor Nick's School of Needlepoint, come on over and get something to eat," dad says while still laughing at his own sense of humor. He turns and heads back out the door of the clinic still snickering like a hyena.

"Ok. All finished. Let's get her some Cephalexin, so the laceration doesn't get infected, and a tetnus shot. Mandara, please tell her to take the stitches out in ten days," Doc Nick says while admiring his nifty work.

Mandara hands a suture removal kit, which basically just contains small scissors and tweezers, to the patient and explains to her what it is and how to use it. Laney returns with the medicine which she explains to me what it is.

"This is an anti-biotic called Cephalexin. We will have her take two pills a day for ten days and Mandara has already told her to look for signs of infection of the wound and also if she gets a temperature or starts feeling ill. If so, then she should return to us before the ten days and we can examine her to make sure the wound is not worse."

"I think you did a fine job Doctor Nick." I attempt to console him.

"Well thank you Lily. Your daddy ain't happy unless he gets to *Hee Haw* me a little, but revenge is sweet. I'll get him back. Always do," Doctor Nick replies with a sinister grin on his face.

"Sounds good to me. Make sure that you do it in front of me, so that I may have a laugh at both of y'all expense."

I get up and head toward Moira who is talking with Laney and Gala.

"There is food next door if you two would like to get some lunch."

89

I inform them as I place all my kit into the left and right cargo pockets of my pants, causing the pockets to balloon outward as if inflated with helium. I even decide to keep one of the Kelly forceps after I disinfect them with Betadine.

"Moira, you and Gala go with Lily and I will help out Jia Li until you two get back. Then I will take a lunch," Laney responds.

"Sounds good Laney. Thanks. See you in a bit," says Gala.

We file out of the door to the clinic and turn left toward the other building. I glance around to the right side as I exit the clinic and can see a lot of people still waiting to be seen. Nobody seems angry. Amazing. It is much hotter now and my shirt is reminding me of that fact by sticking to my back from the humidity. The sun seems even brighter having been inside all morning. I watch all the trees sway back and forth slowly in a very light breeze. They must be forty to fifty feet tall. I know some of them are coconut, but not sure what the rest of them are. Some seem to be wrapped in vines and others have a strange fruit, at least I think it is a fruit, growing out of the branches. The many shades of greens and browns are thicker near the bottom of the trees almost creating a natural fence around the clearing except for the dirt roads and trails leading to the clinics.

"What the? Hey!"

I blurt out as my right hand scrambles into my cargo pocket searching for my sunglasses.

"What's wrong Lily,?" Moira asks nervously as she and Gala stop walking and face me then follow my gaze toward the clearing edge.

"Oh. It is nothing, I don't think."

I untangle my sunglasses from the other stuff in the cargo pocket and put them on as quick as I can hoping to cut down the glare of the sun. I scan the edge of the clearing again.

"No I just thought I saw someone over in the trees there watching us. They aren't there now." I explain as I search in vain. They both look at me and then again to the edge of the clearing where I am focusing my stare.

"Well there are a lot of people here now, so I would not be surprised if one or two are in the jungle," Gala reassures me. "Maybe looking for a bathroom."

"I understand, but this person looked like someone I saw at the airport after we landed. They were driving a car and picked up a passenger on our plane."

I keep scanning the area, but I am not seeing anyone.

"Sister, you just need a drink and some food in your belly. I am sure it was nothing. Let's go eat something," says Moira.

"You are probably right," I reply but I still can't shake the feeling of having seen that person before.

CHAPTER XII

Maybe it was an illusion with the humidity and all. Something to eat should fix me up. We walk past the open area between the two clinics, where the large outdoor oven made from concrete is located, and the Indian woman who was cooking in the smoke earlier this morning, is cooking again except she is standing in a different batch of smoke from before. She doesn't seem to be bothered by it. Her poor lungs! The woman has silver-black hair pulled back into a ponytail. Her sari is a bright blue and yellow. She has an assortment of different size pots on top of a smooth section of the stove in front of her. Some are in the oven cooking and some look empty. The fireplace I saw this morning is several feet from the oven, but doesn't appear as permanent. There are cinder blocks stacked up on three different sides with a pile of sticks and small logs of wood blazing away between them. On top of the fire is a very large round pan, maybe about two feet in diameter, and has some kind of food cooking in it. On the ground near the fire are three more pans like the one cooking over the fire. They are only several inches high, maybe five or six, and it looks like they are getting ready to be cooked since there is stuff that I don't recognize in each of them. There is an Indian gentleman stirring the contents of the pot. Smoke is pouring out from under the pan. I wave hello and the gentleman waves back to me. I look back toward the other clinic. Ally is standing out in front of the building chatting it up with Kenneth and Brandon.

"Hi there," I offer.

Ally looks at me. "Hey babe. What you been up to?"

"Really interesting morning so far. Learning lots from Moira, Gala, and Laney who is still working in the clinic. Your dad even gave me a suture class. It was very cool. Hi Brandon. Hello Kenneth. Are you two taking care of my friend here? She can be a handful at times." I reach out and pull Ally's hat down over her eyes.

"Me? What about you? Hey Brandon, take her. She is all yours now," Ally readjusts her Paris hat from France and pulls me toward Brandon.

"Don't get me in trouble Ally," Brandon catches me. How secure I feel when he has a hold of me. Focus Lily! "You hungry? Follow me," Brandon says as he points around the corner of the clinic. I follow.

"Sort of starving. I can use a bite to eat." We turn the corner and there is now a blue canopy set up covering the concrete patio next to the building. It is covering a large area. There are about six rows of people sitting next to one another on bamboo mats. They each have a small green flat piece of what looks like paper in front of them being used as a plate. There are some Indian folks moving about from person to person spooning food out of silver colored buckets and placing it on their green paper in front of them. There doesn't appear to be any color missing from the color spectrum, because of all the different mundum-neriyathum sarees worn by the females. The most bright, vivid, and colorful picnic I have ever been to. The Indian gentlemen all are wearing the common white dohti bottoms with different colored button down shirts.

Ally and I follow Brandon to a set of bamboo mats on the ground and we sit down. Kenneth and Brandon are the bookends and we are between them. A nice looking Indian woman comes over to us and Brandon speaks to her in Malayalam. She places a green paper in front of each of us. It looks more like what we would call a place mat that you would get under your plate in a fancy restaurant, or even a bar-b-q joint, back home. She then takes her silver bucket and puts a scoop of what looks like rice onto the green paper in front of us. Brandon says, "nanni" to her and she smiles, nods her head, and moves on down the row of people.

"Brandon what does nanni mean?" I ask curiously.

"Oh I just told her thank you."

Next a gentleman steps in front of us carrying drinks. Again Brandon speaks to him in Malayalam.

"Minaral velamundaakum dayavayi," he says rapidly, I think.

"Something mineral, right?" Ally rattles off. "Where are the forks?" she adds.

"That's correct. I asked for mineral water for us, and your right hand is your fork," Brandon smiles as he dips into his pile of rice. We follow his lead. The Indian gentleman places a bottle of mineral water in front of each of us and moves on. Another gentleman appears in front of us and puts a piece of some kind of meat in front of us, but I don't recognize it.

"It is fish," says Kenneth in between chewing his rice.

"Thanks for clearing that up, but what is this stuff?" Ally points to the creamy stuff the next Indian woman has placed on our mats.

"That would be curry. Careful, can be a bit spicy," Kenneth answers.

"We don't have any spoons," I add.

"Don't need any," Brandon points to the woman seated next to him. "Do what she does."

We look over and see that she is using the flatbread to scoop up the curry. She isn't sweating or short of breath, so I take the bread and scoop some of the curry and take a bite. Wow! Yep spicy. So much for the warning. I gulp some of the mineral water down trying to put the fire out on my tongue to no avail. I try not to let on that there is an inferno going on inside my mouth.

"Hey that is pretty good curry. Never had it before. Not quite as hot as our buffalo wings back home." I grab the piece of fish and take a bite. Not bad. Now I know what the Indian gentleman was cooking in the large pan over the fire. The fish. He had cut it up into many pieces, so that there was enough to feed everyone. Lots of people have showed up to be seen in the clinics since we started this morning. It is very cool that they are being looked after and fed lunch while they wait to be seen.

"Brandon what is this stuff called," Kenneth asks.

"That would be jackfruit. They hang in the trees and you have to climb up and get them. Then you cut them open and inside are many little jackfruits." He dips back into the last of his curry. I don't even see any sweat on his forehead. Must be a pro. The sweat would be pouring down my face if it wasn't for my hat. Another Indian gentleman stops in front of Brandon with his silver bucket. He has his hand on his large spoon and about to serve Brandon. Brandon waves him off, thanks him, and then folds his paper mat up. "You have to wave them off and fold your plate up, or they will serve you all day long," Brandon instructs us, so we do the same.

I look around, but don't see our parents anywhere. I decide to pop into clinic one. "Hey y'all, I'm going to find my mom and dad and see what they are up to."

"Sounds good to me. I'll go with you," Ally follows me.

"Thanks for showing us how to eat the lunch Brandon. You can come with us." I offer an invitation.

"Ok then. Right behind you," says Brandon, as he and Kenneth follow us into the other clinic.

We make our way up to the front of the building where the tables and chairs are set up. Mama is sitting next to dad who has just removed a tongue depressor from a small girl's mouth. He then takes an otoscope, which has a light on the end of it, and looks into his small patient's ears. She is sitting on what I assume is her mother's lap.

"All right then. No OE or OM. TM is intact. No excessive cerumen and no insects. Good to go." My dad says this in medical talk. I don't have a clue.

"Hi mama. What did dad just say?"

"Hi baby. He said there is no otitis externa. No otitis media. The tympanic membrane is intact and no ear wax. How is it going next door?" Mama and my dad smile as the patient is carried out by her mother.

"Good so far. Busy. I saw Doc Nick do some sutures. Another patient with high blood pressure. Pinworm infection."

"Sutures that my daughter could have done quicker," dad says again except this time to my mother. "All we have been doing is mostly check-ups and physicals. Nick is stealing all my glory."

"Yeah yeah we know dear. I am sure Nick has a different version of *your* story," mama shakes her head at dad. "Did you eat yet?"

"Yep. We just ate. I really liked the curry," I say as I turn and face Brandon, but he doesn't seem convinced.

"Mrs. Morgan, Lily did very well at lunch. She did mention something about buffalo wings which I think I have to try the American version when I can get there. Had some in England at a pub once, but they weren't real hot."

"It's a deal. When you come to America, I will take you for some hot wings," I blurt out absent mindedly. Wow. Coming to America. Did I just ask Brandon for a date?

"Brandon, you know you are always welcome and you can stay with us," mama puts the invitation out there. Ok I am officially embarrassed again. The best looking male specimen of the human race in my house. Holy crap! I decide it's time to get back to work before mama buries me any deeper. So much for that.

"Kenneth you are welcome to come also since you hang out with Brandon when he is in England." Mama is doing a fine job without a shovel.

"That would be a good idea. I could come down from Columbus to visit Kenneth, oh and Brandon when you come to visit," Ally speaks. When? It is definitely time to go before mama has us married.

"Back to work now. See y'all later," I say as I head to the door.

"Brandon keep an eye on her will you please?" Mama asks him.

"Sure thing Mrs. Morgan." He turns and follows me.

"And please call me Abby," mama requests.

"Ok Abby. See you in a while. Bye Doc." Brandon tells my dad who is already examining the next patient.

"See ya later son." Dad apparently is on mama's let's-marry-off-our-Lily wedding team. Oh boy. I grab Ally on the way out the door.

"Where is the bathroom at?" I ask her.

"Follow me sweets. Boys, we will catch up with you in a minute," she tells Brandon and Kenneth who continue on to the other clinic.

"There is a ladies room behind the clinics. We have to go between the buildings, past the big outdoor kitchen. Follow me."

We make a right turn by the big gray concrete stove. I wave hello again to the Indian lady who is still cooking. Still standing in the smoke. Hidden from view by the stove, are two smaller white structures with the same peeling paint job as the clinics. They are both single story buildings, like the two clinics, but the roofs aren't as high. They are several feet apart from one another. On the top corner of the one nearest clinic two, is the word LADIES in black painted letters. On the other building the word GENTS is also in black letters. Narrows it down. I follow Ally through the open doorway. Inside there are two stalls with thin shaky wooden doors used for an attempt at some sort of privacy. There is no toilet paper, so I pat my hold everything cargo pocket just to make sure my TP is still with me. Yep. Still got it. That's a relief. I open the door to the stall in front of me. It's even thinner than I thought; barely hanging on by the hinges.

"Hey Ally, I think someone stole the toilet," I shout to her in the next stall.

"That hole in the floor with the footpads on either side of it, is the toilet," Ally replies followed by some heavy laughing. "It's not that bad. I was in here earlier." She tries to console me.

"Ok, but if I fall over you better not tell anyone and you better not laugh." Reassured by Ally's expertise, or should I say *expertease*, I guess I have no other choice.

"Good luck honey." She is still laughing.

We finish our business and head back outside. Ally passes me some alcohol hand cleaner from her cargo shorts. I take some, wash my hands, and give the cleaner back to her. She turns to walk back up the gentle slope to the clinics, but I grab her shoulder.

"Ally come here for a minute." I pull her arm toward me and lead her back behind the concrete walls of the bathrooms so that we can't be seen.

"What's wrong dear?" she sees the seriousness on my face and senses the change in the tone of my voice. "This isn't about the guys, is it?"

"No Ally. It's not. When I left the other clinic before, to go to lunch; some movement in the edge of the clearing, in the jungle, caught my eyes. It was a person. A man. A man with long black hair. It was the same man I saw pick up Mr. Handsome at the airport when we landed," I relay my concerns.

"What?" she says with extreme surprise in her voice. Her eye brows are raised and she stares at me with an equal amount of anxiety.

"You are not joking Lily, are you?" She only calls me Lily when we have a serious conversation. "You saw Mr. Handsome at the airport?"

"Yes. I watched him get into a car, one of those Tata's, and it was driven by the man I saw before lunch."

"Did Mr. Handsome, or him, see us at the airport?"

"I don't know. I didn't think so, but I am not sure."

"It might have been some coincidence, or even someone entirely different. There are a lot of people here. A lot with black hair too. Maybe he is connected with the medical clinics in some way." Ally keeps staring not knowing what to think.

"I am positive it was the driver. If he is connected, then that doesn't explain why he was with Mr. Handsome. Something just doesn't feel right about any of this. You believe me Ally, don't you?"

"Yes I believe you. I just hope it was a coincidence and not the fact that Mr. Handsome is upset because of the way I treated him at the airport in France, and then he had his pal follow us." Ally cracks a bit of a smile. "Talk about holding a grudge, right?"

"Should we tell somebody about it?"

"I think we will be ok and I think there is a logical explanation for it. Are you sure a coconut didn't fall on your head?" Ally smiles and gives me a quick hug trying to alleviate my fears, I'm sure." Let us get back to work."

CHAPTER XIII

We make our way back to clinic two, the one I was in this morning. There is still a line of people waiting to be seen. No one seems upset. Everyone is going about their own business until they can get inside.

Doc Nick is back up front seeing patients. Sakurako and Doctor Hiro are here, as well as Laney and Moira. Gala is giving out some medications to a patient and Mandara is translating for her. Brandon is talking with Doc Nick and Kenneth is taking an inventory of supplies.

"Hi. We are back. Where did François go?" I ask thinking we are missing someone.

"Hey there Lily," Doc Nick says, "François, Noella, Petra, and a few others went to the other clinic site."

"You mean next door?"

"No. I mean there is another clinic DHW is running. It's about five miles from here. It's closer for the people who are coming from that direction. There are a total of two clinic sites. This one, and the other one," Doc explains.

"I see. Do they have enough help?"

"Yes Lily. They are staffed pretty well. We keep in touch with them by the shortwave radio," Gala tells me and Ally.

"Welcome back Lily. I will help you out and Kenneth will help Ally," Brandon says as he pulls a chair out for me.

"Sounds great. On to the next patient." I retrieve my stethoscope and supplies from my cargo pockets giving the threads a rest from the strain of my pink kit. "Did I miss anything interesting?"

"No. Mostly just check-ups and physicals," Moira looks over and tells me. "Let's get a set of vital signs on this next patient. Mandara tells me that she has a past medical history of diabetes, so we will need a finger stick to determine her blood glucose."

"Ok Moira. I'm on it." I take the blood pressure cuff and place it on her arm and Mandara tells her what I am doing. I smile at her and say, "hello." She responds with the same hello. After her blood pressure, I take her pulse to determine the heart rate, and then count her respirations. I skip taking her temperature and grab the glucometer. Mandara explains to her what I am going to do next and the patient says ok. I take an alcohol swab and clean off her left ring finger. Next I take a test strip and insert it into the glucometer which turns it on. A couple of numbers flash on the screen and then it says to apply sample. I turn to Brandon and say, "Careful there is going to be some blood; I don't want you passing out on me."

"Good one Lily. I've poked my share of fingers, but thanks for the warning." He pats me lightly on my shoulder. I catch Doctor Nick looking, concerned I'm sure.

"Here I go..." Brandon puts his hand on top of mine.

"Wait just one second." He lifts my hand up slowly and grabs the lancet that I am about to use on the patient to get the blood sample.

"Let's flip this over and put the sharp end facing the patient, so that we don't poke our finger accidentally," he returns the lancet to me pointing it the correct way.

"Sorry about that. Thank you Brandon." He shakes his head, but not in a condescending way. "Little poke."

Brandon translates that for me. I put the lancet against the patient's finger and depress the button on the side causing the spring to release and a tiny needle pokes the skin. I pull the lancet away and give the finger a light squeeze. A good size drop of blood forms on the finger. I take the glucometer and put the tip of the test strip against the blood. The machine sucks up the blood and within five seconds I have a reading.

"Moira, her blood sugar is 104." I put a small Band-Aid on the patient's finger and relay the rest of the vital signs. Moira writes them down.

"Good job Lily. Doc is going to finish the physical and then I think she can go. Her blood sugar is about where it was last time that she had it checked," Moira relates to me. Doctor Nick finishes his examination and tells her she is ok to leave.

"I'm not making you nervous, am I?" Brandon catches me off guard.

"What? No. Of course not," I reply trying to sound confident, but probably not sounding to convincing. World's best looking guy sitting next to me. What's there to be nervous about?

"Glad to hear that. Let us see who is next," Brandon says. "Moira, are we ready for the next patient?"

"Yes Brandon. Next one please," responds Moira.

A frail looking elderly gentleman sits down in front of us. I place the blood pressure cuff on his left arm and pump it up. Brandon checks the pulse in the patient's right wrist and counts the beats to get his heart rate. He then counts his respirations.

"Can I borrow this?"

Before I can respond, Brandon takes my pink stethoscope out of my ears and puts it in his. He gets up, steps behind the patient, and places the stethoscope on the patient's back listening to the lungs.

"Thanks." Brandon drapes the scope around my neck. Dumbfounded, I don't know what to say. I try to regroup my thoughts.

"Doc Nick" he shouts "There are wheezes in both upper lobes of the lungs."

"Thanks Brandon. Send him down to me. I will probably give him a couple of Albuterol inhalers and send him on his way. I actually remember this gentleman from last year," Doctor Nick replies.

We continue seeing patients for the next several hours. Brandon checks their pulses, respiratory rates, and listens to their lungs when needed if it looks like a respiratory patient. Brandon shows me where to place the stethoscope when listening. I in turn keep checking their blood pressures, except I hand Brandon my stethoscope when I am done. After a while we switch jobs, so I can get more experience doing all the vital signs. I find it more interesting doing vital signs on real people, and the more you do, the better you get. I appreciate the experience. After a while I think it's time for a break.

"Moira, do you mind if we take five?" I ask trying not to sound too desperate.

"Yeah, absolutely. Go stretch your legs. We got things covered here." Moira goes back to work.

I look around and don't see Ally or Kenneth anywhere. Oh well, not the time to speculate.

"Brandon, let's go stretch." I get up from my chair and start toward the door.

"Sounds good. I will grab us some beverages," Brandon says as he disappears into the back room for a few seconds and reappears with two bottles of the cold water. He hands one to me and I follow him out of the clinic. This time I put my sunglasses on first, so I don't burn up my eyes in the bright Indian sunshine.

Outside, the sun is brilliant. The forty to fifty foot tall trees are still gently swaying in the light breeze. I concentrate on the trees of many different types, some with vines wrapped around them, some with what looks like fruit on them and some without fruit. This gives me an excuse to go explore them a little closer, or at least a little closer to where I saw Mr. Handsome's friend, which happens to still be on my mind. Just too odd to be a coincidence.

"Where do you want to go Lily?" Brandon offers if on cue.

"How about over to the edge of the clearing right there?" I point off to the right, just past the other side of the vehicles. "You can tell me what kind of trees those are."

"Sure, follow me and I will teach you about the trees of India," he says with a bit of a smirk and pleasant tone in his voice.

Brandon starts to head too far off to the left, but it isn't the spot I am interested in. I redirect him to where I want to investigate. "What are those trees called?" I point to the right and up at the large green watermelon shaped fruit hanging from the cluster high up in the tree. The bottom looks like a coconut tree, but the fruit is different. We reach the very edge of the clearing where I think Mr. Handsome's buddy was standing. The green-brown grass is about as high as my mid thighs. It looks crushed at the base of one of the trees in front of us and there is more crushed grass leading from directly behind the tree off into the jungle almost like a pathway, but only used once or twice. Whoever it was stopped at that tree and didn't continue to the edge of the clearing which would have left an opening on the edge, interesting, or maybe smart, but more like on purpose than a coincidence.

"Papaya. They grow in a cluster and the men here will pull up their dohti, the long baggy dress-like pants so to speak, tuck it into their waist band, and climb up the tree to get them," Brandon explains, but doesn't notice me checking out the area. I continue my distraction and point to the left at another cluster of trees with thick looking brown vines wrapped around their trunks.

"What kind of trees are those over there?" I take a drink of water nonchalantly.

"Pepper trees. Probably left over from the spice trade hundreds of years ago." Brandon takes a drink. I turn to the left and walk along the edge of the clearing having confirmed what I suspected. Why would Mr.

Handsome's sidekick be here? Why do I even remember him? There was something about his face; a scar or something. I wish I at least knew Mr. Handsome's real name, so I don't have to call him 'Mr. Handsome.' I decide not to worry about it. There are more important things on my mind. Not even realizing it, Brandon is walking so close to me that my shoulder is lightly grazing against his arm.

"So, Brandon, won't your girlfriend get mad at you for escorting me around?"

"My girlfriend? Maybe if I had one, but I don't. I'm single and usually very busy with school and everything. What about you?"

"What about me?" I play along as we continue to walk the clearing edge.

"Do you have a boyfriend?" he asks more determinedly. "I don't want to intervene if you are seeing someone."

"No I don't have a boyfriend. Kind of busy like you I guess with school and soccer. I will be a senior in high school when we get home. It will be my last year for soccer unless I play in college."

"So you plan to go to college; what do you want to study?" Brandon asks.

"I would really like to study art history, maybe at a European school. That would be awesome, but my parents think it would be more practical to pursue a career in the medical field. Nurse, doctor, or something like that." I explain.

"It all sounds good. You should go with your dreams though. Follow your calling," Brandon says reaffirming me.

"Where do you go to school Brandon?

"I just finished my first year at University College London in, of course, London, England. My main studies are in engineering, primarily civil, environmental, and geomatic. I've also been taking archaeology classes for what they call in the U.S. school system, a minor. Almost continued studying Latin which I learned some during my college prep years."

"Got it. Major is engineering with a minor in archaeology. Sounds very interesting, and difficult. Why didn't you go into medicine like your parents?"

"I always wanted to do some good for people who don't have much to begin with. I could have gone into medicine; my parents would have liked that, but I thought just digging a well for water, so that people have something to drink, or proper sanitation just seemed to appeal to me more. My parents supported my decision. The developed world takes a lot of things for granted. I have always had a desire to give to people who not only have a need, but also seem so appreciative when you do something for them. It is like you and your parents traveling all the way to India just to help out. These people really are thankful for that."

"I understand Brandon. That's why I haven't decided yet about a college major."

"You can do both. There is nothing wrong with majoring in art history either. Whole entire cultures are celebrated through art. It's how they trace their history and pass it on, one generation to the next."

"So how did you end up at University College London? Why there?" I ask curiously. We keep walking past some of the trails and dirt roads getting closer to the clinics.

"UCL as they call it, is a major research school. They spend and receive hundreds of millions of dollars just for research. Always topped ranked in numerous research disciplines. Everything from medicine to nanotechnology. The person who discovered the Nobel gases was a professor of chemistry at UCL. Plus a lot of famous people have attended UCL, including world leaders such as a former prime minster of Japan. However, the most famous of these persons is Mahatma Gandhi. You probably just know him as Gandhi, the leader of India's independence. Hey if it's a good enough school for a little man from India then it's good enough for me, right?" Brandon lets out a couple of chuckles and takes a drink.

"Wow! I see. It does sound like a good choice. I will have to keep UCL in mind. It looks like there aren't too many patients waiting to be seen." We hurry to our clinic having lost track of time.

"Yeah, you're right." Brandon responds.

CHAPTER XIV

Clinic two is empty inside except for some of our staff. The Indian folks outside are volunteers. Laney is up front by Moira and Mandara. Ally is sitting down next to Kenneth who looks like he is inventorying the supplies left after the first full day of seeing patients. Doctor Nick is talking to Hiro and Sakurako. I don't see Doctor François anywhere and it looks like a few others are not here either. Come to think of it; I haven't seen Pareet or Jillian all day, so I ask Doc Nick.

"Howdy everybody. Sorry we were gone for so long. Lost track of time, ya know," I offer apologetically.

"Don't worry about it," says Doctor Nick. "We were winding things down when y'all left. Couple of more check-ups. That's about it."

"Where is Pareet?" I ask. "I haven't seen her all day."

"She was in the clinic next door, but then went with Jillian, Noella, François, and the others to the clinic located over yonder." Doc Nick points off into space. "It's like our clinic outpost in the middle of nowhere."

"I thought we already are in the middle of nowhere Nick," says Brandon as he walks over to Doc Nick and pats his arm.

"We are about finished here for the day. A couple of folks have volunteered to stay the night and keep an eye on the equipment so that it isn't stolen. I am just going to throw a small first aid kit in the car and then we'll gather up the crew next door and head back to Singh's house. See y'all in a couple of minutes." Doctor Nick heads out of the clinic. Hiro and Sakurako follow him.

"So what happened to you guys?" I ask Ally and Kenneth.

"Kenneth went to show me his equipment," says Ally happily at the same time lightly slapping Kenneth on his knee.

"What kind of equipment?" I inquire having got my attention.

Ally faces Kenneth. "What do you call that thing again?"

"It is a cardiac monitor-defibrillator." Kenneth answers.

"That's right. He showed me so much stuff that I couldn't remember everything," says Ally.

"I see. Kenneth, how do you and Brandon know each other?" I ask trying to figure out their friendship.

"Well, back in London, Brandon happens to work in his aunt's and uncle's restaurant. It is the best Indian food in the city. Whenever we are out on an ambulance call; we make it a plan to always stop there for lunch or dinner. One day, about a year ago, I was talking to Brandon at the restaurant and he started hanging out with me and a few other ambulance workers. He has even done some ride-a-longs with us as part of the crew to see what it was like." Kenneth takes a deep breath. "Brandon is one busy guy. He told me about the clinics staffed here by volunteers and I decided to come and help out. Great guy, but very busy. He is always helping out somewhere." Kenneth takes another deep breath trying to recuperate from his long story.

"And you work in a restaurant? Do you cook? If so, you're a keeper," Ally gracefully offers and turns her attention back to Kenneth. "What about you? Do you cook?"

"Yes I cook and Kenneth just comes to the restaurant and eats everything!" Brandon answers.

"Everyone ready to get back to the house?" Carilyn shouts from the front doorway.

We all get up and start heading outside. I take one last look around to see if I have everything. I decide to keep all my things with me because they were gifts. Four of the Indian folks are staying behind at the clinics. I find my mom and dad outside standing next to one of the Land Rovers. My dad has my beige carry-on back pack hanging off his right shoulder.

"Hi mama. Hi daddy. Let me take that from you and I will put my blood pressure cuff and my stethoscope, or "ears" as they are sometimes called, in there. Less to carry in my over-stuffed pockets." I leave my EMT scissors, pen-light, and Kelly's in my cargo pocket.

"Sure honey. It's as heavy as a baby elephant. Good first day?" my dad asks.

"Yep. Learned a lot. Can't wait for tomorrow," I say as I head to the green Land Rover that we rode in this morning. The back hatch is open, so I toss my pack in there. Brandon comes over, checks to see if anybody else has any gear that they want to put in the back, and then shuts the hatch.

Brandon says to me, "since Pareet is at the other clinic, you can ride up front with me." He walks around to the front passenger door and opens it for me.

"That's ok. I'll ride in the back with Ally." I tease.

"What?" Brandon says with a crinkly forehead.

"What?" Ally echoes like a parrot.

"Wow! JK. Just kidding..." I smirk as I hop in to the front passenger seat. "Thank you kindly mister."

Brandon shuts the door and heads to the driver's side of the Land Rover and climbs in. Laney and Moira get into the back seat and Ally and Kenneth get into the third row of seats. My mom walks up to Brandon at the driver's window.

"We'll follow y'all to Singh's house," my mom tells us. "Don't go to fast; remember how Jim got lost the last time we were here."

"Not a problem Abby. My co-pilot will keep me in line," Brandon looks over at me and winks his right eye in a reassuring fashion.

"That's what I'm afraid of. Moira, Laney...keep them in line."

"We can do that Abby," Moira replies then laughs.

Ludwik and Gala hop into our vehicle at the last minute. Ludwik behind me and Gala sits next to Kenneth in the far back, sandwiching him between her and Ally.

Ludwik turns around and asks, "Kenneth, you going to be ok back there?"

"Yes mate. I think I can handle it. How about you? Will you survive sitting next to Moira and Laney?" Kenneth responds.

"I have everything under control Ken. Thanks for asking. All set let's go." Ludwik slaps the back of the seat.

Brandon starts the Land Rover, turns on the stereo again, puts the four-by-four in drive, and starts out by making a big circle turning around in the clearing and heading back out the trail we came in on. As we drive past the trees where we were standing just a short while ago; my mind drifts to the tree Mr. Handsome's friend was standing next to. I still can't figure out why he was there, but I decide to refer to him as "Mr. Hair" from now on. Long and black hair. I haven't noticed too many Indian men with long hair. Maybe that's why he stood out. We continue past that tree and I turn around to check my dad's progress. They are following us. That's good. At least they aren't lost yet. I am looking forward to getting back to the house, so that I can freshen up a bit. I am sitting next to my dream guy and I feel like I just finished six hours of soccer practice.

We bounce along down the trail, very slowly, descending down to the dirt road we turned off of earlier this morning, which seems like a long time ago. Brandon brings the Land Rover to a stop and takes it out of four-wheel drive. He glances right to check for traffic and then pulls out onto the flatter dirt road turning left. He checks the driver's side mirror for a second to make sure my dad is following and then accelerates a little faster. After a bit of traveling on the flatter dirt road, we come to the paved one. Still quite a few cars and trucks bustling down the road with the occasional horn beeping away. Brandon checks left and then turns right joining the flow of the river of cars.

I peek into the passenger side mirror and see my dad pull out onto the road behind us. He must have cut somebody off because I can hear multiple horns blaring now. Well I can't blame him. Come on. A guy from Alabama driving down a back road in India, what do they expect? I laugh to myself. I relax and slouch back into the seat taking in the view which is pretty much a lot of green trees on both sides of the road. Interesting enough, they all seem to have a billboard nailed to each one. Not the hand written kind, but ones advertising for major products and services.

It is strange to see when we seem to be traveling through the jungle. The yellow and black sign for Western Union is one that jumps out of the jungle at me that I recognize. Plenty of buses loaded with people on the road going both ways. All bright and personalized, or so it seems. A very large truck with what appears to be huge logs, more like whole trees, tied to the sides of the truck is coming toward us.

"Hey Brandon are we going to fit?" I ask him.

"No problem as long as the logs don't fall off. Six logs is a lot trickier. This is normal. If it can be transported, Indian ingenuity will find a way," he chuckles.

Two logs on each side of the truck held on by rope. Brandon slows as he navigates through the tiny spaced left on the road for us. The truck is yellow and red with decorative multicolored fake flowers hanging over the top part of the windshield. There is a large imposing 'T' in the middle of the truck's grille which once again stands for Tata.

"You guys ok back there?" Brandon asks.

"Yes we are fine," Moira replies.

"Traffic is kind of tight here, isn't it?" says Laney.

Ally and Kenneth are lost in their own chatting. We make our way around the truck and soon catch up to a couple of Piaggio rickshaws. Their little engines whining away like a buzzsaw. Yellow on top with green on the bottom. There is a small tan license plate with black letters and numbers written on two lines one over the other. Several people are aboard the one in front of us and how it is not doing a wheely with only the one wheel in front to keep it on the ground, I'll never know. Out of nowhere, a motorcycle zips by with a man driving and a woman passenger sitting sidesaddle in her colorful sari. Wow! Hang on dear and I wish her good luck silently.

Brandon slows down and turns left onto another road. We travel up a small hill a little ways and I soon see the large tan concrete walls surrounding Singh's house. Both sides of the big white gate are already open and Brandon makes a right turn on to the dirt driveway. He creeps down the small slope and stops underneath the car port and turns off the engine. I open up my door and climb out to stretch my legs. I shut my door and lean back through the window.

"Nice driving Brandon; it was a good ride," I say.

"Thanks. Glad you liked it. I think everyone is going to get cleaned up now. Then in about an hour or so, we should be eating dinner," Brandon replies.

"What about your mom and dad and Pareet? Aren't they at the other clinic?" I wonder as I head around to the back of the vehicle to get my pack. Everyone else is climbing out and following me to do the same.

"They will be here shortly. Ludwik talked to them on the shortwave radio before we left and they were just leaving about when we were." Brandon pops open the back gate and we off load our stuff. "Here they come now," Brandon points up the driveway.

We all look to see one of the other Land Rovers, the red one, coming down the driveway, which is about twenty yards long and flanked on one side by about a two foot high stone retaining wall. The rest of the front of the property has what look like coconut trees planted sporadically around the yard. I missed those this morning in all my excitement to get going.

"Hey girlfriend, you ready to get washed up, or what?" Ally asks me as she grabs my arm and we head to the house.

"See y'all later, see ya Brandon," I say as I am being dragged along.

"I will see you in a while Lily, see you too Ally," Brandon says.

CHAPTER XV

Ally enters the house through the kitchen and heads up the steps to the second floor. I can barely keep up with her. She opens the door to the room we are staying in, runs through it, and bounces on to the bed. She lands on her back with her legs flying in the air.

"So, you getting along with Kenneth ok?" I ask, but already knowing the answer. I put my pack on the floor next to my bed and sit down facing Ally. She sits up, lets out a big breath of air, and puts her face on her hands.

"Wow! How did we get so lucky? Two hot guys and no competition. What more could us girls want? One for each of us. Pretty cool, doll." Ally jumps up and grabs some things out of her duffel bag. "I am off to the shower and then some dinner. Kenneth said the Karups' have something planned for everyone later on after we all eat."

"I wonder what that could be? Yeah we are lucky to have met them. I knew it would be worth coming here. We are helping people, learning a lot, and we each have a prince."

Ally heads off to the shower almost skipping out of the room. I gather the things I need for the shower, so I can go as soon as Ally is back. I kick off my hiking boots and lay back on the bed. I can hear chains clanging down the road off in the distance. Elephants going home for the day, I guess. Something catches my attention out of the corner of my eye. I turn toward the window and notice that the little red and gold butterfly has returned. It is bumping its wings up and down in a hover just above the window sill. I get up and walk over to it and put my right hand out extending my index finger. As I get to the window, the butterfly lands on my finger. Instantly there is a bright flash of golden light. I rapidly shut my eyes. When I open them I find myself in a beautiful courtyard type garden that looks exactly like the one from my visions.

"It is you. The one from my dreams. Who are you? Where am I?" She is just staring at me. Looking me over or checking me out or something.

"It is nice to finally meet you Lily," she states in a calming, low voice. "I am Ellora, the Princess of Andhari, an ancient kingdom of India. My family once ruled half of ancient India. Everything from what you would call modern day Bangladesh to Tamil Nadu and Kerala. And from Kerala to the sands of Gujarat and every bit of the lands in between. All of the mountains. All of the rivers and waters. From the grasses to the stars; it was once called Andhari."

"But what do you want with me? Why am I dreaming of you Princess Ellora?" I plead her for answers. "Why are you in my head?

"Lily, you are not dreaming. I need you. You are the one I have chosen." Princess Ellora says calming me, relaxing me.

"I don't understand. You need me for what? Why me?"

I feel myself walking toward her almost like she commanded me to do so. We are now face to face. I try to comprehend her breathtaking beauty. Her hair matching the shade of her skin. Her red and gold sari blowing gently around her body, yet I cannot detect a breeze. The little butterflies are hovering about her as if ordered to be there. The golden light ricocheting off of her elaborate jewels and sparkling gold staff. Totally mesmerizing me in a hypnotic kind of trance.

"This isn't real. You are not real. I'm just having another dream about you. This is something I've made up in my mind," I continue to plead with her, but her facial expression doesn't change.

"Lily, I wish that was true, but I have chosen you. The gods have chosen you. There is no one else that they or I, can trust. Inculpability will trump tyranny. I have waited over two thousand years for you. Two thousand years so that I may pass on an extraordinary gift. Something exceptional. Something awe inspiring. You are the one. The only one, pure enough for me to bestow this upon. No one else, but you. I know you will use it wisely and you will inspire people," Princess Ellora tries to explain.

"This is all so confusing to me. I'm just Lily from Alabama," I say trying to discourage Princess Ellora from choosing me.

"You don't know it yet, but you are a leader and protector. I know you will do what is right with this gift, for the gift will only listen to you."

"When Princess Ellora? When?" I keep staring at her, still mesmerized.

"Soon Lily, soon...," her soothing voice fades away. I shut my eyes.

"Lily. Lily. Darling! You awake or what?" I hear a familiar voice. "What are you doing on the floor? I think the bed is a bit   softer pumpkin," Ally says as I open my eyes to see her leaning over me with a towel wrapped around her head.

"I think I just dozed off. I was looking out the window and voila here I am on the floor," I say trying not to let her in on my fantastical dream this time. Sooner or later she must start to think I am losing my marbles.

"Oh, ok then. Well let's get you up and in to the shower. You're next and the line is getting bigger."

"Ok Ally. Thanks for waking me up. I probably would have slept all night," I say to her still trying not to let on about the dream, but I think she knows better.

"See you downstairs when you are finished doll. Laney is next for the bathroom after you," says Ally as she heads off down the hall.

I jump up and head to the bathroom. Laney is just coming out of her room and I tell her I will give her a knock on her door when I am done, so that we can keep the shower line moving. I am quickly in and out of the bathroom, so that I don't hold everyone up. The shower was refreshing and much needed. I head back to my room giving a couple of knocks on Laney's door along the way. My hair is pulled back into a loose pony tail. I put on my tan cargo shorts and a crimson t-shirt with a big giant white 'A' in the middle of the chest. I step in to my 'Roll Tide' flip flops and head downstairs. There is nobody in the main room, so I head to the kitchen which is also empty. There are voices coming from outside around the back of the house and I head toward them.

I walk under the car port again and turn left to find a long row of tables set up near the edge of the house. They are joined end to end and covered with white table cloths. There is an elaborate amount of food already set up on each table forming a colorful palette with all the different types of fruit, curry, vegetables, and things I don't recognize, all looking very tempting. In front of each of the different foods is a small white index card folded over and standing upright with the name of the food in Indian and the English translation underneath it. I spot Ally and sit down next to her with a large assortment of fruit in front of me. On the card is the word- pazham, which must mean fruit. Ally has a variety of vegetables in front of her and the Malayalam word is bashyayogyamaayasasyam. Yep not going to attempt that one.

"What's up girlfriend?" I say admiring Ally's sign.

"I was thinking you fell asleep on me again. Dig in. Everyone is eating. It is very informal. I know these are veggies, but I am not going to try to pronounce the Malayalam word for it." She points to the placard by the vegetables. "Pareet told me the top word is the traditional Malayalam writing for it; which kind of looks like ancient Sanskrit. Under that is how you would pronounce it in English. That is usually pretty long in some cases. Then Jillian and Pareet were nice enough to put it into proper English."

"I see. It looks confusing." I start to load up my flat green paper.

"Yeah, can be. The Karups' do it for all the new guests when they come over. Makes a nice transition and learning experience all in one."

Ally digs back into her food. Kenneth comes over and sits down next to Ally. Pareet and Jillian are still putting out food and drinks.

"Hi there. It all looks delicious," I say and wave hello as they pass by in front of me on the other side of the table.

"Hi Lily, how was your day?" Jillian asks.

"Great. Busy, but I learned a lot. Happy I made the trip with my parents. Thanks for this wonderfully looking dinner. Do you need help serving or setting up?" I offer, feeling bad not being done with my shower sooner. Pareet, how was your day? We missed you."

"No. No. Thanks, but we are just about done," says Jillian looking eloquent in her blue, white, and yellow sari.

"It was good. The other clinic is also very busy. I will join you two in a minute," Pareet responds, as she continues to pour drinks for everyone. "This is chaaya, or tea, as you call it. There is sugar on the table being passed around."

"Thanks Pareet. It all looks delicious," I say while trying to figure out what to eat. Everyone is walking around the table like being at an exuberant buffet. I get up and join the procession. I read the cards describing what each food item is, and when I don't recognize it, I take a small sample to try it out. As I near the end of the table farthest from my seat, I see Brandon lighting tiki torches. I look back and see that there are six torches running down the length of the house all evenly spaced apart. He doesn't see me. I sneak up on him.

"Hey there fella, do ya need a match?" I say as I stop at the end of the table.

"Hi. Thanks, but I think I got this. I don't want you to burn yourself," Brandon says as he is still holding the lighter in front of the top of the torch as a big whoosh of flame launches in to the air. Brandon jumps back, with a startled look on his face. All of the guests turn and look our way. Cheers and a round of clapping erupt from both sides of the dinner tables.

"Hey Brandon mate, do you need a medic?" shouts Kenneth from his seat next to Ally.

"Bravo! Bravo! Brandon," says Marco in his thick Italian tone before Valentina can restrain him from applauding Brandon's misfortune.

"Maybe I should get a fire extinguisher. Are you sure I can't be of some assistance before I eat this yummy food y'all prepared for us?" I offer.

"Nope. I'm pretty sure I've been distracted enough. See you in a minute when I am done here," he says as he double checks himself for burns.

"Distracting? You don't mean me, do ya?" I say as I give Brandon a wink with my right eye. What the heck did I do that for? Focus Lily. "You are losing control every time he is near you," I say quietly to myself.

"Save me a seat. I will be there in a minute," says Brandon still trying to catch his breath.

"I will save you a seat just as soon as a dial 9-1-1 India to get you some assistance," I laugh a bit at my little joke and head back to my seat as Brandon smiles, shakes his head a bit, gives himself another once-over, and goes about his tiki torch lighting project. I wave to my parents from the other side of the table as I walk past them. Dad laughing. Mama shaking her head.

"What are you two doing over there? This isn't a bar-b-q," Ally says in a long exaggerated southern drawl.

"I think I distracted Brandon, so I figure I better get my food and sit down before more accidents happen."

"Good idea sweetie," Ally says as she goes back to eating and her own conversation with Kenneth.

The sun has about dropped behind the trees causing just a slight orange glow in the sky. It's still pretty warm out with not much wind blowing. Everyone is eating and lost in their own conversations about the day, the trip, and India. Pareet is next to me and Brandon is next to her. I still can't figure out why no one is sitting across the table on the other side from us. I feel like we are in a Da Vinci painting.

"Pareet, how come nobody is sitting on the other side of the table?"

"Oh, that's because in a few moments when it is darker, we will be doing something special for all of the guests. As a matter of fact I have to go change and so does Brandon and my father," she explains but still leaves me confused.

"Ok. I will help your mom clean up the dinner table."

"Sounds good to me. See you in a little while." Pareet stands up and looks to her right at Brandon. "Come on Brandon. Let's get ready. Dad is already inside."

"We will see everyone in just a little while," says Brandon, as he and Pareet disappear around the corner and into the house.

Ally and I both get up and join Jillian and a few others who are helping to clean up the tables from dinner. We follow Jillian into the house and kitchen with our arms full carrying bowls of food that were not eaten. We store everything in the kitchen and Jillian tells us to head back outside and to have a seat. We still don't know what is planned for us, but once back in our seats I can sense some excitement in the air. The tables are clear except for people's snacks and beverages. It is completely dark out now except for the light coming from Brandon's torches that he lit earlier providing a waft of kerosene in the air. Jillian walks to the other side of the table and stands in front of all the guests.

"Attention. Welcome everyone. My family and I, and the people of India would like to thank all of you for making the trip to our country and our home. Singh, Pareet, and Brandon have put together a demonstration of the ancient Indian art of kalarippayat. Some of our guest who have been here before will have seen this, but hopefully it will be new for most of you. We usually try to present a different demonstration of the art each time. They will be demonstrating weapons tonight," Jillian says as she makes her way to the end of the tables. Another round of clapping goes off as Jillian walks up to a small boom box and turns on some background music which sounds like drums beating and cymbals crashing.

"Ok everyone first up is Singh," Jillian says. "He is using metal weapons which are called ankathari, and specifically, the valum parichayum, or the sword and shield."

Singh appears and centers himself in front of the tables, but about ten feet away and I can see why. He is wearing a white tank top and white loose fitting long pants. There is a dark red sash tied around his waist forming a triangle over his right hip. In his left hand is a small round gold colored shield. It might be only twelve inches in diameter, decorated with a small protruding point in the middle. In his right hand is a shiny silver sword. It has a slight curve to it on the opposite side of the blade which gets thicker as it extends from the handle. I recognize it as being one similar to what Brandon was practicing with when I first saw him very early this morning which now seems like a long time ago. Singh has a serious look on his face.

Singh begins by facing toward us. He then turns to his right, rapidly, extending the shield outward. He leaps to the right and thrusts the sword directly out in front of him while simultaneously bringing the shield back to the left side of his body. Singh jumps up in to the air turning one-hundred and eighty degrees and landing facing to his left now. All in a blur. My eyes try to keep up with his movements, but he is already thrusting the sword to the left when my eyes catch up. The music in the background intensifies his motions. Singh drops into a deep squat position, suddenly he leaps straight up facing us. Both of his legs continue upward into a full split while at the same time he jabs the sword out in front again toward the crowd, us. We all clap hands and cheer for Singh. He repeats several more moves without jumping, but turning instead to the left, right, and back to us again. All of it looking really impressive and nothing like I have ever seen before. Jillian narrates some for the crowd giving the background and the history of kalarippayat.

Pareet enters from the right. She is also dressed like Singh with white loose long pants, loose white shirt with short sleeves, and a red sash tied around her waist forming a triangle over right hip. She has the same kind of shield in her left hand and the same kind of sword in her right.

Singh and Pareet face each other and bow. They both lean way back on to their right legs, almost in a one legged squat then leap toward each other in the air. They both swing their swords at one another making the swords come crashing together in a violent metallic thunder. Sparks fly from the metal blades of their swords producing an unexpected fireworks display. My heart skips a few beats. The guests all respond with a collective gasp followed by clapping. Pareet and Singh land and step back a few feet from one another. They then circle each other, almost the way animals will circle each other in a fight. Eyes locked upon each other, and once they both are parallel to the dinner table, they launch through the air again, but this time they bang into the other's shield also creating a light show of sparks. Still facing one another, Singh on my right and Pareet on my left, they dip in to another one legged squat and launch again. The swords crash together, but this time they don't step back. Instead they connect with the swords back and forth several times making a continuous spark shower. We all clap thunderously.

"Wow this is good stuff. Ain't nothin' like this in Alabama," Ally yells while still clapping her hands together. Pareet lets out a small almost unnoticeable smile, yet keeps her focus at the task on hand. Singh and Pareet continue the display for several more minutes before setting the swords and shields aside.

"Next Pareet and Singh will demonstrate some verum kia, also known as empty hands fighting, or fight without weapons," Jillian explains to all of us.

Pareet and Singh face off and bow again. They each step back. Pareet steps toward Singh with her right hand throwing a simulated punch. Singh intercepts the punch with his left arm, steps behind Pareet and twists her right arm behind her. Pareet ducks under Singh's arm and reverses the position holding Singh with his arm behind his back. The crowd erupts. They face off again. Pareet steps toward Singh throwing a kick with her left leg at his head. He blocks the kick with his right arm and swoops Pareet's legs out from under her. He lowers her gently to the ground. While doing so, Pareet wraps Singh's arm with both of her legs, grasps the wrist of his right arm, and flips him over her. Singh lands on his feet. Wow! Ally is right. This is good stuff. They next demonstrate the dagger, which Jillian tells us it is called a katara. They dazzle us for over thirty minutes and I can't help think about how tired they must be since everyone has been awake since early this morning.

I start to wonder what happened to Brandon. I don't know if he is part of the demonstration, or maybe he went to sleep, which I can't blame him for it if he did. The banging drums and crashing cymbals stop. Pareet and Singh take a bow for us. We give them a standing ovation. Cheers, thank you's, and bravo's come from all the guests. Jillian walks over to the boom box again and hits a few more buttons and cranks up the volume. I realize it is the band from Italy that we listened to in the car. A strident gothic metal tone of low guitars, slapping bass, and machine gun like drums resonates from the speakers. Preceded by a few notes from a medieval sounding keyboard. A beautiful ranging female voice starts to sing accompanied by a a deep growling male in flawless harmony.

"Next is Brandon with a special demonstration for you all to enjoy. He is using the wooden staff, what we call here— the kettukari," Jillian says loudly, barely audible over the music. "The staffs look like long straight brown sticks."

There is a whooshing sound coming from my right. Myself and the rest of the guests hear it at the same time and look that way. The orange glow from the tiki torch near that corner of the house seems to be getting brighter. As the glow intensifies, Brandon appears from around the side of the house. In each hand is about a four foot long staff as Jillian described, but both ends of the staffs are wrapped with some sort of material which has been lit on fire producing a brilliant red-orange-blue flame. Brandon keeps walking parallel to the row of dinner tables. As he is doing this, he is spinning both staffs simultaneously so fast, that it looks like he is holding one continuous circle of flame in each hand. Impressive! He stops when he is centered in front of the tables and continues to twirl the staffs like nothing I have ever seen. Brandon is just on the other side of the table and close enough in front of me that I can feel the heat coming from both staffs. He is wearing a black tank top, black loose long pants, and has a red sash tied around his waist forming a triangle over his right hip just like Singh and Pareet. He has a red bandanna tied around his forehead trying to keep the sweat off his gorgeous face, but I can see the perspiration forming on his cheeks. His fit chest and muscular arms are shining in the light of the flames. I can feel my mouth start to dry up watching this. Suddenly I feel a hand on my leg and I look down then at Ally.

"Oh my wow...are you seeing this?" she says squeezing my leg tighter.

"Focus Ally. Nothing like this at all back home is there?" I say as I redirect my attention back to Brandon's performance, and pry Ally's hand off my leg.

And I am telling her to focus. Yeah, right. Just when I thought it couldn't get better, Brandon throws a kick to the front, a kick behind him, and then somersaults in place, all while continuing to spin the flaming staffs. He looks at me and we lock eyes for a split second. I smile and wink at him again and just as quickly, the staff in his right arm goes flying out of his hand and tumbling across the grass. Wow, I did it again. Brandon stops, feeling embarrassed I'm sure. He stands there for a few seconds with a disappointed look on his face, sweat pouring from his body now, and panting just a bit trying to catch his breath. Everyone stands up and gives him a round of applause. No teasing whatsoever. Just good job's, excellent's, and a fantastico from Marco. Pareet runs over and dumps some water on the burning staff lying on the ground and then takes the one from Brandon and puts water on that one to put out the flames. Brandon takes a bow and then walks around the end of the table and sits down next to me.

"Brandon that was incredible," I say exuberantly. Pareet comes up to Brandon and hands him a white towel. He takes the towel from her.

"Thanks sis," he says as he pats his face, chest, and arms dry. "Thanks Lily. I am usually better than that, but something caught my eye, just for split second, and that's when I dropped the staff." He continues with the towel; this time running it through his hair leaving it pleasantly messy. He puts the bandanna on the table and drapes the towel around his neck.

"What do you mean only for a split second?" I tease him some more.

"Do you want to go for a walk with me," Brandon catches me by surprise.

"Yes."

I get up from my chair and tell my parents that I will be heading up to bed. Ally looks at me and gives me a 'yeah right' wink and goes back to talking with Kenneth.

"Goodnight everyone. I will see y'all in the morning. Thanks Singh and Pareet for the demonstration; that was fantastic. Thanks for dinner Jillian."

"You are very welcome. Goodnight," they respond together.

Mama gives me a smile and she and my dad return to their interesting conversation with Hiro, Sakurako, and Jia Li.

I follow Brandon to the right of the house back toward the carport.

"Where did you have in mind Brandon?" I ask. "It's kind of dark to be going outside the gate. Aren't there big animals out there?"

"Yes there is that's why we are going inside, sort of."

He takes my hand and leads me through the kitchen and then up the steps. We walk down the main hall together and make a right turn past my bedroom. We end up at the opposite end of the house from the bathroom. Down the end of this small hallway are a set of white French doors with sheer white curtains covering the eight panes of glass in each door. Brandon opens up the doors and leads me outside on to the balcony.

"Oh I see. Inside then outside," I say stupidly feeling a bit nervous alone with Brandon. Not scared nervous, but nervous because of how I am feeling about him right now. It's as if some kind of emotion inside of me keeps getting stronger every time I am near him.

"Yes outside and safe from everything except giraffes, I suppose." Brandon and I walk over to the white concrete railing and peek down on the remaining guests illuminated by the tiki torches. Ally and Kenneth are nowhere to be found. I am sure she will fill me in later about their whereabouts.

"Hey this is kind of like my very own Juliet balcony, but bigger and with a better looking guy than that Romeo dude," I blurt out not realizing what I just said.

Brandon gives me a surprised look with his face glowing different shades of orange in the flickering light of the torches. We stare at each other. Our eyes locked on to one another's.

"It is a lot better to look at you for a bit longer than a few seconds, and you see how distracted I become when that happens. Can you imagine what I will be like after five minutes of looking at you?" He takes both my hands in his.

"N..no...ope," I struggle to get a one syllable word out. Not good Lily.

"I can't explain what's happening to me Lily, but this is a first for me. I have never felt a connection like this with anyone before. I don't know how to explain this," Brandon looks away for a second and then back at me.

"I feel the same way Brandon. I don't think I ever met anybody like you before. I feel the same connection. I am not usually like this. You have me tripping over my own feet. I can barely get my words out when I am around you. It has been automatic, like a switch came on when I first saw you," I let my heart speak for me this time. "I am very at ease around you."

121

"Me too Lily. I do have a confession to make though," he says. "I have dreamed of meeting you for over a year now. Ever since your parents showed me your picture and told me all about you the last time they were here."

"Well they have kept you a pretty good secret from me, but it was worth the wait," I say almost out of breath as Brandon puts a hand on both of my shoulders and pulls me to him ever so slowly so that our faces are only inches apart. I can feel the warmth of his breath hitting my lips. He moves even closer, his mouth moving toward mine. Neither of us saying a word. Just before our lips make contact, he moves his mouth to my forehead and presses his lips softly against my skin for several seconds leaving behind the most gentle kiss I have ever received. My legs wobble and I feel faint. His hands drop from my shoulders and wrap around my lower back. I cling onto him, burying my head into his firm chest. I can feel the dampness from his still moist shirt. Unconsciously, I inhale deeply taking in his pleasant scent. It is comforting like his muscular arms around me. I feel safe for some reason.

"I won't rush this Lily," he says tenderly.

"Thank you Brandon. I don't think I would want you to."

CHAPTER XVI

The next morning I wake up to the sound of my alarm beeping quietly under my pillow. I glance over to see Ally tucked under a thin blanket in her bed. Glad to see that she made it back last night because she wasn't here when I went to sleep, and that was kind of late even for me. I will bombard her with questions later, but first I am on a mission. I get out of bed slowly, so I don't wake her up. I fumble around in the dark a bit until I locate my black yoga pants, slip into them, and then my sneakers. I change t-shirts and head to the bathroom and brush my teeth, wash my face, and pull my hair back slapping another hair tie around it.

I tip-toe down the steps quieter than a mouse, so I don't wake anybody up. I bump into a chair as I make my way through the kitchen. Someone in the other room lets out a muffled snort. I go out the door to the carport and turn left making my way to the back of the house. There is still a faint smell of kerosene coming from the tiki torches as I walk past them; all though they are not burning now. Just enough light exists to see the tables from last night.

I lean back and raise my arms over my head to stretch. I can't believe how stiff my body feels right now. I bend slowly at the waist and reach for the ground, stand straight up again, and then back toward the ground once more. My palms settle on the prickly grass. The back of my hamstrings burn slightly as my muscles resist the warm up. I stand up again and widen my stance with a leg out to each side. There is a sharp sting on the back of my neck. I quickly swat at whatever it was, but I don't feel anything. I bend to the right and then to the left. Then I bend and reach for my right toes, swing to the left and grab my left toes. My calves are next to be stretched and then I find the blue and white soccer ball. Feeling pretty warmed up, I grab the ball out from underneath the first table, drop it on the ground in front of me and start to dribble it around the yard alternating from right foot to left foot. About five minutes passes.

"Good morning. You are an early bird, aren't you?" a now familiar voice says from behind me. "You wouldn't be trying to show me up, right."

"Good morning. Not a chance Brandon. Why, do you feel shown up?" I turn and pass the ball to Brandon at a steady speed. He traps it with the bottom of his foot; stopping the ball dead.

"What do you say?" he passes the ball back to me using the inside of his right foot. "Fifteen and fifteen?" Brandon says while flashing me that beautiful smile of his.

"What?"

"Soccer for fifteen and then kalarippayat for fifteen?"

"Sounds good to me Brandon."

He jogs up to my side and we begin to trot slowly around the yard in a large square pattern. He passes the soccer ball to me and then I pass it back to him. We alternate for the first fifteen minutes. Switching sides and using both legs to make the passes back and forth. Outside of the foot and inside of the foot. Brandon is better at soccer than he is leading me to believe. I didn't think he played much, but I can tell he has some skill with his feet.

"That's fifteen minutes. I am thoroughly warmed up. My turn now. We will start with some basic movements, so follow my lead," says Brandon hardly out of breath.

"Ok Brandon," I respond like a player listening to their coach when receiving new instruction.

I position myself on his right side and watch his movements. I start out by putting my hands together with the palms touching in the traditional namaste greeting. Next I bend the right leg and squat down keeping the left leg extended and then switch legs bending the left leg and extending the right leg. We are only inches away from the ground, almost sitting. Next we stand back up, bend the right leg again, but this time we extend the left leg far behind us and then do the same thing on the opposite side. When we stand up this time, Brandon brings his right leg up in a high methodical kick, fast, but not to forceful. My quads are burning, but I won't let it show. He continues.

"Ok. Now with the other leg. Let's go back down again, but come with the other leg for the kick. We are not looking for full power here, so that we don't pull a muscle or injure ourselves," says Brandon in that instructor's kind of tone. We repeat this sequence several more times.

It is starting to get lighter outside now and it's easier to watch Brandon's movements. I catch a whiff of coffee in the air and turn to see my dad and Doc Nick chugging their morning mugs.

"Looking good y'all. We didn't want to interrupt," my dad says as he swooshes down another mouthful; steam still coming from his cup.

"Hey there. Good mornin' you two. Did we wake you up?" I ask.

"Nah. We are up early all the time when we get together. I think it is left over from our army days. Brandon, how long have you been doing that martial arts stuff?" Doc Nick asks.

"About eighteen years, I think. Well, dad says he started teaching me when I was a baby. He said I was pretty good at it while still in my crib."

"I believe him," Doc Nick says as he continues drinking his coffee with my dad. "Jillian said breakfast will be ready in about half an hour. See y'all inside."

"Ok Doctor Nick, Doctor Jim," Brandon responds.

"Bye y'all," I say. "Another five minutes Brandon?"

"Sounds good to me. You are doing very well. You have great balance and muscle control which are the keys to kalarippayat."

"Thanks Brandon. You are a good teacher."

We continue with more kicks and then finish with a cool down using stretching. It's a good morning workout overall and I am beginning to like the ancient Indian martial art. I tap the soccer ball so that it rolls back under the table and ends up against the house. Brandon leads the way and I follow him back into the house.

"See you in a little while at breakfast."

"Same time tomorrow Lily," Brandon says.

"Definitely. Wouldn't miss it."

My bedroom is empty when I get there. Ally must be in the shower. I pick out some clothes for the day and ready my things for a shower. Ally comes in the room after several minutes.

"Good morning sweetie. You were up early today," she says.

"Yeah. I went outside to work out. Brandon came out and showed me some of that martial art he does and we passed the soccer ball around for a bit. How did you make out last night? You weren't here when I went to bed," I inquire.

"Make out all right. Kenneth was all over me. He is awesome! We have to stay for a couple of extra weeks."

125

"No you didn't. You were kissing already?"

"Heck yeah. What did you and Brandon end up doing? You seem to disappear and I couldn't find you two."

"Oh, we just hung out on the terrace," I offer trying not to give too much away.

"Not believing you. Tell me more," Ally demands staring at me while she finishes getting dressed.

"You know me. I won't kiss and tell. We...just talked. Did you know Brandon has actually been in London for two years. One of them was a preparatory year for University College." I try to change the subject not expecting Ally to buy it.

"That's nice, and?"

"And he is so sweet and yes we have to stay longer." I give in.

"I knew it. Well jump in the shower sister and I will see you at breakfast," says Ally as I head out of the room and down the hall to the bathroom.

After the shower, I walk back down the hall to my room and see Kenneth coming the other way.

"Good morning Lily. How are you today," Kenneth asks.

"Hi there. I'm good and you?"

"I am great. How's Ally this morning?"

"She is fine. You made her very happy last night," I say as I squeeze by him.

"That's good. I hope she didn't say too much."

"Don't worry Kenneth, you are still a gentleman in my eyes."

"That's good. I wouldn't want you to think any less of me. I really like Ally," Kenneth says as if it was a confession. "I didn't mean to keep her up so late."

"Your secret is safe with me. See you at breakfast."

I get to my room and put on long blue cargo pants with my tan safari shirt with the pockets all over the front and tabs on the shoulders hoping I don't look too ridiculous. I look for my hiking boots, lace them up and head for breakfast.

Downstairs I find just about everyone up and getting some breakfast. It looks like nobody is sitting down, but instead taking the food with them and heading out to the cars.

"Good morning Lily. We are grabbing some food and eating it on the way to the clinics," my mama informs me.

"Ok. I have everything I need for the day already stuffed in my pockets." There are cups of orange juice already poured, so I drink one down and take one for the ride. I grab a bunch of fruit and some idlis rice cakes as I head outside to the cars.

Brandon already has the Land Rover started and is holding the passenger door open for me.

"Thanks. I didn't realize I took so long," I say apologetically.

"That's ok. We are following everyone else this time. My parents are leading the way." Brandon waits until I am in the car and gently shuts the door. He goes around to the other side of the Rover, makes sure the door on the house is locked, and then jumps into the driver's seat.

We back out from under the carport and head up the driveway turning left. I can see the other two Land Rovers in front of us as they slow for the right turn. Brandon steps on the accelerator pedal and almost catches up with the others before they turn. One by one, we make the right turn and join in with the morning traffic. Brandon has the stereo on as before and reaches up to adjust the volume, but this time he turns the music down instead of up.

"Lily, I have to ask you for a favor."

"Sure Brandon. What can I do for you?"

"Can you feed me while I drive," says Brandon as he gestures with his right thumb to the console between us.

"Um...Ok," I say not really sure what he means, but I see a paper bag on the console.

As I open the top and peek in, I see that it is filled with fruit and idlis. I reach in and grab a banana. Brandon is trying to avoid the traffic and in the process is swerving a little. I peel the top of the banana and hold it toward Brandon's mouth.

"Good luck with that Lily," says Pareet from behind me. "You know Brandon has been a little distracted around you lately. Like he has two left feet, right?"

Brandon looks over his shoulder at Pareet.

"GOAT!" yells Kenneth from behind us.

Brandon's eyes widen as he swings his head back around to the road in front of him. He swerves the Land Rover hard to the left and then to the

127

right. The banana makes contact with the right side of Brandon's head becoming banana mush. Instant heavy laughing comes from the back seats.

"Everyone all right?" Brandon says with concern taking a deep breath at the same time.

"I didn't know you wanted some goat with your fruit salad there, mate," says Kenneth with his sarcastic English tone. "You never offered that on your restaurant menu in London; something to consider maybe."

"Sorry Brandon. There's another banana in the bag if you want me to try again," I offer trying to establish some order in the car.

"Anything less dangerous?" Brandon responds while concentrating on the road and vehicles dodging at him.

"Nope. All the other fruit will probably knock you out if we hit a goat."

"Or elephant," says Ally to add to the humor of the moment.

"Hey it's a good thing Marco is in the other car," says Laney from the far back seat. "He would have fun with this for a while."

"Brandon, do you want me to show you how to drive this fine English piece of car?" says Ludwik in his German accent.

"Hey hey, Brandon's doing good now," I say as I turn around to see Ludwik sandwiched between Laney and Moira. "He is happily chewing the other banana." Another eruption of laughter.

"How did all the guys back there get lucky to sit between all the girls?" I ask.

"It's our charming personality, good looks, and wonderful sense of humor!" Ludwik responds. "You need to see some German driving skills though."

We continue down the road. Brandon keeps eating. Traffic is heavy like yesterday. The sun is at its full brightness. I put my sunglasses on. It feels like the temperature will be hotter today. Everyone settles in to their own conversations by seat. The girls in the back chatting with Ludwik. Pareet and Ally both are chatting with Kenneth. I am listening to the stereo, the sounds of the traffic, and the wind coming through my open window. I take in all the scenery like before and admire Brandon from the passenger seat. He is like a magnet that won't let go of me and I don't want him to. This trip is really going to be too short, so I plan to make the most of every moment, for sure.

"Hey Brandon, the turn is coming up just past the third elephant," says Kenneth. "And make sure you give it the right-of-way."

I hear a grunt come from Kenneth as Pareet gives him a soft elbow to his gut.

"Be nice to Brandon or you can ride that elephant the rest of the way," says Pareet pointing out the window to a mammoth grey pachyderm as Brandon navigates the Land Rover steadily around the elephant.

Brandon makes the turn and soon catches up to the rest of our small convey. One by one, the vehicles slow and make the right turn onto the rough dirt trail and head up the hill to the clinics. We bump our way up to the clearing. The night-shift is standing outside with cups in their hands. I can see smoke coming from the outdoor kitchen fireplace. There are large black pots cooking on the open flames. It looks like the same cooks from yesterday and whatever is in the pots, smells delicious. As we get closer, I can see it is Tushar and Mandara who stayed behind last night along with a few other Indian people whose names I don't know. There is a small crowd of brightly dressed Indians in front of both clinics. Men, women, children, and babies. Some are standing. Some are sitting on the ground. It looks like mostly the women are holding the babies. It doesn't look like any emergencies, so that's good. Brandon brings the Land Rover to a stop next to his dad's vehicle. We pile out and head around back to the open hatch to get our things.

"Y'all want to work in clinic one with me today, well at least for the morning?" says my dad as he comes walking up to our group.

"Yes that sounds good. Everyone ok with that?" Laney replies.

One by one everybody agrees and we head to clinic one. Once inside, we can see there are already patients sitting in the chairs. I head to the back row of tables and put my things down, organizing my stethoscope and blood pressure cuff in the process. Everyone grabs a chair and does the same.

"Ok. Looks like we are open for business," says my mama.

"I am going to check the shortwave and see how the other clinic made out last night and what kind of crowd they have for today," Ludwik says as he trots over to the radio.

"Sounds good Ludwik. Ok. Looks like Carilyn, Nick, Sakurako, Jia Li, and Gala are in clinic two," my dad says with some organization in his voice. "Pareet, who is first?"

One by one the patients come forward and sit down in a chair. They explain their problem to Brandon and Pareet who are translating for us today. Well at least for the patients who don't speak any English. Surprisingly, some do. I settle into a routine like yesterday. I take their blood pressure. I count their pulse rate and their respirations. And I check their blood sugar when appropriate. For the patients with breathing issues, I place a pulse oximeter on their finger to get a reading of their oxygen saturation. I listen to these patient's lung sounds trying to learn the difference from what is normal and what isn't. Like yesterday, Brandon helps me. When there is something abnormal, my mom, Laney, or Moira, double checks what we find. The morning goes by fast. We see mostly check-ups and physicals. Past patients with mostly high blood pressure and chronic breathing problems like asthma, which mama explains is from smoking and cooking. Meaning, the cooks who are constantly breathing in the smoke from their concrete ovens.

"Do you guys want to break for lunch?" mama asks us.

"Sure, if you don't need us right now." Brandon says.

"No. Go ahead and get something to eat. The patients are stopping for lunch. We'll handle anything that comes," my father responds.

Brandon and I get up and head out the door with Kenneth, Ally, Laney, Moira, and Ludwik. The air outside is hot, it must be close to ninety-five degrees or better. We take a left turn and walk around to the side of the building where we ate lunch yesterday. It's full of people, but we manage to locate a spot and the bunch of us sit down on the mats layered on the ground for us. Ally is next to Kenneth. Ludwik doesn't seem to have any complaints sitting between Moira and Laney. Brandon is on my right and Pareet is on my left.

The food is colorful like the lunch from the day before. I even get a bit more daring and try some curry again. This time it's not as hot and my tongue thanks me for it. I feel bad being waited on, but Pareet tells me not to worry. I actually enjoy not seeing any fast food for a change and placing the food on the green paper mat is an easy clean up. What a great system. It's one big colorful scene with all the different sarees and I hope there is time for a trip to buy one for myself and Ally.

We make small talk during lunch before Brandon finally suggests another walk.

"Sounds good. Y'all want to come with us. Brandon is going to show us around the jungle," I offer.

"Yes. Wait for us," Laney says as she and Moira stand up along with Ludwik.

"We will see y'all back at the clinic," says Ally as she and Kenneth get up and head off in another direction.

We take the opposite route around the clearing that we walked yesterday actually starting near the trail that Brandon said leads to the tea plantation. He is giving a great tour and everyone is listening to his knowledge of the trees and the area history. I am more interested in seeing if Mr. Hair is out there anywhere today. Maybe I just imagined the whole thing. We make a right turn on the edge of the clearing and eventually come to the spot where Mr. Hair was standing yesterday. The grass is still flattened near the tree and I can still make out the trail he left behind when he walked away from the tree. So much for my imagination. I am almost half tempted to follow it, but can't figure out how to tell Brandon without him thinking I am nuts.

Brandon finishes the walk and explanation about the snakes causing me and the other girls in his tour group to let out a few screeches. We head back to the clinic.

Inside there is a patient lying on some mats on the floor. My dad is on his knees listening to the patient's chest. It seems to be a girl around my age. I can hear loud wheezing coming from her pursed lips which look dusky almost matching the color of her purple-blue sari. My mom is placing an oxygen mask on the patient's face. She reaches into an orange hard plastic case and twists the valve open on the green oxygen tank. An excited Indian lady, who I think is the patient's mother, is talking with Pareet who is translating.

"She says her daughter was stung by a bee. She is allergic to them," Pareet explains.

"Ok. Let's get some vital signs. Moira, we are going to need intravenous access, so let us get an IV going," my dad says calmly in his emergency doctor mode now. "Normal saline please."

"I am on it Doc." Moira grabs some supplies from the table.

I kneel down by the girl's left side, opposite from my dad. I place my blood pressure cuff on her left upper arm and begin squeezing the black rubber bulb inflating the cuff. I slowly open up the valve near the rubber bulb to release the air in the cuff. The needle in the gauge moves to the left, but I am not hearing any correlating sounds in my stethoscope, the lub-dub. The first lub-dub being the top number, called systolic, of the blood pressure and when the lub-dub disappears, it provides the second number, called diastolic, which is the bottom number of the blood pressure. The numbers pass by- 160, 150, 140, 130, 120. Nothing. Stay calm Lily. 100 and then 90 and I still don't hear anything.

"Dad, I am not hearing anything. I can't get a blood pressure," I say with concern, trying not to panic.

"She has a faint radial pulse in her wrist so I know her blood pressure is at least 80 systolic," dad says in response to what I told him. "Not good. Laney lets draw up 0.3 milliliters of high dose epinephrine and go ahead and give that sub-q please."

Moira has a rubber tourniquet around the patient's right arm and is about to attempt the IV stick.

"What size catheter do you want Moira?" says Brandon as he holds several in his hand.

Moira rubs the girl's arm with an alcohol swab on the opposite side from the elbow. They told me this area is called the antecubital fossa and is a preferred choice for IV starts in an emergency. I glance at the pulse oximeter on the index finger of the patient's left hand. It says oxygen is 88% and the heart rate is 64.

"Let's have an 18 gauge please," Moira asks for.

"Here you go Moira," says Brandon as he hands Moira a green IV catheter.

"Let's give a breathing treatment and see if we can get the airways to open up," says my dad. "Albuterol 0.5 milligrams in 3 milliliters of normal saline, please. Wait, let's double that dose."

Laney steps around to the girl's left side and kneels on one knee. She rolls up her sleeve, cleanses the area with alcohol, and then injects the epinephrine in to her shoulder.

"Epi is onboard, Doc," Laney says it as if it's just another day at work.

"IV is in," says Moira as Brandon places a piece of white hospital tape across the IV catheter to hold it in place. Moira has a small IV extension set, about three inches long, attached to the catheter. I grab the IV fluid and hand Brandon the end of the tubing. He takes it and plugs it into the extension set. I open up the roller clamp and watch the clear IV fluid begin to drip into the plastic chamber.

"Dad, how fast do you want the IV?"

"Let us run it wide open. She will need at least one liter of fluid maybe two so we can correct the hypovolemia," dad says calm as can be. "Ok. We have a good IV. Let's give her 50 milligrams of IV Diphenhydramine and Methylprednisolone 125 milligrams also IV."

"I will get the Diphenhydramine," says Laney. "Do you want Ranitidine next?"

"Good call Laney. Yes she can definitely use a histamine blocker, so how about 50 milligrams IV and run that over fifteen minutes please," my dad adds. He then turns his attention to the girl's mother.

"Pareet please ask the mom if her daughter has any other history of medical problems, any other allergies, and also see if she is taking any medications on a regular basis. Tell the mom it was a good job in removing the bee's stinger."

"Sure thing Doctor Jim," Pareet says as she translates the questions to the patient's mother.

"She said there are no other medical problems, medications, and no allergies except for bees."

"Thanks Pareet. If you could explain to her that we will have to watch her daughter over the next six hours to make sure she will be ok, that would be great. Also, tell her we will be sending some medicine home with her, including some Epinepherine in case she is stung again. Her daughter will have to take Prednisone and Diphenhydramine for the next four days. I don't suppose there is an allergist that we can send her to. They might be able to desensitize her to the bees."

"I will tell her of this," Pareet says and begins to translate.

The patient is starting to look better. Her lips aren't as dusky like before. Her respirations are slower. The pulse oximeter on her finger is showing an oxygen saturation of 99% and heart rate of 82. The only thing we don't have is a current blood pressure, so I kneel down by her left arm again and hope that this time I will hear something. I pump up the cuff and slowly let the air out again. 150-140-130. I hear my lub-dub at 124. I watch the needle move slowly to the left and when it is on 78, the lub-dub disappears.

"124 over 78," I excitedly yell out while my stethoscope is still in my ears. Everyone looks at me and smiles. I take the scope out of my ears. "Sorry. A little louder than I thought, right?"

"Great job everyone. Thanks for your help," my dad says to everyone as the girl's mother cheerfully shakes his hand. "Thank you," he says a bit embarrassed. "They did all the work." He points to all of us. Pareet translates.

The clinic is empty except for us. Everyone was redirected to the other clinic while we had this emergency. We make the girl more comfortable with some blankets used as pillows. It's not long before she decides to sit up, so we move her to a chair. I help clean up the mess that we made with the IV and syringe wrappers and put the oxygen away. Ludwik goes back over to the radio and Kenneth disappears in to the supply room. The clinic feels like it is about one hundred and five degrees in here now and I am hoping for some air.

"Hey nice job girlfriend," says Ally. "Let's get some air."

"Mama, is it ok if we go outside for a couple of minutes," I ask.

"Yes, get a cold drink first and go get some air," mama says.

We head over to the supply room. Kenneth is gathering up some replacements for the stuff we used. Ally opens the small fridge and takes out a couple of bottles of water and hands one to me.

"Kenneth you want to come with us," Ally asks.

I was hoping for some girl time, so much for that.

"No. That's ok. I will catch up with you when I get the resupplies," says Kenneth thankfully.

Ally and I head out the front door and make a right turn toward the bathrooms. I take in the crowd of people still in front of clinic two and make a note to help them out after the break. We continue to the bathrooms and for some reason I can feel myself start to become saturated with sweat. My steps start to stagger and I can't figure out why, but my balance is off.

"Hey Lily, are you all right?" says Ally. "You don't look so perky."

The sun, all three of them, begins to fade in front of me...

CHAPTER XVII

"Hello Lily," Princess Ellora says to me, dreaming I hope.

I find myself face to face with her again. This time we are walking through magnificent courtyards. Bright white solid marble walls about ten feet high decorated with thick spiraled columns on top which are capped with a white cover that looks like marble. On the bottoms of the walls appear to be giant relief sculptures depicting battle scenes with men and animals, possibly tigers. The columns match the solid wall in height making them about twenty feet high total. All the walls look to have vines of red and white ivy growing up their sides. There is a walk way, like a ledge, on the inside of the walls and I can swear that I can see tigers sitting on the ledge peering out through the columns as if they are guarding the place. I tell myself that I am having one kick ass dream, and continue.

The air is pleasant and smells magical. The ever present red and gold butterflies are following Princess Ellora. We walk down several gray-white concaved marble steps worn out slightly in the middle from people, and maybe animals using them. That must have taken hundreds of years, if not longer. As we turn the corner, I jump back and scream. There is a man, or beast, that has to be about eight feet tall. He has brown and white wings jettisoning from behind his back and extended outward to the right and the left. He has a human face, but it looks like white feathers for hair hanging down both sides of his face stopping at his shoulders. His muscled arms are resting on his hips. His heavily defined light brown chest is bare all the way to his waist where thick brown feathers begin, enveloping both legs and stopping at his feet which are dangerous looking yellow talons that look like they could pierce steel.

"What is that?" I say as I latch on to Princess Ellora's left arm and step behind her.

"It is ok Lily. He is friendly and one of my only allies that I have left. His name is Garutte."

"Garutte, I am sorry. It's just that I have never seen anything, I mean anyone, like you before," I say as I step around Princess Ellora and toward Garutte extending my hand as I do so. As I get closer, I can see that the feathers on his head meet at his overly large pointed nose; dare I say, like a beak.

"It is nice to finally meet you Miss Lily." He shakes my hand ever so gently as his wings flap slightly creating a breeze that moves my hair back. "You are the one."

"I have been hearing that a lot lately. You know my name?"

"Of course we all know who you are," he says as a large tiger with more orange color on its head and front legs and mostly black color toward the hind end and back legs, including a solid black tail with a little orange color on the very tip, steps around Garutte and brushes against my left leg. It almost looks like it is wearing an orange shirt with black pants. I freeze, not wanting to move.

"That is Kalio. He won't hurt you," Princess Ellora says trying to calm my worries. I don't feel too reassured, but I let this dream continue.

"Why am I here Princess Ellora? Why do people keep telling me that I am the one?"

"Lily many thousands of years ago, a king from a rival territory of Andhari, plotted and then killed my father, although it could never be proven. He sent a sorceress in disguise to poison my father. After doing so, he married my mother planning to join the two territories, so that he could reign supremely over half of the known world at that time. My mother's name was Kasara and a descendant from the gods. My father was Kalkita. The only memories I have of him is on his white horse, looking very proud and mighty. He also came from the gods, but in human form like my mother."

We continue walking with Garutte on one side of us and Kalio on the other as if having personal protectors. Mesmerized, I try to keep up with Princess Ellora's story.

"After King Shivalla had poisoned my father using a secret formula, known only to demons and their offspring, he was able to convince my mother that they should marry. She still did not know it was King Shivalla who was my father's killer," Ellora continues further.

"I don't understand what any of this has to do with me," I say in exasperation.

"You will. After my mother was married to King Shivalla, I became his step daughter. It was soon realized what his true purpose was and he set out to conquer all of the kingdom of Andhari to add to his ambitious conquests. My mother's forces were able to fight back for many years, but eventually she was killed in battle. She had managed to take back half of our kingdom before she died. Myself being older when it happened, knew I would have to lead to save the people from King Shivalla's rule."

"I think I understand what you are saying Princess Ellora, but I am just Lily from Alabama in America and I am just here, in India, on a trip with my parents," I say as we make our way around the lush green grounds of the courtyard, or more like fortress, now that I think about it.

"King Shivalla had a tiger farm which he used to raise tigers just to be slaughtered for their parts. When a battle came up he would force the tigers, with the help of his demonic allies, into battle to fight for him. It was the demons who could cast spells on the tigers and they went to their deaths. The tigers had no choice. I soon discovered that I had inherited powers from both of my true parents and was able to rescue all of the tigers from King Shivalla's tiger farm. In turn, they swore their allegiance to me."

"You can communicate with the tigers?" I ask.

"Yes Lily, and soon you will too, for the one that I rescued first will be yours and she will do anything you ask of her to wrestle your world back from the demons of King Shivalla. She is named Panthera..."

I hear Brandon's whispering voice. "Hey Lily, please wake up, please. I beg you. Come on I need a soccer partner," says Brandon.

CHAPTER XVIII

My eyes feel heavy beyond belief. It's like they are anchored shut. I struggle to open them, one blink at a time. There is a cloudy image of a man in a chair between my bed and the window. The blinking continues. More and more, the light invades my eyesight and I struggle to focus. The man has dark hair and is reading something, a book maybe. Slower than slow I try to make out his form. The room starts to come into focus first and I realize I am still in India. It is the bedroom. I squint and let out a soft moan.

"Lily!" that ever so familiar voice says. It is Brandon.

"Lily, you are awake. Are you ok. Talk to me," he says.

I try to answer, but my mouth is like sand paper. I look at my left arm and then follow the tubing up to a dripping IV bag hanging above me. I look back at my arm and spot the dressing on my left antecubital fossa, emergencies only? What?

"What...what happened? Why am I in bed? Where is everyone? Why are you sitting there?" I spit out as I try to work my tongue into words.

"You have been unconscious for two days. Your dad thinks it was a mosquito bite. Maybe some kind of pre-malaria or something. We have been taking turns keeping a watch on you. How are you feeling?" Brandon says as he puts the book down and leans toward me taking my left hand in his in the process.

"Something did bite me on the back of my neck that morning when we were training together, but I took my doxycycline like I was supposed to."

"That's good. You seem to have fought off whatever it was," Brandon says reassuringly. "We were getting ready to transfer you to a hospital in Kochi today; your dad was hoping it was the flu."

"I have been out for two days? I feel ok now. I want to get up and go to the clinics. They need my help. What time is it?" I ask.

"Take it easy for a bit. The clinics are ok. It is almost eight o'clock in the morning. How about something to eat? You have been on IV fluids for two days. You must feel pretty drained for sure," says Brandon with fatherly concern.

"No. Really. I feel good. Just had to get my eyes open."

"Your eyes opened as soon as a butterfly landed on your forehead. It was kind of humorous, all things considered."

"Was it a red and gold butterfly?" I ask impatiently.

"Yes. How did you know?" Brandon leans toward me from his chair.

"Lucky guess. I sort of dreamed about her, I mean it. Come on help me up. I need a shower."

I sit up and extend my hand toward Brandon. He gives me a tug. Surprisingly, I don't feel dizzy or anything. He helps me up to a standing position and I expect to fall, but nothing. If anything I feel strong. Brandon clamps off the IV, disconnects it from my arm, and puts a bandage over the small hole left behind. It doesn't bleed. He checks my pulse.

"Heart rate normal. You didn't flinch when I pulled the IV catheter out. Hum? Let me take your hand and I will get you to the bathroom. After that you are on your own, unless you need your back scrubbed, in which case I am your man," Brandon says jokingly while I consider the offer.

I smile at him. He walks me down the hall.

"So, you were watching over me for two days," I say.

"No. Not the whole two days. We all took turns. I was watching over you for just the past three hours. It was my turn. I really had to convince your parents, and Ally, that you would be ok. That was the only time except for checking up on you about every hour that I was awake. Actually I didn't sleep too much. None of us did," Brandon explains.

"Ally is more protective of me than my parents," I say as we get to the bathroom door. "See you in five minutes, ok?"

"I will get some stuff ready in the kitchen," Brandon says as he leans close to my cheek and gives me a soft peck. "Glad you're back. I was missing you."

The shower was much needed. Feeling refreshed now, I look out the window to check the weather. It looks clear, so I opt for shorts and a white polo shirt. I grab my back pack and double check for sunscreen, sunglasses, camera, and hairbrush. All the necessities. I decide to put my flip flops in the pack, just in case.

Downstairs I find Brandon sitting at the kitchen table. He has a plate of food out. Fruits and such. I take a glass of juice and swallow it all in one gulp.

"You must be thirsty," Brandon says a little shocked at my drinking skills.

"Yep. Can I get a refill sir?" I hold my glass out in front of him and he tops it off. I drink the second one down. "Did they leave us a car?"

"Yes. Why?"

"Show me India."

"Ok. Let's go," Brandon says with a big smile on his face. "I already radioed your parents, so they know you are all right."

"Sounds good to me."

I take a piece of fruit and an idlis and follow Brandon to the green Land Rover. We head up the driveway and Brandon turns right this time.

"If we go north we will run into Chinnar Wildlife Sanctuary. If we go south, we will end up at Eravikulam National Park. Either of those places interest you?"

"Yes. What happens if we go east or west?" I inquire.

"I will tell you what, let's go west on highway 49. I will take that to the Mandabar coast and then head down highway 47, which runs down the coast. There are no scenic drives quite like this one. I think we will eventually end up in Thiruvananthapuram. You probably know it as Trivandrum. We will finish with some shopping, a girl's best friend, right," says Brandon while navigating the traffic.

"Please. Only if you do me one favor. Can we call it Trivandrum for the rest of the ride?"

"Sure we can Lily. Sit back and enjoy the trip. If you don't mind, can you find 93.5 Red FM on the radio. It is usually what I tune into when I head toward Kochi."

"Sure Brandon." I start pressing buttons on the car stereo.

"You don't have anything against Hindi-English radio, do you?"

"No Brandon. I am game for everything."

"Good. It's the Malayali way," says Brandon.

We settle in to the drive. I take in the country side as before. All the people. All the traffic. The different colors. Cows in places where you don't expect them. The occasional elephant. People just going about life. I just take it all in. I am happy to be with someone like Brandon. I can't picture doing this with anybody else. We pass through the occasional small town. The buildings seem all connected in a row on each side of the street. The edge of the buildings line up right next to the edge of the roadway. What looks like telephone and electrical wires connecting all of the shops. Almost two hours goes by.

"We are just south of Kochi, so I will be taking highway 47 now all the way to Trivandrum. How are you feeling?"

"I feel great Brandon. Really. I am loving all of this and glad to be with you." I take Brandon's right hand with my left and give it a tight reassuring squeeze and lay them both on the center console.

It's not long before the ocean comes into view. Vivid aqua blue water dotted with white caps that look like white sprinkles of candy. The salty ocean air permeates through the car. I pull out my camera and take some pictures. First of the ocean and then Brandon driving. He tries to pose, but is more concerned with the other vehicles. I snap a few more pictures of the people on the beaches. The Indian women are wearing their long sarees for their bathing suits. The men are in their pants and dohti's. The men and woman have their clothing pushed up their legs to almost make shorts. The men's dohti's are pulled up between their legs and tucked into the waist. I don't see any bikini's anywhere. Interesting. Saves money. Brandon pulls over at what would be the equivalent of a rest area. A couple of small shops selling drinks, food, and gasoline.

"I will get us some snacks and drinks. There are bathrooms around the side of the store over there," he points to the left side of the building.

"Meet you back here in a couple of minutes," I say as he is about to get out of the Land Rover. I tug him toward me and kiss him gently on his lips catching him off guard.

"Wow. What was that for?" he responds and returns the kiss.

"That's for taking care of me," I say as I hop out and head to the bathroom not believing I just did that, but it felt right.

After returning to the car, I find Brandon is standing by the passenger door. I climb in to the passenger seat and settle in for the rest of the trip. He shuts the door and heads to the driver's side, gets in and starts the Land Rover.

"All set? We are topped off and I got us snacks and drinks. Help yourself. We're not that far away from Trivandrum," he says.

"Off we go then," I say as I open a bottle of water and hand it to him.

"Thank you. If you want to, try to find Radio Mirchi."

"Ok Brandon. What number am I looking for?"

"98.3 is the station number. I usually tune in when I get down the coast farther from Kochi."

It's not long before I start to spot signs for Trivandrum and soon we arrive. It seems more modern and developed than some other areas we have been through. We drive down paved four lane streets here and there and the traffic doesn't seem as crazy.

"How about we shop first?" Brandon offers. "I just wanted to drive you through on a quick tour, but we are actually going to Balaramapuram. It is where the materials were all hand woven for the royal families. The people, called Shaliars, or hand weavers, were brought here on orders from those royal families. I think you will like it. There are over five-thousand hand looms in this city."

"Sure. Sounds interesting. Surprise me."

"I know a place where we can get you outfitted properly."

Brandon drives for about another half an hour and pulls up in front of an older looking building with several shops advertised on the store fronts. We park the car. Brandon meets me on the passenger side, takes my hand, and we walk to the shop that has the smallest, almost unnoticeable sign on the door. There is nothing hanging in the front display window.

"This place has been here for a couple hundred years. They don't advertise, yet everyone knows of it by word of mouth. I think we will find you something that you will like here," says Brandon as he holds the door open for me.

"Please, lead the way," I say.

There is a nice looking Indian gentleman who greets us in soft spoken Malayalam. Brandon returns the greeting and I offer the namaste with my palms together. Brandon explains that he wants something special for me. The gentleman disappears behind a door in the back of the shop and an Indian lady returns with him. She stares at me for just a second. They say something to each other before she approaches me. She is about my height, maybe sixty years old, and has graying shoulder length hair.

"What did they say Brandon?"

"I am not sure. I couldn't hear them. That's a first. I have been here before with my family."

The Indian lady introduces herself as Atmaja, takes my hand and leads me over to some shelves of materials along the wall.

"Wait here," she says and heads to the back room where she came from.

"What's going on?" I ask Brandon.

"I don't know. This never happened before," he says in a tone not reassuring to me.

He seems as surprised as I am. The door opens and Atmaja walks through carrying the most spectacular looking black and gold material I have ever seen. She walks up to me and holds out her arms showing me a close up of the detail in the material. She explains to Brandon that the material is only for the most special of people. It has hand stitched gold borders. There seems to be miniature gold pearls through out the fabric. She holds it closer so that I can touch it. Silk is the first thing that comes to mind. There is intricate gold decoration between all of the pearls. She explains these are called keri. They look like miniature tiger stripes. I am blown away by it.

"Brandon, I don't think I can afford this," I say with disappointment.

"You don't have to pay for it," he says with equal disbelief. "Atmaja said there is no cost to you because you are the one."

"What? I don't understand."

"She said you are the one. What does she mean Lily?" Brandon says puzzlingly.

"I don't know, I swear."

Brandon looks at me not knowing what to think. Atmaja and the Indian gentleman start taking my measurements. The gentleman explains that it will only take about thirty minutes and I will have a choli, the tight fitting shirt worn under the sari, and the mundum neryathum, or the Malayalam sari. We walk around the shop and browse the different fabrics. Every couple of minutes a different person comes out of the door in the back of the shop, where the hand looms are located, nods, and gives me a namaste greeting with their palms together. I return the greeting each time. Brandon looks on with amazement.

"I don't know what is going on Brandon. I have never received this much attention before."

"Yeah, I am kind of jealous. Feeling a little left out."

"I will make it up to you," I say soothingly as I take both of his hands and face him. "I have to get something for Ally, my mom, Carilyn, and my aunt back home. What do you suggest?"

"It is already taken care of. That was the extra-long exchange we had in Malayalam. And they said there is no charge."

"Am I dreaming? I couldn't possibly take these for free."

"They insist, but won't tell me why, so we will honor their wishes," says Brandon.

Atmaja returns with a humble look on her face almost as if she is proud to serve me. She takes the bottom piece of the sari and wraps it around my waist. It fits perfectly. She has me go into a changing booth and put the choli on. It is beautiful. Solid black except for gold trim short sleeves and gold trim around the neck line. I come back out and can see Brandon's jaw drop. Atmaja takes the final black and gold piece and drapes it diagonally across my left shoulder to my right hip, and joins the two ends with a small gold tiger pin. Atmaja takes my hands and bows to me. I return the bow thanking her with every ounce of exuberance that I have.

"If I wasn't speechless right now, I would tell you that you are the most beautiful woman I have ever seen," Brandon struggles to say. "Will you marry me?"

"Thank you Brandon, and yes, you are first on my list."

"You have a list?"

"Yes. With one name on it. Please tell them how thankful I am of their graciousness."

"I will."

The sari is almost too nice to wear, but Brandon pleads with me to leave it on. All the workers come out and I greet and thank all of them. Atmaja wraps up the rest of the items and explains to Brandon that they just might need a hem along the bottom and hopes they fit my friends and family. She also wrapped up a small package and handed it to me saying not to open it until after we leave. Brandon and Atmaja converse a little more in Malayalam. We say our goodbye's, still feeling pretty humbled and head back to the car.

"Thank you again Brandon. I wonder what that was all about. I feel bad that they did not want any money."

"You are welcome."

"What did Atmaja mean by the word vishu?"

Brandon hesitates with the answer. "She said Vishnu."

"What is Vishnu?" I ask curiously.

"Still want to see India, or do you want to head back?"

"Take me to wherever you want to take me," I say as I open the other package not feeling too upset Brandon didn't answer my question. "Wow!"

"What is it?"

"It looks like a small solid gold band. Maybe to hold my hair back."

I decide to try it on. The band is flat and about a half inch in width. The middle of the band comes to an upward facing point in the center forming a triangle just bigger than the width of the band. There is a small tiger's face embossed into the gold. The band is open in the back and I slide it under my hair; it fits just right.

"Beautiful! This even looks like real gold."

"That's because it is."

"Stop it! I am just Lily. Nobody would give something like this away for free. Hey look. There is a pair of black sandals too Almost like a Cinderella story going on here, don't ya think?" I say with some of my Alabama twang slipping out.

"Right. That might explain things. Anything for my Cinderella."

Brandon matches it with a proper British accent.

CHAPTER XIX

"I know another place you will like."

"I am still all yours," I say as I run my hands over the new sari that I am wearing. I thought it would be hot, but it isn't.

We leave Balaramapuram and continue south, still on highway 47. I can't figure out why the shop owners were so nice to me, but am happy it happened. I admire the scenery once more wondering where Brandon is taking me. There can't be too many things that can top what just happened. Maybe twenty or thirty minutes passes and a magnificent view of the ocean comes into sight. Brandon gets off the highway and heads toward the water. He pulls the Land Rover over in the sand only about fifty yards from the water and turns off the motor. The sounds of the waves breaking against the white sandy beach are audible.

"Welcome to Kovalam beach," Brandon says as he gets out of the Land Rover. I follow and meet him in front of the car, being careful where I step trying not to ruin the new sari. I choose bare feet and pull the bottom of the sari up just enough to clear the sand.

"It's beautiful Brandon. I'm just a simple girl from Alabama. I never expected a trip like this. Thank you."

"I will grab a bag from the back of the car and we will go for a walk, ok?"

"Yes. Sounds great to me."

Brandon kicks off his sandals and rolls up the bottom of his khaki pants above his calves which look like they were chiseled onto his lower legs. His sleeves on his white button down shirt are already rolled up to his elbows. He puts our sandals in the back of the car and locks it up. The small pack is over his left shoulder. He takes my left hand with his right and we head toward the edge of the water. We reach the water and start walking to the right toward the sun. I hold up my sari with my right hand to keep it from getting wet. The ocean feels as warm as a bath. I can see Brandon's reflection bouncing off of the sun lit water making me feel like I am walking with a bronze god.

The beach isn't crowded, just a couple of people here and there, or a family enjoying the water. There are some small hills along the edge of the beach forming a natural border. The occasional palm tree stands guard over the sands. Ally won't believe me when I tell her about all of this; neither will my friends back home. I decide I better get some pictures and stop for a moment to fish my camera out of the pack.

"Brandon, I need to prove you are real, that this is really happening, so how about standing near that palm tree."

"Sure thing. Only if I get copies," says Brandon as he puts the pack around both shoulders.

I take some pictures of Brandon by the palm tree and then of him standing in ankle deep ocean water. He does the same of me then places the camera on a small rock.

"What are you doing?" I ask.

"Hurry. Smile. I set the timer."

He runs back to me stumbling and falling into the water as he reaches me. The camera goes off.

"That should be a good one," I say supportingly.

I help him up. We pull each other together tighter, almost simultaneously, with my thought matching his, and his mine. We instantly kiss, passionately, like we have been waiting our whole lives for this experience. Brandon's legs give out and he falls backward with me landing on top of him. I can feel Brandon's heartbeats crash through my chest like the waves crashing around us. We continue kissing. He rolls to the side and we are both half in the ocean and half on the sand. We kiss more. I run my hands through his wet hair and he clutches his unyielding grip around me tighter. We continue for what seems like an hour, before neither of us can catch our breath. He struggles with his words.

"Lily, I don't want this to be over in a couple of days from now when you have to leave," Brandon says while staring into my eyes. "We should probably get up before anyone starts to complain. We are usually a little more reserved here."

"It won't end. I won't let it. Someway, I won't let it." We stand back up and I search for my sunglasses. Brandon locates them in the water, wipes them off with his half dry shirt, and hands them to me. We take a long walk hand in hand down the beach before heading back to the car. Brandon takes some more pictures, of us, and the beach.

"Hey look at this one, the camera went off when we had our arms around each other, kissing."

Brandon shows the picture on the camera to me.

"That's the best one. I will never lose it," I say wondering how the camera went off at just the right moment. We eat some of the snacks at the car and drink some bottled water. Not wanting this moment to end, but knowing we have to head back, I reluctantly get into the passenger seat and settle in for the return trip. I am still in shock of how the day has gone. Awaken from a two day sleep where everyone thought I was sick, to spending time alone with Brandon walking on a beach in southern Kerala.

We head north back up highway 47. The traffic is spread out, surprisingly. I catch myself gazing at the puffy cotton clouds in the sky when I swear the front of one cloud in particular turns into the shape of a giant white and gray tiger. It looks like it is running, or in motion, moving with a purpose. The body is made up of the cloud, but it is the tiger's face that is full of anger and rage. Even the eyes look like red flames shooting from the skull. There appears to be some kind of black shield on the tiger's head coming to a point in the middle of its forehead. And then it is over. It is back to a normal cloud again.

"Wow! Did you see that?" I ask Brandon.

"See what?"

"It was a funny looking cloud. It was as if it looked like an animal, but just for a few seconds," I say not wanting to sound too crazy. "Did I fall asleep?"

"No. You have been awake the whole trip. You must be tired. I will stop for some gas and take a break here shortly."

The ride back is long and seems to go by in slow motion since my vision of the tiger. Brandon most likely thinks I am nuts, but I hope not. We stop once for fuel and food. The folks at the gas station seem to be taken aback when they see me, especially in my sari, but in a respectful way. It could be of all the ground-in sand that is still on me; I don't know. I receive some stares and even some bows. I thank them to be polite. I can swear that one of them says the word mahatma to me. We continue our trip. About another two hours pass.

We finally pull into the driveway of Brandon's house just as it is getting dark. Everybody comes out to welcome us back. I hop out still in the sand covered sari and gather my things from the Land Rover. Ally runs over to greet us, followed by my parents. The look on their faces says it all. Ally and I exchange a big hug. I can tell she is excited to hear about my adventure away for the day.

I press my mouth next to her ear and whisper, "wait a little while and I will tell you about the trip."

She gives an understanding nod and lets go.

"Hey mama and dad. We had a great time. I know y'all wanted me to rest, but I felt pretty good when I woke up."

My mama wraps her arms around me at the same time my dad does the same. Yep, group hug.

"We were starting to worry about you two," mama says as she lets go and gives my attire a quick up and down look from my head to my sandals. "This is beautiful. It must have cost you all of your spending money."

"Just about mama. Brandon took me to a shop where they make everything with hand looms. He got me a good deal on the sari and I have one for you and Aunt Bess." Hoping she buys my story I hand her a pink colored sari with light blue flowery trim. Her mouth seems to get stuck open for a moment when she sees it.

"It is gorgeous. Thank you Lily. Thanks for taking her Brandon," she says as she holds up her new sari against her chest and spins around quickly to show the ladies standing and observing the gifts.

"Mrs. Morgan. It was my pleasure to take Lily and show her a small piece of India. She is great company," says Brandon. "And I believe Pareet and my mom are going to take you and the rest of the woman volunteers to Kochi tomorrow after the clinics close down for the day. Some kind of a ladies only shopping thing."

"Yes. She mentioned that, but thanks for bringing back these gifts. They are stunning," mama says as she continues to admire her new sari.

I hand out the sari we decided should be for Carilyn. It is yellow with intricate green designs throughout the soft silky cotton material. She does the same as my mom and all the females let out another gasp. I give the other package containing the sari for my Aunt Bess to my mother for safe keeping. I can see Ally waiting impatiently for her sari, I'm sure. I decide to give it to her upstairs.

"Ally, I need to freshen up a bit. Can you help me?"

"You betcha. Let's go. Hey y'all, see ya in a bit," Ally responds and grabs my hand as she drags me in to the house. I catch a glimpse of Brandon and give him a see-you-in-a-minute look. He nods.

"Hey, wait for me," says Pareet as she follows us.

We enter the room we are staying in and I set my pack and things on the bed and sit down. I grab Ally's sari, which is wrapped in plain brown paper and hand it over to her. She sits down on her bed and takes a deep breath in as she unties the string holding the paper wrapping together.

"Holy crap Lily!" she says as she slowly stands up letting the material dangle to the floor. "You got me my favorite color, purple." She continues to hold the sari in front of her.

"Well, actually the nice lady at the shop picked it out. This is the first time I am seeing it. It is awesome. There are little black and white designs on it that look like small flowers," I say as I rub my hands over the sari. Feels nice but different from mine.

"Here, put the bottom piece on and I will help you with the rest," says Pareet as she takes the white colored choli and hands it to Ally. "The shirt goes on next." Ally slips the choli on and then Pareet takes the last piece and folds it over long ways several times and then drapes it over Ally's left shoulder and brings it across her waist to her right hip. "There you go. You look amazing. You two can wear them to dinner now," Pareet adds.

"So tell us about the trip," Ally says.

"It was great. We drove down the Mandabar coast to Trivandrum. Then to a town just past there and that's where the sari shop was located. It had a long name."

"I know of the place. It is the best one in all of India, I think," Pareet adds.

"Yes. The people were so nice to me and Brandon. They wouldn't even take money for the sari. Then we went to the beach at Kovalam, just for a walk, but as you can see, I fell into the ocean and got sand all over my sari."

"I was once told that the shop that you went to use to make sarees for royalty, and even gods, so legend has it. I lived here my whole life and have never seen a sari like yours Lily. It is truly one of a kind."

"Thanks Pareet. It is amazing. I'm starved. Is there food outside? I smell the tiki torches burning."

"Yes. Let's go show Ally off to everyone. Kenneth will love this sari on you. How did you and Brandon get along? You must have some kind of a magic spell on him," Pareet adds as she makes a final adjustment to Ally's new attire.

"We got along great. He is very special. I like him. Why do you ask?" I say feeling a bit confused. Pareet makes uncomfortable eye contact with me.

"Well, it's just that he was hurt really bad in his last relationship and he was going to dedicate himself to his studies. Brandon said he was not going to see anyone. No girlfriends until after he was done with school, so I just don't want to see him get hurt once more. I am not sure he could handle it," says Pareet.

"I would never do anything like that to him. I really care about him," I say in my defense.

Pareet leaves the room and I follow. As I go through the doorway Ally grabs my shoulder.

"What was that all about? And?" she says in a whisper.

"I don't know *and* he was wonderful Ally."

We make our way outside to the tables by the house. The torches are burning brightly against the now dark cloudy sky. Guests are sitting on both sides of the tables making for more intimate conversation. We approach Carilyn and Doc Nick who are sitting with my parents, Noella, and François.

"Hey that looks fantastic on you," says Carilyn as she reaches for Ally's sari, gliding her hands over the material. "Very soft and I love the design pattern. Looks all hand made."

"All of it. I love it. I will only wear it on special occasions," says Ally.

"Let me see ya," Doc Nick says. "Wow that is neat looking. Probably looks best on you, but I might give it a spin later. Is it my size?"

"No dad. You can't wear it. We can get you a dohti tomorrow."

"I already have a dohti. He is sitting right there," Doc Nick says as he points across the table at my father. The people who hear the joke chime in with a combined laugh at dad's expense.

Dad responds, "So there's this American doctor named Nick from Alabama and an elephant and they go into a bar. The doctor says: a can of beer for me and how about a bag of peanuts for my girlfriend here." Everyone laughs again, but harder this time.

Carilyn zeros in on my dad. "Hey wait a minute, are you referring to me Jim?"

"No way Carilyn, but did I ever tell you about the lady Nick met when we were in Bangkok?" says dad as he tries to save himself.

"I am not sure I want to hear about that one," responds Carilyn.

"Don't listen to him. They were never in Bangkok, right Jim?" says mama.

"No comment Abby." Dad smiles, looks at Nick, and laughs as mama gives him a light smack on his arm.

We finish eating some of the food left out. I tell everyone about our trip down south to the tip of Kerala. They all enjoy it, although I feel bad that everyone had not gone with us. But most of all I am happiest to have spent time alone with Brandon. A couple of hours pass by. Brandon who squeezed into a seat at the next table down from us, finally gives me a nod with his head to say 'let us get out of here' and I wink 'ok' back to him.

"Hey goodnight mama and daddy. I am going to head up to bed. Catch y'all in the morning." I reach over and give each of my folks a hug and then tell everyone else good-night. Ally and Kenneth follow our lead and also get up and leave for some alone time. Brandon meets me at the end of the tables.

"Wow. I was starting to think that we were just going to make silly faces at each other for the rest of the night," says Brandon as he takes my hand.

"What, I don't mind making faces at you." I pout my lips at him and laugh. "Follow me. I know a place where we can go."

"By all means then, lead the way Lily," Brandon says submissively as I grab his hand and tow him along behind me.

I take him in to the house and through the kitchen, up the stairs to the second floor, make a left down the hallway, and then a right turn back out on to the balcony where we were alone together a couple of nights ago.

"Interesting," he says playfully. "Do you come to this place often?"

"Yes. I bring all of my boyfriends here."

"All of them?" Brandon says as he takes over and leads me to an outdoor couch that looks big enough to seat four people comfortably.

"All one of them," I say as I turn and lock my left leg behind Brandon's right leg and push him onto the couch cushions. He lands flat on his back and I climb onto the couch settling next to his left side.

"I did not expect that."

"I have a great teacher," I say. "Can I ask you something?"

"Sure Lily. Anything."

"What did that nice lady at the loom shop mean by the word vishu? I heard her say it several times when you two were talking," I ask hoping for an answer this time.

"You mean Atmaja. Well, Indian mythology says that when things are out of balance in the world; the gods will send a god to earth to bring that balance back in order. It is said that this god will appear in human form. Legend has it that there have been nine or ten Vishnu's that we know of incarnated in human form."

"What did that have to do with the conversation Atmaja was having with you?"

"She said that it was an honor to be in the presence of a Vishnu and that you will make things right again."

"I will? She was joking, right? What about the tenth Vishnu? Who was it?" I choke a bit as I comprehend what Brandon just said, but pry for more information.

"She didn't specify if it was me or you, so I just thanked her for the nice comments figuring she was off her loom so to speak, but you are definitely a goddess in my eyes Lily. She did mention something about the tenth Vishnu being a woman and that the one before that was a man on a white horse."

He reaches up behind him and pulls a smaller cushion under his head for a pillow. Then he slides his left arm under me and around my back. I slip my right arm under him and lay my head on his chest kind of half looking at the balcony railing and the cloudy sky. He then wraps his right arm over me resting it on my lower back. At this moment I feel entwined as if we are one.

"Brandon?" I say as I pick my head up just enough to make eye contact with him in the starless night.

"Yes Lily?"

"I think I love you," I say expecting to somehow be rejected and dropped off the couch to the balcony floor. Instead his grip tightens around me. I can make out his eyes staring at me from the glow of the tiki torches extending over the railing.

"I think I love you too."

I slide up closer to his face. "I won't hurt you."

"I know," Brandon says as our lips come together. We begin to make out passionately. It feels like a continuation from the beach and it feels right. His fingers spread out on his hands as he works them slowly up and down my back. I wrap my other arm around him and we turn toward each other now lying on our sides. We continue to kiss, squeezing each other tighter and tighter until finally we can barely breathe. We relax at the same time as we compete for each other's oxygen. The kissing slows. I eventually lay my head back on to his chest and close my eyes.

"Lily?" I hear as I open my groggy eyes.

"Yes Brandon?"

"It's midnight. We fell asleep. I will walk you to your room."

"Ok Brandon," I say in a partial moan as we begin to untangle.

We reach the door of my bedroom, open it slightly, and I can barely see Ally in her bed. That's good. Early night for her. I pull Brandon toward me and do a quick check looking up the dimly lit hallway in both directions making sure no one is heading to the bathroom.

"Goodnight Brandon. I love you."

"I love you too Lily," he says as he lowers his face toward mine and I raise up on my toes a bit. We kiss again very slowly for what seems like five minutes until I hear a door opening behind us. We stop and I jump into my bedroom closing the door quietly.

"Hey Doctor Jim. Are you heading to the bathroom too?" I hear Brandon say coyly on the other side of my closed door. I smile. Close call.

CHAPTER XX

The next morning I wake up to what sounds like pouring rain outside of the bedroom window. I look over at Ally and she is still sleeping. I decide to head downstairs anyway. I grab my black yoga pants, another t-shirt, and sneakers and put them on. Quietly, I sneak out of the bed room and stop off at the bathroom to brush my teeth, gargle, and just generally wash up to look presentable although; I don't expect Brandon to be up to train with all the rain outside. I tip-toe down the steps, pass through the living room, and then the kitchen. The main kitchen door is already open, but the screen door is closed. Maybe someone forgot to lock up last night. Oh well. I head out through the screen door and to my surprise; Brandon is under the carport and already stretching.

"Hey there. Good morning," I whisper as I walk up to him.

"Good morning. I thought for sure that you would sleep in because of the weather," he says as we throw our arms around each other for a wake up hug. We stop for a second and reading each other's minds again, kiss just for a few seconds.

"We can work on some kalarippayat, but I think kicking the soccer ball will be tough with all the cars in the way."

"I agree Brandon. What do you want to teach me today?" I say as I stretch out my legs and then rotate my waist a bit to warm up my core.

"Some basic self-defense. This is a rubber knife, because the whole thing is blue; I will show you how to defend yourself against it since your take-downs are already pretty good." He has a hard time to keep from smiling over that one.

"Sounds good," I say as I face Brandon. "What do you want me to do should I ever be attacked by a rubber knife?"

"If you weren't so cute I would be pretty mad, well my teacher would be."

"I know. I'm sorry," I offer in an apologetic tone even though we are both laughing.

"As I come at you with the knife, I want you to step to the side out of the way of the attack and at the same time turn your body sideways making yourself a smaller target. Grab the attacker's wrist with your hand that is closest to the knife." I follow Brandon's instructions as we slowly practice the movements. "When you have the attacker's wrist, pull the arm toward your chest as your other arm comes up and hits the attacker below their elbow which will hyper-extend their arm. The pain will usually cause them to drop the knife." We practice slowly as I try my hardest to maintain focus being this close to Brandon.

"I think I got it. What do I do after they drop the knife?"

"Lily, the best thing to do is run. Find a way to escape. You never want to keep fighting. Once you are not in imminent danger anymore, then run."

"I understand Brandon. Let's practice some more and then we should probably get a shower and breakfast."

"Sounds good. You are a natural and a quick learner. How often do you lift weights Lily?" Brandon surprises me with the question as he simulates another knife attack.

"I didn't think you noticed. I train with weights twice a week even when it's the off season and I am not playing soccer."

"No really. I can tell. Your shape and your muscle tone is excellent."

"Thank you for the compliment Brandon. You're not so bad yourself." We exchange a quick hug and kiss once more and then sneak back inside to get ready for the day.

It is lighter outside now and I can see around in my bedroom without turning on any lights. The first thing I notice is my sari which I left hanging up on the closet door. It is spotless like it was sent to the dry cleaner overnight and returned to me this morning. Not a spot of sand or dirt on it anywhere. I grab the material and pull it to my nose and expect it to smell like the ocean sea water. Instead, it smells fresh like it was washed in flowers. I don't understand it because the second thing I notice is Ally, and she is still in bed. Who would have washed it?

"Ally it's time to wake up."

"What time is it? It is too early." She moans and rolls over.

"I am heading to the shower. Did you clean my sari last night?" I figure I would ask.

"What? No. I would have if you asked me to."

"I know you would have. Ok see you in a couple of minutes."

The bathroom is empty when I get there. I start my shower, but I am having trouble concentrating. First of all there are my dreams which are more like visions. Then there is that Vishnu thing Brandon told me about. Now my sari apparently cleaned itself. It is all starting to freak me out. I hear a quiet knock on the bathroom door and I start to move a little quicker.

"I will be out in a minute," I say trying not to wake up the house full of people.

"Take your time," an accented female voice responds.

I finish up and eventually open the door to find Valentina waiting against the wall.

"Sorry I took so long."

"No. You were pretty quick. Are you ok? You seem elsewhere."

"Yes I'm fine. I am just lost in thought."

"Anything you want to talk about?"

"I appreciate the offer, but really I'm fine. I get excited when we head off to the clinics. You know, always happy to help." I bluff. My thoughts are elsewhere.

"I understand. See you in a bit. Oh, I was told Gala is going up to the other clinic today along with Moira, Laney, and a few others. I think doctor Nick and Carilyn will be going there too."

"Oh. Ok. We'll have to ride together again," I say as I head back to my room. Ally is awake and admiring my sari.

I finish getting dressed. Kind of miserable weather outside, so I decide to wear my long khaki pants with the cargo pockets and my goofy matching safari shirt. The one with the big loops on the shoulders. I look like Ranger Lily of the park service or something, but that's ok. Ally heads off to the shower. Several minutes pass and my thought wonders again to what Brandon told me about the ninth Vishnu being a man on a white horse. I think back to what Princess Ellora said about remembering her father riding a white horse. Could it be? Is Princess Ellora, from my dreams, the tenth Vishnu? Maybe Brandon is the eleventh Vishnu? I decide to attribute everything to the stress of this whole experience— out of the country for the first time, finding the man of my dreams, and the fact I will be leaving soon and may never see Brandon again. That is even a worse thought and I quickly crush that idea. Ally returns from the bathroom.

"Hey doll, can I borrow some clothes? I forgot to wash them. Maybe just a shirt will do." Ally asks me as she digs through her duffel bag.

"Absolutely. My crimson colored t-shirt with the big letter 'A' on the front is clean." I hand my favorite t-shirt to Ally hoping I see it again in the future. "I know where you live so if I have to come to Georgia to get it then I will."

We share the laugh and finish dressing and gathering our things for the day. I grab my small back pack, double check that all of my pink kit is in it, and head downstairs. Ally follows. I enter the kitchen just as I see the green Land Rover backing out from under the car port. Brandon's driving. My heart skips a few beats, but I get it under control. The car looks full.

"Good morning Jillian. Did I just see Brandon leaving?" I nervously ask.

"Good morning Lily. Yes don't worry. He was taking the other volunteers to the third clinic, but he should meet us at ours by noon or so. He told me to tell you to have a good day."

"Oh. Ok. Thanks," I respond with relief that I will see him later on.

"You really like him, don't you?"

"Yes I do." If she only knew. "I will miss him and everyone else when we leave."

"See. I knew it. You two make a really cute couple. Maybe you can go to school in England next year." Jillian says surprising me that she is trying to fix me up with her son, or maybe everyone knows about us.

"I would consider it if there was some way, but I don't know right now."

"I understand. Well, eat up. Long day ahead of us. You and Ally can ride to the clinics with Pareet and me today." She hands me a plate and I fill it up with some fruit and rice cakes. Ally arrives and says good morning and we head out to the black Land Rover. The sky is dark gray with thick flat clouds and it looks like the rain is coming down harder. I peek in to my pack and retrieve my pink Paris hat and put it on.

Ally and I climb in to the Land Rover along with Valentina, Marco, Petra, Noella, and François. Pareet sits in the front passenger seat and Jillian drives. We follow the same route down the dirt road and make the right turn on to the paved one joining the traffic flow. The temperature has dropped a couple of degrees making all the motorcycle riders and rickshaw passengers cover up from the rain to no avail. It seems to be turning into a monsoon or something. Ally is fumbling through her back pack.

"Oh great," she says in frustration.

"What?"

"Nothing. I forgot my hat."

"Relax. I will make you one out of banana leaves," I offer.

Jillian drives us to the clinics swerving here and there and dodging the occasional animal and human. I wonder about Brandon, missing him deeply already. I try not to let it get me down, but can't help it. At least I can try to be upbeat for everyone else so they don't have to suffer with me. I know Ally is already feeling the same way about Kenneth, but neither of us want to think about leaving India and our beaus.

Jillian finally makes the right turn for the clinics. She slows to a stop, places the Land Rover in to four-wheel-drive low range and begins to crawl up the slippery washed out muddy trail. The windshield wipers turning in unison with the mud clogged tires. The Land Rover struggles with the lack of traction, but after what seems like another hour, we arrive at the clinics. There are two extra blue canopies set up in front of the clinics covering a bunch of rain soaked people. The sky is almost black and the rain doesn't seem to be giving us a break. We park as close to the clinics as we can. At the same time, we open our doors on the Land Rover, make a dash to get equipment out of the back, and then sprint for clinic one.

Inside we find a dry Doctor Karup staring at us while he sips a hot tea. I didn't even realize he spent the night here at the clinic. Hiro, Sakurako, and Mandara are here also. My dad follows us into clinic one and heads for the big silver metal coffee pot. It is the kind that makes a bunch of coffee all at once for large groups. He pours a cup for himself and then joins Singh to plan out the details for the day.

"Sounds good Singh," says my dad as he walks over to our group huddled by the coffee pot. "Ok. Here is the plan. It doesn't seem like there will be a large turnout of patients today. So, for now it will be Pareet, Petra, Ally, Lily, Kenneth, and Mrs. Morgan staying here. Mandara will stay to translate for us. Jillian, Tushar, and Jia Li, along with Hiro and Sakurako, and François and Noella, will run clinic two."

"You forgot about me," says Singh as he takes another drink of his tea. "Can I be on your team Coach?"

"Sorry Singh. I'm not awake yet. You can stay here with us," says my dad as he takes another drink. "That will give us at least two docs per clinic."

"Sounds good to me Jim," Singh says as he gets out of the plastic chair he was sitting in. "I will wash up and join you in a minute."

The group divides up and the clinic two folks top off their coffee cups before heading back out in to the monsoon. I feel happy staying inside for now and pick a spot at the end of the row of tables against the back wall to put my stuff on. Everyone staying here picks a spot for their things and we settle in for the day. I am hoping to be busy to take my mind off of Brandon not being here. I'm already wondering where he is, what he is doing, and when will he get here. I want to spend every minute I have left of this trip with him. I would have gone with him to the other clinic if I had known he was going, even if I had to ride on the roof of his Land Rover. A couple of people are waiting to be seen, so I focus on work.

An ill looking Indian gentleman comes up to us and Mandara guides him to a chair. She speaks to him in Malayalam and then relays his symptoms to us. I take his vital signs. First his blood pressure and pulse rate at his left wrist. Then I count his respirations and take his temperature with a battery operated oral thermometer.

"Jim, it sounds like malaria," Mandara says as my ears perk up having never heard that phrase before. "He reports being outside about a week ago on a boat in the backwaters and said the mosquitoes were terrible. He is complaining of feeling pretty weak today. He has a headache and the chills saying he can't get warm. Also complaining of being short of breath without much exertion."

"Yes. It sounds like it. I wish we could draw some blood for lab work and get a sputum sample. What's his vitals Lily?"

"Dad his temperature is one-o-two. His heart rate is one twenty six and respirations are twenty-four. I can't tell if he is sweating or if it is the rain."

"He is probably diaphoretic, sweating. Ok. Petra let's give this gentleman Quinine Sulfate 600mg by mouth three times a day for seven days and Doxycycline 100mg twice a day for seven days. I also want to give him three Pyrimethamine tablets now just one time. Some

Acetaminophen sounds good too. How about a gram every six hours for the fever." Dad gives the orders as he finishes examining the patient.

Petra retrieves the medications as Mandara translates the instructions to the patient. I try to watch Petra give the medicine, but find my thoughts drifting elsewhere, specifically, Brandon. I look over at Ally and Kenneth who are taking care of some other patients. Dad is off to another patient already. Singh and Pareet are seeing someone else, but I feel alone without Brandon being here next to me.

Mandara gives some follow up instructions to the patient telling him to return if his symptoms get worse and to make sure he takes all of the medication. She then waves over the next patient. It is a nice little old lady dressed in the brightest sari that you can imagine. Yellow, blue, and red designs flow from the sari. They appear to be hand embroidered and intricate. She looks at me and nods; kind of the same way the other Indian folks have, as if to say: I know who you are. I give her the namaste greeting back and say good morning.

"Mandara, what can we do for her today? She doesn't appear to be sick or in any distress. A checkup maybe." Mandara talks to her in Malayalam as I gesture to the chair in front of me.

"Lily, she says she just came to meet you and that the word has traveled fast. There may be others coming to meet you also," says Mandara with a quizzical look and her eyebrows raised crinkling her forehead. I have a feeling I know why, but decide to just play it off as the unusual tourist.

"Jeepers," I mumble to myself. "Tell her I am flattered, but I am just here helping out. Does she want me to take her blood pressure?" Mandara translates.

"No. She said she was just happy that you are here."

The nice old lady gets up from the chair, half bows, half nods to me again, and leaves. Wow, this is getting to be a little too much for me. Now I am really lost. Where is Brandon? The morning drags on. It seems even darker outside than what it was. I can feel the wind whip through the open windows every now and then. We keep seeing more patients that were brave enough to travel in this weather. I continue with the vital signs and the occasional check of their blood sugar remembering to hold the lancet correctly before I poke their finger. Just the way Brandon showed me, but then I think of him even more, not that I ever stopped. Where is he? We eventually make it to lunch time. Ally walks over to me giving me some pouty eyes feeling bad for me I am sure.

"Hey girlfriend, let's get some lunch," she says.

"Ok."

"Cheer up. He will be here. He is probably just helping out the other clinic. They might have gotten a lot of patients today. That's all." Ally puts her arm around me and we head out of the clinic around the corner to the lunch area with Kenneth.

The water run-off from the rain has crept under the edges of the makeshift dining area forming what looks like a small medieval mote. We pick some dry spots and sit down, but soon realize we are going to have to get some takeout. We load up our green place mats with food, grab a bowl of curry, and scramble back to the clinic.

"Hey y'all," says Ally to the rest of the people in clinic one. "You have to get some takeout 'cause it's too windy and rainy."

"Sounds good. Be right back," says my dad as the rest of the people and workers follow him.

Kenneth clears the equipment off of the table. I head into the back room and get drinks for us and set them on what is now our picnic table.

"Man, it is like a monsoon out there. I thought it rains pretty good in London, but this is really something," says Kenneth as he digs in to his food. "That river forming around the dining area reminds me of the Thames."

"What the heck is that?" Ally asks.

"Oh. It is the big river that runs through London," he says as he chews his food eating rapidly like all paramedics do, I guess. "You know the one. Big Ben. London Bridge. All that sort."

"That is called the Thames? Then Mini Thames is outside," Ally says. "Hey Lily baby, he will be here, smile."

"I know. I just miss him terribly right now." I keep eating, but I am not really tasting anything. I tell myself to enjoy the food, but I am elsewhere right now. My dad comes back in with a bunch of food and he has found my mama. Pareet and Petra return also carrying their food carefully.

"Hi mama. Hi dad. You two look like you just took a shower," I say as I slowly peck at my food.

"I've never seen this much rain before. It is like a little hurricane," my mama says as she picks out a chair and sits down.

"It is a good storm, but at least it isn't snow." I say as if we get snow in Eufaula.

"Hey. They need to get better take away containers. I'm spilling everything," says Petra as they sit down at the table joining ours.

"I know. This is fun isn't it? Pretty normal for us," says Pareet as some of her rice falls to the table as she sets down her green mat.

"Ladies, what are you drinking? We have water, water, and water," Kenneth adds as he stands up to get some drinks.

"There seems to be plenty of water out there." Singh points to the doorway. "In case we run out."

"How about a coffee if you're offering Kenneth," Petra says.

"Your wish is my command." Kenneth stands up and heads over to the coffee maker and returns with two steaming cups for Petra and Singh, knowing that Singh would not say no to coffee like my dad.

"Thank you Kenneth," they both say almost at the same time.

"All right then. I have to head to the bathroom," says Ally. "Anyone else coming?" She nods to me and Kenneth.

"Yep. Right behind you," Kenneth says as he collects our lunch plates and heads to the garbage can.

"Wait for me," I say knowing I can't refuse Ally's request for company. I take a second to dig in my back pack again to find my pink Paris hat and throw it on as if it will act as some kind of an umbrella. We head to the door and peek outside. It is still raining pretty good.

"One. Two. Three. Go!" Kenneth calls out as the three of us dash out of the clinic, turn right, run past the smoking concrete brick stove, and then turn right again and down the small hill toward the bathrooms. A few Indian folks standing under the outdoor kitchen canopy admire our determination to stay dry. We reach the bathroom and Ally slides in the grassy mud nearly slamming in to the men's room and falling before Kenneth catches her.

"Hey sugar, did you want to use the bathroom first? I want to stay here a second and talk to Kenneth. Oh, and can I borrow your hat until you come back?" Ally asks me while Kenneth stands leaning his back against the bathroom wall with his arms wrapped around Ally.

"Yeah. Sure thing doll. Dang you two make a heck of a sweet couple," I say as I take off my hat and put it on Ally's head with the bill facing backwards. "I guess you really did leave yours at the house."

"You know me. See you in a minute," Ally says as her and Kenneth give each other a peck on the lips. It is more than I want to see right now so I head in to the bathroom. A few minutes past and Ally finally joins me inside.

"I saved you a hole in the floor. Don't stumble. The floor is a little wet. I think it's from the rain. I hope it is from the rain."

"Thanks Lily. Stop worrying. Brandon will be here and you two will have the rest of the afternoon to make googly eyes at each other."

"Thank you. I didn't know I could miss someone this much, especially that I haven't known him all that long. Crazy, isn't it?"

"I feel like that about Kenneth. What are we going to do when we have to leave?" Ally asks me.

"I am trying not to think about it."

"You're right. Sorry for bringing it up," Ally says as she gives me a quick hug. "Let's get back to work. You know. Try to stay busy, ok?"

"Sure thing Ally," I say as we head back outside.

We leave the bathroom and Kenneth intercepts Ally for another kiss.

"Lily baby. I will meet you back at the clinic in a second," Ally says as she wraps her arms around Kenneth one more time.

"Ok," I say and head up the small hill toward the outdoor kitchen.

As I near the top of the hill, I spot the roof of the green Land Rover. My heart starts to hammer away in my chest and I can feel myself getting short of breath. I catch a glimpse of Brandon coming out of clinic two. His back is toward me.

"Brandon!" I yell, but he keeps walking toward the green Land Rover. He walks faster like he is trying to dodge the raindrops. I don't think he heard me because of the rain and wind.

"BRANDON!!" I scream louder as I slip trying to catch up with him. He turns his head and looks at me with angry eyes for a second, but walks even faster. He reaches the Land Rover, opens the driver's door, and gets in. He slams the door shut and starts the Land Rover.

I scream as loud as I can, "BRANDON!!!" as I run toward him.

He stomps on the gas pedal spinning the Land Rover's tires as he turns the car around heading back out of the clearing. He stares at me through the passenger window as he drives past me and keeps going. I drop to my knees and immediately begin to cry trying to figure out what just happened. I put both hands on my thighs as I settle to the ground. My tears are flowing faster than the rain splashing off my face. I feel a hand on my left shoulder as Ally drops to her knees in front of me.

"Are you ok? I saw the whole thing. What was that all about?"

"I don't know Ally," I say struggling to get my words out as the tears continue. She hugs me tighter.

"Well. Come on. Let's get you inside." Ally stands up and takes my hand trying to pull me up with her.

"NO! I can't let my parents see me crying like this!"

"They won't notice. We are soaked like wet rags. Come on we will sneak you in to the back room and get you cleaned up," says Ally as I ever so slowly try to stand, but I can't feel my legs under me. It's worse than running twenty miles in a soccer game. My legs just won't work.

"Hey! Lily! I asked you not to hurt Brandon. I told you he couldn't handle it, but you did anyway!" Pareet says from behind me.

"Back off!" Ally screams at her. "What are you talking about?" Ally pulls me up to my feet and I turn to face Pareet as she storms up to my face. Ally steps in front of me blocking Pareet's path.

"How can you defend her after she was just kissing Kenneth!" Pareet says stopping a couple of inches from Ally's face. "Isn't he your boyfriend?"

"What? What the heck are you talking about Pareet?" Ally stares at Pareet demanding an answer.

"Brandon said he just saw Lily and Kenneth tongue wrestling down by the bathrooms," says Pareet angrily still looking like she wants to kill me.

"Wait. Wait. Wait! Oh no. Ally look at you shirt. Isn't that Lily's shirt? Is that not Lily's hat? Long blonde hair. Almost the same height. Similar bodies?" Kenneth says as he steps between Ally and Pareet separating them. "Pareet, I think I know what happened. It was Ally and I that were kissing by the bathrooms. Lily was inside the bathroom. Ally borrowed her clothes this morning. Brandon must have thought Ally was Lily. I know he has seen Lily in the pink hat and this t-shirt before." Kenneth points to the big 'A' on my t-shirt that Ally is wearing. "Pareet, where was Brandon going?"

"He said he was going home, to the house, and that everybody can walk home tonight," says Pareet as the tone in her voice returns to normal conversation level. "I am really sorry Lily. It's just that..."

"It's ok. You didn't know," I say as Pareet throws her arms around me and buries her head on my right shoulder. I return the hug. As she pulls back to look at me, there are tears in her eyes.

"Ok then," says Kenneth as he lets out a big sigh. "Let's wait a bit and try to raise Brandon on the shortwave radio at the house."

"Ok Kenneth," I say feeling like this has been the worse day of my life.

"Now can we get out of the bloody rain?"

"Yes Kenneth," says Ally as we start to walk over to clinic one hoping not too many people saw this whole mess.

CHAPTER XXI

Pareet apologizes again and heads back inside clinic two. Ally, Kenneth, and myself walk up to clinic one and enter through the door hoping my mama went back in to the other clinic and that my dad is too busy to notice my distraught face. Thankfully he is examining a patient and is facing away from me. We walk down the right side of the building past the radio and in to the back room where the extra supplies and refrigerator is located. Ludwik follows us.

"Hey, are you guys all right?" Ludwik asks in his thick German accent.

"Yeah. Everyone is ok. Just a little mix up. Can you call Brandon at the house in about an hour," Kenneth asks.

"Sure. No problem. Is there anything else I can do for you guys?"

"I don't think so. We just need to reach Brandon."

"Ok Ken. I will work on it," Ludwik says as he heads back out to the radio. He stops at the door for a minute and turns to Ally. "I almost forgot Ally. Your parents said hello and wanted me to check up on you. I will tell them you are fine, yes?"

"Yes. Thanks Ludwik. We are all fine. Tell them I will see them later at dinner," says Ally.

"Ok. Sister, let's find a towel. You have French poodle hair right now," says Ally as she wraps a towel around my head. I grab the ends and dry my face off. Then I dry my hair the best that I can. Ally hands her hairbrush to me and I run that through my hair trying to get the knots out of it. I take one of my hair ties from my pocket, grasp my hair in to a pony tail and put the tie around it. Ally hands me my hat back and I figure I should put it on to hide my face a little bit, so my dad doesn't see what a mess I am. Ally and Kenneth finish getting cleaned up, grab some water, and the three of us leave the supply room and sit down at the table closest to the supply room door in case I have to go in there and cry. We join in the treatments of the next patients. I try to focus on taking some blood pressures on the next several patients.

At least an hour goes by and I keep flashing a peek over at Ludwik sitting in front of the shortwave. He keeps shaking his head side to side indicating he has not talked to Brandon yet. I try to tell myself that maybe it is too soon and that he will be there in another thirty minutes. I can't even remember how long it takes to get to the clinics. Please get a hold of Brandon I say to myself trying to pass the thought to Ludwik. Thirty minutes goes by and Ludwik shakes his head again. Another hour passes and still Ludwik shakes his head again. I lose count of how many blood pressures I have taken. How many pulses? How many respirations that I have counted? It's all a blur. Every time I look at Ludwik, it is still no. He shakes his head at me as if to say he is sorry, but I know it isn't his fault.

The number of patients thins a bit. Maybe only five or six in our clinic being treated and probably not many more than that next door. I keep working until we have seen them all, yet quite a few stay inside trying to wait out the storm I guess. Probably twenty, or so, hanging out with us. Mandara is talking with them and translating for my dad from time to time.

I get up and head over to Ludwik.

"Any luck Ludwik?" I ask wishing he has made contact with Brandon and that he is on his way here.

"Nothing Lily. I have tried everything. All my connections are right. It might be the weather or maybe Brandon just has their radio at the house turned off."

"Thanks. I know you are trying your hardest."

I walk to the front door and stare out in to the clearing hoping that maybe I would see the green Land Rover pull up to our clinic. But nothing. If Brandon does come, I can promise it won't go like it did earlier. It is still raining. The sky is still dark. And I am wondering when the sun will return. I look toward the kitchen and can see several Indian folks cooking up some kind of food. Their dedication is remarkable. I admire that. I can't quite see the doorway to the other clinic, but I am sure mama will be up here soon because it is getting late and they will decide on who will be watching the clinics tonight. At this point I feel like volunteering, but would rather explain to Brandon what had happened. Maybe he will come back and the both of us can stay here tonight alone just to be with each other. I decide to head to the back room again to freshen up again just in case he shows up.

My dad waves to me as I pass him. He is still talking to the other folks. Singh and Mandara are both translating for him. I check in with Ludwik again and still nothing. I head to the back room only to find Ally and Kenneth kissing again.

"Excuse me," they stop quickly. "If you two are done with the inventory, I would..."

BANG! BANG! BANG BANG BANG! BANG! BANG!!!

"What the hell is that?" says Kenneth as he heads to the doorway. "It sounds like gunfire or something."

"Move move move!!" Kenneth yells as he jumps back from the doorway as bullets fly past him hitting one of our blue supply boxes from home leaving it peppered with holes. I see IV fluid leaking out of it.

"What is it?" Ally screams as she is grabbed by Kenneth and pushed toward the window.

BANG BANG BANG!!!!

"Bandits or something! They are all in black! They have black masks over their heads! Move Lily!" he says as he drags me to the window. He picks me up and almost throws me out of the window. I glance to my right only to see Ludwik lying on the floor of the clinic with what looks like blood coming from his legs. There is smoke smoldering from the shortwave radio. Oh no!

"Jump!" Kenneth screams at me.

I half fall, half jump landing on the wet muddy grass next to our outdoor eating area, rolling to a stop. I look up to see Ally dropping down on me. I quickly roll to my side and she just misses landing on top of me. She makes a grunt as she lands. Kenneth is half out of the window when a black covered arm reaches around his neck and drags him back in to the clinic.

BANG BANG!!

"Ally run!" I grab her arm and start dragging her toward the clearing edge. I don't know where to go. Think Lily think! We duck behind the blue canopy covering the eating area.

BANG BANG BANG BANG!!!!

A burst of what I am now sure is machine gun fire rips through the canopy leaving the top of it looking like the top of a salt shaker. The tea plantation pops into my head.

"Ally run. Stay with me!" I yell as I hang on to her arm pulling her with me like conjoined twins. We sprint as fast as we can to the trail that Brandon said leads to the tea plantation. We make it to the trail as a row of bullets sprays the rubber trees in front of us leaving an oozing of latex dripping from them. I hear the noise of a vehicle, its engine sounding like it is screaming. I look off to my right to see the green Land Rover being sprayed with bullets all along the driver's side. BANG BANG BANG BANG!!! TINK TINK!! SMASH! The back window shatters with an explosion of glass. Brandon is driving. The Land Rover is sliding violently out of control. Mud and wet grass flying from the tires. He turns to the right heading toward the trees where I last saw Mr. Hair. The Land Rover disappears and then there is a loud crunch of metal and trees coming together. Oh no! Not Brandon too.

We keep trying to run as fast as we can, but the mud won't let us get any traction under our feet. I feel like I am stuck in quick sand. We run. We slip. We fall. We get up and slip some more. The trail is barely wide enough for a small car to pass through. The trees thicken and change quickly from rubber to the ones with the brown vines wrapped around them. The branches at the tops of the trees overhang on each side of the trail almost forming a thatched roof making it almost like running through a dark tunnel. I can still hear gunfire coming from the area of the clinics, but it is not as loud now. We must be making some kind of distance between the attackers and us. As soon as I think that, the mud dirt and grass explodes in front of me. Nope! I turn to see several small black dots running toward us up the twisting trail. Not good shots thankfully. If it were Alabama deer hunters, they would have had us by now.

"Lily! I gotta stop! Please I can't run no more. Let's hide," Ally begs me.

"We have to keep moving! Keep running!" I yell over the sound of the wind and our heavy breaths. "A little farther. Brandon said the tea plantation is up this trail. Somebody there can help us," I say trying to reassure Ally and myself.

We break from the trees on to a trail surrounded on both sides by lush vivid green plants. About three to five feet tall packed tightly together. There are little white flowers and green leaves. Tea? Not the way I wanted to see it for the first time. The slope of the hill seems to be going straight up. It is definitely steeper. Farther up the trail I can see other paths leading to the left and to the right. I can almost make out the entire tea plantation on this slope. It is segmented almost like a corn maze back home, but more like city streets.

Ally is barely able to walk fast now yet alone run. I am feeling it too. We keep moving up through the tea plantation about another fifty yards and then turn right on to one of the other grass and mud paths leaving perfect foot prints for the bad guys to follow. The tea plants are too thick to run through and the path is to muddy to hide our tracks. I lead Ally off further to the right until we come across another path leading higher up the slope kind of like zig-zagging our way through the plantation.

The top edge of the slope is bordered by thick trees forcing us to turn right on to the last path. We reach the end of that path and are now stuck in the corner of the plantation like a couple of wet cornered rats. Not a good feeling. We duck down behind the tea plants the best we can. Ally lays down on her back. I try to spot our pursuers hoping that they gave up. I see some movement about half way up on the other side of the tea plantation. So much for that.

"Lily what do we do," Ally says between gasps for air. "I don't want to die."

"We are not going to die. Don't talk like that. This is all a bad dream. Let me think for a second." I look around trying to figure out where to go. There is bright movement in the trees to my right. It seems out of place with the wind and rain. It is the red and gold butterfly hovering.

"Hello there. I was hoping you would show up."

"What?" Ally struggles to sit up. "Who are you talking to?"

"Nobody. Come on, crawl in to the trees," I say as I direct her to where the butterfly just was.

We both crawl in to the thick trees while I catch another glimpse of the butterfly moving slowly between the branches. My pants are almost completely brown from the mud and dirt. My hiking boots feel like I am moving two giant wet sponges, but I continue to crawl pushing Ally in front of me following the butterfly. We crawl for about another thirty yards weaving between the tree trunks until I can make out what looks like a rock wall jetting straight up in front of us. I start to wonder if snakes come out in the rain and then decide we have bigger problems.

"Oh great. There is a wall in front of us," says Ally as she spots it also.

"Just keep going. Maybe we can lay down in here and then try to find the house where the tea plantation people live or something," I say trying to think of what to do next. The butterfly is almost right up against the rock wall. We can't climb up the wall. It is to sheer and I can't even see the top of it. The ground is mostly covered in wet dirt and tree branches. The smell of century old decaying leaves and who knows what else, stings my nose. We keep crawling. I am almost right on top of Ally's legs.

"Lily what is that cracking noise?"

Before I can answer, the ground beneath us gives out dropping us down in to darkness. The tree branches dirt and rocks drop with us. We both scream out as we land with a splash and thud in to what must be a hole of some kind. There must be about three or four inches of water. Ally lets out a moan. I find myself lying face down across her legs. The drop must have been eight or ten feet. I push myself up on to my hands, roll off Ally, and look up from where we just fell from. I inhale deeply trying to catch my breath. The air is thick and stale. I feel the same as an ancient archeologist does the first time they enter one of those old pyramids.

"Lily!" Ally says in an angry voice.

"What?"

"I am tired of falling. That is the second time today," she says as she sits up in the water. "Sorry, but this is getting ridiculous."

"I know babe. Are you ok? Is anything broken? Let me see if my pen light is still working."

"I think I am ok," Ally answers. "Your shirt is torn, sorry."

"Don't worry about it."

I dig in to my cargo pocket and pull out my pink pen light. I shine it around and it looks like we landed in some kind of cave, not a hole.

"Ok butterfly, I see what you were doing."

"What? Why do you keep calling me butterfly?" asks Ally as she stands up.

"Nothing. Come on. Let's see where this cave goes," I say as I hope my batteries in the penlight will last. "Do you have your pink mini flash light on you?"

"Let me check," Ally fumbles in her cargo pockets. "Yep. Got it."

"Ok. Save your battery. We will use mine until the batteries quit," I say as we start to step into the darkness of the cave. "I don't think Brandon made it."

"What? He was back at the house," says Ally as she tries to brush the mud off her pants.

"No. He was there. At the clinics. He pulled up as we were running to the trail. I saw him driving the green Land Rover. They shot it up and then it disappeared down the hill. I don't think he is alive," I say trying to fight my tears back.

"Don't worry. I am sure he got away. If anybody could do it he can. That's for sure. I am sure everyone is ok. Let's get out of here and find some help."

"You are right Ally."

SPLASH!!!

I turn around with my penlight to see a person wearing all black and holding a large knife glistening in the beam from my penlight. Instinctively, I step back and raise the light to their face as they are pulling off the black ski mask.

"It is about time I caught up with you," the person says, but it is a female voice with an accent I can't make out.

The mask is completely off now revealing long black hair lying over both sides of her shoulders. There is a small scar by the corner of her lower lip on the right side.

"You. It's you. You are a woman," I say realizing that Mr. Handsome's friend from the airport and the clearing is not Mr. Hair, but Mrs. Hair.

"Lily, you know her?" Ally asks with an almost inaudible voice.

"Yes she knows me. Lily is the only one out of your whole bunch that has been paying attention. You're all very stupid," Mrs. Hair retorts. "I have orders to bring you two back to the clinics, but accidents do happen. I think I will have to kill you both and skip the ransom money," she says almost to happily smiling in the process and contorting the scar by her lip making almost another eerie smile.

"We have done nothing to you. Please we are just here to help people," I say finding myself pleading, trying to buy time or something. I try to remember what Brandon taught me this morning about knife self-defense. It seems so long ago. My thoughts are cluttered. Brandon's gone. Parents are at the clinics. Ludwik lying down bleeding. Kenneth being dragged back in from the window. I can make out a pistol in a holster on her right leg.

"Yes. I think you can watch me kill your friend first and then you will die next," Mrs. Hair says as she takes a step toward me waving the knife back and forth across the beam of light I have directed on her face. "Yes Lily. Sounds good, no?"

Suddenly a vision of Princess Ellora surrounded by a red neon glow appears behind Mrs. Hair's head. "Lily, remove the triangle shaped rock from the cave wall." She points to her left, my right. "Grab the crystal," she says as the vision fades.

I quickly shine my little beam of light toward the wall on my right. I hear Mrs. Hair take another step heading toward Ally. Frantically, I work the beam of light up and down and back and forth across the wall. The light starts to flicker telling me that the battery is about to check out on me. Not now! Finally about waist high in front of me, I spot a small triangle shaped rock. It is about the size of my hand. Mrs. Hair takes another step toward Ally splashing the water in the process. I reach for one of the protruding corners and pull. It barely moves. I stick the edge of my pen light against the corner and pry the rock. It makes the whole cave dark now. There is barely any light coming from the hole that we fell through.

"Where you going Lily?" Mrs. Hair says with a cynical voice. "You can't dig through the wall with your flashlight."

The triangle rock gives and splashes into the water. A brilliant small tiger head crystal reflects off the dying beam of my penlight. I grab the crystal as fast as I can. Instantaneously, a flash of grey black and white fur flies by my penlight letting out a deafening roar and lands on Mrs. Hair. She is taken off her feet as I redirect my light to see the knife fly through the air and in to the water. There is a sound of crunching bone and Mrs. Hair is no more. I run the last of my beam of light over the most magnificent white tiger that I have ever seen. It is totally covering Mrs. Hair's body except for her right arm sticking out in an awkward manner from beneath the tiger. I should be scared, but I am not and don't know why. Ally grabs my left shoulder pulling me to her.

"Lily, did you see that? What is that?" Ally says as she turns on her mini flashlight. "Bandits first. Now tigers. What the f...!"

"Ally, it's all right. Calm down. I think it is here to help us."

"Have you completely lost it. This is a bad dream. I gotta to get out of here."

"Ally it is ok. Relax. I even think I know its name," I say as the tiger finally release its grip on what is left of Mrs. Hair's neck.

"It has a friggin name?" Ally says with a still shaky voice.

"Yes. Shine your light toward the tiger." Ally illuminates the tiger moving the beam of light from its head to its tail. It must be fourteen feet long. Wow! Impressive I say to myself as it walks toward me. I reach out with my hand and it lowers its head. Slowly, I touch the tiger on top of its head between two still alert ears as if saying I am still on guard. Carefully I rub my hand on its head.

"Thank you," I say quietly. "I think I know who you are."

"Oh great. You are having a conversation with a bloody tiger," Ally says as the tiger comes over and sits down between us brushing up against Ally's leg in the process. "It touched me Lily."

Just then we hear a crash of noise coming from the top of the entrance of the hole we fell in to. It sounds like fighting and pounding and then some muffled gags.

"What was that?" Ally whispers to me. She shines her light toward the hole above us.

SPLASH!!

A body clad in black falls down in to the water in front of us.

SPLASH!!

A second body dressed in black falls through the hole and in to the water.

A third body falls, no, jumps down in to the hole, landing on the first two bodies which appear lifeless. The person pulls out a flashlight and shines it on the three of us— myself, Ally, and the tiger.

"What? I needed something, or in this case, some people to break my fall, you know, cushion my landing," says Brandon in a calm cool voice. "Hello Panthera," he adds.

CHAPTER XXII

"Brandon!" I scream as I run to him and throw my arms around him. "I thought they got you. I never thought I would see you again." I keep hugging him tightly as Ally runs over to Brandon and hugs him also. He has a rifle slung over his right shoulder and another one in his left hand. I turn back to glance at Panthera and she is just sitting there watching our reunion.

"Brandon, we are so glad to see you. They were going to kill us. Where is everyone? Did you see Kenneth? Are they all dead?" says Ally as we release our hugs.

"Ok. Ok. Try to relax and focus. All I know is that I pulled in to the clearing at the same time the attack must have begun. There were masked people with guns entering the two clinics. The Indian folks who were outside, were already huddled together and being watched by some of those attackers. One of them was tying the cook's hands together. So, I don't think they were there to kill everyone. I think they were going to ask for ransom money or some kind of other demands."

Brandon stops for a second and scans the cave with his flashlight and then the hole that we all dropped through. We let go of Brandon to let him catch his breath.

"Ally, I am sorry, but I never saw Kenneth, and Lily, I never saw your parents or mine."

Brandon leans down and begins to search Mrs. Hair's body. He pats down her upper clothing and works his way down to the feet.

"Here, put this on," he says as he removes something from her body. "It's a bullet-proof vest."

I hand the vest to Ally who insists that I wear it at first, but then puts the vest on.

"I understand Brandon. We have to go back there and help them. We have to get help. We need to call the police or something. I couldn't find the people who work on the tea plantation."

"No. You wouldn't have because they don't live here. There are no phones near here either. We have to get back to the camp and steal one of the other vehicles because mine was shot up pretty good, unless," he pauses for a second. "Maybe I can sneak in and use the radio. Here, this is her pistol." He hands me Mrs. Hair's gun and I stick it in my waist band behind my back like I've seen on TV.

"Not possible Brandon," I say as he returns a puzzled look. "They shot the radio and Ludwik too."

"Oh no. I took a rifle off of each bad guy up top there," he says gesturing to the hole again. "Ally, this is yours." He hands Ally a rifle and she hangs it over her shoulder with the sling.

"What is it?" she asks.

"AK47's I think. Push the latch down by the trigger and it will fire, I think. Ok we have to find a way out of here. I only had one semester of geomatics, but looking at the topography of the cave," he thinks for a moment. "The cave must circle around the mountain and I bet there will be some kind of exit not far from the bottom of the tea plantation, I hope."

"I hope so too," says Ally as Panthera lets out a soft grunt.

"It looks like Panthera is ready to get out of here to."

We turn as Panthera stands up and starts to walk back in to the darkness of the cave. It must be seven feet in height and looks wide enough for about five people to stand shoulder to shoulder. More man made than naturally formed I think. I wonder who dug this and when. It must have taken forever.

"Looks like she knows where she is going," Brandon says as we follow the massive tiger. "Ally, let's just use your flashlight to conserve batteries. When yours goes then I will turn mine on. This cave could be longer than I am guessing."

"Good idea Brandon. We are just so happy to see you," adds Ally as the beam of light from her flashlight bounces off the walls, the water, and Panthera.

"By the way Lily, that tiger makes a way better knife defense than anything I could ever show you," says Brandon as we slosh through water as quietly as possible.

"Thanks anyway. I was having a little bit of trouble recalling exactly what to do with that knife. How did you know about Panthera?" I decide to ask.

"Well, Panthera is one of those things that was only supposed to exist in legends and mythology, but I knew there was something about you that I couldn't figure out from the first time I met you."

"Like what?"

"Little by little it was all starting to add up, but I didn't want to believe it because it isn't supposed to be real, hence mythology, right?"

We keep walking through the cave as Ally's light starts to flicker, the beam ever weakening, illuminating less of Panthera walking ahead of us. It feels like we are walking down hill now, but not too steep. There is less water and the surface feels like sticky clay. The cave splits in to two tunnels and we follow Panthera to the left. I ask Brandon to continue.

"It finally occurred to me at the shop that we got the sarees from. When Atmaja spotted you; I pretty much knew that you are the eleventh Vishnu."

"The what?" Ally says while tapping her flashlight against her leg. "That's about it for my light."

"Ok Ally. Here is my flashlight," says Brandon as he turns on his light and hands it to her. "A Vishnu is a god sent to earth in human form to set the balance right between good and evil."

"My best friend is a god? I mean goddess? I always thought you were special. Wow! I can't believe it. So none of this is a dream?"

"No Ally. It is all real and I think Panthera can help us when we get back to the clinics," Brandon adds.

"I hope my parents are ok. They were at the third clinic. You don't think they were attacked too, do you?"

"I don't know Ally. We will get to them, I promise."

"Thanks Brandon," says Ally as we travel down the cave. It is steeper and we are almost walking on rock, some of which is loose making it treacherous unless you are a mountain goat, or maybe a tiger with paws the size of large frying pans. I no sooner finish my thought when Ally begins to slide almost out of control taking the flashlight with her and leaving Brandon and I in the dark literally.

"Help!" she yells as her voice fades in the distance followed by a muffled, "thank you." We move as fast as we can to catch up with her. Brandon leads and I hang on to his arm. He carefully chooses his steps until we finally reach Ally who happens to be leaning comfortably against Panthera standing sideways across the cave.

"Wow, she is something, ain't she?" Ally says as she strokes her hand down Panthera's back. "I am really getting tired of falling today, really tired. Hey guys, it looks like it has gotten flatter and I think I can hear water running up ahead of us."

"You ok?" I ask.

"Yes," she responds while wiping mud from her legs.

"Listen," Brandon adds. "It has definitely leveled off here. It almost sounds like a waterfall further down the cave, doesn't it?"

"Yes it does. Let's go," I say anxiously. I start walking next to Panthera, even a little in front of the range of Brandon's flashlight. The urge to get back to the camp and help my parents is overwhelming.

"Easy there. Wait for us. I think I know where this cave ends and we can't just run out in to the open. The bad guys might know about it too if they did their homework," says Brandon as he catches up with me and Panthera.

"Wait for me you two," Ally says with a demand in her voice.

"Brandon?"

"Yes Ally."

"I just want you to know that it was me kissing Kenneth outside the bathroom. I borrowed Lily's shirt that morning, but you never saw me because you left for the other clinic pretty early. And I had just grabbed her pink Paris hat as she was going in to the bathroom hoping it would keep me dry."

"I know Ally. I am real sorry about that. It just happened very fast and I overreacted. I was kind of in shock, you know?" Brandon says as he takes my hand and holds it tightly. "I should have known better. It wasn't until I got to the house that I actually figured it out. I know Lily would never do anything like that to me." He squeezes harder and turns his face toward mine. "I love you Lily and I am really really sorry."

"I believe you Brandon. I love you. Now let's go get our families back," I say as we reach a waterfall blocking the cave exit.

"Ally, turn the flashlight off, quickly," Brandon says in a quiet stern voice.

"Ok. It's off," says Ally as Panthera stands just on the inside of the cave behind the water cascading in front of us in the black night. She raises her nose up and takes in as much of the air as she can.

"What is she doing?" Ally whispers.

"She is trying to sniff out any bad guys."

"Got it," Ally responds.

"If I remember correctly, this is like one of those wedding cake type waterfalls." Brandon tries to peek out between the streams of water. "I can't see too much; I am not sure what level we are on. It might be the top of the cake which would be challenging, or we could be at the bottom. Maybe somewhere in between."

"Is that good or bad Brandon," I ask.

"It depends," Brandon exhales deeply. "It is a seventy five footer."

"Oh. I see." I approach Brandon cautiously. "What do we do?"

Panthera looks back at us almost like she is sizing us up. Maybe she needs to know how many of us to catch or how far we can jump. She turns her head back around, grunts, and steps through the left side of the waterfall. She disappears for a second and then sticks her drenched head back through the water and grunts again.

"I think we go through the water right here," Brandon says as he points to where Panthera's head was poking through a second ago. "I will go first and take a look."

"Be careful Brandon," I whisper to him.

"Always am."

He steps through the water. My heart sinks to the bottom of my chest. A minute passes. I start to worry. Just then a wet arm barely visible with the lack of moonlight pokes through the waterfall and in to the cave. The fingers waving us forward.

"Go ahead Ally. Take his hand and then I will go next."

"Ok Lily," Ally says nervously as she grasps Brandon's hand. I hear a soft male grunt from the other side of the water.

"Sorry. To tight," she says while stepping through the water and disappears.

Several minutes pass until I see Brandon's wet muscular arm again. I grab tightly and step through. Instantly, I am soaked almost like standing in one of those new fancy showers with water coming at you from all angles. I find myself pinned to another jagged rocky wall on a two foot wide damp dirt path. Panthera is about twenty feet down the path waiting for us. Ally is behind her.

We slowly creep down the path until we clear the large pond of water below us, ending up on wet grass, and finally standing among a bunch of thick trees providing us some cover.

"Hey," Ally whispers to us.

"What is it?" Brandon asks.

"I thought cats don't like water. Panthera went through that waterfall without any problems, even stood in it for a while."

"That is just one of those myths Ally," says Brandon. "We are lucky because we were about fifty feet up that waterfall and it would have made a heck of a splash if we fell in to the water."

"What now Brandon?" I ask still wanting to get back to the clinics.

"We have to carefully, and as quietly as possible, walk down to the bottom of this slope. The clinics will be about a quarter of a mile off to our left. We will probably intersect the tea plantation trail and come around to the front to get a better view of the attackers. There had to be at least ten that I saw just as I pulled in to the clearing. Hopefully they are too distracted to send out a search party for their missing sidekicks."

"Looks like she is ready," Ally points to Panthera who is now walking down the slope very slowly with her ears flicking back and forth like small radar dishes looking for a signal.

"Brandon, does this mean that my best friend has magical powers?"

I intercept Brandon before he can answer.

"I don't feel any different except for the fact that I don't feel tired anymore."

"Ouch!" Ally says in a loud muffle. "Watch that tree branch that I walked in to."

"How come you didn't see it? It was right in front of you," I ask.

"Are you kidding me? It's pitch black out. There is no moon and it must be like midnight or close to it."

"Ally is right Lily. It is one a.m." Brandon looks at his watch. "You mean that you can see in the dark?"

"I couldn't tell how long we ran for. It is a big mountain that we ran up. Then we tried to hide waiting for the darkness. I assumed it was almost daybreak and maybe it was getting light outside. Somehow I now have excellent vision in the dark."

"Ally, to answer your question, I think Panthera is Lily's magical power," Brandon whispers. "She must be able to pass on her natural tiger abilities to Lily someway."

"Wow, so it's kind of like tiger-Lily. That's still pretty cool. If she starts hopping around purring then I know that you are right with your assumption," Ally says in a chuckling whisper.

We slowly continue toward the camps. The ground levels out again as we reach the bottom of the hill and turn left. I watch Panthera as she continues to lead us through the jungle. My vision feels sharp and acute. I can see Ally stumbling over fallen tree branches, struggling to keep upright and not drop the gun off of her shoulder. Brandon has tan cargo pants on. The left pocket is torn. The right one is stuffed with items he took from the attackers. He still has mud and dirt caked on his shirt that the quick waterfall shower missed cleaning. I wonder how he subdued the two attackers outside of the hole, but quickly change my thoughts knowing he did it to save us. Knowing that he is with us gives me hope that we can get to the clinics in time to help everyone. Panthera suddenly stops and crouches. I tap Ally in front of me and she squats down, slowly sliding the gun off of her right shoulder and pointing it out in front of her. Brandon freezes and then does the same. I look around to see what Panthera has spotted; it looks like two men standing on the tea plantation trail. I can hear them somewhat, but they are speaking a language I don't recognize. It is not Malayalam. One of the men looks very angry and is pointing at the other bad guy. Panthera awaits patiently watching the two of them as do I. She is frozen still; not even a twitch from her over defined musculature. The angry bad guy turns around and starts walking back toward the clinics. My heart should be pounding away, but it isn't. I feel as calm as Panthera.

The angry one of the two is no longer in sight. Panthera creeps forward stopping about ten yards from the lone bad guy who, I figure, must have been looking for the Mrs. Hair party of three. I wonder if he knows that they will not be joining them for dinner this evening, or any other. The bad guy has one of those AK rifles slung over his left shoulder. I turn around to make sure Ally and Brandon are still behind me. They are and they are both kneeling down on one knee. Brandon is holding the rifle he took from one of the bad guys across his left leg with the barrel pointed at this attacker on the tea plantation trail. Ally is just behind Brandon with her AK still pointed out in front of her. I look back at Panthera again. She hasn't taken her eyes off the bad guy yet. I send her a message mentally telling her it is ok to get rid of this bad guy so we can get to the clinics and our families.

The bad guy takes a few steps toward the tea plantation unknowingly passing to Panthera's left. I can swear that I see Panthera's fur darken, almost completely black as she steps out on to the trail. The attacker turns around facing Panthera probably sensing someone, or something, is watching him. He moves his head side to side struggling to see, but he can't spot Panthera for she has blended in to the darkness. With another blur, she is up on her hind legs. Her front paws come crashing down on to the bad guy's shoulders. He drops the AK as she buries her massive fangs into the side of his neck. The attacker's arms go limp and Panthera quietly lowers his body to the grassy trail. She pulls his lifeless form off the trail and into the high grass next to me. I smell the metallic odor of blood. She releases his neck and starts walking toward the trail again. Just then, three sambar deer scamper for their lives when they see Panthera approaching, but she isn't interested in deer meat right now.

I walk over to Brandon and Ally. When I reach Brandon, I cup both of my hands around his ears and whisper.

"Brandon, Panthera just killed one guy on the trail, but he had a friend with him who looked upset."

He cups his hands around my right ear the same way.

"That's good and bad. It is good because we know there must be people still alive at the camp, or the bad guys would have left." He takes a breath and then exhales warm air directly in to my ear. "It is bad because they will probably know that the 'chick who plays with knives' is not coming back. I hope they don't take it out on our families."

"You're right. Let's move out. Hang on to my belt and make sure Ally grabs on to you. We will move in a single file behind Panthera," I whisper to Brandon again as I stand up. He does the same.

"I didn't even see her take that guy out. I didn't hear anything either. She is good," adds Brandon.

She is good. I don't feel afraid, even though I know I should. I watch Brandon pass the word to Ally as she stands up and grabs Brandon's belt. We move as silently as we can behind Panthera. Her color seems to have turned back to the white, black, and grey pattern she had when I first saw her in the cave. I watch the thick broad black stripes move back and forth with every step she takes. We cross the tea trail. As I do, I instinctively look left and right making sure it is clear both ways. I don't know why because Panthera already has done this. The four of us continue through the jungle slowly turning to the right in an arc like pattern. I don't know how Panthera knows that this is the route Brandon described taking. Maybe she heard him. I am just glad my best friend and the love of my dreams are not freaking out while trekking through the jungle in India, at night, and with a tiger escorting the way.

We move for about another hour turning right and inching closer to the clearing edge until we can finally make out two buildings and some of the Land Rovers. I can see Brandon's green Land Rover about thirty yards to my left almost hidden in the trees from where he crashed it earlier. The bullet holes up and down the side of the vehicle are prominent in my newly acquired night vision. I can smell leaking gasoline and radiator fluid. I can't believe he survived the destruction and then escaped in to the jungle.

I stop and squat down again. Ally and Brandon do the same forming a small huddle around me. Panthera keeps watch on the clearing.

"I can see a bad guy in front of each clinic carrying guns. There was also one guy who went down the hill by the dining area," I relay to Brandon with my hands around his ear again. He relays the information to Ally in the same manner.

"There might be more. Let's get to the guy by the dining area. If we can get rid of him then maybe the ladder is still on the side of the clinic and we can use it to get a peek in to the supply room. I can't make out the radio antenna on the roof. It looks like they must have destroyed that also," Brandon whispers with concern.

Ally cups her hands around my left ear. "I wonder if they damaged all the cars. I can still smell the brick oven. Why would they stay so long and how would they be contacting anyone for ransom demands if that's what this is about?"

I answer back, "They might have left some of the vehicles undamaged to make their escape. Maybe they have their own radio or satellite phone to arrange a ransom. We can use that to get help," I whisper in to Ally's ear trying to reassure her.

Panthera stands up and changes herself in to solid black again blending in to the darkness. She quietly moves around the clearing to the right heading toward the dining area. She keeps herself about five feet inside the edge of the tree line hiding the way only a cat could hide as she prowls toward the next bad guy. We follow as quietly and slowly as possible. We reach the side of the first clinic. The attacker on that side is just passing under the window we had jumped from. There is no light coming from inside the clinic that I can see. An almost invisible Panthera crouches across the clearing approaching the bad guy. I can't say that I feel sorry for him because of what I saw them do to Ludwik. Fifteen feet. Ten. Five feet. Boom! Panthera is on him taking him down to the ground without any noise. She drags him down the hill and leaves his motionless corpse behind a nice looking jackfruit tree. Suddenly I feel a little hungry. Odd thought at a time like this. Brandon sneaks over to the body, searches him quickly, stuffs something in his cargo pocket, and returns to us.

"More ammo," he whispers. "These guys are packing heavy heat, but this one did not have a vest on Lily." He hands Ally a bullet filled magazine for the AK and she puts it in to her left cargo pocket making sure the flap is buttoned closed. "I would have grabbed the gun too, but I think Panthera bit it and bent the barrel in the process."

"Let's look for the ladder," I say as I start walking in a crouch heading to the first clinic. Ally and Brandon follow. Panthera is next to me on my right.

We reach the edge of the building just below the window. Brandon heads to the dining area and returns a minute later without any ladder.

"Not there," he whispers quietly as he makes his way to the bottom of the hill looking for the ladder.

As he reaches the bottom of the hill, I spot the barrel of an AK coming around the edge of the clinic. Oh no! I reach behind my back for Mrs. Hair's pistol stuffed in my waist band. Brandon doesn't see him. This is bad. I start to run that way bringing the pistol up in front of me hoping it will shoot when I pull the trigger. The bad guy turns the corner and is face to face with Brandon only a couple of feet away. Not good. The bad guy is wearing night vision goggles like the funny ones my dad use to tell me about when he was in the army flying in the helicopters. Brandon is blocking my shot even if I could hit the guy. The bad guy freezes for a

185

second and starts to bring up his AK to aim at Brandon. I run quicker. Whoosh! I see Panthera's two massive front paws come up over the top of bad guy's shoulders pulling him backward off of his feet. He hits the ground with a muffled thud. His AK drops to the ground. Panthera smothers him ending the close encounter. Brandon leans back against the building and lets out a deep sigh.

"Wow," he whispers almost inaudibly.

I reach the bad guy and pat down his pockets to find two more AK magazines fully loaded, a knife about the size of a small car, and when I pat his chest, I feel the hardness of a bullet proof vest. I unstrap the vest and pull it off of him. Panthera stands guard. I can smell the blood oozing from her teeth. She runs her tongue over her mouth trying to clean the nasty taste of bad guy away, I am sure. I turn to Brandon.

"Here, put this on. Don't argue," he starts to resist. "Trust me. Panthera will protect me. Brandon puts on the bullet proof vest just as Ally reaches us and I give him the oversized knife.

"Are you guys all right? I never saw that bad guy, but she did," she points to Panthera. "Dam she is good. What now?"

"Let's work our way around the clinics and clear the perimeter. Then we can deal with whoever is inside. By the way, do you like my new stylish sunglasses?" Brandon whispers more clearly now that he puts on the bad guy's night vision goggles.

"Yes. They are nice," I respond feeling like I am talking to a robot with two pointy things sticking out of his head for eyeballs. I hand him the bad guy's ammo. He takes one and hands the other magazine to Ally. We continue around the back side of the clinics heading to the bathrooms. In my mind, I hope nobody heard the commotion, although the bad guy will probably be looked for when he doesn't check in. There is a smell of gasoline lingering in the air. I glance to my left and spot the generator tipped on its side without any power cables attached to it. We move a little quicker. As we get to the edge of the clinic, I swear I hear someone talking. I think it is coming from the women's bathroom. Panthera heard it too and stops just to the right side of the door; her back side is around the rear of the bathroom and her head and front legs are poking around the corner toward the door. I see two people emerge from the doorway. It is Petra and a bad guy. What if she screams? I have to get to her at the same time Panthera takes out the bad guy. Bam! I hear as I see the giant knife fly through the air and ending up in the bad guy's chest. Petra stands startled just staring at the bad guy as he slides down the outside of the bathroom wall to the ground making a screeching sound on the bathroom's concrete wall. It sounded like an aluminum can being torn in half. I can make out a line of blood on the bathroom wall from where the knife came out of his back. Panthera seems to nod her head to Brandon as if to say nice throw dude. The rain keeps falling heavily and I hope it covers the noise we are making.

I leap to Petra and cup my hand over her mouth just before she starts to scream. I stand in front of her and whisper. "Petra, it is ok. We will help you. You will be ok." I release my hand as she realizes it is me.

"I...I thought you were all dead," she struggles to get out in her Greek accent. "We have people shot inside. It is very bad. The robbers, they want money and things. We have to get help."

"No. It is going to be ok. We will get help," I say as I look for Panthera not knowing how Petra might act to the bunch of us hanging out with a tiger.

I spot her making her way up the hill toward the oven and outdoor kitchen. She disappears from my sight as she crests the hill top. A second later I see Panthera. She is dragging a body back down the hill toward us. She stops half way and lets the limp bad guy fall to the ground. Panthera is almost invisible to everyone else in the dark. Petra doesn't notice. I guess we will take credit for that bad guy out of action.

"What do we do?" Petra says quietly in a shaky voice.

"I have an idea," says Brandon as he runs off in the direction of the other bodies. He returns several minutes later with his arms full of stuff.

"What's that?" Ally asks.

"Here put these on. It is the black pants and shirts the bad guys were wearing," Brandon says instructing us like an old army sergeant issuing orders to their soldiers.

"What?" Ally protests. "Ill. Yuk. No way. Aren't they covered in blood?"

"Just a little bit in spots," Brandon responds. "They are still wet enough and it will buy us the time we need to take out the rest of the bad guys." Brandon pulls a baggy pair of black pants on over his muddy tan cargo's.

Brandon undoes his bullet proof vest. Ally and Petra each take a black shirt and put them on like jackets buttoning them up in the process. Brandon then hands the vest to Petra.

"Petra, wear this please. It is bullet proof," says Brandon.

"Thank you." Petra takes the vest and slides it over the top of her lowering it on to her shoulders and then Brandon fastens the straps around her waist. He then reaches down and picks up the bad guy's AK and hands it to Petra.

"Have you ever fired one of these before?" he asks.

"No," Petra replies as she holds the gun in front of her.

"That's good. Neither have we," Brandon says as he gives her a quick lesson.

"Wait here," I say as I run up to the latest bad guy and pull him down to the bathroom. Brandon and Ally look startled as I start to pull the guys black fashion attire off of him.

"Yes Petra, we just took this guy out before we got to the bathroom," I explain as Ally and Brandon hear my little fib. "Ok. Let's put these two in the ladies room."

"Sounds good to me," says Brandon. "Don't tell anyone I was in the ladies room. I will never hear the end of it."

"We won't," I say laughing silently to myself.

We drag the bad guys in to the bathroom and put one in each of the two stalls and then shut the doors. I spot Panthera in front of the men's room looking at me like it is time to get moving.

"Wait. Put these on," says Brandon as he passes out three black ski masks and then puts the fourth one on his head and redoes the goggles.

"Follow me," I whisper. Panthera leads me around the bottom of clinic two and then half way up the slope on the other side of the building. Ally is behind me then Petra and finally Brandon watching behind us with the night vision goggles. I have to say we look like a small imposing force. I hope this bluff works long enough to get the bad guys inside the clinics. My new uniform is a bit baggy. They will definitely think that this bad guy has gone on a diet. The bottom of my pant legs are dragging under the heels of my hikers even after trying to roll them up. Suddenly, Panthera leaps forward. I hear a small thump and then something that sounds like air escaping from a balloon. She drags another bad guy down to me.

"Nice going Panthera. Thank you," I say as I run my hand down her back. She gives me a you-are-welcome look and heads back up the hill. I pat the guy down quick. Another pistol, small flashlight, and gum. Gum? I take a piece and put it in my dry mouth. It taste like peppermint. That's nice to know- bad guys with fresh breath, great. I chew a bit and then spit it out. I start to move up the hill and spot another item, yes!

"Ally," I whisper. "Put these on."

She takes the night vision goggles from me and puts them on. Forget imposing force; now it looks like we are the Martian Traveling Circus. Yep, it's official. Come get your tickets everyone. Petra looks on with concern. I put the other pistol in my not ripped cargo pocket and continue up the hill. I can see the corner of the clinic to my left. Two Land Rovers, one of which appears to have flat tires, but no sign of Panthera. Thump again! She comes around the corner dragging another bad guy from the front of the building. Surely they must be missing their buddies by now. No! I spot another rifle barrel coming around the corner behind Panthera. In an instant, Brandon races by me just as the bad guy comes around the corner. He stops in front of Brandon and says something in the language that I don't understand. Brandon replies, but I don't know what he said. The guy steps around Brandon to his right and freezes as he comes face to face with Panthera. He tries to raise his rifle in a panic, but it is too late. Panthera leaps up and takes the bad guy out dragging him down the hill and dropping the body just behind us.

Petra looks startled. I try to whisper an explanation. "Petra, the tiger is with us. Don't be afraid," I add as I put my arm on her shoulder.

"What? Where did it come from? I don't understand," Petra says as she takes a deep breath.

"I will tell you later, but right now we don't have time."

"Petra," says Brandon as he joins our little huddle. "How many attackers were in the first clinic?"

"There were three inside. They all have guns and stuff," Petra says as Ally joins us. "Maybe some of these attackers were from inside and there might be less. I was never in the other clinic building, but I think all of the clinic workers were moved in to building one."

"So the second clinic might be empty?" Brandon asks.

"Yes it could be empty," says Petra. "Everybody that I know of was with me. Your father is with me Brandon, but your parents are gone Lily.

Jillian and Pareet are gone too Brandon.   I never saw François or Jia Li though. I don't know what happened to them," Petra adds with sadness in her voice.

"Ok then. I will check out the second clinic," says Brandon.

"Wait. No. Let me come with you. I can pass for a bad guy."

"No Lily. I will be right back." Brandon turns and slowly walks the last five feet to the corner of the clinic. He peers around to the left and then disappears. Time seems to stop for several minutes. Panthera returns to my side and nudges up against my leg I guess to reassure me that Brandon will be ok. Ally is watching behind us with her rifle pointed down the hill toward the back of the clinic. Petra is standing with her back leaning on the clinic foundation. Brandon returns. He is shaking his head side to side making the night vision goggles look like the antennas on a caterpillars head.

"Not good," he whispers. "The clinic is empty except for several bodies. There is blood everywhere."

BANG!

"Oh no they are killing the hostages," Petra says. "If their demands were not met then they said they would kill one hostage every hour."

"How are they communicating Petra?" I ask.

"I think it is a satellite phone. It has a big antenna on it. They only turn it on once an hour, but I think they are talking to one of their own people and not a negotiator."

BANG!

There is another gunshot followed by a loud scream from a woman. We all instinctively move to the corner of the building. Brandon leads with Panthera next to him. One by one we go around the corner of clinic two turning left and head toward the outdoor kitchen. My sense of smell seems as sharp as my vision is now. The metallic bloody odor permeates my nostrils again as I pass the clinic door. I decide not to look inside the clinic and instead I look left and right and don't see any bad guys. Brandon stops for a second and points to his left. It is the ladder Ludwik used to put the radio antenna on the roof of clinic one. Brandon walks back to me crouched over. He cups his hands around my right ear.

"I will take the ladder down around the clinic and come in through the window. There can't be many bad guys left. Wait five minutes. Go to the front door and just walk in."

"Ok, Brandon be careful," I say as Brandon sneaks over to the ladder, slings his rifle over his back and disappears behind the giant concrete stove. I relay the plan to Ally and Petra. We slowly walk to the side of the door of clinic one and wait. Panthera stands guard ready to leap in to the clinic if needed. It would be a lot of explaining to do if she does.

"Are you ready?" I ask Ally and Petra softly.

Petra adjusts her ski mask to make sure it is covering her face, points her gun toward the door and nods. Ally follows suit and does the same.

"Ok, one, two, three, go."

I turn left and enter the clinic. There is a small lantern on the table where the shot up radio is and one bad guy sitting next to it holding an AK across his lap. There appears to be dried blood on his black cargo pants. He turns and sees me, but does not react. I nod at him. I look left and see another bad guy standing in the corner only a couple of feet from the entrance. He also has an AK and is wearing a vest with what looks like a contraption on it with different color wires protruding from it. A white wire seems to be dangling from his left black sleeve resting casually in his left hand. Oh no. Petra sees him and heads toward him. I spot a third bad guy to the rear of the building by the triage tables. There is an AK in his hands and a pistol strapped to his right leg. He stares at me through the eye holes in his black ski mask trying to figure out what is different about me, I am sure. I nod again. Between him and us are all the hostages sitting on the floor. They look at us with fright on their faces. Thump! A not so good sounding noise comes from the supply room. The bad guys all look in that direction. The guy by the triage tables starts to head that way. I look back at Ally who is looking at the bad guy sitting next to the lantern. Ok. Everyone has someone. Ally moves toward him. I start walking to the supply room and Petra heads to the bad guy by the entrance. I get about half way there when I spot Brandon kneeling just inside the doorway.

"Now!" I scream.

We raise our guns. Petra yells something in Greek to the bad guy by the door and he drops his AK on the floor. I don't know if he understands Greek, but she points her AK at his head and he puts his hands up in the air. A universal language I guess. The guy by the radio starts to stand when Ally reaches him with her gun pointed at his chest. He thinks otherwise and drops his AK as Ally screams at him in

Alabamian and even I don't understand it. I keep moving toward the last of the three attackers as Brandon stands and exits the supply room with his AK raised turning right and getting the bad guy in his sights. The bad guy keeps moving toward him screaming in a foreign language. He starts to raise his AK while almost running now. Instantly he is swept off his feet landing with a smack on the clinic floor. Singh appears from in front of the table and with another move knocks the attacker flat on his back and then renders him unconscious with a vicious strike from his right hand to the attacker's face. Singh picks up the bad guy's AK and stands up.

"And that my friend is called kalarippayat. The oldest martial art in the world," Singh says with command in his voice.

CHAPTER XXIII

"Is everyone all right," I say as my eyes scan the hostages looking for my mama and dad. I don't see them. I don't see Jillian either. I glance at Brandon as he lifts off his night vision goggles straining to see in the low light of the single lantern. I am sure he is looking for his mom. I spot Noella standing up in the corner by the triage tables. She breaks in to a run toward the attacker Singh just knocked unconscious. She is sobbing and screaming something in French. It doesn't sound like compliments. Noella reaches the attacker and begins to kick him in the face, head, and body. I look around and realize François is not here. I seem to understand now. Singh grabs Noella and pulls her off the attacker, trying to calm her in the process.

"Dad, where is mom?" Brandon asks as he meets Singh by the sleeping attacker.

"They took her and Pareet. They took the Morgan's too," Singh replies. "Let's find something to tie these bandits up with."

"Ok. I will get something," Brandon says as he looks through the supply box scattered on the floor.

"Well it is good to see you again Lily."

I hear someone say in a thick German accent. I look to my left and spot Ludwik trying to sit up. He is leaning on his right elbow next to the clinic wall. Both of his legs are wrapped in white bandages with what looks like dried blood saturating the material. Both pant legs look like they were cut up the middle long ways and are lying to both sides of his legs. He moans in pain as he continues to sit up.

"Ludwik! You're alive!" I say as I start to walk through the hostages who are now beginning to stand up.

"Danke, yes. Yes don't look so surprised."

"Hey don't worry about that old sauerkraut. He is as tough as they come," Kenneth says in a happy voice. "We put some bandages on his legs, but couldn't do anything about his mouth," his voice now exuberating a sense of relief."

Kenneth is lying just to the left of Ludwik's legs. His face is grotesquely swollen. His left eye is completely closed and he is unable to open it. It looks like they beat him up pretty good, but he is alive. I peer toward the doorway of the clinic. Panthera is standing there blending in to the darkness like a chameleon blending in to a tree branch, watching over us. No more attackers in the area; that's for sure.

"Kenneth!" Ally yells out. She lowers her AK and begins to move to her right toward Kenneth. Oh no! In an instant the bad guy Petra was guarding leaps forward stopping in the doorway of the clinic. He raises his left arm in the air and clutches the contraption on his chest with his right hand. It is not just a white wire in his left hand, but a switch. No! He is going to blow us up!

"Get down!" I scream as I begin to run toward him. He drowns out my words by yelling something. I can't make out what he is saying. The hostages are still standing as they begin to look in the attacker's direction. I move faster than I have ever moved before. It must be part of my new gift from Panthera. My acute vision narrows in on his left thumb as he begins to press down on the black button. I get close enough to try kicking him, but can't get to my gun in time. I leap in to the air bringing my left leg up first and then my right leg and falling backward at the same time. As my legs pass one another, I feel my toes inside of my right hiking boot connect just under the attacker's chin smashing his jaw bone in the process making a sound like a snapping wish bone. His head contorts upward making his body fly to the doorway.

"That's called a bicycle kick, jerk," I say to myself. "Perfected by Pelé." I continue the backward somersault through the air landing on my feet. The attacker continues out the door as I see Panthera's paw come up over his right shoulder sinking her dagger like claws in to his upper chest wall and dragging him off in to the dark.

BOOOOOMMMM!!

There is a huge explosion in the clearing followed by a shockwave of hot air rushing through the clinic knocking me off my feet. I land on my back struggling to catch my breath. I lay stunned for a moment. I look around and don't see anyone standing. People are coughing and moaning.

"Anyone hurt!" I struggle to yell while spitting dust out of my mouth in the process. The lantern was knocked over making it pitch black for everybody. I get to my feet and give myself a once-over. No injuries. I brush off some of the straw on my shoulders from the wood and thatched roof. I run my fingers through my hair picking the rest of the debris from my hair. One by one everyone starts to check in. "No injuries here," and a couple of "I can't hear anything's." I spot Brandon standing up. I feel relieved. Panthera! I run outside. Panthera is lying on her left side in the middle of the clearing in a newly formed crater about ten yards wide, her massive body nearly filling up the entire hole. I continue to sprint to her, jump down in to the crater, and drop to my knees when I reach her. I throw my arms around her head.

"No Panthera, please no. Don't die. You saved us. I need you." I struggle to get my words out. Something isn't right. I release my hug and tap my right hand on her shoulder. It feels hot from the blast. What? It is hard like iron. She lets out a soft moan. I lift my head and scan her body in the dark. Armor. "You have armor." It encloses her entire face and covers all of her body extending down the tail and legs. There are tiny relief sculptures on the armor similar to what I saw at Princess Ellora's castle. "Battle armor!" Panthera raises her head and looks at me with her glacier blue eyes. A sense of relief consumes me. There is life in my white tiger's eyes. I catch a smell of singed whiskers in my dust filled nostrils.

"You will be ok," I whisper to her as she rolls over on to her belly. She shakes her head and slowly stands up. She lowers her face to mine and in an instant the black battle armor seems to dissolve into her fur. I look for blood, but don't see any.

"You are one crazy cat," I say quietly as I hug her head again.

There is no sign of the attacker except for a smoldering black singed boot lying next to one of the Land Rovers which now has no windows.

"Lily!" Brandon calls out as he runs up to the crater. "Are you ok? How is Panthera? I don't see a mark on her."

"She was wearing battle armor when I got to her. It kind of retracted back in to her fur, I think. She looks ok except her whiskers got singed."

"Here give me your hand," Brandon says as he leans over the hole and extends his right hand to me. I grab hold and climb out.

"How is everyone?" I ask since I ran outside before checking on everyone. The remaining bad guys are tied up.

"It looks like there are no major injuries. I am going to try to get a Land Rover running; probably that one on the end," Brandon says as he points to the silver one covered with dirt and no windows. "It looks like one of the tires is flat, but I don't think there is time to change it."

"I will meet you there in a minute," I say as I head back inside the clinic.

"Lily, you are ok?" Ally asks as she runs over to me and throws her arms around my back.

"Yes. I am fine. Did anyone call for help?"

"I don't think so. They can't find the satellite phone and the radio is shot up," Ally responds.

"Petra, where is the bad guy with the satellite phone?" I ask anxiously.

"That guy that blew up had it in his chest pocket," Petra says.

"Well there is nothing left of him except for half of a boot. I don't think we can use that to call for help."

"Hey, wasn't there a phone in the guy's shoe on that American TV show," says a familiar voice. It is Marco trying to lighten up our serious situation. I hear a few chuckles in response. "Somebody go check his boot for a dial-tone."

"Vait, vait, vait a minute," Ludwik says with the heavy accented 'V' sound instead of the western pronunciation. "Bring me that scrap of a radio over here."

Marco makes his way over to the shortwave radio lying on the floor after being knocked off the table from the blast, picks it up, and carries it to where Ludwik is lying on the floor.

"Here Ludwik. Tell me what to do," says Marco.

"Let's open it up to see what is left of its guts," says Ludwik.

Marco pulls out a multi-tool and begins to unscrew the back cover of the radio to get to the inside. He next removes the metal case entirely and shows it to Ludwik using a flashlight. Singh walks over to help along with Valentina.

"Ok. Get me some bratvurst, veisswurst, and some schnitzel," says Ludwik with a pronounced frown on his forehead.

Marco and Singh look at each other then back at Ludwik. Valentina looks confused.

"I don't understand Ludwik. Why do you want food and drink at a time like this?" says Singh with concern.

"Why? Because I have a better chance of making a radio out of bratvurst than this hunk of metal. Transistors kaputt! Resistors kaputt! Semiconductors kaputt! Inductors kaputt! Control board looks like what you call sviss cheese!" Ludwik sounds off. Again exaggerating the "v" in swiss.

"Ludwik, is there anything you can do?" asks Valentina as Ludwik pauses, stares at the radio remains, and then answers.

"It is really, how you say, going to be old school. I might be able to spark a signal. Maybe bounce our frequency off a carrier signal. The bullets chipped the radio pretty good. Maybe get something together to at least send out some Morse code, but the amplifier is shot, so we might not be able to receive anything back," Ludwik says with heavy frustration in his voice.

"Lily!"

I look to the door and see Brandon standing there waving a let's get going wave.

"Ally," she looks at me kneeling next to Kenneth. "Stay here. Brandon and I will head to the other clinic."

"No way Lily. I am coming with you," Ally says as she, kisses Kenneth on his lips, stands up, and grabs her AK lying on the floor. "Kenneth, we will be back in a little while. You will be ok."

Brandon looks at Singh who intern nods at him knowing he won't be able to change his mind.

"Seeing how well you did here; I feel for the bad guys," says Singh. "I will send somebody out on foot to get help while they work on the radio."

"Ok dad. We will be right back, I promise," Brandon says.

Ally and I catch up with Brandon at the doorway. His pockets are over stuffed with ammo for the AK's. I decide just to keep the two pistols. He hands us each a bottle of water and we head to the Land Rover.

"Wait. I will go too. You might need a medic," says Valentina who has a tan first aid pack thrown over her shoulder. Valentina and Marco embrace.

"Here take this." I reach in to my cargo pocket, pull out the extra pistol, and hand it to Valentina. There is no time to dress her in bad guy black.

"Good. Let's go!" she says. "Wow what a hole!" she adds looking at the crater as we climb in to the silver Land Rover. The red one looks destroyed and I know Brandon's green one got shot up and is in the jungle somewhere. There is a crunching noise coming from beneath me as I shift around on the chunks of broken glass lying on the seat.

I scan the clearing for Panthera, but don't see her and begin to worry. Was she summoned back to Princess Ellora? Will I ever see her again? Is that it for my magical powers? My vision is still keen although it must be around four o'clock in the morning. I don't feel tired, yet everyone else looks exhausted. I am not even that thirsty. Instantly, I feel a small object in my left hand. I unfold my fingers from around it and to my amazement; it is the tiger crystal from the cave. I realize that Panthera is still with me.

"The ride might be a bit rough. We only have three tires with air in them. The back tire on the passenger side is flat, but we have to get going."

"No problem Brandon. Drive it like you stole it!" Ally yells from the rear seat behind Brandon.

I feel Valentina grip the back of my seat bracing herself for what I am sure will be an interesting ride. Brandon throws the already running Land Rover in to reverse gear, stomps on the gas pedal, and turns the steering wheel hard to the left causing the Land Rover to spin around one-hundred and eighty degrees. He heads down the trail leading in to the clearing driving as fast as he can. The Land Rover bounces madly from side to side trying to stay on the remaining three wheels. Branches scrape the sides of the vehicle and enter through the glassless windows. I continue to duck out of the way, so I don't catch a branch in the face. We continue bouncing and swerving. Ally and Valentina are hanging on the best they can, but all four of us fly off of our seats nearly bumping our heads on the Land Rover's roof. The vehicle begins to slide sideways. Brandon turns the wheel hard to the right. The passenger side rear of the Land Rover makes contact with a thick stout coconut tree. I recover from the impact as Brandon keeps going. Thump!

"What was that?" asks Valentina.

"Coconut!" Brandon replies as it rolls off the hood, and in front of the only remaining headlight illuminating the coconut in the process, before Brandon runs it over with the vehicle making a squishing sound in the mud.

We make it to the flat dirt road and Brandon struggles to turn the Land Rover left and back toward the paved single lane highway. He steps on the gas pedal harder accelerating the vehicle as fast as it will go. We pass a blue Tata car parked on the side of the road. It is like the one I saw at the airport picking up Mr. Handsome. He wasn't at our clinics. We took the ski masks off of the bad guys and I didn't recognize any of them. Was he the one that blew up? No. Wasn't his voice, I am sure. He might be at the other clinic. The one we are going to now. Maybe he is the mastermind and the one making the phone calls. Oh no. If he was calling every hour then we don't have much time before he realizes something is wrong. If there are other hostages alive then he might...I don't want to think about it. My parents are there. So are Ally's. Brandon's mom and sister are there. So are Gala, Laney and Moira along with our Indian friends.

Brandon reaches the paved road and turns left heading away from his house. There is traffic on the road even at this hour. Brandon starts to weave in and out of the cars and trucks and buses and of course rickshaws and motorbikes. The early morning wind rushes through the window lacking Land Rover's interior. The back end of the Land Rover is fishtailing back and forth nearly hitting the other vehicles. The flat tire keeps going whop, whop, whop; sounding like a helicopter. Sparks, from the almost bare metal rim, light up the road behind us. There is the smell of burning rubber throughout the Land Rover. Brandon keeps turning the steering wheel side to side trying to maintain control of the Land Rover. He must look like a total nut of a driver even by Indian standards. The Indian drivers answer back by blowing their horns at us. The rain pelts my face through the opening where the blown out windshield used to belong. Brandon squints to see in between the wind and water ricocheting off his own face.

"Brandon, we don't have much time. Petra said they call every hour. It must have been at least fifty minutes," I say.

"It isn't much farther. I never drove this fast to get there before, but the turn off is about another mile. We will park about half way down that road, shut the car off, and run the rest of the way. If we lose the dark; well then I think we're in trouble," Brandon says as he swerves the Land Rover sideways around a green rickshaw causing the tires to skid loudly and the people to shout back at us even louder over the roar of the engine.

"Lead the way Brandon!" Ally yells.

"Yes. We will follow you," Valentina says as I turn to see her saying something to herself. Maybe praying.

Brandon slams on the brakes and slides almost to a stop as he turns right on to a dirt road flanked by thick jungle on both sides. He travels down this road a little slower. It has a gradual incline, but not steep like the one leading to the other clinics. It seems more narrow. All of us look out for bad guys; maybe there is a guard or someone to give them warning. I don't see anyone. Brandon brings the Land Rover quietly to a stop and turns off the single headlight and then the engine. We listen for several seconds. The jungle is oddly quiet. We jump out of the vehicle.

"We have about a quarter mile further up this road before we get to the clinic. The building is similar in size and is rectangular with just the single entrance. The clearing isn't as big and it is flatter, so there is no sloop when we get there. Unfortunately, it is all up hill on the trail, but not too steep. Ready?" says Brandon after relaying the information.

"Ready Brandon," Ally replies firmly as she holds her AK in front of her at a ready position.

"I am ready too Brandon," says Valentina as she puts both of her arms through the shoulder straps and slings the first aid kit on to her back.

"Do you want me to carry that pack?" Brandon asks.

"No no. I will be fine. Marco and I hike in the hills around Firenze when we are not working."

"Ok Valentina. Lily?" Brandon says in the form of a question.

I coax him to look in to my left hand as I release my fingers showing him the tiger crystal. He pulls on a black ski mask and affixes the night vision goggles to his head tightening the strap in the process. He nods with approval. Ally follows suit and dons her ski mask and night vision goggles.

"Valentina?" I say.

"Yes?"

"We sort of have a friend helping us. Don't be alarmed," I offer calmly.

"Ok."

I gently toss the crystal on to the trail in front of me and whisper Panthera's name at the same time. Instantly she appears. Valentina jumps back. Ally stops her from falling. Valentina struggles to see without night vision goggles.

"It is ok. She is a friend," says Ally as we all start to jog toward the clinic.

"Is that a tiger?" Valentina stutters trying to speak. "Does she have a name?"

"Yes. Her name is Panthera," I say quietly as I follow Panthera who is in a steady trot now. "It is sort of a long story."

"I bet it is. Hi Panthera. She is p..p..pretty," Valentina responds.

We continue up the trail until we get about fifty yards from the clearing when I notice Panthera turn all black again. She stops her trot and begins to walk slowly with her head down and eyes and ears fixed straight ahead. I signal for everyone to stop. We all crouch down. Ally and Brandon have their AK's ready for anything. Valentina is holding her pistol with two hands out in front of her. She looks like she has held a pistol before, so I am not too worried about her, but she isn't camouflaged in black like us and isn't wearing bulletproof vests like Brandon and Ally. Panthera crouches and begins to creep forward. I scan and spot one unsuspecting bad guy standing just off the trail about thirty yards in front of us. A sentry. And he is smoking. Doesn't he know smoking is bad for him? He inhales on his cigarette lighting the end of it up like an orange bull's eye on a paper target. I catch a whiff of the cigarette smoke as it travels down the trail to my nose. Yuk. He must roll his own. Panthera is only four feet away from him. I am glad Valentina can't see this, although she is a medic. In a lightning quick pounce, Panthera takes the bad guy down sinking her fangs into his neck and cutting off his air so that he can't scream. Panthera literally bites the fight out of him. She drags him off the trail and leaves the body under some drooping green tree branches that nearly touch the ground. The cigarette smolders in the wet grass. Panthera steps on it as she returns to the trail, looks at us, and then turns right continuing to the clinic.

We continue up the trail until near the open clearing. Panthera goes left, remains in the cover of the trees and knee high grass, and we follow. I can make out two Land Rovers and a car. It is also like the blue Tata I saw at the airport. My heart skips a few beats like it has many times before on this night. Can Mr. Handsome really be here? Or was he in the other Tata we passed on the road near the other clinics? We continue quietly around the entire clinic ending up a few yards from where we started. Brandon and Ally's heads are moving back and forth scanning with the night vision goggles. It looks clear. Panthera begins to approach the clinic from the front right side keeping just out of sight behind the black Land Rover which looks intact and not shot up or blown up. That's good.

The three of us stick close to her as she comes to a sudden stop. I can hear people coughing inside the clinic followed by some moans. Not good. Injuries? Who? I brush those thoughts aside. Panthera lowers her head; her ears pointing forward again, twitching just a bit. I can see her nose vibrating trying to smell the threat. I peer up over the hood of the Land Rover and see a bad guy lighting up a cigarette in the doorway of the clinic. He yells something off in the direction of the trail we drove in on. There is no reply from his buddy and he looks angry. The bad guy probably thinks his lookout fell asleep. Nope. He turns and says something back toward the clinic and begins to head to the trail while putting on night vision goggles. An AK hangs from a sling in front of his chest. Oh no. Who are these people? How could they have this kind of gear? Panthera turns to her left and follows him on the other side of the vehicles. She reaches the end of the Tata and stops. The bad guy gets to the end of the car and turns. He walks past Panthera, who is still all black, and continues to look for his buddy. He yells out one more time. Again. No response. I hear a tree branch snap from the area where we left Valentina. The bad guy mutters something under his breath and just about reaches the trail when Panthera runs at him from behind. He starts to turn to face her, feeling her massive feet hit the ground behind him, I am sure. As soon as he completes his turn; Panthera leaps the last ten feet. Her right front leg is extended out in front of her. All the claws on the paw are protruding like individual razor sharp swords. She lands on her other three legs. Panthera strikes the bad guy with the right front claw raking him from the top of his face down across his chest opening four giant crevices in his body. I hear a rush of air escape from his now shredded lungs. An odor that reminds me of standing at the butcher's counter at the supermarket, drifts my way. Ally and Brandon look at me with their frog like night vision eyes protruding from their faces. I know they can't smell the carnage from here, but because of my enhanced senses when I am around Panthera, I can. I will never forget the smell. The bad guy tumbles backward in to the brush. Instantly, she sinks her fangs in to his neck to finish him off. Another blur. I have never seen anything as fast as Panthera in my entire life. The cigarette just now lands and extinguishes itself in the dirt. I guess smoking *really* is bad for you.

The wet ski mask feels like I have a sponge clinging to my face. Brandon points to the door of the clinic and holds up two fingers. I nod in agreement that two of us should go inside doing what we did at the other clinics. It worked before. If we fool the bad guys just for a minute, maybe we can overtake them here also. I start to tell Ally to wait here and she shakes her head no. I look back at Brandon and show him three fingers. He nods in agreement, but then whispers in my ear.

"Ally and I will go in first. Wait ten seconds and then follow. The bad guys inside, however many there may be, are only expecting two bad guy friends to enter through that door," he points at the clinic.

"Ok. Ally, got it?"

"Yes," she whispers while shaking her head up and down looking somewhat like an aardvark with the goggles protruding five inches from her face. We stand up and start walking toward the single story building. It is white with only one door in front flanked by two open windows on either side. There are no curtains or screens. There are no side windows in the back like the one we escaped from at clinic one. I follow Panthera to the left side of the clinic. Brandon and Ally head between the Land Rovers straight for the door. Brandon slides the safety off on his AK and Ally follows suit.

I wish them both good luck silently in my head hoping this turns out ok not knowing how many bad guys are in there. Panthera and I stop on the corner of the building ducking just below the window. I feel calm as Brandon and Ally enter the clinic. I start to count 10, 9, 8... Brandon says something, but I don't know what language he is speaking. Someone replies back to him. Suddenly Brandon yells. I hear footsteps running the length of the clinic. 4, 3, 2, 1, go! I get up and run in to the dark clinic with my pistol held tightly out in front of me. Ally is off to my right. She has a bad guy sitting on the floor. Her AK is pointing at his chest. His gun is lying on the floor beside him. Ally walks slowly over to him and kicks his AK away from his reach. Brandon is at the rear of the clinic with his AK pointing at another bad guy, no it is another woman, bad girl I guess. She has an AK lying at her feet. Brandon is motioning for her to move away from the hostages with his AK. I begin to glance around and realize the hostages are all lying on the floor blindfolded with their hands tied behind their backs. I see a man wearing a familiar shirt. A tan goofy looking safari shirt like the one I have. It is my dad. He looks alive. I continue to walk toward him looking for the rest of our people from the medical mission. I spot Laney. Her face is bloody, but she is moving.

"Who is there?" a muffled voice says. "What's going on?"

"Mama!" Ally shouts out. "It's us. You are rescued."

"Ally?" Carilyn responds confusingly.

I begin to move down the left side of the clinic stepping amongst the hostages trying to reach my father. Panthera stays outside not wanting to show herself unless absolutely necessary. That means less explaining to do. As it is, we will have to think of a good story of how the three of us saved three clinics from heavily armed bandits.

"Dad?"

"Lily?"

"Yes. We are here. Everyone will be ok," I try to sound as reassuring as possible. "Where is mama?"

"She is in here tied up somewhere I think," my dad says as he tries to sit up.

"We will find her," Brandon says.

The hostages start to realize that they are out of danger and begin to try to sit up. I hear people conversing in Malayalam.

"Ally watch that guy," says Brandon. "I will get something to tie him up with and this woman in front of me here."

"Hey, if you cut these ropes off of me, I would gladly tie those two up for ya."

"Doctor Nick!" I keep moving toward my dad and Doc Nick.

"Yes. The one and only," says Ally's dad. His shirt is ripped, but he looks uninjured. "Who booked this vacation by the way?"

"I thought you did. You're not my travel agent anymore," my dad says laughing. "What took y'all so long?"

I put my pistol in my waist band behind my back and reach in to my cargo pocket for my EMT scissors to start cutting the ropes off of these people. Unexpectedly, a lady wearing a bright green, white, gold, and red, sari stands up next to me on my left side. That's weird I thought everyone was tied up. She has a green scarf over her face. She seems a lot taller than most of the Indian women I have met so far, maybe six feet tall. In an instant she reaches around my right side and pulls me toward her. Her arm squeezes around my throat. I can barely take a breath. I drop my scissors on the floor while a struggle to breath. She drags me toward the wall until she can't go any further.

"Let me and my warriors go and I will not kill her," says a male voice in what might be a Mediterranean accent.

It is not a woman, but a man wearing a sari as a disguise. I feel cold steel pushed against my head. It is his own pistol. A sense of doom begins to overwhelm me. I try to make eye contact with Brandon. He turns back around in a single motion and swings the butt of his AK across the chin of his female attacker instantly rendering her unconscious. He begins to walk slowly toward my bad guy with his AK pointed at him. Ally takes a step back from her bad guy and tries to keep him covered while backing Brandon up at the same time. The bad guy presses his pistol harder in to my temple making me wince in pain.

"What's going on?" my mama says in a sleepy voice.

"Drop the gun and I won't shoot you," says Brandon sternly.

"Shoot who? Not my Lily," my mama replies.

"Let us go and your Lily will live," my bad guy says as Brandon gets to within ten feet of him. Some of the Indians are moaning. I hear sobs from somebody.

"Maybe you did not hear me. Drop the gun buddy and I won't shoot you!" Brandon says again, but louder.

"Brandon?"

"Not now mom. Kind of busy." Brandon says.

"Brandon's here?"

"Pareet give me a second," Brandon replies as he squeezes his AK tighter and peers down the barrel through his night vision goggles.

The bad guy begins to crush my throat with his forearm. I begin to choke. I feel a tear begin to form, break away, and flow down my left cheek. His hot breath permeates through my ski mask on to the back of my neck making me cringe.

I see Ally looking my way unable to make eye contact because of the night vision goggles. Suddenly the attacker she was guarding jumps up slamming in to Ally's rib cage knocking her on to the floor. She lands on a group of hostages who moan in protest after feeling Ally's weight on top of them. The bad guy starts to run for the door. In an instant the masonry wall explodes to the left of me as Panthera's massive paw crashes through the twelve inch thick barrier sending chunks of stone and cement on to the hostages. Her claws extend outward as she pulls her front leg back through the wall while sinking her claws into my bad guy's skull in the process. There is a crunching sound as he releases his grip from around my throat as I fall forward to the floor gasping for air. I turn around to see the bad guy get yanked through the wall as he reluctantly creates a new man shaped doorway. He begins to fire his pistol blindly in to the air as he disappears in to the darkness. Then total silence.

"Lily!" screams my father.

"I am ok dad. Wait I am coming over to untie you."

"It's all right everyone. You are all safe now," Brandon begins to say. "No more bad guys left."

"Ally?"

"I am ok Lily," she says as she begins to get up, untangles herself from the hostages, and stands up.

We begin to remove blindfolds and cut the ropes off of the hostage's hands. Everyone looks weary and tired, but except for some bumps and bruises, I don't see any major injuries. My dad will have to get with Doc Nick and check the hostages. I reach my dad's side and lower his blindfold. He blinks hard several times trying to focus as I pull the ski mask off of my head.

"A little early for trick-or-treat, ain't it?" he says as he admires my attire. "It sounded like the wall blew up."

"It is a long story," I say as I throw my arms around him. "Let's get everyone free and call for help."

"The other clinic?" he asks.

"Some bad injuries and some dead, but I am not sure who," I reluctantly say.

"I understand," my dad nods as he turns to search for my mama.

"Dad, what time is it?" I ask.

"Don't know, but looks like it is first light outside." He points to the new doorway. "They took my watch."

I can see early morning mist rising about two feet high from the grass. I don't hear any rain beating off the thatched roof. Maybe the storm has finally passed. I cut several of the Indian volunteers free and make my way over to my mama. My dad finishes cutting her hands free with a scalpel from a supply box. She stares at me in disbelief then looks at Ally and Brandon who have now shed their night vision goggles and ski masks.

"I was a little worried about y'all when you disappeared in the supply room of the other clinic." She wraps me up in a tight hug. "All the gunfire. The shouting. The chaos. I had a feeling you guys were ok because the bad guys seemed very upset with y'all." She releases her hug as tears begin to fall from her eyes.

"Don't cry mama. We are ok. Help is on the way. Well, it should be if they got the radio working."

Mama stands up and wipes the tears from her eyes. Back to nurse mode once more. She begins to go amongst the people and checks for injuries. Brandon has Jillian and Pareet freed from the ropes. The three of them embrace. Ally is crying with her mother and Doc Nick.

BANG! BANG! BANG! BANG!

Gunshots are heard from where we left Valentina. We instinctively crouch. Some of the volunteers scream. Someone yells out, "not again!" I head out of the new doorway pulling my pistol from my waist band and run toward Valentina. I feel Brandon's presence behind me. We reach the trail entrance just as Valentina steps in to the clearing holding her pistol with both hands, the barrel still smoking. Brandon and I stop running when we reach her.

"What happened?" I ask. "Are you hurt?"

"No I am molto bene. Very fine. Bad guy ran out of the jungle at me. He had a gun. I started shooting, but then your how should I say, cat got him. Shredded him like a ball of yarn."

"Yeah she does that on occasion," I offer not knowing how to explain all of this when we finally get some help. "Please, if you can keep her a secret; it would probably be best for everyone."

"I understand. I won't say anything," Valentina replies.

I hear footsteps running up behind me and turn to see my dad with one of the bad guy's AK47's in his hands. At the same time I feel something protruding in the palm of my own hand. I slowly open up my right hand to see the tiger crystal. I close my grip and say thank you Panthera. I place the crystal in my front pocket knowing we are safe.

"Everyone ok?" says my dad as he scans the jungle with the AK47.

"We are good Mr. Morgan. Valentina scared off the last bad guy. He won't be back," Brandon says.

"How can you be so sure? I mean these guys were professionals." My dad moves his head side to side, his eyes straining to see into the jungle.

His right hand is squeezing the pistol grip of the AK tightly as his index finger rests on the trigger. The butt of the rifle stock rests firmly against his right shoulder. He points the barrel of the rifle from one tree to the next making sure it isn't a human about to attack us. "By the way, how did you guys manage to take out all the bad guys and what was that explosion in the wall from?"

"James," says Valentina as I hold my breath and brace myself. "Lily, Ally, and Brandon got very lucky. That is all." I exhale and wink at Valentina. She winks back, gives me a half smile, and continues to try and change the subject avoiding my dad's questions. "Now let's get everyone loaded up and head to the other clinics. There should be help there by now. They might even be headed here, I hope."

"You are right Valentina. Let's go," my dad says as the four of us head back to the clinic.

CHAPTER XXIV

We walk back to the clinic building as people are filing outside probably for the first time in twelve or fifteen hours, maybe longer. Everyone looks ragged and worn out from the ordeal. Valentina sets down her first aid pack and begins giving everyone a quick once over as Doctor Nick fills her in with what injuries he has found so far. She pulls out some white cling dressings and some white tape and starts to bandage one of the Indian folks who has blood dripping down his face landing on his dohti checkering it with red blotches. I glance at Doc Nick's lower arm and spot a heavily bleeding gash that I did not see before. Gala and Moira appear uninjured and are sorting through hostages.

"Doc, are you ok?"

"I think my arm needs a couple of stitches Lily; are you up for it?"

"Um, I will get a suture kit and a… fix ya right up."

The stitches go in without a hitch. Doctor Nick talks me through it. Hope he doesn't mind the few crooked ones, but at least his wound is closed. My mama and Carilyn are handing out water to the rescued hostages. Brandon walks over to Jillian and Pareet. The three of them embrace in a quick family group hug before Brandon runs off down the trail to retrieve our Land Rover. Ally and I interrupt our mothers for a second and the four of us embrace as Ally begins to cry.

"Mama, it is really bad at the other clinics. Some people are dead," Ally explains through her sobs.

"I know baby. It will be ok. You guys saved us. Y'all are heroes," says Carilyn. "Thank you."

"Your mama is right. Thank you from the bottom of my heart," my mama adds.

My dad retrieves the new doorway making bad guys' pistol off of the grass and puts it in his left cargo pocket of his safari pants. He then joins the group of us waiting by the vehicles.

"Listen up everyone," my dad says. "We are going to load up everyone in the vehicles and drive back to the other clinic site. We don't have any life threatening injuries, so we will re-organize a formal triage once there."

"Hey Jim," yells Doc Nick as he peeks into the Tata. "The keys are in it. I can get four people in the car."

"Ok Nick," my dad replies. "Let's load up! I will put the prisoner in the back of the first Land Rover. Make sure we have all the weapons and bring extra water and medical supplies. Whatever will fit. Essentials like trauma kits and IV's." He looks at the new white bandage on Doc Nick's arm. "That looks like my daughter's work."

"It is Jim," says Doc Nick as my dad raises his eye brows a bit.

"Mama, I will ride back with Brandon. There won't be enough room in the two Land Rovers and the one Tata."

"Ok Lily."

"Mama. I will ride with Brandon and Lily," Ally says.

"Ok Ally," says Carilyn as she hugs Ally once more.

Everyone turns their heads toward the sound of Brandon's Land Rover as he breaks in to the clearing. I hear a few gasps from the folks who have not loaded up in to a vehicle yet. He parks next to my dad and climbs out. My mama begins to cry.

"I can't imagine what y'all must have gone through," says my mama as she gives the shot up blown up Land Rover a once over.

"Don't cry Mrs. Morgan," says Brandon as he exits the sorry looking vehicle. "It still runs, but I do need the spare tire off of Doctor Jim's roof there." Brandon points to the Land Rover my dad will be driving.

Brandon retrieves the jack out of our Land Rover while my dad and Nick get the spare tire. Brandon loosens the lug nuts on the wheel with the flat tire as Doc Nick jacks up the Land Rover. My dad pulls off the bent wheel with flat spots all along the rim. Doc Nick and my dad look at each other as they toss the wheel aside and mount the new tire on to the Land Rover. Brandon tightens the lug nuts as Doc Nick lowers the Land Rover and pulls the jack out from underneath. He places it in the back of our Land Rover as Brandon gives the lugs another quick turn to make sure they are snug. The whole tire change takes less than five minutes.

Brandon puts all of our AK's in the back of our vehicle in the cargo area; I set my pistol in there with Valentina's also. There are already two AK's lying in there. Brandon must have found them in the jungle from Panthera's earlier work. One of them has the brown wooden stock bit off of it. Teeth marks are clearly showing. Doctor Nick has the remaining AK with him, the one from the female prisoner, in the Tata.

"All right, let's go!" my dad says once more.

We are able to get ten people into each of the first two Land Rovers that were already here at the clinic. Two Indian gentlemen sit in the back of the first Land Rover guarding the prisoner. Doc Nick takes three people with him in the Tata. Valentina and Gala ride with us. Laney and Moira are in the second Land Rover.

It is a somber mood as we drive back to the other clinics. Nobody speaks. Each buried in their own thoughts. Traffic is still crazy around us. Horns are still blaring. Rickshaws are still swerving. Nobody knowing yet what all of us have just been through. The sun is just about completely up now. I feel the warmth of the summer day begin to take over from yesterday's rain. Once again, the wind blows in my face through the front of the windshield-less Land Rover. At least this time things are calm and there is not as much of a sense of urgency. It feels more like dread not knowing who was killed and not wanting to know. I feel bad for Noella already knowing François must be one of the bodies in clinic two. I hear a whop whop sound heading toward us. I look at Brandon and he looks at me.

"It's not another flat tire," he says.

Just then, as the sound intensifies, I look up to see two black helicopters fly over the top of us heading in the direction of the other clinic we just left from.

"Who was that?" I ask.

"Indian military," Brandon replies. "They must be on the way to the clinic we were just at. That means Ludwik's radio made from Bratwurst must have worked." He takes my hand and squeezes making a little smile in the process.

"Sounds 'bout right to me," I say as I return the squeeze. "We will let them know what to look for when we get to our clinics."

Our small convoy continues down the road and eventually makes a right turn to the side road leading to the clinics. One by one the Land Rovers reach the trail and begin to turn right. Doc Nick pulls the Tata over knowing it won't make it up the trail. There is no sign of the other Tata. I wonder if Mr. Handsome was here all along. There is no way he could have been at the other clinic and escaped us and Panthera. Maybe it was somebody else altogether. Maybe Mr. Handsome was the one making the phone calls for demands. Either case he will be short staffed now unless he hires some temps. I kind of hope he was the last one that Panthera got and this other Tata was just a coincidence. Doc Nick climbs out of his Tata as we pull up. Brandon slows down.

"Hey Doc I will come back for you as soon as we off load all of the passengers," says Brandon.

"Sounds good to me, but I will start walking. Watch your back. There can still be bad guys around," says Doc Nick.

"You too. Be right back."

We slip and slide up the trail which looks even more tore up than before as if an army tank drove up the trail churning up all the dirt and mud in the process. We pass by the coconut tree we hit earlier this morning. There is a large chunk of its bark missing which I think is now part of the coconut Land Rover, ours.

As we finally enter the clearing, four massive flat black military like trucks come in to view. They have a solid rectangle like enclosed box on the back kind of like a cargo truck, but there are no windows, just a single door at the rear of each truck. The front has a large sloping windshield protected by steel mesh and an angular grille which has the word UNIMOG in the center in subdued black letters. There is a brush guard and winch mounted on the front of each of the trucks. All the trucks are riding on massive off-road tires almost three or four feet tall with wide aggressive treads. What appear to be radio antennas, protrude from the roof of the cab. We continue past them and park just before clinic two. Serious looking Indian men wearing a green, black, and brown tiger stripe like uniform seem to be patrolling the outskirts of the clearing. Each one looks like they are carrying a machine gun of some sorts and I can see a pistol strapped to each of their thighs in a black holster. They all seem to be wearing a radio microphone dangling on the sides of their green painted faces. They are all wearing one of those floppy jungle hats also camouflaged. It looks like they all are carrying water in one of those carriers strapped to their backs. They all appear to be wearing body armor over their chests.

We shut off our Land Rover and get out. It looks like everyone else is up by the first clinic, so we head that way. Two of the serious looking men are at the Land Rover with the prisoner. They lift her out of the back and place her on the ground on her belly. One of the men puts plastic handcuffs on her. She begins to move and doesn't appear to follow his directions. He raises his hand and in a swift motion, slaps her in the back of her head. She gets the message. They stand her up and cut off the makeshift roller bandage that was restraining her hands and then march her up to the front of the black trucks.

Singh is standing there talking with one of the serious looking men, except this one is wearing a black beret with some kind of shiny emblem in the middle of the front. His rank probably. Must be the commander. They are standing next to a flat black colored Mercedes 4x4. I think my dad told me once that they are called a G-Wagon. I can tell by the square boxy shape. Antennas are sticking up from the G-Wagon's roof like the black trucks and there is steel mesh covering the windshield, side windows, and the rear window. It also has a winch and brush guard to protect the grille. Its off-road tires got a workout coming up the trail this morning judging by the amount of mud stuck in the tread. I catch up with my dad and the others.

"What's going on dad?" I ask.

"Hang on a second," he points toward Singh. "Here he comes now."

"Hello everyone," says Singh. "I just talked to the officer in charge. He said both sites are secure and everyone is accounted for. Brandon is telling him now about the other location by the cave at the top of the tea plantation." Singh looks at me and Ally. "I did not know you two ran so far." Ally and I nod at him. "Well, anyway, the officer says it looks like the bad guys, at least most of them, were killed by a tiger. A very big tiger." Singh looks at us again. "It is very fortunate that this tiger chose last night to do its hunting. It is also a good thing that you two were not eaten by this tiger. It is a good thing Brandon was not eaten either."

"Um...Wow. I guess we are very lucky," Ally says with a stutter in her voice.

"Yeah. We had no idea. I thought it was just a couple of bad guys," I say as my dad gives me a 'yeah right' kind of look.

"The Colonel thinks it would be very very bad publicity if word got out that a man eating tiger was on the loose, so he said in his report that he will just mention that the attackers were overwhelmed by a group of hostages that escaped and then came back and rescued the rest. He also asked if we could keep the tiger thing a secret. It could hurt tourism and all of that kind of stuff," Singh says as Brandon returns.

"Sure thing dad, by the way, who are these guys?" Brandon asks.

"This is India's Force One anti-bad guy unit. Highly elite. Kind of like U.S. Army's Delta Force. They still seemed a little perturbed that they didn't get to kick some bandit butt, excuse my language," replies Singh.

"Singh?" I ask. "Who didn't make it?"

"Jim should I tell her?"

"Yeah. Go ahead Singh."

"Lily," Singh pauses and takes a deep breath. "Jia Li, François, and our translator Tushar were killed." His voice lowers. "Tushar tried to intervene and was beaten and then shot."

"Did we get all the bad guys?" asks Ally.

"The Colonel thinks everyone except for the one making the phone calls to the negotiator. He believes they were being made at a different site than from here. Force One was notified as soon as the first ransom call was received by the Indian officials. It just took a while to figure out if it was a hoax or not and also who and where the hostages might be."

"Singh, why were our camps chosen? I mean, we treat everyone equal. We never had a problem like this before," asks Doc Nick.

"The Colonel thinks it was just random. Possibly from our Doctors Helping the World website even though only the volunteers on the trip with us knew the exact dates and times we would be operating the clinics. Target of opportunity I guess. Who can say for sure," explains Singh.

"Singh, did they identify any of the attackers?" I ask not sure if I should tell anyone about meeting Mr. Handsome in the airport in Paris.

"The Colonel says the tiger did a good job in making most of them unidentifiable, but they have several prisoners. They said they will make them talk," explains Singh as he curls up his bottom lip into his dark mustache. "Well anyway, Force One is assuming care of all of the Indian folks. They will make sure that they all get back to their villages and homes. All of the volunteers will be released after giving statements to the intelligence officer. I think Ally and Lily are the last to see him. He is standing next to the Colonel."

"Ok dad. We will go talk to him," says Brandon as he gently grabs my hand and leads Ally and I over to the Colonel and the Force One intel officer standing at the hood of the G-Wagon. He has a lap top computer opened up and is typing into it as we approach.

He stops typing as we inform him and the Colonel who we are. They both look at our disheveled bad guy uniforms. Brandon begins and tells

214

them the whole story for us in Malayalam, well at least our unofficial version. No need in taking the three of us to the loony farm if we can help it.

"So let me get this straight, Brandon rescued you two from the cave," the intel officer says as he points to Ally and I.

"That's correct," I say.

"Yes that is right," says Ally.

"Then you three were able to sneak back to the clinic and over power the attackers," the Colonel adds as the intel officer types some more on his keyboard.

"That's correct sir," says Ally.

"That's right," I say. Some more tapping on his keyboard.

"Then you three and the paramedic from Italy drove in a blown up Land Rover to the third clinic, over powered a couple more attackers, and another tiger ate the rest of the bad guys," the Colonel says.

"That sounds about right sir," says Brandon.

"Yep, I agree with that statement sir," says Ally.

"Yes sir, I agree with them two," I say while glancing at the colonel's black name tag which reads PATEL. Kind of young looking for the rank of Colonel.

"Two tiger attacks in one night. Almost ten miles apart. Multiple scum removed from the earth. Sounds good to me. Nice work," the Colonel says as he extends his hand. The intel officer follows his lead. We shake hands and say our goodbye's. "Lieutenant, do you agree with their statements?"

"Yes sir I do," the intel officer replies. "However, it might be a good idea to have a different press release than bandits. That's not good for tourism either."

"Yes. You are correct. No tigers. No bandits," the stern looking Colonel replies.

"Are we free to go?" asks Brandon.

"Yes, just leave the bad guy's clothing behind and you are free to go," the Colonel says.

We quickly strip off the bad guy black and lay the muddy crusty clothing on the hood of the G-Wagon. Brandon retrieves all of the weapons and piles them also on the hood, says goodbye one more time, and we locate our parents.

"Mama, where is Kenneth?" Ally asks.

"They took Kenneth, Ludwik, and a few of the more serious injuries by helicopter to Kochi. There is a hospital there that can treat them and we should see them tomorrow. Both had fractures and they think Ludwik's bullet wounds aren't as bad as first suspected. We have to wait and see," Carilyn replies empathetically.

CHAPTER XXV

After giving our respects to Novella; Brandon, Ally, Moira, Laney, and I, head to our blown up Land Rover for the ride back to Brandon's house. Petra and Gala, along with Jillian, Carilyn, and my mama, decide to stay with Novella for support.

Brandon drives once again. As he backs up the Land Rover, I can't help but survey the clinics and the clearing. The damage and carnage that took place here has me lost in my own thoughts. I try to figure out what happened last night, but come up short of answers. It feels like a dream, but I know it is real. I casually glance at the others in the vehicle with us and they all seem to be in their own worlds. Nobody is saying a word. I guess everyone is trying to decipher what happened.

We head down the trail for what will probably be the last time. The Land Rover is making screeching sounds that it isn't supposed to make, at least not when it left the factory, but it keeps going. After bouncing down to the bottom of the worn out trail, Brandon makes the left turn. The Tata is still parked there. Doc Nick had walked up to the clinics because the car could not get up the trail. Something catches my eye in the grass behind the Tata. A reflection of some kind. Shiny from the sun's rays bouncing off of it.

"Brandon, stop here for a minute," I say.

"Ok, what for?" he replies as he pulls over just past the Tata.

I open my door and jump out.

"I saw something."

In the grass is a small circular thing. I bend down for a closer look. I think someone lost a contact lens, but there is something unusual about it. It is brown in the middle. A brown contact lens? I decide to keep it just in case it belongs to one of our volunteers. I get back in the Land Rover.

"What did you find Lily," asks Ally.

I turn toward the back seat.

"Well, I think it is somebody's contact lens, but who would be wearing brown contact lenses?"

"That's a good question," says Brandon." I do know your eye sight is probably better than theirs right now seeing how they are missing that contact lens." He puts the Land Rover in drive and we head off to his house.

I hold the lens up to my right eye and try looking through it not knowing what to expect.

"Hey this is odd," I say surprisingly.

"What is?" asks Laney.

"Does anyone of y'all wear contact lenses because this one doesn't seem to make my vision blurry or anything like what happens when you put a friend's eye glasses on who has really bad vision."

"Let me see that," says Laney. She holds it up to her eye. "No. You are right. I think someone was just wearing the contacts to change their eye color but why?"

"Maybe one of the bad guys?" says Moira.

"Possible," responds Brandon. "Hang on to it and we can turn it over to my dad. He can give it to the authorities."

We reach the paved road and Brandon makes the familiar right turn and joins in with the rest of India's traffic. Horns beeping, cars swerving, and people shouting. The usual daily motorist routine. People oblivious to what had occurred last night. Maybe they are better off not knowing. About an hour passes before Brandon turns on to the dirt road leading to his house. He then makes the right turn on to his driveway. The Karup's house is a wonderful sight. A sense of relief comes over me. Brandon turns off the engine, but it seems to keep running for a few seconds longer despite not having a key in the ignition. We all climb out of the battered Land Rover which now looks out of place against the back drop of Brandon's home.

"Well, she did her job, but it looks like we might need a tow truck to get her out of here," says Brandon.

"Maybe a tune-up and some touch up paint," adds Ally as she kisses the hood of the Land Rover.

"If you all want to head inside and start to get cleaned up, I will get some food and drinks out. Pareet and some of the others should be coming in a little while."

"Sounds good Brandon," I say as everyone nods in agreement. "I will give you a hand."

"Thanks," he replies.

Ally, Laney, and Moira head up stairs while Brandon and I stop in the carport to slip our muddy shoes off before entering the kitchen. We pull out some of the usual fruit, drinks, and left over rice cakes. Brandon says that should be good for now and we will most likely cook up some meat tonight. I grab some bananas, an idlis, orange juice, and water. We sit down at the kitchen table. It seems awkward at first because of the silence. Neither of us saying a word. I decide to initiate a conversation not knowing if Brandon really wants to talk.

"I don't understand Brandon."

He swallows a bite of his idlis, takes a drink of water, and pauses for a minute.

"What do you mean," he says.

"I mean Princess Ellora lead us to Panthera."

"Go on," he replies with concern.

"We couldn't save those other people. Why couldn't we get to them quicker?"

"Lily, you can't beat yourself up over what happened or the way things happened. Sometimes the evil in this world has to really show itself before someone can respond to it. I think that is what happened. Princess Ellora and Panthera are only there to help after this evil appears. It would be nice to be able to prevent everything that is bad before it happens, but it just doesn't seem to work that way. Not now. Not in the past. And certainly not in the future. We can only do the best that we can when the time arises," says Brandon.

"I think I understand what you are saying. I just hope that next time we can put a stop to things earlier," I say.

"I hope there is no next time," Brandon adds. "I think the shower might be open. It sounds like you are next then I will jump in and maybe our folks will be back by then."

He stands up and comes around to my side of the table, takes my hand, and I stand up. We embrace for a few moments.

"Ok. See you in a couple of minutes," I say as I head up the stairs to the bedroom.

Ally is already showered and changed. She is lying on the bed with a blue towel wrapped around her head. Her eyes are shut and she seems to be asleep. She looks exhausted. I quietly walk over to her and cover her up with a very light blanket. Then I slip out of my clothes, put a bathrobe on, and head for a shower. After that I get dressed and head back down to the kitchen.

"All yours Brandon."

"Ok. Thanks. Where's Ally?" he asks.

"Oh, she is sleeping. I didn't want to wake her."

"Good idea. Laney and Moira came down for some food and headed back up to their room. They said they were also going to lay down for a while."

"What about you? Aren't you tired?"

"Yeah. I guess it is starting to catch up with me, but I will sleep tonight once I know everyone is back here," he pauses.

"What's a matter?" I ask.

"I got the clinic on the radio; my dad gave Novella a sedative. They are going to take her to the hospital. My mom, dad, and Mandara are going with her."

"I feel so bad for her and the rest of them."

"I know you do. Hiro and Sakurako are going to accompany Jia Li's body to the morgue and begin making arrangements to return her home to her family in Hong Kong. Everyone else should be back here within the hour," explains Brandon.

I decide to go outside and just walk around the yard for a while. The temperature is warm and the sun is bright. I have no idea where my sunglasses are. The air is fresh. The birds in the trees are making their usual chatter. Off in the distance I can hear another elephant clanging its chains down the road, once again taking its owners for a walk. I find it somewhat strange that everyone and everything just continues on with life. It almost feels normal except for having lived through it. I guess the Colonel is right, maybe it is for the better that all the people don't know what happened last night. I continue my walk around the yard until I hear some cars coming near the house. I turn to see a couple of the big boxy square Land Rovers pull in to the driveway. It looks like everyone is back except for Brandon's parents. I turn the other way and continue to walk. I hear what sounds like someone kick a soccer ball. I was right. It rolls just past me. I turn to see my father.

"How you doing there?" he asks as I retrieve the ball with my foot and kick it back to him.

"I am ok. A little worried about everybody else though."

"Lily, none of this was your fault. Don't beat yourself up about it. If anything, we told you it would be a safe trip, so we apologize for that. We had no idea that any of this would happen. Y'all are heroes. This could have turned out much worse."

My dad walks over to me and gives me a hug. I think maybe he is right. We head back inside the house. Petra and Gala are trying to eat a light meal. Brandon is pouring drinks for them. One by one they stand up and give me a hug. I look at Brandon.

"Just a thank you Lily. We didn't get a chance to at the clinics," says Gala.

"You are very welcome," I reply and then exchange a hug with Petra.

"Don't worry about your cat thing. I will not tell anyone. You are all heroes. Thank your cat when you see her next time," she whispers in to my ear.

"I will. You are welcome."

Carilyn and Doc Nick follow with the hugs and then my mama.

"You did good out there. I am proud of you," my mama says.

"Mama, if it wasn't for Brandon and Ally; it could have been really bad."

"I know, but you guys are heroes. Y'all saved a lot of lives," she says as she releases her hug and keeps both of her hands on my shoulders.

"Where did Pareet, Marco, and Valentina go?" I ask.

"They went upstairs to get washed up," Brandon says. "I think they will eat a little snack like everyone else and then catch up on some sleep before dinner."

"Ok then. I think I will check on Ally and maybe take a nap."

"We will see you later baby," says my mama as she gives me a kiss on my cheek.

I nod at Brandon and head up to the bedroom. Ally is sleeping soundly. I can't imagine what she is feeling inside. I just hope she recovers from this horrible experience without any lasting damage. I decide to crawl into bed with my best friend, slide up behind her, and throw my arm over her. I don't want her to feel alone. I drift off to sleep.

When I wake up, I spot the familiar orange glow of the tiki torches radiating outside the bedroom window. The faint smell of kerosene is flowing in the air once more. Ally is no longer lying beside me. I get up, slip into my sneakers, and head downstairs. A couple of people are sleeping on the living room floor, but covered with blankets, so I'm not sure who they are. I walk through the empty kitchen which is only lit up by a single candle and then out the door by the carport. I make the left turn and another in to the backyard to find several people awake talking quietly. Brandon is here and he has a somewhat depressed look on his face. Ally, who looks almost recovered, and her parents are here. My folks are here and so is Jillian.

"Hey y'all, what's going on?" I sit down next to Brandon. "Sorry I slept for so long. What time is it?"

"It is almost midnight," my dad answers.

"Hey baby," says my mama.

"Yes," I say as I grab another banana off of the table.

"We have some good news and some bad news," she says.

"Go on mama. Just tell me."

"Lily, the clinics are closed now. They were going to stay open for several more days, but because of the things that happened we decided it would be better not to re-open them right now."

"I understand. What does that mean?"

"Well we are going to leave India the day after tomorrow," my mama explains.

"Can't we stay? We don't have to go home right away," I feel my heart begin to sink as my eyes begin to fill up with tears knowing I will only have Brandon in my life for one more day.

"We talked to Carilyn and Nick and decided that because we do have some time left on the trip that we are going to stop off in Italy on the way home. We all know how you and Ally are big art nuts and we thought maybe a quick stop in Rome, Florence, and Milan would kind of be a help in dealing with everything that happened here." I can't believe it. I don't want to leave.

"If that is what y'all decided then I guess that's what we will do. I hope I can come back here and visit someday soon though," I say hoping nobody can detect the grief in my voice.

"We will all come back honey," says my dad. "Here I fixed you a plate."

My dad slides a plate of food over in front of me. I begin to pick at it wondering if I will ever see Brandon again.

"Lily, don't worry. I think you will have a good time. It might be a once in a lifetime trip. Hey, I will come and get some of those chicken wings and bar-b-q's you told me about," says Brandon supportingly, but I can feel him hurting inside like me.

I finish eating the best that I can and say goodnight to everyone. Brandon and I get up and head to our usual spot on the terrace. We sit down beside each other on the outdoor couch.

"Do you have the crystal on you?" asks Brandon.

I reach in to my front jean pocket and pull it out showing it to him in my hand.

"Good. Here is a nylon cord that you can put through that loop on the back of the crystal. You can wear it as a necklace. Keep her with you at all times," he says.

"Thank you," I respond as I slip the thin black nylon cord through the loop.

Brandon brushes my hair over my right shoulder as he takes the ends of the nylon cord and ties it in to a knot behind my neck. He puts my hair back behind me as I let the little tiger crystal dangle on my chest. It seems to sparkle every once and a while from the moonlight hitting it.

"It looks good on you," he says.

"Thank you Brandon," barely comes out of me before I begin to cry.

"What's wrong Lily," he asks as he puts his arms around my back pulling me against himself.

"We only have one more day together."

"Well then, we will have to make it a special one."

He takes both of his thumbs and wipes away my tears falling under my eyes, places his hands on both sides of my face, and kisses me firmly on my lips. We stay on the couch for about another hour just admiring the moonlight, the stars, and each other.

"Come on, I will walk you to your room," Brandon says as he takes my hand and leads me to my bedroom. "See you early in the morning. We should get on the road by seven."

"Sounds good. I will see you then." We kiss each other goodnight.

I shut my door and listen to Brandon quietly make his way down the hallway to his room secretly wishing we were spending the entire night together. Ally is peacefully sleeping not making any noise except for an occasional breath. I can only hope that she will not be affected by all of the traumatic events that have unexpectedly unfolded on this trip. I slip in to bed, let out my own deep breath, and wait expectantly to have a dream tonight.

CHAPTER XXVI

The next morning I awake at 6 a.m. Ally is already up and dressed. Her parents are going to take her to Lakeshore hospital in Kochi, near Ernakulam, to visit Kenneth. Singh and Jillian are going to go with them. They want to see how Ludwik and Novella are doing. Pareet is going to take the rest of the volunteers in to town also just so everyone can kind of take their minds off of what happened. It took some pleading, considering that my parents did not want me out of their sight, but they are allowing me to spend my last day in India with Brandon. I couldn't thank them enough and understood if they said no.

"Hey there sweetheart. You get any sleep?" says Ally.

"I think I got a couple of hours. How about you?"

"I feel a little better. I just can't wait to see Kenneth. What does Brandon have planned for y'all today?"

"He said it will be a surprise."

"I like your new necklace. It kind of stands out. Why don't we paint it so it isn't so noticeable. It would suck if some pickpocket ran off with it," says Ally as she digs in her makeup kit and retrieves some burgundy nail polish.

"You are right. Go ahead and paint it."

I hold the tiger crystal as Ally covers it with the nail polish. It does the trick. I never thought about it, but it did look almost like a diamond; now it looks more like a cheap harmless charm I picked up at a souvenir stand selling trinkets and such. Perfect.

"Nice job Ally. It looks good."

"Thanks. You should go and get ready. I will say bye to Kenneth for you. He will understand if y'all don't make it there to see him. He knows how tight you and Brandon have become."

"Ok. I will see you later," I say as we give each other a big hug.

Ally heads out the door and I go and get washed up. After a quick shower, I put my white cargo pants on with my crimson colored polo shirt that I have been saving to wear for a special occasion. I decide to leave my hair down, parted in the middle and resting in front of my shoulders. I go easy with the makeup. A little eyeliner and some lip gloss. The shirt has a small University of Alabama elephant on the upper left chest. Me and Al, the elephant, head down to the kitchen. Brandon is sitting in a chair and turns around when he hears me coming.

"Wow. You are truly beautiful," he says as he stands up and wraps his arms around me.

"You're not so bad on my eyes either," I respond after a serious morning kiss. "Is everyone gone already?"

"Yeah. They all skipped breakfast to get on the road early. I think we will do the same if you don't mind."

"I don't mind. Lead the way."

We go outside to find that they left one of the Land Rovers for us that wasn't damaged, another silver one.

"How did they all fit in the other Land Rover? It must have looked like a clown car."

"It did," says Brandon as he lets out a chuckle. It feels good to hear him laugh again.

Brandon heads out of the driveway and turns right this time traveling the same way we drove in on the first night we all arrived. At the end of the dirt road he turns left on to the paved road and joins in with the morning traffic. I don't think I will ever get used to the cars, trucks, rickshaws, and buses going every which way, but I am really starting to enjoy watching all the folks go about their daily life.

"We have about thirty-five miles until we get to Muvattupula and then from there, it will be maybe ten or fifteen miles to Kochi," explains Brandon as we continue through the rolling green hill country.

"Lead on. I am all yours."

"That's good to know. We can grab some breakfast near Munnar, or just keep going."

"Let's just keep going. I can wait," I say.

The sunrise is behind us and it is starting to get brighter outside. I tune the radio to Red FM and relax in my seat. Brandon nods in agreement with the radio idea. I make a mental note to buy some sunglasses because I have no clue what happened to mine. I am not really sure where my pink Paris hat ended up either. Maybe I will add a new hat on to my shopping list. I am definitely getting a dohti for Uncle Jake. I find myself starting to count down the hours that I have left with Brandon. I am not sure how I will cope with leaving him tomorrow morning. I do my best to change my thoughts. A few car horns blaring helps me. It is like rush hour around Birmingham Alabama times ten, plus cows and elephants. That's how I decide to explain it to my friends back home. Brandon makes the occasional controlled erratic swerve to avoid the other traffic. I can tell he has done this many times even though he is only a little older than me. I don't have many miles on my driver's license. Too busy with school and soccer I guess. It isn't long before we reach Muvattupula. I feel myself getting excited knowing we are getting close to Kochi. It will be nice to get out and walk around with the local people. I wonder what Brandon has planned for today? It doesn't really matter as long as we are together. We finally leave the lush green hills and mountains and to my surprise, the city of Kochi comes in to view. I wasn't expecting to see white high-rise buildings. They look like they might be apartment complexes with an occasional office building thrown in to the surroundings. Brandon continues on the highway and I even see the dreaded sight of airplanes taking off on the edge of the city.

It isn't much longer before we finally pull in to the city and Brandon makes his way through the congested streets.

"Well I hope it is still ours when we get back," he says with a slight smile referring to the car. "Do you like boats? We might go for a boat ride later."

"Boats are ok. I live near a lake back home. This area looks different. Is this Fort Kochi?" I ask.

"Nope." He points across the water. "That is."

After a very short ride across the bridge, we arrive. I don't notice any high rises over here. He parks the Land Rover and says goodbye to it hoping it won't be stolen.

"Welcome to Fort Kochi. Most of the historic trading happened around here. Let's get some food. There is a street vendor just down the street there," he says pointing to his left. "I stop there all the time when I get in to the city. They have the best appam and I smother that with payasam." Brandon's grin gets bigger.

"Sounds good. What is it?" I ask as Brandon takes my hand and we head down toward the vendor he is talking about.

"Appam is a rice pancake that is soft in the middle and the edges are just a little cooked, making them crunchy. The payasam is a topping made from molasses, spices, and coconut milk. Usually they will throw cashews and raisins on it to."

We dodge in and out of people walking all different directions. We pass under a small green awning extending from the front of what looks like a news stand. I glance at all of the newspapers on display until one in particular catches my eye, not because it is written in English, but because of the headline: ROBBERY ATTEMPT FOILED BY CLINIC WORKERS. Brandon and I look at each other and keep heading for some food. No words needed.

"That really does sound good. I can't wait."

After a few more minutes of walking, we arrive at the street vendor. It reminds me of getting warm peanuts at the Peanut Festival back home in Dothan. Two cooks working out of a small trailer and a female taking orders through the opened side window. The wheels seem to have been taken off of this trailer making it look like more of a permanent fixture. I can't tell if the missing wheels were planned, or maybe borrowed ten years ago. Brandon orders for the both of us in Malayalam. He hands me my appam and thankfully he got me a fork.

"It can be a bit messy," he says as he kind of rolls his appam up like a cigar and starts eating from one end.

I decide to skip the fork and eat like a local. I roll the appam up and attempt to bite in to the end of it not realizing that the payasam is starting to ooze out of the other side. Just when I figure that out, a clump of it lets go and slides down my chin.

"Hey there, you got a little something on your face," says Brandon chuckling as he reaches for a napkin off of the counter. The nice lady doesn't say anything as she looks at me, but I can tell she is laughing hard inside at my expense.

"Fork?"

"Probably a good idea for first time appam eaters," he replies as he wipes my chin for me leaving a slight stickiness behind.

I laugh and grab the fork. The appam is almost the same size as the plate, so after several minutes I finally finish it. I wash it down with some bottled water. Brandon thanks the kind staff and we continue down the street.

"Thanks Brandon. That was only slightly embarrassing. Should I worry about the rest of the day?" I ask jokingly.

"Yep."

"What's next Brandon?" I try to pry as we stop in front of what looks like some kind of store. I gaze into the large glass picture window and see a display showing tattoos, I think.

"Matching tattoos already?"

"Henna."

"What?" I ask.

"Henna. Ancient body art. Comes from a plant. They grind it up in to a paste and use it to paint artistic renderings on people. Goes on orange and then dries to a darker brown. Not permanent, but will last a while. It is usually done for special occasions, but I think it has become popular worldwide."

"Ok. My mama might be upset if it doesn't wash off," I say jokingly.

He holds open the door for me and we walk inside. It looks like they are just getting things ready for the day's customers. Brandon speaks to them in Malayalam. One of the ladies with jet black hair down to her lower back and wearing a bright yellow and red sari points to a chair. I walk over and sit down. Her left arm is bare and I can see that it is almost completely covered with what must be henna art.

"Brandon?"

"Yes?"

"She isn't going to do my entire arm, is she?"

"No. I asked her to just go around your left wrist and left hand," he explains without laughing, so I believe him.

She lays out some small paint brushes with very fine bristles on the ends. Next she sets out several small dishes about the size of a cereal bowl back home. They appear to be filled with a dark color paste. She takes a small ceramic stick and stirs the mixture.

"Ready?" she says in broken English, gives me the same kind of special look I received at the sari shop, and smiles.

"Yes," I reply.

She takes a wet cloth and washes my left hand and wrist.

After that, she takes one of the paint brushes, dips it in to a bowl filled with the dark paste, and begins to paint on my left wrist. Maybe an hour passes and she finishes. It looks like a swirling design that reminds me of fine delicate tree branches, but I can swear part of it consists of words. It seems the tree like branches curl off of each of the words blending the whole design as if it was one continuous tattoo. She sets down her brush.

"All done," she says with a big smile. "You like?"

"Yes. I like it very much," I say to her.

Brandon leans in closer for a better look.

"That is perfect," he says then turns to the nice lady and says something in Malayalam as he hands her a handful of rupees.

"Am I seeing things, or did she write something on me?" I ask while admiring her beautiful work.

"Yes. I asked her to do it," says Brandon.

"And?"

"It says: follow your calling in Malayalam."

"I already am. Thank you."

I stand up and thank her for my very first henna tattoo and then turn and give Brandon a great big hug.

"What's next?" I say. "This was a big surprise. I can't imagine anything better than this. Thank you. I love it."

"You're welcome Lily. Let's get that dohti for your uncle," says Brandon as we wave goodbye to the nice ladies in the henna shop.

We head down the street a bit further from the car leaving me to wonder about Brandon's joke about the Land Rover still being there when we get back. After passing by about ten more shops, we cross the busy street and go in to a store that has a display of Indian clothing in the front window. I admire all the stacks of materials piled up on the shelves along the walls. It looks like dohti's and sarees and shirts of all kinds are sold here. Brandon leads me through some display racks in the middle of the store until reaching one with white dohti's hanging from it.

"This is a traditional dohti," he says as he lifts one off the rack and holds it in front of him as if to model it for me. "How tall is your uncle?"

"Well, I think he is about six feet tall." I reach out and run my hands over the silk smooth dohti. "But I think he will look funny wearing this with his brown and tan cowboy boots. I never see him wear any other shoes. He might even shower while wearing them. I should ask my aunt."

"That's funny. You're joking, right?" Brandon says with a short burst of laughter.

"Nope."

"Oh, well let's get him this one. You can always get your aunt to hem up the bottom for him, or do what we do, just pick up the bottom of it and have him tuck it in to his waist band. I think white matches everything, so I wouldn't worry about the cowboy boots."

We head over to the checkout counter and Brandon insists on paying. I let him. The nice Indian man behind the register puts my uncle's new dohti in to a brown paper bag and Brandon puts it in to his small black back pack. I say thanks to him and the store clerk and we head back outside. We pass by what looks like a beautiful church of some kind. It has a sand colored exterior and after straining to look up I notice two pyramid looking structures on top of the roof giving it a unique profile.

"What's this building called?" I ask Brandon as we continue walking down Jacob Road going by what the faded street sign says.

"That is Santa Cruz Basilica. I am going to take you to my cousin's Malayalam cultural center. I think you will like it. I come down here and train in kalarippayat when I can. We put on shows for locals and tourists. Sometimes it is the best when we can get a tourist to join in."

"I am not sure I like the smirk on your face. What do you have planned for me?"

"Maybe a little bit of kathakali, but first we have to get you painted," he says with a prolonged snicker.

We make a left after leaving the clothing shop and continue walking away from the Land Rover. Brandon leads the way down the street until we reach another intersection. We cross the street to the opposite sidewalk and turn left. It looks like there are some stand-alone buildings on this road; not the joined together two story types that I was getting used to seeing. As we continue down the street, I happen to glance at a small blue car driving toward us. I instinctively squeeze Brandon's hand and with my other hand I reach up and grab my tiger necklace.

"What's wrong Lily?"

"That car. It's blue like the one I think was at the clinics. The same one I saw a guy get in to at the airport who was with the nice lady in the cave." The car continues past us. It looks like a family of fifteen is crammed in the front and back seats. I turn and watch it until it disappears at the end of the street from where we just came.

"It is ok. You're with me. I won't let anything happen to you. I think if there was a bad guy left, he is long gone after losing his whole squad of goons."

"I know you are right Brandon, but I think it will be on my mind for a long time." I release my death grip on his hand.

"That's why we are here." He turns the other direction and points to a light orange two story building trimmed with wooden columns forming spirals on both outside corners. "This is my cousin's cultural center."

"I know. We need to get our minds off of the past two days. I thank you for that."

Brandon leads me up to the large brown wooden door and pulls on a thick braided rope. I actually hear a bell chime from inside.

"I like the door bell," I say with light banter in my voice.

"I will let you pull the rope next time," Brandon replies with a smile.

The large door opens and we are greeted by a strikingly beautiful woman around my height with jet black straight hair parted in the middle and resting past her shoulders.

"Welcome. Come in," she says with almost perfect English.

"Hi Meera. This is Lily." Brandon points to me as she extends her hand to me. "And Lily, this is my cousin Meera."

"Nice to meet you Meera," I say as we shake hands. She looks to be around twenty-five and stunning like the rest of Brandon's family.

"Hi Lily. Brandon told me all about you. Follow me. The others are getting ready."

Meera leads us to what looks like a reception area decorated with Indian paintings on the walls and wood carvings of what I think might be Hindu gods standing in the corners. There is a solid wooden counter in front of us about five feet long and four feet high. A single lamp on the counter is providing the only light. A wood paneled wall is behind the counter. Off to the right and left sides of the counter are open doorways leading to another room. Meera leads us around through the entrance on the right. She stops and bows before entering the next area. Brandon does the same and I mimic their bows the best that I can. The three of us enter a larger open area that looks like a small arena. Maybe forty feet long and twenty feet wide. There are two Indian guys doing what I know now to be kalarippayat. Both are only dressed in white baggy pants stopping at their knees and a red sash tied around their waist. No shoes and no shirts. They are both muscular and ripped with maybe a 2% body fat. Wow! They stop after seeing us enter and walk over to greet us. A small trail of sweat follows on the teak colored wood plank floor.

I try not to stare and continue looking at the rest of the arena. Directly to the front of us at the opposite end from where we are standing is an elevated stage the same width as the arena. There are a set of stairs in the right corner leading up to the stage. On top of the stage and to the rear and centered is what looks like a small altar or a wood bench seat of some type. Above that is a small angled thatched roof supported by two wooden posts in the front and attached to the back wall of the arena in the rear. The wood is a bit darker than the shiny teak colored floor. I look up to see a second floor balcony just above the stage on the right side extending all the way around the arena in a horse shoe shape to the left side of the stage. There is a small wood wall in front of the chairs to keep observers from falling in to the arena, I assume. Back on the ground floor that we are standing on; I can see about four sconce lights along the left and right side walls. They seem to be giving off a soft yellow glow because they are not very bright. It feels comfortable and informal in here yet I can sense a sort of discipline in the air probably when training.

"Lily these are my brothers, Bansi and Bali, Brandon's better looking cousins," says Meera playfully as the one pointed out as Bali grabs Brandon and trips him to the floor, falling next to him.

"Getting sloppy cousin," says Bansi as he helps Brandon up while Bali is laughing on the floor. "Pleasure to meet you Lily."

"Nice to meet you too," I shake hands with Bansi as Bali gets back to his feet.

"Nice to meet you Lily," says Bali as I shake his hand. "Our sisters and other brother are expecting you.

"Oh. There are more of you?" I ask.

"Yes we will teach you an Indian dance from kathakali, but first we have to get your makeup put on and we have a costume for you."

"Thanks Bali. It sounds fun," I say not knowing what to expect, but enjoying the idea of taking my mind off of other things. "What exactly is this place?" I ask.

"This place started out as a training center for kalarippayat many many years ago and still is. That is why we bow when entering the training floor," explains Brandon. "Over time our relatives incorporated ancient and traditional Malayalam theater called kathakali which involves dance, music, makeup, and generally tells a story based on Hindu mythology. It was a way to get the word out to the common masses. Because a lot of the people did not speak Sanskrit, which was the original language kathakali was performed in, the dances use gestures that everyone can understand," Brandon explains.

"What's my role going to be?" I ask anxiously.

"You are going to follow Meera through that door behind you and I am going to the door behind me to let's just say: get ready for the performance."

"I hope there is no audience coming to watch," I say.

"You will be wonderful Lily," replies Meera.

"See you in a little while," says Brandon as Bali and Bansi grab his arms and lead him over to the door in the wall across from where Meera is taking me.

Meera leads me to the door, opens it, and I follow her in to another room. This one is smaller with a table running along one wall and a mirror hanging above it which is being shared by two females in makeup and elaborate dress. Their faces are lit by the six large round light bulbs sticking out of the wall in a horizontal row above the mirror.

"Hello this is Lily, Brandon's friend from America," says Meera as the two girls turn around.

"Hello Lily. I am Parvani and this is my sister Kriti," Parvani says while standing up and extending her hand. I return the hand shake and do the same with Kriti.

"Nice to meet both of you," I say as I scan over the makeup supplies lying across the table.

"Are you ready?" asks Meera. "Have a seat in the chair and we will get you changed for your performance."

"Yes. Ok. Brandon didn't tell me too much about what I would be doing."

"Don't worry. Brandon just said to make your last day in India a memorable one," says Kriti with a big grin showing through the white makeup on her face. It has been so far I say to myself.

Parvani has me pull my hair back and out of the way of my face. She then takes a cloth and applies a clear cream to my face and explains it is to keep the skin soft and protect it from a rash or anything that might develop from the makeup after it is removed. Next she takes a makeup brush and applies a yellow paint covering my entire face. She adds thick black lines around both eyes and extends them toward my ears making it almost look like I am wearing a mask. After that, using a smaller makeup brush, she applies red paint to my lips, but spreads it past the edges making them appear larger. Then she adds the red paint below my eyebrows and on my eye lids. Next she takes the black paint again and puts a heavy thick line covering both of my eyebrows. She completes the look by adding a red tear shaped mark in the middle of my forehead.

"What do you think Lily?" I look at myself in the mirror trying to find an answer.

"I like it. I can't wait to see the finished product."

They all look at me and smile not knowing if what I said was good or bad, I'm sure. Kriti goes to a closet behind us and retrieves some kind of costume from it. It looks like an oversized white dress with red and gold trim around the bottom and waist line. This is getting interesting. I stand up and slip it on. I look in to the mirror one more time and get ready to walk back out to the arena area. Kriti stops me.

"Wait, we have one more thing," she says as she retrieves an elaborate looking white and red head dress with a black wig attached from a shelf next to us.

"Sorry."

"This piece is for your head."

She takes the head dress and places it on top of my head. The edge rests just above my new eyebrows and the long black wig drapes over all my hair, so no blonde is showing. Finally she takes two large yellow ears and attaches them to the sides of my face with some kind of sticky adhesive so that I can't see my real ears.

"Perfect. All done. Let's go see how the boys are doing," says Meera.

"Great. I love it. Can you take some pictures for me?" I ask as I fumble with my hands trying to retrieve my camera from my pack while I try to figure out who I am supposed to be.

"Yes. Of course. You are now a princess which usually has a yellow face. Brandon will be wearing green face paint because he is your prince. So, now we will have a small demonstration of kathakali," says Parvani on que as if she had just read my thoughts. She teaches me what I am supposed to do.

"Sounds fantastic to me. I really appreciate y'all doing this for me," I say wondering if they literally meant Brandon is my prince for real.

We head back out the door we came in and end up in the arena. I try not to trip over my new dress which is covering all of my feet. I reach down to pick the front of it up to try to help me walk better. When I look back up, my attention is immediately drawn to the stage. A large green man is sitting on one of the chairs in the middle of the stage. Well, at least his face is painted green. As, I get closer to him, I can make out black paint around both eyes joined like a mask and an extra amount of red paint on his lips and a touch of it on his forehead. He has a large head dress also, but it is more exuberant than mine covered in gold, black, red, and green colors. He seems to be wearing some sort of gown, but it appears masculine not feminine. The base of it extends wildly out to the sides. Yep, we definitely look like gods of some sort. That's for sure. I can't keep from smiling as I approach him. His cousins have the same attire on that they were wearing earlier except they are wearing a red vest and now they are sitting on the floor in the corner of the arena holding what looks like some kind of fancy wooden guitar and drums that look like bongo's. I guess that they must be the band. I feel a little nervous as Brandon stands up and meets me at the top of the stairs. Kriti and Parvani each take one of my hands and help me up the steps.

"You look beautiful Lily," says Brandon through the makeup.

"Thank you. So do you," I reply trying to be respectful and keep from giggling just a bit.

"Ok. Well, basically I will move around you and perform a piece from one of our Indian mythological stories about a prince admiring his new bride for the first time. Bali and Bansi will be playing the veenas and sitars, guitar looking instruments, and Balavan, my other cousin who just arrived, will be playing the drums.

"Nice to meet you Lily," says Balavan.

"Nice to meet you too," I say as Brandon takes my hand and leads me to the wood bench seat under the thatched roof and has me sit down. I try not to trip or fall in my new cumbersome attire. Brandon's is a lot bigger than mine, but I can tell he has worn his costume before. It seems to have more gold and red on the front and back. Meera takes my camera and snaps some pictures for my scrap book. Kriti and Parvani are not dressed as wildly as Brandon and I am, yet they still look impressive. They explained that they dress like this on most days for the performances and teachings they do while working at the cultural center. Kriti is wearing what looks like a one piece sari. Snug at the top, but a little looser around the bottom by her feet. It is turquoise and yellow with a red sash that she has draped across her left shoulder and joined at her right hip. Her black hair is pulled back and tied in what we would call a bun on the top of her head. She has a small gold band just above her forehead holding her hair flat. She has several gold necklaces around her neck coming to rest on her upper chest and bracelets on both wrists. Parvani is wearing something similar except her sari is mostly maroon with a gold sash which happens to be inlaid with a striped pattern done in silver. Her hair is done up the same way as Kriti's except her gold band on her head looks more like a small crown rising up only about two inches. The white makeup on their faces is done lightly and almost unnoticeable. Their eyes are heavily accentuated with black makeup, or what we would say in Alabama: a little *extra* eyeliner. Bright red lipstick tracing the outline of their lips, unlike Brandon's and mine, and small ruby like jewels on their foreheads and sides of their noses, complete the look.

The band starts playing as Kriti starts to sing in Malayalam, I think. Brandon begins to move around the stage as if he was performing for a sold out concert. To the left. To the right. Spins around. Making gestures with both arms and hands. The twang from the funny shaped wooden guitars, with the very long neck on them, resonates through the arena. Bali and Bansi keep plucking away at the strings. The bottom of the guitars, or veena's like I was told, rests on the floor. Bali and Bansi are sitting beside them and reach high up on the neck of the instrument with one hand and continue to pluck the bottom with the other hand. Balavan establishes a beat with the bongo looking drums sitting in front of his crossed legs. Meera takes some more pictures of the performance and then gives a condensed translation of Kriti's singing.

"Lily, Kriti is basically telling the audience about the way Brandon found his true love and that his true love is going to take his hand in marriage to be his princess."

I try to speak, but realize that some of the makeup has made my lips stick together. I struggle to separate them, but nothing. I nod my head to let her know that I understand what she said and then go back to trying to get my mouth open. Brandon continues for about another ten minutes until he takes my right hand and stands me up. He pulls me close to him, well as close as the costumes will let us and then kneels down before me making himself look like some sort of upside down colorful mushroom stuck on the floor. Kriti raises her voice louder and the band follows suit and then stops all of a sudden. Everyone is quiet.

"Lily," says Meera. "He wants to know if you will marry him and be his princess."

My lips tug at one another until separated just enough to squeak out a muffled, "yes."

I think all of his cousin's chuckle at the same time realizing what happened. The band picks up the pace as Brandon stands up and begins to spin wildly around the stage. I follow his hand gestures as instructed by his cousins. Both arms down with my hands bent at a ninety degree angle at the wrists. Both hands to my right. Both to the left. I then simulate a wide circle with my arms. I repeat my part several more times while Brandon pretends to react to it. Brandon then has me walk around what would be a fire on the floor seven times. He slows to a stop in front of me and takes my hand again and leads me to the wood bench seat under the thatched roof and sits me down. He stands in front of me, takes off a gold necklace and places it around my neck, bows to me, and then takes a seat beside me. The music stops and everyone claps. That was intense.

"What did you think?" Brandon says while trying to catch his breath. I can see perspiration oozing from beneath his green forehead.

"I loved it. Kriti is an amazing singer and you are quite the dancer. Do you do windows too?"

"Sure, if we had some," he says laughing.

"Then you are a keeper."

"Well anyway, that is kind of a condensed version of a prince from long ago who unexpectedly finds his princess. The performance is about another hour in length, but since I think there are a few more things that I want to show you, I cut it short. Let's get out of our costumes and swing by the hospital to see how Ludwik and Kenneth are doing."

"You were wonderful. Everyone was wonderful. Thank you," I say as I get the rest of my mouth unstuck hoping my lips are still intact. Meera gives me the black wig as a gift to remember the occasion by.

"What did you glue my ears on with?"

"Spirit gum," she replies hugging one last time.

CHAPTER XXVII

After getting changed, cleaned up, and saying goodbyes, we head back outside in to the warmth of the Indian sun. I snap a few pics of the cultural center and we head back up the street toward where we left the car. I spot what looks like a small souvenir stand on the way with sunglasses for sale and pick out some cheap oversized white framed glasses with black tinted lenses.

We make it back to where Brandon parked the Land Rover and he looks surprised to see it still in the parking spot.

"Hey look," says Brandon as he points up ahead. "They left the car, so I guess we don't have to walk to Lakeshore Hospital."

"That's good news Brandon." We reach the vehicle and Brandon unlocks my door. I wait a second to let the heat from the bright sun escape from the Land Rover and then climb in. We head off to see our friends.

"It shouldn't take too long to get to the hospital," says Brandon.

"Ok. I just wanted to tell you thanks for everything so far. I have never quite had an experience like this before. Thank you."

"You are very welcome. I have never experienced anyone like you before, so I think we are even." He holds my left hand and glances at me for only a second not wanting to wreck one of the few running Land Rovers in the heavy traffic. "The hospital is about another three miles from here."

About a half an hour goes by when Brandon finally turns on to a small paved road flanked by green trees on both sides. We pass under an unassuming archway that has Lakeshore Hospital written on it. As we round a corner an unexpectedly large white building comes in to view. It must be at least ten stories high. The front is dotted by small rectangular windows aligned symmetrically floor by floor. On the second or third floor directly in front of us, is a round, almost flying saucer looking part of the hospital jettisoning from out of the front façade of the hospital. I notice a large blue Lakeshore Hospital sign on the top of the roof. There is a row of continuous tinted glass windows wrapping around the bottom floors of the building.

"Wow! I did not expect anything like this. It looks more modern than the two hospitals back home in Dothan."

"Where?"

"Sorry. The big city nearest to where I am from."

"Oh. Right. Yes. Not everything around here has a roof made from tree branches. Come on," says Brandon while smiling at the same time.

I get out and Brandon leads me to the entrance. We go inside to find what looks more like the lobby and check-in desk of a five star hotel than the information desk of a hospital. Brandon walks over to the counter, says hello, and gets the room numbers that we need. I can't help admire the size and the cleanliness of the waiting area. Nobody looks angry. The pleasant well-dressed lady at the counter directs us to the elevator. We exit the elevator and turn left like the lady told us to when we see the nurse's station and eventually find Kenneth and Ludwik in the same room. Brandon knocks and enters the hospital room. I follow not knowing what to expect.

"Hey there slackers!" Brandon says a bit too loudly. Ally who is sitting in a chair facing the windows spins around. "It is too nice to be cooped up in here all day. Lily and I are going to smuggle you two out inside a dirty linen cart. It's the only one we could find." Brandon laughs as he shakes Kenneth's hand and then heads to the bed by the window and shakes Ludwik's hand.

"Dirty linen?" responds Kenneth. "No thanks. I will stay here. Have you seen what my roommate does to his linen despite the ten sponge baths since he was admitted with that scratch on his leg."

"After a day with Kenneth, I will take you up on your offer," says Ludwik.

"Hey y'all. I thought ya was going for the day," says Ally.

"No way. We did some running around, but had to come see how our guys were doing," I say as I glance at the thick white cast on Ludwik's left leg protruding out from underneath the peach colored blanket. There is some kind of shiny metal contraption connected to the cast with pins or bolts. It runs the length of his cast toward his bare foot. There is a small sand bag dangling from the end and resting near the floor, but not touching it. Oh, I think it is called a traction device to keep the bone aligned. Red, white, green, and black wires stick out from under his hospital gown and the end is connected to a small heart monitor mounted on the wall above him letting off the occasional beep when he tries to adjust his position. There is an IV running in to his right hand infusing clear fluid from the bag of fluid hanging from the ceiling on an IV hanger. Otherwise he looks good and I am glad to see him.

Kenneth looks good too. His face is less swollen. His arm is in a green sling lying across his chest. It appears bandaged near his shoulder and ends just pass his elbow. His hand looks bruised judging by the black-purple colors. An IV catheter is in his other hand, but he doesn't have any fluids running. He is wearing the same kind of un-manly flowery hospital gown like Ludwik's. He has his legs covered by the same kind of peach colored blanket. Ally is holding his hand on his good arm.

"Hey tell my roommate, that if he drops his blanket on the floor one more time, I am going to request a room change. Please, will someone get him some underwear?" Kenneth says simulating pressing his call bell.

"Where is everyone?" I ask having expected to see the rest of the volunteers here.

"We told them to go shopping and see some of India before they left. There was no point in staying here with us. I am good. I can get up and use the toilet and Ludwik, well he has a nice nurse today," Kenneth adds while Ludwik laughs.

"I see. So when do you and Ludwik expect to get out of here and head home?"

"Well, Lily I think I will be here another day or two," Kenneth says.

"It will be at least a week, maybe two before I can go. At least that is what the doctor said. Gala and Petra said they will help me with the trip home since they are kind of like neighbors," says Ludwik. "Hey why don't you two take off for the rest of the day. Enjoy India. There is no need to waste it here stuck inside with us. I have the best nurse and if they are busy, well then Kenneth can empty my bedpan."

"No way! This guy eats to much bratwurst!" Kenneth protests.

"Ally, why don't you go with them and see some sites."

"Not a chance Kenneth. I am staying here until the last minute."

"I really appreciate it Ally," says Kenneth as he pulls Ally closer for a kiss on her cheek.

"Are you guys really sure? Do you want us to get you anything?" Brandon offers.

"No really. Go," Ludwik says.

"You two take care of yourselves," I say. It was really nice to have met and worked with the both of you." I turn toward the door.

"Hey," says Ludwik.

"Yes," I answer.

"Thanks again for saving our arses as my roommate likes to say."

"You are very welcome. Get well soon."

"Lily baby, I will see ya back at the house later," says Ally.

"Ok. Bye."

"Bye Brandon."

"We will see you tonight Ally. See you later Kenneth, Ludwik," Brandon says as he shakes both of their hands.

Brandon and I head out of the hospital and back to the car. I can't help feeling somewhat depressed for what happened to Kenneth and Ludwik and the fact that they have to stay in the hospital. I hope to see both of them in the future when they are healed up. It is mid-afternoon and I start to wonder where Brandon is taking me next. It really doesn't matter as long as we are together. I know the time is passing by faster than I want it to.

CHAPTER XXVIII

"Are you up for that boat ride?" says Brandon catching me off guard a bit.

"You mean like a ferry ride except this time to a secluded island?"

"Well not exactly, but kind of."

"Sure. Wherever you want to take me is fine with me. You know that, but I thought you were joking about a boat ride."

"Nope. Ok. We are heading to Alappuzha. Italy has Venice and this is our version. Lots of waterways, canals and such. I have reserved a..." he hesitates for a moment. "Well, a boat to take us around."

"Why do you say 'boat' like that?"

"They actually used to be like barges transporting rice and other things on the backwaters of Kerala, but now some are more like houseboats. I hope you will find it interesting."

"Absolutely. I am with you. Keep leading the way."

"Alappuzha isn't too far, so sit back and enjoy the ride," Brandon says sarcastically.

We continue through the traffic filled streets. The horns blowing as usual. I turn up the Red FM on the radio. Rickshaws darting at us from all directions, at least it seems that way. Swerving around the big red and yellow buses with KSRTC written across the front. It must be the local transit system. I've seen enough of them so far today that I don't bother asking. I still can't tell how the ladies keep from falling off of the motorcycles while riding side saddle. Brandon continues driving and I don't want to distract him with my silly questions. He eventually gets back on to highway 47 and heads south again in the same direction we went when he took me for my sari near Trivandrum. We travel for about another hour.

It isn't much longer until I see some water, a river I think. Brandon heads for another parking area and brings the Land Rover to a stop.

"Well we are here. Welcome to the Alappuzha. I am going to that building right there," he points to a small white single story structure that has a big sign on the roof reading Backwater Cruises in both English and Malayalam.

"I will wait here and enjoy the scenery." I glance at a bunch of funny, but interesting looking boats tied up to the docks. Most of them have a dark, almost black, bottom which looks like wood. The front comes together in a little point. Right behind that appears to be a seat and wheel from which I assume the boat captain must sit and pilot the boat. But, the most interesting part is a large light brown wall that seems to come up from one side of the boat, extends upward to maybe a second deck, and then ends up on the other side forming a complete roof. It looks like it is made from interwoven bamboo straps or something similar. The boat itself must be a good fifty feet long and the roof runs almost the whole length of it except for where the captain sits. I can see some crew members moving about on most of the boats getting ready to leave with tourists. Brandon returns.

"Hey these are pretty neat looking. So they used to be rice barges, but now used more as houseboats for tours of the backwaters?"

"Yes. You are catching on and ours is right there," Brandon says as he points to the boat in front of us that I was just admiring.

"No way!" I yell probably a bit too loud again. "Where are the rest of the passengers?"

"It is just you and I," he finishes grabbing our stuff from the car, locks up, and leads me to our boat.

"Wow. Really amazing. Thank you."

"You are very welcome. They serve dinner on the boat and you can even go on an all night cruise. They have beds. I booked us for a dinner cruise so that I can get you back to your parents before sun-up," he says humorously.

"Dinner on a boat sounds great," I say as one of the crew members helps me climb aboard. He is a nice looking gentleman dressed in a crisp white long sleeve button down shirt with even a crisper white dohti covering his legs.

"These are actually called kettuvalloms which means houseboat in Malayalam," Brandon explains as he follows me and climbs on board.

We walk down the middle of the boat and I can see a small kitchen and several bedrooms. There are large square windows covered with bamboo like shutters that can be propped open if needed. We reach a small set of stairs and the other gentleman with a bushy thick black mustache is standing by them. Brandon says hello to him and introduces me in Malayalam. He extends his hand.

"Welcome aboard Lily. You sit back and enjoy the trip. Beautiful weather," he says as he gestures with his left hand pointing it to the front of the boat.

"Nice to meet you," I offer as I return the hand shake.

"We are headed up, the half ladder, half stairs, here to the upper deck," Brandon says.

"Ok." We climb the stairs and I can see a nice comfortable looking wooden seat that looks like it should be in a park somewhere. It is the kind with open slats across the back rest and the seat. It is facing the front of the boat for maximum viewing and sightseeing. There is a wooden railing just in front of the seat. I walk over to the edge of it and look down to see the captain just starting the motor making a quiet rumbling coming from the rear of the boat. And to my right I watch as the other crew member pulls the ramp, that we used to get on the kettuvallom with, on to the bottom deck. The lines are already untied and we slowly drift away from the dock. The captain heads toward the sun which must be south and slightly west of us by now, giving the time of day. We leave the dock area and the other boats and before long, head into a narrow portion of what looks more like a canal than river. The captain makes a hard left turn, almost ninety degrees I would say judging by the angle, and continues on. After a couple of hundred yards, he makes a right turn which also looks like a right angle. The other crew member appears and hands us each a glass of juice and then disappears.

"This is phenomenal Brandon. It must cost a fortune. Can I help pay for it?" I ask feeling bad.

"Not a chance. My treat. I am just happy you are here with me," he says as he takes my hand. "We have a few more turns coming up and then the water opens up and the turns aren't as harsh."

"I love it. I have to get some pictures." I retrieve my camera and take some pics of Brandon sitting on the seat and then standing next to the railing. I couldn't have asked for a better back drop. Wide open waterways flanked on either side by palm trees and vegetation in ten different shades of green. At some points it is so thick that I cannot see beyond the jungle. At other points I can see fields, farms, and crops. The occasional house pokes through the greenery. Some look more newer than others, but I can't imagine taking a boat every day to get home. Some have thatched roofs and others look tiled. The captain continues navigating through the backwaters passing by other kettuvalloms in the process. All different sizes with differently styled roofs. Smaller boats, of various types, mostly being paddled by hand, drift past us going the other way. The other crew member appears again with a serving tray filled with fresh fruit. We sit down.

"The main course will be here shortly," says Brandon. "We eat it for lunch a lot, but I thought it would be a better dinner for us."

"I think you know by now that I am easy to please. I am in to whatever you are," I say while continuing to take in the scenery and Brandon. About another thirty minutes passes until our chef returns. This time he has a larger serving tray in his hands leaving me spellbound as to how he climbed up the ladder. Brandon takes a table from the side of the deck and places it in front of us. The chef places what I think are metal plates down in front of us, to my surprise. I was expecting green paper place mats. He then sets down several other dishes of what look like rice, vegetables, and some things I have not seen before. He has more beverages for us and fills our glasses again. Brandon and I thank him and he goes back down the ladder again. The sun is behind us now and I figure we must be heading east.

"This food looks incredible. I was..." Brandon interrupts.

"Paper plates, right?" he says while laughing.

"Well, yeah, maybe. I'm sorry."

"No need to apologize. I can request them for you."

"No. That's ok," as I look at all of the food trying to figure out how to eat it. Brandon spots my befuddled gaze.

"This dish is called thali. It basically refers to the metal plate. What we do is put the banana leaf down first, then some water over that. We then put a bunch of rice on top of it. Next we add dhal, or lentils, both yellow and soupy which are called sambar. Plus some mixed vegetables, some people like them fried, but I eat the healthy steamed ones. Mix all this up together or one of the side dishes with the rice and eat."

"Thanks for the instruction," Brandon says as I watch him roll the mixture into little bite size balls of food. I follow expecting to squish the ball and drop it into the water for fish food, but to my surprise, manage to eat several as Brandon looks on with some amusement, I'm sure. He lets out a small laugh.

"Very good. When you are done with that, these things here," he points to some kind of fried dish that looks delicious, but not to healthy, "are called aloo tikka, or fried mashed potatoes." He laughs again, but louder this time.

"But you said..."

"Hey, every now and then I cheat on the diet."

"I admire your will-power any ways," I say smiling back at him. "Excuse me for just one second."

"Sure thing."

The captain continues the trip and feeling concerned, I stand up and look down to see that he is eating and our chef has pulled up a chair beside him and is also eating. I return to my seat.

"I was worried that they didn't get to eat, but it looks like they are doing very well."

"They are fine. We will be coming up on the halfway point shortly. By the time we get back to the car and make the drive to my house, it will be dark. Maybe nine or ten o'clock."

"That's ok Brandon. Don't worry about keeping me out to late," I say reassuringly. "I can sleep on the flight to Italy."

We continue our lazy backwater cruise. Brandon looks as depressed as I feel, but he is doing his best not to show it. The day is ticking away and I continue to take in as much of India as I can not knowing if I will ever get back here again. Somehow I will see Brandon after I leave here in the morning; I just haven't figured out when or how. Maybe I can go to school in Europe to be closer to him. Anyway, I decide to try to relax the best that I can. I let my hair down and try to fluff it up a bit by running my fingers through the tangled ends. I thought it would dangle somewhat, but the boat is going just fast enough to create a breeze making my hair wave around. I catch Brandon checking me out, I think. His eyes focus back toward the water. I wonder if he likes my hair down or pulled back? He begins to talk as if he just read my mind.

"I like your hair down. It is flowing nicely in the wind," he says while trying not to stare at me.

"Thank you. You can look at me if you want to."

"I do. It is a little different here. I didn't want you to think I was rude or anything like that."

"Never would I think that of you. Would the Captain mind if we stood up by the front of the boat?" I ask.

"No I don't think he would. Come on," Brandon says as he stands up and extends his hand out. I take his hand and we walk the few feet to the railing. He puts his arm around me pulling me next to him firmly. We watch the water rippling past on either side of the boat. We head through a wide section almost the size of a small lake. The Captain keeps the boat toward the right side as a couple more small two or three person boats travel past our left side going the other way. The lake edge is curved and after several minutes the Captain completes his right turn and we are now facing the sun. It is brilliant orange, but it is sitting low in the sky, very low. It appears to be only inches off of the horizon meaning the day is almost over.

"It is beautiful Brandon," I gush out.

"A beautiful sunset for a beautiful person," he says while he steps behind me with his right foot and wraps both arms around my waist. His face is next to mine with his chin almost resting on my left shoulder. Our ears are almost touching.

"Hey you tricked me."

"Why do you say that?"

"Well because I did not know this would be a sunset cruise." I reach up and place my hands in front of me resting them on top of Brandon's. "Any more beautiful surprises for me?"

"Nope. Fresh out. I was just hoping you would like it."

"I love it. I love you. It is absolutely breathtaking, like you."

"Thank you. I just wanted you to remember this forever," he says as he leans his face forward. I turn toward him until our lips make contact. We kiss softly for what seems like several minutes neither of us letting go of our grip on one another. We finally stop and watch the sun start to disappear below the horizon. The sounds of the boat breaking through the shallow waves in the water adds to the serenity of the moment. I never would have dreamed of a moment like this. We just continue standing there as the Captain continues to navigate his way back to the dock. About another hour passes by while the green vegetation on the canal banks turn from green to black in the darkening sky. The sun has been replaced by the moon reflecting off of the mirror like water. Eventually our starting point comes in to view. The dock and parking area is lit up by soft street lamps. The Captain brings the kettuvallom to a stop alongside the dock and turns off the motor. We make our way down the stairs, past the kitchen and bedrooms, and to the ramp leading off of the boat to the dock. The Captain and his one man crew are waiting for us.

"Thank you so much for an amazing cruise," I say while shaking their hands. They thank me in English and they ask Brandon something in Malayalam. He answers them in Malayalam, but thanks them for the cruise in English. I just nod and smile naively. We walk up the ramp and head toward the car.

"What did the Captain say to you?"

"They were both wondering where you got your cheap looking tiger necklace, asked if it was a gift from me, and told me that they thought I could find you a better one."

"What did you say?" I ask as I look down to see my Panthera necklace dangling on the outside of my shirt. I quickly take it and drop it on the inside of my shirt letting it rest against my chest trying to keep it from plain sight.

"I said your necklace was from a cheap souvenir stand in Delhi, possibly made in China." He laughs as we reach the car. I hug him one more time and climb in. Brandon shuts my door, gets in to the driver's side, starts the Land Rover, turns on the headlights, and we drive away. It isn't long before we are back up the coast and heading east again on the very winding highway 49. I can't make out the overly green scenery in the dark, but we pass now familiar towns like Muvattupuzha and continue toward the area near Munnai. We pass by the couple hundred cars heading the other way, at least it seems that way, and reach our turn off. Brandon heads down the paved road for about another half hour before finally reaching the dirt road that his home is on. He makes the turn and continues another couple of hundred feet and then turns left in to the drive way. It looks like the remaining intact Land Rovers are all there. I can see the glow from the tiki torches illuminating the car port and back of the house. I climb out and Brandon retrieves my shopping bags and back pack and we follow the orange glow to the back yard.

We round the corner to find my dad and Singh alone at one of the tables. Each of them has a drink of some kind.

"Hey y'all. Sorry we were gone for so long. How is everyone doing?" I ask as I walk over to my dad and give him a big hug.

"No need to apologize. We were just waiting up for you two to make sure you made it back and didn't runaway together," responds my dad with a quiet laugh.

"Thanks for waiting. Singh, I want to thank you, Jillian, and Pareet, for everything. I have really had a great experience: all things considered."

"You are most welcome. Anytime you want to come back and visit is ok with us. We have enjoyed meeting you in person."

"Dad, what time is wake-up?" Brandon asks.

"Let me see." Singh looks at his watch in the dim light. "It is ten O'clock now. I think we will have to get up at six o'clock. Everyone else is back and in bed I think."

"Ok. Well goodnight dad. Goodnight Doctor Jim. I will escort Lily to her room and see y'all in the morning," replies Brandon as both of our fathers stare at him admiring his new language skills, I'm sure.

"Goodnight y'all?" I say sarcastically as we head in to the house trying not to wake anybody up. The kitchen is empty except for the smell of a recently cooked meal. We pass by a few soft snoring folks in the middle room. Despite there being no lights on, I can see Marco and Valentina sleeping on cots like they were on a camping trip. Brandon follows me up the steps to my room. I slowly open the door so that I don't wake Ally. I peek in to see her sound asleep in the bed closest to the door.

"Well goodnight Lily," Brandon whispers in to my ear. He turns to walk away. I grab his hand and lead him in to the room. We quietly shut the door. I put my shopping bags and back pack down, and pull him over to my bed. He looks surprised, but doesn't say anything. We stand between the window and my bed facing each other in the orange tiki torch moonlight. I slip off my shoes and everything until I am just wearing my shirt and shorts. I climb under the thin blanket holding one end up giving Brandon a cue to join me in case he hasn't figured it out yet. He takes off his shirt, shoes, and pants, leaving on his red and blue striped boxers, cute, and climbs in to bed with me.

"Don't ask. They were a gift," he whispers.

"Not saying a word," I respond trying hard not to make a bigger smile than the one I already have.

We wrap our arms around one another until our chests are touching. I kiss him tenderly on his lips. He reciprocates and we drift off to sleep locked in our embrace.

For some reason I awake. Brandon has his relaxed arm over me. I look at Ally's alarm clock on the night stand between the bed and the green numbers are showing a four, three, and a zero. Ally appears to still be sound to sleep. I can actually hear voices coming from the kitchen. Part of my new found senses I guess. I ever so gently slide out from underneath Brandon's arm. There is a skip in his breathing, but he doesn't awake. I sneak out of the bedroom and tip toe down the stairs until the voices are clearer. I freeze for a minute when I pick up the conversation.

"...yeah. I have no clue either. I mean tigers and the kids didn't get hurt. How the heck did they rescue everyone? I know you said Brandon is good, but those bad guys were pros, AK47's and everything."

"There are some puzzling pieces Jim. Force One never found the cave at the edge of the tea plantation or the pond and waterfall that they described either. Just the two bad guys and the bad girl piled up at the edge of the plantation."

"Yeah. It is confusing. Singh, any word on the ring leader?

"Well Nick, the only thing that Force One found out was that they believed he was working for some military contractor out of North Carolina. Mercenaries, more or less. Whatever you want to call them. It's just a preference of titles. The company supposedly went out of business after their wrongs in Iraq and elsewhere, were exposed. I believe the Colonel said they were even deployed to New Orleans after your Hurricane Katrina. I didn't even know that one. So, what he said is this company which still exists, but under a new name, had an operator working for them that was so secretive that they didn't even know his name. He wouldn't allow his picture to be taken. No fingerprints. Nothing. Paid in cash. The Colonel was able to make contact with the company and all they would say is that this guy was the absolute best that they have ever seen. Best soldier. Run fifty miles with a one hundred pound pack on his back, no problem. Shoot a target with a pistol from three hundred meters away, no problem. Demolitions, the best. Parachuting. Scuba diving. Hand-to-hand combat. Evasive driving.

Mountain climbing. The best. Even speaking many different languages. The most interesting was that he was one of the best hackers they knew of. There wasn't anything that this guy couldn't do. They even thought he once attended a professional special effects makeup school near Pittsburgh Pennsylvania."

"Wow that is really something making me wonder even more how Brandon, Lily, and Ally rescued us. I feel very lucky now."

"I know Jim," Doc Nick says. "Singh, was there anything else about this guy, anything at all? Nationality? Anything?"

"There was one thing that Ludwik thought was interesting. He said some of the attackers moved like they were former KSK, the German special forces. Ludwik served as a communications expert with them at one time," Singh responds. "Truly an international mercenary all-star team, I guess. They thought that the leader went by a nickname according to some of the guys who worked with him."

"What is it?" my dad asks.

"Sapphire."

"Did they say why?"

"Only that it was something about his eyes."

"What? Like he had blue eyes?"

"No Nick."

"I don't understand."

"They thought his eyes were each a different color."

I quietly head back up the steps, enter my bedroom, and retrieve a few things for a shower, then slip over to the bathroom. It must be getting close for everyone who is traveling today to be waking up. While in the shower, I try to contemplate what I just heard. I find it scary. Mr. Handsome could be anywhere. Could look like anyone. How the heck does anybody find him? I just hope he is out of India, seeing how he lost his whole team of sidekicks. I rush through the shower and return to the bedroom. Brandon is gone. I can see light protruding from under his closed bedroom door at the end of the hallway. The alarm clock is making its annoying beeping sounds and Ally is swatting at it to no avail. I walk over and give the clock a good whack to quiet it.

"Thank you," says a groggy Ally. "What the heck time is it?"

"It is five o'clock. Waky waky sweetheart sugar pie."

"I'm up." She slowly sits up and slides her feet out from under the blanket. "Did you have a good time after y'all left the hospital?"

"Yep, Brandon took me for a river cruise on a houseboat. It was really neat. I have a bunch of pictures from all the stuff we did. You can look at them when you want to," I say feeling bad about Ally's beau being cooped up in the hospital.

"Great. I will check them out on the flight. Shower time. I'm packed, so I guess I will see you downstairs." She gets out of bed and stretches her arms over her head. "You and Brandon do anything else?"

"Nope."

"Yeah ok Lily doll," she laughs as she leaves for the bathroom.

I finish packing all of my things up, make the beds, and try to make the bedroom as presentable as it was when we got here. I grab my duffel and carry-on back pack along with some of the shopping bags, and head back downstairs. I try to remember to look surprised to see everyone and pretend I didn't overhear their conversation a little while ago. I enter the kitchen.

"Hey y'all. Good morning."

"Good morning Miss Lily. How did you sleep?" says Jillian.

"Great. Thanks for everything."

"Oh, you are welcome. Please come back anytime you want. Our door is always open for you. Matter of fact, I think it is always open any ways." She draws a laugh from the men in the kitchen.

"I will definitely do that. Right dad?"

"Yes Lily. We will return."

"How was your day with Brandon?"

"It was wonderful Miss Jillian."

"There is really a lot to see and do here. It wasn't hard for Singh to convince me to move to India with him. Grab some food. I think we will be leaving in about thirty minutes."

"I agree. I can see why," I say as I help myself to some tea and fruit from the table. Eventually Ally and Brandon come down to the kitchen. Pareet, my mama, and Miss Carilyn, along with Valentina and Marco, round out our travelers this morning. I say goodbye to Laney, Moira, and the rest of the volunteers and head to the Land Rover.

We load up two of the cars and head off to the airport. Back across curvy highway 49 for the last time, at least on this trip. It takes us a couple of hours to reach Kochi International Airport north of the actual city by about fifteen miles or so near Nedumbassery. The sun is already bright in the eastern sky. It feels good to have driven through the green hilly country side one last time. The heavy traffic. The colorful people. I'm already missing the elephants. We pull up almost to the exact spot where I saw Mr. Handsome get in to that blue Tata. I flinch for a second and start scanning the crowds of people looking for him. Knowing I am being ridiculous, I snap myself out of it.

We all climb out of the Land Rovers. Brandon and Singh retrieve some luggage carts and we load our bags on to them. It was a good idea to leave the blue medical containers with the Karup's for future use. After checking our bags, we head to the security screening area. I know Brandon can't follow me through because he is not flying. I am already crying inside, but don't show it. The mood is somber, but Singh tries to lighten things up with a few jokes.

"Ok Jethro, you are going to Alabama. I say again A-L-A bama. Don't get off the plane in Dubai. It is the wrong country. What you want to do is keep going a little bit farther to the West. Got it or do I have to write it down for you?"

"No Singh. I think I can find it, but I don't know about Jim the Extraordinary Explorer over here," says Nick as everyone begins to exchange handshakes and hugs.

"Hey you two. Please come back," says Pareet as Ally and I share a group hug with her.

"Absolutely. And anytime you want to come visit, please do. You are always welcome."

"Thanks Lily. I will. Bye."

"Bye bye Pareet, says Ally.

"Remember to look us up when you get to Florence. We will show you around and take you for a ride along on the ambulance with us," says Valentina as she gives me a big hug. Her voice lowers to a whisper, "don't worry about your cat. That secret is safe with me. I didn't even tell Marco."

"Thanks Valentina. I will see you in Florence in two days after we stop in Rome. It is too bad this flight was full or you would be flying with us."

"Remember also that you can take the Leonardo Express from the airport to Rome. It is the slow train. And validate your tickets in the yellow boxes by the train tracks before boarding or it can be a hefty fine."

"Got it. Thanks again. Marco, see you in two days."

"Good Lily. You will enjoy Italy. Arrivederci," he says while hugging me.

Everyone continues with their goodbyes as I grab Brandon and lead him off to the side away from everyone. My mama nods in agreement.

"Brandon, I don't want to sound cliché, but let's not say that 'G' word. Instead, let me say I will see ya soon."

"I will see you soon too." He takes both of my hands in his.

"I love you Lily. I mean that. Be safe and take care of that gift of yours. I don't think it is the last time you will need it. It is my feeling. If you ever just say the word, I will stop whatever I am doing and come to you. I promise. No matter what."

"I know you would. The world isn't as big these days. I will e-mail you when we land. You be safe too. I love you more than anything." We embrace and kiss one last time. I catch Ally out of the corner of my eye snapping our picture.

"One more thing, thank you for saving me and Ally, our folks, and everyone else. I really don't know what I would have done if you weren't there with us."

"I think you would have done all right. Remember, we all had help," he says as he nods to the necklace hidden under my shirt. "No crying; it's not allowed."

"See ya," I barely say in an audible voice.

"See ya too," says Brandon with that big beautiful smile of his.

We all head through the security check point and on to the boarding area. I pass through with no issues. I guess Brandon's nylon cord for my necklace was a better choice than the gold one from him now in my luggage. Only about twenty minutes go by before we board the airplane. I make my way to my seat and sit down next to the window. Ally's idea. The engines start and we get pushed back. As the plane turns to the left, I spot Brandon in the observation area of the khaki colored terminal. His right hand is pressed up against the tinted glass window. I place my left hand against the airplane window. He winks at me which makes me crack a comforting smile that I hope he can see.

CHAPTER XXIX

"It is hard to believe that four days ago I was in India. Now I am staying at the Leonardo Da Vinci Hotel in Milan. Rome was awesome. We did all the touristy stuff: the Vatican Museums, the Pantheon, the Colosseum, Piazza Navona, and the Spanish steps. Walking across the ponte Angelo was cool looking at all the statues on either side. My mama said *Roman Holiday* staring Audrey Hepburn was filmed near there. Trevi fountain was amazing! Ally and I tossed in a coin. I enjoyed it all. We took the fast train up to Florence. That was neat. Almost felt like flying. Nice interior with it almost like being in a restaurant. We had two seats together and a table in front of us with two more seats on the other side facing us. An aisle ran next to us and there were more seats on the opposite side. We all sat together. I absolutely loved Firenze. Valentina and Marco gave us a tour that only the locals know about. Of course we went to the common sites, but then ate at some local ristorante. We were the only tourists. I really loved the Uffizi Museum. Spectacular!! It made me definitely want to study the art history thing even more. We walked over the ponte Vecchio bridge at night time eating pistachio gelato. It came with a little plastic spoon and a miniaturized ice cream cone stuck in the top. The lights on the bridge made the gold in the windows of the jewelry shops sparkle that much more! Michlelangelo's David at the Academia was impressive. I mean the detail down to the toenails was striking and no Ally and I did not snicker at him. The ambulance ride along was great too. We climbed in a little white and orange ambulance that I think might have been a Fiat and ran three calls with Marco and Valentina alternating as the paramedic. The really cool part is that they park their ambulance right next to the Duomo. Literally, right on top of the bell tower practically. You can almost see Ghiberti's bronze doors from the ambulance parking spot. It made it convenient to climb up to the dome of the Duomo. Lots of tourists though with it being August and all. We did some shopping near our hotel by Palazzo Davanzati and then jumped on the fast train up to Milan, or Milano, as the locals call it. Tunnel. Daylight. Tunnel. Daylight. I didn't know if I should keep my sunglasses on or off. So now we are in Milan. We are getting ready to get some breakfast in the dining room and head out for the day. I think we are trying to get to the Duomo which they said you can get up on to the roof for some spectacular views, and then some shopping while we walk over to Castello Sforzesco. Marco even told me there is a soccer, I mean, Football Store behind the Duomo, so I will definitely have to check that out. I saved the best for last. You won't believe it, but my dad and Doctor Nick were able to score some tickets for a soccer game between A.C. Milan and Inter Milan at the San Siro, their stadium! Can you believe it? Marco and Valentina have a Doctor friend in Milan that hooked us up. Anyway, I wish you were here with us. I will e-mail you again when I get a chance. I miss you. I LOVE YOU, Lily" I click on the send button hoping Brandon is waiting for it.

"Hey there doll, you ready?"

"Yep. I am all done Ally. Let's eat and then mama said remember to get the passes for the Metro at the check-in desk." Ally and I finish with the free hotel computers and head off to the dining room.

After eating, the group of us buy our passes from the front desk and head outside. We walk to the end of the parking lot toward some brown apartment buildings and turn right on to the sidewalk. The girl at the front desk said the street is named Via Senigallia. Today we all agreed to take the bus and subway, or Metro as it is called here, back to the Duomo. Last night when we got to Milan, we actually took the surface train to the hotel. It was only about a hundred yards or so from the Bruzzano station. More of just an outdoor train platform than a station. We continue up the sidewalk flanked with tall green hedges to the bus stop. The street is lined with small cars parked along the curb. I almost walk into a lime green garbage can mounted to a pole as we approach a blue car that reminds me of the Tata back in India. On the back I see the brand name Citroen. My heart relaxes. We pass by a few more apartment buildings on our left and a small grassy area that looks like it is a small park maybe for walking dogs and keep going another fifty yards. It looks like some large rust colored office buildings with mostly glass sides are right next to the bus stop. One of the other guests in the hotel even said there was a mini-mart with excellent pizza, and a McDonalds around the corner if we follow the sidewalk around next to the highway. I think the lady was from England. She said it was the closest McDonalds and also advised that the one near the Duomo closed down, but did have a nice view of the Prada store at one time.

It isn't long before we see the big green bus get off the highway and make its way toward us. The big orange LED lights above the driver reads: ZARA. That's our bus. The driver loops the bus with the three axles, including one in the middle making the bus bend in half, around and all six of us climb onboard.

"Dad. You forgot to validate your ticket again," says Ally.

"Thank ya baby. I don't think I will ever get used to the public transportation thing."

"Weren't we supposed to take the number 52 bus? Comasina or something like that?" my dad asks.

"Either one will get us to where we are going, but Comasina takes a couple of minutes longer because it passes through another neighborhood," my mama explains.

One by one we stick our Metro passes in to the yellow box on the pole, the machine clicks a few times, and we pull the tickets out with the date and time stamped on them. We pick a seat in the rear of the bus which is almost empty except for three other people. The driver pulls the bus out, rounds the corner to the right, and makes his way across the highway eventually going left. It is a short ride when the bus turns right again and we begin to head down a city street with buildings and business on both sides. Traffic is heavy, but not anything like India. The female robot bus voice calls out the names of the stops as we approach. "Astesani." "Rossi." We pass by some kebab shops. The bus robot continues. "Stelvio." I peer to my right after seeing the street sign for Valtellina. One building in from the corner I spot the pale grey exterior of the club Alcatraz. Marco and Valentina said that was the last place they went to in Milan to see a concert. I make a mental note to stop there if we have time. I snap a picture from the bus window. "Imbonati." "Carbonari." "Maciachini." That should be our stop.

"We get off here for the Metro," says Carilyn.

"Follow me. I know where we are going," says Doc Nick.

"I doubt it," adds my dad followed by his usual laugh after conversing with Doc Nick.

"Oh boy you two," mama chimes in.

"This way," Ally says as she points to the Metro entrance.

"I feel better following you baby."

"I know you do Lily," she replies.

We head down the several sets of stairs until we reach the turnstiles with the validation slot in the top. After a quick check once again at the signs overhead, we validate our tickets, and continue on to the subway platform. I admire the yellow trim along the walls and ceilings making it almost foolproof to get lost. It only takes several minutes before the next train arrives, the doors open, and we squeeze onboard. The morning rush hour is just about over, but not quite. We peek out of the windows and count down the stops. People get on and off at each stop with what seems like more people heading to the Duomo, which is the next stop. The train slows to a halt. One by one we swiftly climb off on to the platform. I hear a few "scusi's" and "permesso's" as we exit. The girl at the hotel said to use them when getting through the crowds.

The six of us make it off in one piece and find our way up to the outside world once again. As I get to the top of the stairs, my heart flutters, this time for a good reason.

"Ally, that is incredible," I say excitedly.

"That is definitely the Duomo," she responds. "Isn't it amazing?"

We exit the Metro and enter the piazza. It must be the size of a giant soccer pitch, four of them. Concrete instead of grass though. Flanked on two sides by six or seven story tall buildings all joined together in a row resting on arched columns, so it seems. Loads of tourists are moving about in all directions possible. Pigeons are trying to keep pace looking for a handout, I'm sure. I glance to my left to see a green somewhat tarnished statue of a man on top of a horse. On the steps leading up to the statue is a large statue of a Lion reminding me of something. I am not sure which monument that is, but find it kind of neat that there is a giant Ray Ban's sign affixed to the top of a building also in my view making for a nice contrast to the horse and rider. New and old I guess. We keep heading toward the Duomo. Off to my far left I spot the old train station that Valentina told me about. I think it is called the Vittorio Emanuele. There is a huge arched entrance way flanked on both sides with a double set of columns supporting one another. The exterior is like a cream color. I can make out the arched glass ceiling as we pass by. There are several large blue and white police vans parked near the entrance making for a nice show of security making me feel relaxed. The police officers are dressed in dark blue fatigues with dark berets on their heads. We continue on. Carilyn and Ally are taking pictures of the Duomo and piazza. I snap a few for myself. Off to my right is a giant video screen in the corner of the piazza. Probably used for shows I assume. I look back behind us to make out a department store called La Rinascente just like Valentina said. Kind of upscale but worth checking out if we have the time.

I focus my attention back to the Duomo. One of the most gothic structures that I have ever seen. It is supposedly made completely from marble giving it an off-white grayish exterior color. The center dark bronze doors seem to be matched with smaller doors off to both sides of the bottom of the Duomo. There are windows matching the shapes of the doors throughout the face of the structure. The windows look like even they are decorated with rose like sculpting. There is a statue of some kind almost everywhere that I can see covering the Duomo's surface. Especially interesting are the gargoyles. We walk up the set of long steps stretching across the bottom of the Duomo. I head straight for the giant set of arched bronze looking doors in the middle of the Duomo. They seem to be sculpted. The detail is amazing. Biblical things I think. I take some close-up pics.

"Hey, how about a group photo?" my dad asks as he digs his miniature camera tripod out of his corny yet useful black fanny pack. He unfolds the legs and places the tripod with his camera resting on top of it on the ground, sets the timer, and runs to us lined up in front of the bronze doors. I still cannot get over the number of spires jettisoning above the roof of the Duomo.

"Smile!" Doc Nick says. "Run Jim run," he adds for effect.

The camera makes a barely audible click as the flash goes off.

"I think that worked," my dad adds as he retrieves the camera. "Yep. Perfect."

"Great. Now let's get up to the roof of this wonderful building before our time runs out," says my mama referring to the time schedule for tourists.

We head over to the entrance door on the left where it seems everyone else is gathering. There is an Italian paratrooper dressed in green camouflage checking back packs and purses as people enter the Duomo. He has a rifle or machine gun of some kind strapped across his back. I can tell he is a paratrooper by the maroon beret that he is wearing. Dad explained to me once that that is pretty much universal all over the world. Dad even called it the world's biggest fraternity. They take security here very serious; that's for sure. Next to the paratrooper is a sign that has the tourist hours posted. Tourists from English speaking countries can go up on to the roof until noon.

"We are good to go everybody," says Doc Nick. "Elevator around the corner and to the rear of the Duomo."

"What, no steps?" my dad asks sarcastically.

"Honey, you can take the stairs, but the rest of us are taking the elevator," says my mama.

We laugh and head to the left side of the Duomo, walk past another entrance for the Metro, and continue to the back corner where we find the door leading to the elevator. We each get out our Euro's and head inside. A man is waiting to take our money, but explains only three of us will fit in the elevator at one time.

"Carilyn, you can go up with Ally and Lily. I will catch the next one and make sure the boys don't get in to trouble while we wait."

"Ok Abby, but remember they can be sneaky. Keep your eyes on them. We don't need an international incident," Carilyn says as the elevator door opens and the three of us climb onboard with the elevator operator. It is kind of snug inside, but we make it up as high as the elevator will go. The door opens and we step out into a tiny hallway and turn right. We continue on to make room for some tourists going back down on the elevator. As we step back out into daylight; I am in total awe. Everything is marble. We can look to our right over the edge of the Duomo. Spires and statues everywhere making me wonder how the place was built being over five hundred years old. It supposedly wasn't completed until the twentieth century. Wow! I have no clue. Ally and I snap away taking pictures of all the ornate detail. Even the spires have their own decorations that look like exploding flower petals wrapped around in a spiral pattern continuing to the tops of each spire. It isn't long before the elevator returns and my mama, dad, and Doc Nick climb out and catch up with us. We keep walking down the narrow walkway back toward the piazza. We duck under a few low arches and finally reach the steps that we are looking for. We turn left and begin to climb the marble stairs each of which is worn out in the middle of the step from all the foot traffic making everyone's footing tricky. Eventually we reach the roof. Immediately I turn left and follow everybody gazing up at the gold statue affixed atop the tallest spire in the middle above the front of the Duomo.

"Isn't that beautiful?" my mama says.

"Hey there is one of those giant binocular things," says Ally.

"How much is it?" I ask.

"One Euro," says Ally as she retrieves a coin and puts it in the slot and turns the silver handle. She presses her face up against the eye pieces and moves it toward the gold statue. "Wow! Take a look Lily doll."

I walk up to the giant binocular machine and for some reason glance down and see the name VELLARDI embossed on the handle. The machine maker I guess. I peek through the eye pieces and am instantly blown away by the detail of the gold sculpture. Again I try to figure out how they managed to get the statue up there.

"It's the Madonna! She is beautiful," I exclaim.

"I think this placard says it has been up there for two hundred years," says Ally as she reads the small grey metal sign attached to the binoculars.

"Hey another group picture," says my Dad. "Women only Nick."

"Ok. Ok," says Doc Nick as he stands by my dad. "Jim, you join them and I will take the picture."

"Funny one. I would, but I know you will probably just get all of our feet knowing your camera skills."

"Boys, sometime today. We have a game to get to," Carilyn says.

Ally and I stand in the middle with our mom's on the outside of us. We put our arms around each other and wait patiently while my dad gets down on one knee trying to get the Madonna in the back ground of the photo. I know it is tricky because she is quite high up.

"Smile...got it," my dad says as he checks the picture to make sure he got us. "Yep, everyone and the statue."

"Dad set the timer and you and Doc Jim come join us," says Ally.

Doc Nick props the camera up under the giant binoculars and runs over to us just as the camera's red flashing light goes off.

"Let me check," Doc Nick says looking at his camera. "Yep, got it. Can't let that amateur picture taker show me up."

"Hey dad, can you take a pic of me and Lily together?"

"Sure."

Ally and I walk past the giant binoculars and sit on top of what looks like a giant square piece of marble using it for a seat. We throw our arms around one another and face back to the camera.

"Ready dad," says Ally as we crack big smiles hamming it a bit.

"Got it. That should turn out good."

"Thanks dad," Ally replies.

Our parents walk down the length of the roof toward the Madonna. There is a small raised slope section a couple of feet high running the length of the roof. Doc Nick and my dad walk down on top of it, but our moms stay to the sides on the flat parts. The roof is closed off on all sides by sculpted or maybe cast marble fencing, more like walls. There are ornate cutouts through the fence which you can look through to check out the skyline of Milan. The city appears pretty flat. The Duomo is the tallest building from what I can tell, at least nearby anyway. I step closer to one of the cutouts and look down into the piazza. The people look like ants from way up here. I guess the Duomo's roof is not the place to be if you don't like heights. I look back to my right. Supposedly you can see Switzerland from Milan on a clear day. Despite being sunny and clear, there is just enough haze in the sky keeping me from seeing the Alps. I look back toward the piazza and the Ray Ban sign. I can barely make out the roof line of the San Siro breaking up the Milan horizon in that direction. Wow! The soccer stadium must be huge.

"Too bad the guys weren't here to enjoy this with us."

"I know Ally. Wouldn't that just be the best. Maybe we can plan a trip to come back to Italy in the future."

"How cool would that be?"

"We have to check our e-mail when we get back to the hotel."

"I am glad to hear that Kenneth is up and about."

"Yeah, a couple of weeks of physical therapy after the bandages come off. He said the flight to England from here only takes about ninety minutes, if that."

"Well let's gather up the folks and head down now. I think it must be noon by now."

"Sounds good Lily," Ally says lost in thought.

All of us make our way back down to the ground level and head to the soccer store, or Football Store as it is called here. The blue and green sign for the store jumps out at me and I jog to the doors admiring the soccer items in the display window as I enter. Ally and our parents can barely keep up with me. I enter the store and turn left heading up a short set of steps. The store is full of stuff for any soccer fan. Jerseys, t-shirts, soccer balls, and all sorts of collectibles. You name it; it looks like it is here. I see mostly A.C. Milan and Inter Milan, but spot stuff from other teams including one of the English leagues. Ally catches up with me as I walk past the sales desk and turn right in to a smaller back room. Bath towels, bath robes, and sandals with the Milano team's logos.

"Hey Lily," says Ally as I turn around to see her holding up woman's underwear. "Do you want these A.C. Milan collectible woman's undergarments? I am sure they might be worth some cash someday," she asks teasingly.

"No. I think I am good after getting our laundry done in the hotel last night."

"How about the Inter umbrella?" she asks while trying to open the thing.

"I don't think there is enough room back here to open that," I say as Carilyn walks around the corner.

"Let's keep it simple. How about some soccer jerseys?"

"Ok mom. I will wear Inter and Lily will probably get A.C. Milan"

"You read my mind Ally doll." I grab a black and red A.C. Milan team jersey without any numbers on it. I figure I would cheer for all of the players. Ally gets a blue and black Inter jersey and we head to the checkout counter. I also pick up a miniature black, red, and white soccer ball with the A.C. Milan name and shield on it: vertical red and black stripes next to the red cross and 1899, the year they were established. ACM is above the shield. We lay our items on the counter and the nice girl asks us if we would like to have a name and number put on the back of the jerseys. I decide not to only because we our pressed for time.

"Hey that's a good choice Lily. You two will definitely get some attention in the stadium," my mama says smiling and shaking her head. She then looks at Ally. "Did you want the Inter earrings to match?"

"I think the jersey will do for now," says Ally as the girl behind the counter puts our purchases in a bag for us. I give her my best "grazie" and she says "prego." We head back outside where our dads have managed to stay out of trouble.

"What did y'all buy?" my dad says.

"A couple of jerseys."

"Which team?"

"Both," I answer.

"Oh boy," he says not sounding too reassuring.

"What Doc Jim? We are tourists. The locals would suspect that," says Ally.

"Yep I know, but I told you the fans are very passionate about their teams. More so than the American sports."

"Ok. Where to next Jim," my mama asks.

"I think the castle is next. Let's head around to the other side of the Duomo and we can take the street in the corner of the piazza. It will lead right to it."

"Lead on Jimbo," says Doc Nick as he wraps his arm around Carilyn and we continue on our way.

We make it back to the piazza and head for the corner to our left dodging excited tourists along the way. We pass by the Metro entrance and make a small right turn leaving the piazza. At the very far end of the street, I can make out the brown bell tower of the castle. Wow again I say to myself. We continue past outdoor cafe's with their tables and chairs set up on both sides of the street. Some have awnings to keep the sun off of the people enjoying their lunch and some have no awnings. I glance at a few jewelry shops making me reach up and touch my tiger necklace under my shirt just to be sure it is still there. It is. I look over to my left to see a pastry shop of some kind. The food in the window looks delicious making my mouth want to drool a little. I do my best not to.

We reach an intersection at the end of the street, pass by a couple of newsstands and souvenir shops on the corners, and cross the street. After another minute, we have a full view of the big brown castle. Its walls must be at least thirty feet high made of stone with small square holes throughout the walls everywhere that I can see. I don't know if they are for drainage, or maybe for archers shooting arrows, or something else altogether, but they add to the unique detail of the walls. The bell tower is situated right in the middle of the front wall and has an entrance just below it that people are walking through. There seems to be another man and horse sculpture on the bell tower and a clock that doesn't have numbers or look like it is working.

"Hey y'all, how about a picture by the fountain right here and then I can set the timer and get one of us with the castle as the back drop," says Doc Nick.

"Sounds good honey," replies Carilyn.

We all gather in front of the two tier white concrete fountain. It is pretty with separate jets of water shooting around the edges back toward the center which has more water spraying from the middle. I can see through the clear water that the bottom is layered with coins that people have tossed into it, but not as many like Trevi fountain in Rome. Doc Nick snaps the pic, programs the self-timer, and then sets the camera on the fountain. We switch positions and put our backs facing the castle. Doc Nick runs over to us, throws his arm around my dad, and plants a big kiss on his cheek just as the red light on the camera stops blinking. We all crack up.

"Thanks Jim," says Nick. "This will look good in my scrap booking project."

"How about one in the water Nick?" my dad says as he wipes his cheek off with his hand.

"Boys!" mama interrupts them. "Let's continue this wonderful self-guided tour."

"Yes dear," they both respond in stereo.

Doc Nick retrieves his camera and we head through the castle entrance actually coming out into an open courtyard. The walkway seems to go off in different directions leading to museum entrances in the corners of the castle. Kind of neat, but I know we're short on time, so we keep casually walking toward the next open doorway about twenty yards in front of us. I snap a few pictures of the courtyard and Ally. We go under the next passageway and to the right I see what looks like a very long, but shallow swimming pool. Maybe it is one of those reflecting pools or something. Next to it is a giant geisha; at least I think it is. The statue is wearing a blue flowery kimono, I think. What an interesting spot for her to be? We continue past her and under some hefty looking iron gates that look like they could crash down on us and exit through the thick walls to the other side of the castle. Off to my left and right appears to be an old mote of some kind. There is no water in it, but instead rich green grass lines the bottom. Still, it must be a thirty foot drop to the bottom. I take a quick picture.

We enter some kind of a park just outside of the castle. There is a souvenir stand to my right as we continue walking. The awning is covered with green, white, and red Italian flags blowing about for sale. I can make out some A.C. Milan and Inter Milan merchandise also. There is a nice Inter flag with their black, blue, and gold logo in the middle of it which is the team's initials, the I, M, F, and C, in gold stacked on one another surrounded by a blue and black circle. There is a gold star on top letting everyone know that they have won multiple championships in their league similar to A.C. Milan. Next to the flags are red and black, black and blue, and green white and red, scarves flapping in the light breeze. To our left is a food stand vendor. We walk down a slight hill on the paved asphalt road just for a bit before stopping. The park itself looks to be pretty big with the usual park stuff: trees, grass, and benches lining the sides of the road here and there. Most are filled with people, probably tourists, taking a rest.

"Let's turn around here before we get lost. I think we have to catch the Metro now and get to the stadium," says my mama.

"Mama, what is the name of this park?" I ask.

She fumbles through her small guide book for a second as we head back up the hill.

"Sempione," she answers.

"Thanks for checking."

"Hey Nick," says my Dad while pointing to the snack stand.

"Yeah Jimmy."

"Didn't you want to get some focaccia from the food vendor? That is the only Italian dish that you've been eating since we have been in Italy. I mean, if you would learn another Italian word you could jazz up your diet..."

"Boys!" Carilyn and my mama cut them off together.

Chuckling our way back through the castle; we come out by the fountain again and head toward the Metro. My dad spots the now familiar big red and white Metro sign with just the 'M' on it and we head down the steps in to the station. It turns out we are at Cairoli. We validate our twenty-four hour passes and walk down some more steps until we reach the platform. The subway stops and we all jump in to a car. The doors shut and off we go again. I am really starting to enjoy the subway thing once again having never been on one until I got to Italy.

"Hey remember that we have to change trains at Pagano to make sure we take the right line to the San Siro," Carilyn says.

"We got to the Metro Line 1. That's pretty good," says Nick.

"Yep. The red one, right?" my dad chimes in.

"Yes dear. You did very well. Now let the women take over, you know, so we don't get lost," my mama says.

I laugh and watch the walls at the different stations looking to see where we are: Cadorna, Conciliazone, Pagano. That's us.

"Everyone off!" shouts Carilyn.

"Except the boys, right," my mama adds.

We follow the signs to make sure we get on the RHO line and not Bisceglie. After boarding what we think is the correct line, we pass by Buonarroti, yep, the right line, and get off at Lotto, and exit to the street.

"There James, that wasn't too hard was it?"

"No dear. You did very good. What street are we looking for now?"

"Ok. Look for Caprilli," says Carilyn as she checks her tourist map. We stay to the left walking along Lotto.

"There it is," Doc Nick says pointing off to the left.

The six of us leave the roundabout and make a slight left up Caprilli. I take in the sights of the tree lined neighborhood. It seems like mostly small apartment type buildings only a couple of stories high. Off to the right is a large grassy area. It definitely is not residential.

"I thought there was a bus that took us to the stadium?" Ally asks.

"There is baby, but the J and N sightseeing tour is much more fun, isn't it?" says Carilyn.

"I hope we don't walk past it and miss the stadium all together."

I laugh at Ally's last remark. We reach another small roundabout and stay to the right.

"Ok. Here is Moratti," my dad says.

We continue walking up Moratti past a few more buildings and I gasp as I see the San Siro come in to view.

CHAPTER XXX

We keep walking as the San Siro Football Stadium comes in to full view. It is massive! Maybe over one hundred feet tall. Giant white cylindrical concrete towers surround the outside of the stadium as we approach. They kind of look like they are zebra striped with the sloping walkways appearing to be the black stripes. Maybe even more like giant thick black and white candy canes. An easy exit from the seats at the top of the stadium, but probably quite the work out going up, at least it looks like that so far. Protruding over the upper edges of the stadium are massive red girders making it look like it is still being built, but giving the stadium an unexpected contrast to the white concrete. The layout of the seats on the inside look like they makeup black horizontal lines on the outside of the stadium giving the concrete towers competition for my attention. It looks that way, but it is probably the walkways at different levels. Mama reads over the directions that she got from our hotel's front desk.

"Let us see here. Ok. We are looking for gate 14. She said the word is ingresso. Look for Ingresso 14," mama says as we focus our attention to the black metal fence surrounding the stadium.

"I think that means entrance honey," says my dad trying to get a word in. "Down there to the left seems to be where we need to go."

"Lead the way Polo," blurts out Doc Nick.

"Yeah yeah, here this way down Achille," my dad replies.

"I think we are actually heading in the right direction," says Ally as we both continue snapping pics of the stadium. We pass by what I think is a ticket office due to the amount of people waiting in line making me glad that we got ours in advanced. It is the last week of August and the first game of the season. What were the chances of attending this match? Our group reaches an entrance to the stadium. We pull out our tickets and are waved through the gate. A man in a uniform glances at my dad's ticket. The gentleman then points to the right of the stadium, so we keep walking. I remain in awe of the mighty structure. Nothing close to this in Alabama, maybe the stadium in Birmingham, that I once played in during the state soccer championship game, but I don't think so. There is some kind of other structure next to the San Siro to my left. It might be a horse racing track, or maybe bicycle. We stay to the right and start passing by gates. Ingresso 3. Ingresso 4. Each with their own flat round roof I guess to keep spectators dry as they enter. Reminds me of little flying saucers again. We pass by some more gates. Ingresso 7. Ingresso 8. There are several parking lots to the right of us that are filling up with cars and buses. We keep walking farther around the stadium. I can make out Ingresso 15 as we make a left turn.

"What's our gate again?" asks Ally.

"Ingresso 14," answers Doc Nick.

"I see it," Ally says pointing straight ahead. The gates and black iron fence are closer to the San Siro now. Actually kind of right under it. We reach fourteen and hand over our tickets as we pass through the turn stile. The ticket checker scans the bar code and hands me back the ticket. Yeah! Souvenir from the game. I will frame it when I get home. Now we are only feet away from entering the San Siro. I can't believe it. On the pavement in front of me is the word MUSEUM painted in yellow. It has an arrow pointing left. Right next to that, also painted in yellow is the word STORE with the arrow pointing straight.

"What section are we looking for?" Doc Nick asks. The ticket says blu."

We stand there and look up at the three signs mounted on the stadium wall. The red one says ROSSO and the arrow is pointing left. The middle one says BLU and the arrow is pointing straight. The green sign says VERDE and is pointing to the right.

"What the heck does verde mean?" asks my dad with a confused look on his face.

"I am pretty sure that it means green," replies my mama.

"How did you know that?" he asks.

"Follow me Marco," Doc Nick says as we head up ramp seven. Doc Nick leads us up the ramp and onto a concourse. He checks his ticket and then looks at the numbers posted by the entrances leading to the seats.

"Here we are. Section 110 is to our left," Nick says as he checks our tickets one last time. "Sorry we aren't sitting together."

"It is fine dad. I still can't believe we are at the friggin game!" Ally exclaims.

"Now the four of us will be in Section 214. It is kind of up above y'all. If you need anything, come get us," says Carilyn.

"Do y'all have enough money for snacks and stuff? My mama asks.

"I think we are good for now," I reply as we bounce off to our seats.

"Remember, we will meet here at the end of the game, so don't go anywhere," Carilyn adds.

"Ok mom," says Ally.

Ally and I enter the San Siro and I am flabbergasted. Our whole end of the stadium is covered in blue seats. The opposite end is covered in green seats. Two of the mighty concrete towers are visible in the corners flanking the green section, at least the tops are. Unlike the stripes of walkways on the outside, they have little round windows over the exposed part reminding me of the castle. To our right the seats on that side of the field are all orange. The seats to our left are all red. It must look awesome when it is all empty, but right now the seats are probably three-fourths full with fans still filing in. The grass field looks so perfect that I can swear it is painted green. There is one giant rectangular opening in the roof above the field. The red girders are exposed along the edges of the roof that covers the fans, but the girders don't cross over the open roof section providing a nice view of the blue sky. We have just enough shade where we are sitting. We sit down in our little blue plastic seats. They are solid one piece and are mounted directly to the concrete. I glance over to the red section and it looks like the seats fold down and are a bit more comfortable. There is a clear four foot high glass wall separating the sections. Upper class. Lower class. Doesn't matter. I am at the San Siro with my best friend about to watch Inter Milan and A.C. Milan battle in the first game of the season!

"Can you believe this?"

"Ally, this is a dream come true, right?"

"You better believe it. I mean look at everyone going nuts and the game didn't even start yet. Giant red and black banners. Huge black and blue banners." She points at the edges of the upper decks. "The crowd is already chanting. How long before this thing kicks off?"

I check my watch, "about five minutes. Let's get our jerseys on."

"Ok."

I reach in to the green and blue shopping bag from the Football Store and pull out our jerseys. I hand Ally hers and she slips it on over her green Ciao Milano t-shirt. Her jersey is black with three thick blue stripes running vertically down the front of it. The Inter crest is on the upper left chest. I pull my jersey on over my Crimson Tide Pride t-shirt. My jersey is black with three thin red stripes running from the collar down each of the short sleeves. The A.C. Milan logo is also on the upper left chest. So far so good. Nobody notices we are sitting together. Fans of two of the biggest rivals in all of sports.

"Look at all of the team scarves waving around. Isn't that cool?"

"Lily doll, I think they are as passionate as those 'Tide' fans are."

"You might be right. Hey I think the game is about to start."

I point down to the field. The players from each team are walking out on to the grass holding hands with kids wearing matching team jerseys. They reach the middle of the field and line up in a straight line. The stadium speakers crackle to life and some music begins playing. Anthems I guess. We stand. The music stops and a few announcements are made, but don't have a clue what is said, it is in Italian. It looks like the team's starting line ups shake hands with the referee and linesmen and A.C. Milan wearing their black jerseys with the red stripes running down the fronts and sleeves, face our direction. They have on white shorts and black socks with red stripes around the tops. Inter is wearing their white jerseys with black and blue stripes on the sleeves over black shorts. Their backs are facing us now, so they will be trying to score in the goal opposite from where we are sitting.

"Do you realize that we can actually get hit by the soccer ball from here if they miss the goal?" says Ally.

"I know. We are almost right behind the goal and just one section above the field. I am glad our parents let us sit together this close to the action."

"Do we keep the ball or throw it back?"

"I think we should throw it back. We don't want to draw any unnecessary attention to ourselves, right?"

"After what we have been through? No you are absolutely right Lil babe." I quickly stop a vendor offering programs for sale, hand her a twenty Euro bill, and buy a program to check out the roster numbers. She gives me change back and I hand her a Euro back for a tip hoping I did it right. The referee blows his whistle and Inter kicks the ball beginning the game. They start passing moving the ball toward the A.C. Milan goal.

Immediately there is a break away from a long pass across the field to my right and the ball goes beyond the A.C. defenders. An Inter player catches up with the ball. There are no offside flags. He shoots toward the lower left corner of the goal and the A.C. goalie makes a diving save to his right. The crowd of about eighty thousand or so, goes nuts.

"Did you see that? Holy crap Lily. These guys are good!"

"Some of the best on the friggin planet!" I shout back at her barely loud enough to hear over the crowd. Up to my left in the red section I can make out what looks like the press boxes. Way above them, in the upper deck, looks like luxury boxes. Who would want to be up there I ask myself? This is where the action is. There is an open section above the upper deck of the orange seats that has a giant TV screen mounted in the middle. Myself and the rest of the fans watch the replay of the Inter shot on goal.

The A.C. goalie drop kicks the ball back in to play. Somebody in black takes it off of their head in the middle of the field. They make some short passes all the way down the field to our corner. An A.C. Milan player kicks the ball and it ricochets off of the Inter defender bouncing out of bounds for an A.C. throw-in. The ball is intercepted by an Inter player. He starts to dribble the ball up the field only to have an A.C. player take it from him. A.C. Milan takes a shot and the soccer ball sails over the goal way off to our right. The fan throws the ball back to the field.

"Wow, this is exciting!" Ally screams in to my left ear trying to compete with the crowd noise. We join in and whoop in unison with the crowd. Shouting noises really, because we don't know much Italian. But it is fun anyway. The teams go back and forth taking the ball up the field. Nobody gains an advantage until A.C. Milan slide tackles an Inter player knocking the ball away from him. The crowd boos, but there is no foul. Another A.C. player receives a pass. He dribbles to our right and sends a beautiful cross to the middle of the goal just inside the eighteen yard box. A group of players from both teams leap in to the air trying to get a head on the descending ball. It bounces off an A.C. player past the Inter goalie and into the bottom left corner of the goal. The fans erupt. Half cheering for the goal. Half yelling at the foul that wasn't called. We both jump up. Ally boos away and I clap for the goal. Just what our jerseys tell us to do.

"Wow! Did you see that? He put that thing in from like fifteen yards away with his head," I holler.

"I saw it, but my dang goalie didn't!"

We both look up at the giant video screen and watch the replay. The crowd boos again. The other half cheers again trying to drown them out. The Inter goalie takes a drink from his water bottle and then whips it into the stands. A fan down to our right jumps up and down with his new souvenir. He is wearing an Inter jersey with matching scarf from the summer collection, I guess.

"This is fantastic Lily. I wish Kenneth and Brandon were here with us."

"Me too. Remind me to check my e-mail when we get back to the hotel. I will send pictures."

"Good idea," Ally says as she snaps some pics of the game. I do the same as Inter takes the ball and heads toward the A.C. Milan end of the field. They make some crisp passes. An A.C. player goes for the ball and takes down the Inter player without touching the ball. The ref signals for a free kick. From our end it looks like they are probably about three yards outside of the eighteen box. The A.C. goalie calls for a wall to be set up to his right. Three Inter players line up behind the ball. The ref steps away from the front of the wall making sure they are the proper distance from the soccer ball. He signals for play to begin. The first Inter player jumps over the ball. The second steps to the right. The third player kicks the ball. It bends around the right side of the wall to the goalie's left and crashes into the back of the net about waist high. The Inter fans go crazy jumping up and down. Ally cheers. I boo as loud as I can to the point that I cannot even hear myself.

"Hey we are tied up sugar!"

"Did you see the bend on that ball? Dang the poor goalie never had a chance!" I scream while we watch the replay on the big screen high above us.

"I am almost hoarse from all of my yelling," Ally says as we sit back down in to our cozy blue seats.

"Yeah, my mouth is pretty dry too. Hey I will go and get us a couple of sodas."

"How much time is left in the first half?" Ally asks as we both look up at the time clock.

"It is at 31:15. There is like fifteen minutes left."

"That's ok Lily. I can wait until half-time."

"No really it is no problem. I will be back in two minutes. The snack bar is right behind us where we came in at and besides, there will be a huge crowd buying drinks at half-time."

"Are you sure you don't mind? I will go with you."

"Please. I will be back in a minute. Watch our stuff and let me know what happens."

"See you in a minute. Thanks sweetie."

I stand up and head around to our left and back through the little tunnel to the refreshment stand. It was a good idea because there is only one other person buying some drinks. I walk up to the counter and hold my fingers up making a "V" for two.

"Colas please," I say as I pull out another twenty Euro bill. The nice girl at the counter takes my money as her co-worker fills up two big colas in San Siro stadium souvenir cups. "Grazie."

"Prego," she replies. Still don't know what it means, but I hope that wasn't an insult; I make it a point to check my mama's guide book for the translation. I walk back through the little tunnel admiring the souvenir cups with the picture of the stadium on them. The crowd jumps up as I enter blocking out any view of Ally. It looks like some team scored. I stop for a second and look up at the giant video screen, but only catch the tail end of the play. I look at the score: A.C.-2, Inter-1. I walk a little quicker so that Ally can fill me in with the details and dare I say, let me rub it in a little.

The crowd sits back down. I look to where we are sitting, but I don't see Ally. Hum? I round the corner and get to our row. I see the game guide lying below the seat on the concrete. It looks like the cover is torn. Great one Ally. That was a souvenir. I sit the drinks down on the concrete and relax back into my seat. I guess she went to the bathroom probably because of the excitement. I guess I should have gone too, so that I can beat the half-time crowds. I think she would have waited for me though. Oh well. I can yell at her when she gets back. I reach down and pick up the game program guide only to find her camera lying under it. The screen on it is cracked. What the? Someone behind me taps my shoulder. I turn around to see a lady pointing down toward the field, but to the left.

"Friend?" she says.

I look back to my right and see a group of policemen. Maybe six or eight of them. Oh no! Ally is in the middle of them. It looks like they are escorting her toward the player's tunnel between the team benches. Was she celebrating that wildly? Something isn't right. I reach up on to my chest and grasp my tiger necklace. I concentrate and focus on the policemen. Dam! It is Mr. Handsome! He is leading the group into the tunnel. How the heck did he find us? Can't worry about that now. I stand up and try to spot our parents. No luck. Here goes nothing.

I run over to the nearest aisle in front of me between sections 107 and 109. I run down the steps until I get to the railing. I leap down to the field just behind the left side of the Inter goal. Shortest distance between two lines? Straight. I sprint on to the field heading toward the tunnel between the players benches. For some reason a glance up to see myself on the giant TV screen. Can't wait to see this replay. The camera was on me pretty quick. Then I realize an A.C. player is dribbling the soccer ball toward me. He is just about at midfield. I can see Ally disappear into the tunnel with the group of policemen. The only Italian I know is grazie and focaccia thanks to Doc Nick's diet the past few days and that's no use to me now.

"Pass! Pass! Pass!" I scream as loud as I can. I feel like I am in the zone. The A.C. Milan player with spiked hair has a stunned look on his face, but kicks the ball to me. In one motion I put all of my force into the kick of my life aiming it at the tunnel. I come off of the ground in the process. My right foot makes solid contact with the ball knowing I hit it as clean as I can. The soccer ball sizzles toward the tunnel striking one of the fake policemen in the back of his head putting him in to instant sleep mode as he falls on his face. Oops! I say to myself. I think the crowd is cheering louder than they did all day. I hope the folks didn't look up at the big screen for the nicely zoomed-in replay. Maybe they think it is just a crazy fan like the ones trying to kiss the players when they run on to the field. Yep that will be my story.

I run pass the reserve players and jump down the stairs and into the tunnel. They all look shocked, and clear a path for me. I land on Mr. Unconscious and continue running on small square red tile. There is graffiti on the walls, but it looks professional. I think I run past a mermaid to my left. Mermaid in Milan? Straight ahead I can see daylight as the red tile changes to concrete and then asphalt. I reach up, grab my necklace, break the cord from my neck, and throw the tiger crystal in front of me. Panthera instantly springs to life as three of the bad fake policemen turn around toward us at the tunnel exit. I don't see Ally. They start to pull out pistols and raise them up to aim. The blur of gray, white, and black fur changes to black battle armor as they begin to shoot. The guns echo loudly in the tunnel as the bullets bounce off of Panthera's armor. I run directly behind her shielding myself. She leaps the final ten feet and takes the three of them down. Their guns go flying, but I don't have time to pick one up. Panthera swings her massive frying pan of a paw across the two bad fakers on her left putting them out of action. She pounces on the bad fake copper to her right who is trying to stand up after Panthera's proper tackle, and sinks her fangs in to his head. He goes limp, permanently, I think. I hope this isn't on the jumbo TV; lots of explaining.

"Nice job Panthera," I say as we reach the outside of the stadium. "Where is Ally?" I ask as Panthera looks to the left, her battle armor already retracted. I follow her gaze and spot a white van. One of the fake policemen is just closing the side door. I catch a glimpse of a black and blue soccer jersey being pushed back down to the floor of the van as the door shuts. Fight Ally. Fight. The driver puts the van in gear and spins the rear tires making a loud squeal as he speeds away toward the parking lot exit. I smell burnt rubber. Panthera crouches as if she is about to run after them.

"Wait Panthera." She stops. I look to my right, left, and back to my right again. I run up behind a black Fiat 500 with my tiger in tow. We stop and look at each other. Her glacier blue eyes focused on me.

"You are absolutely right. We ain't gonna fit in that one." I look at the car parked to the left of the Fiat. It is a Ferrari. I can tell by the jumping horse on the trunk lid. The left side is painted red. The right side is painted green and the middle is painted white. It looks like the Italian flag. Cool! The long narrow European rectangular white license plate above the three exhaust pipes has the name "MASSIMO458" personalized on it in black letters. Well at least I know who to return it to, but how do I get in it. Panthera reads my mind. She walks up to the passenger door, sticks her claws into the window shattering the glass. I open the door. Ok. We are in. I carefully climb across the passenger seat to the driver's seat trying not to cut myself. I pick up a red and black towel off of the floor and wipe the broken glass off of the tan leather seat, so Panthera isn't cut. She climbs in and sits on the passenger seat. The door is still open. I get out of the driver's side and run around shutting Panthera's door. We will have to work on that one. I settle back in to the car behind the steering wheel and try to figure out how to start it. It looks like a spaceship inside. This can't be too difficult. I fly my dad's Piper! Panthera struggles to bring her massive head back in to the car. We scan the dash and instruments at the same time. I flip down the sun visor searching for a spare key or something. Nothing. I reach down under my seat. Nothing.

"Panthera, how do we start this thing? We have to get Ally back!"

We both look down at the console between the seats. It looks like window controls; useful a minute ago. Ignition? Start? Panthera lifts her left front paw and smashes it down on the console cracking the plastic and leather cover. I spot a red button in the lower left corner of the tricked out steering wheel. It says IGNIZIO on it. I give it a push. The engine turns over and the Ferrari is running. Never mind then.

"Thank you," I say as Panthera squeezes her head back out of the nonexistent passenger window. I don't see a gear shift anywhere. I start squeezing the long silver things behind both sides of the steering wheel. An 'R' lights up on the lower right side of the dash. I get the 458 in to reverse and stomp on the gas pedal. The rear tires spin violently as the car reverses. I turn the steering wheel hard to the left and the front end whips around as I slam on the brakes. Smoke from the burning rubber tires fills up the car. I squeeze the paddle like things again and manage to put the Ferrari in to first gear and stomp the gas pedal again. The rear end of the car fish-tails crazily as I struggle to keep the car straight. We head toward the exit where I last saw the van turn right. I squeeze and a lit up '2' appears where the '1' was. I think I am getting the shift thing down now. Lights blink on the top of the steering wheel. Part of the tachometer maybe?

"Don't worry Panthera. I know I have more hours in dad's Piper than I have in a car, but this beats running, right?" She roars loudly. "This is a bit more modern!" I shout.

We reach the exit and pass by a few on-lookers that must be trying to figure out what the heck they are seeing. I hit the brakes and whip the wheel to the right out on to a main road. Horns blare and people scream.

"Sorry!"

I squeeze again and hit third gear. The tachometer is in the middle of the dash, but I haven't found the speedometer yet. The upper left part of the dash has the word RACE lit up.

"Sounds perfect to me."

I speed up trying not to lose control of the Ferrari. That would be bad since I already bought a window and gas, I guess. Well, I hope there is gas in the tank. I decide not to look at the fuel gauge while driving. This will probably make my insurance go up back home. I weave in and out of traffic. More buildings on the left and right. Cars in front of me everywhere that I can see. I go around them trying to avoid vehicles coming the other way. More horns and I think, *hello's*, in Italian. Maybe they think I have a bad case of road rage. That doesn't explain my cat hanging its head out of the window. I glance at her real quick. The breeze is causing her fur to flatten and flow backward like she has a fan blowing on her. She seems to be enjoying herself. I swerve left and then right again to get around traffic. Panthera's butt hits my right arm. She tries to adjust in the seat and ends up moving her bushy tail across my face. I duck under it just in time to see that the road turns to the right. I glance at a street sign. Harar. No wait. Novara. The names change every block; it seems.

The road opens up now. I squeeze the paddle shift again. Fourth gear. I speed up. The Ferrari skids around a turn. I grip the steering wheel so tight that I feel my fingers start to go numb. I relax my grip to get some blood flowing in to my hands. I concentrate on the vehicles far up ahead. I can see two white cars. No. One is bigger. It has to be the van. The gas pedal is on the floor. Now I am starting to lose feeling in my right calf from pressing the gas pedal so hard. I ignore it and try to get the 458 to go faster. Squeeze. Number five on the dash. I am afraid to look at the speedometer. I don't want to take my eyes off of the white van. We must be traveling through a farming area. I don't see any big buildings. This is my expertise. It is just like a country back-road in Alabama. Piece of cake. Spoke to soon. One more apartment building on my left. Back to the farms again. I can see the van about one hundred yards ahead of us. The brake lights come on. They are slowing. They turn right and disappear behind some trees.

I reach the turn and slam on the brakes. The Ferrari does all that it can to keep from skidding. I squeeze the opposite paddle on the steering wheel and the car downshifts. I whip the steering wheel to the right. The back end of the car slides off of the asphalt in to the dirt on the side of the road striking a street sign that I think said "RIZZARDI" making a 'tink' sound. I hope it is just a scratch in the paint job. I stomp on the gas again. The rear tires spin madly trying to get traction. Squeeze. Second. Squeeze. Third. I see the white van turn right again, but this time there is a cloud of dust in the air blocking my view. A dirt road? They then turn left. I only see fields.

"Ok Panthera. I think they know that they have company."

She roars loudly again. I accelerate up to where the van turned and then slow down. I make the turn to see the van cutting across a dirt field maybe a half mile wide. I speed up as I leave the dirt road and turn left in to the deep loose dirt. The Ferrari bounces up and down shaking Panthera and I in and out of our seats. The fat rear tires spin for traction. We are only twenty yards from the white van. I can only make out a row of tall green trees above the dust cloud. There is nowhere else to go. I think the van is stuck in the loose dirt. The van's brake lights come on as I plow in to the back end of it crunching the Ferrari's sloped hood. A burst of gun fire comes from the rear of the van shattering its rear window and the Ferrari's windshield. I duck below the steering wheel with the large black and yellow horse emblem in the middle of it.

BANG! BANG! BANG!

More rounds hit the Ferrari's hood. Panthera leaves the car knocking the passenger door in to the air as she exits. I glance out of the shattered windshield to see that Panthera has already activated her black battle armor. She glistens in the sun light as she jumps across the Ferrari's shot up hood and in through the back window of the van leaving a tiger size hole in the rear door because she didn't quite fit.

BANG! BANG!

More shots are fired. I crawl across the seats and out of the Ferrari landing on my belly in the dirt. The side door of the van opens. I can make out an arm covered by a ripped black and blue Inter jersey.

"Ally, run!"

Half of her body is hanging out of the side door. I can see the look of fear on her face. One of the fake cops leaps out of the van's passenger door, grabs Ally's arm, and yanks her the rest of the way out of the van on to the dirt. Another fake cop runs around the front of the van and grabs Ally's other arm. It is Mr. Handsome with black hair. They lift her up and start to run toward the trees half dragging Ally and half carrying her. They fumble with their guns as Ally fights with them. I get up and start to run after her. As I reach the van's side door, Panthera leaps past me in a blur. The faker on the right turns and tries to fire while Mr. Handsome continues toward the trees. I can hear approaching sirens in the distance.

BANG! TINK!

The fake cop gets off one shot at Panthera. The round ricochets off of her armor. She leaps and takes him down with her left paw dragging across his face and then chest. She keeps running after Mr. Handsome. The sirens are on the dirt road now. Mr. Handsome and Ally are about ten feet from the trees. He continues to drag her. Suddenly, Ally gets her left hand free and shoves Mr. Handsome to the left. I keep running toward them. Panthera leaps at Mr. Handsome's back dragging her claws from his right shoulder to his left hip. The navy blue police shirt shreds to pieces and I can see blood spraying from his back. He drops his pistol as he goes flying off in to the trees and out of sight. I turn to see the Carabinieri, Italian military police, in their distinctive dark blue police cars with the red stripes on the sides driving across the field. It looks like about six or seven police cars in all. Time to hide Panthera. I grab Ally and we run off in to the trees. Less explaining to do. We head left away from where Mr. Handsome was punted. I say thank you to Panthera and put my hand out. She disappears in a flash and I feel the tiger crystal in my hand again.

"Ally, are you ok? Did they hurt you?"

"They ripped my jersey, but I am ok. I think that was the creep from the airport in France."

"I think it was also."

"How did he find us?"

"I overheard our dads talking. They said he was a hacker and some kind of mercenary for hire. He must still be upset about that India thing gone bad for him and his sidekicks."

"Apparently he has more sidekicks. Let's get back to the stadium. I don't want to have to explain this one."

"You up for a run?"

"Yeah. Let's go. By the way, I like your choice in cars."

"Run faster or I might have to pay for it."

Ally and I start running through the trees back toward the San Siro. At least I hope we are heading the right way. We make it out of the trees and on to some back road and keep jogging through some area with houses and buildings spread out. I think the street is Bellaria. Must mean beautiful street or something. We keep jogging. It must be close to ninety degrees out and I can see we are both starting to sweat pretty bad.

"Ally, you did wear a sports bra today, right?"

"You are...Worried about...Support...At a time like this," Ally says in between breaths.

"No. I mean let's ditch the jerseys so we don't stand out. They must have been reviewing the giant TV footage by now. Two blondes wearing Milan jerseys, one A.C. one Inter."

"Ok. I understand. At least you have your khaki cargo shorts on," she takes a deep exaggerated breath. "I have to push my Capri's up, so we look like joggers."

We continue to run as we take off our jerseys and t-shirts. At least they will stay dry and not drenched in sweat when we get to the stadium. We approach a garbage can and Ally quickly chucks her torn Inter jersey in to it. We enter another neighborhood and I can see the red girders of the San Siro poking above the buildings.

"Hey we're getting close."

"Yeah, I see the stadium Ally."

"How do we get back inside? We are supposed to meet our folks in the concourse by our seats," she says as she reaches down and pushes up the right pant leg so they still look like shorts and we still look like joggers.

"I remember seeing some trees next to the outer fence of the stadium. Maybe we can climb over."

"Look up ahead of us," Ally says nodding with her chin not wanting to point. "What do we do?"

"Keep jogging. We are just a couple of joggers. With all the supermodels in this town, he will probably think we are just keeping in shape for the next fashion show," I say as I try not to stare at the Carabinieri standing on the corner about a block in front of us. He is wearing a light blue short-sleeve uniform shirt tucked into dark blue trousers with a red stripe down the outside of both legs. Across his chest is a diagonal white strap holding up his black gun belt and holster. As we get closer, I can see that his pant legs are tucked in to high black boots. A cute looking motorcycle cop. Yes, he standing next to a dark blue motorcycle with blue emergency lights mounted on both sides of the windscreen and rear of the bike. I can now see a BMW symbol on the lower front fairing of the bike. Crap!

"What...do...we do Lily?"

"Act like a jogger and smile at him when we pass by. Whatever you do...don't talk." We are almost on top of him. He turns and looks at us. I can see his head go down to our feet and back up to our really moist faces. I can't see his eyes behind his sunglasses. I panic and crack a smile.

"Ciao," the Carabinieri says as he smiles back at us with his right hand resting on his holster. I keep smiling thinking now we are busted.

"Bonjour!" Ally spouts out in perfect thick French.

His radio clipped to his shoulder crackles to life and takes his attention away from us and back to his job. He says something back in to the radio, climbs on to his motorcycle, and speeds away with the blue lights flashing and siren blaring.

"That was close Lily."

"Hey, good thinking. I knew studying French in Georgia would pay off for you some day."

"I know, right? There's the trees over there," she says pointing across the road toward the San Siro's fence.

"Stop at that souvenir stand on the corner. Maybe we can replace your jersey."

"Great idea Lily."

We finally stop jogging and walk up to the stand trying to catch our breath in the process. I don't feel as winded as Ally looks. After a couple of deep breaths, Ally starts to browse through the soccer jerseys hanging on the racks in front of the souvenir stand. I walk off to the side of the small stand and put my t-shirt back on. The sweat is drying as Ally shops. I keep my A.C. Milan jersey rolled tightly into a black ball. I walk up to a rack with hats hanging on it and pick out a red "CIAO MILANO" cap for me and a pink one for Ally and pay for them. I make sure my hair is hanging down and put the hat on. The 'girl' who ran on to the soccer pitch had a pony tail.

"Any luck?"

"I think this will have to do," Ally says as she holds the Inter jersey up in front of me.

"But yours didn't have any numbers on it."

"Yep. I know, but at least it is black and has the blue stripes on the front. Close enough."

"Are you sure?"

"Trust me. My folks will never remember," she says as she pays for the new Inter jersey. She does the same as me and puts her t-shirt back on. The gentleman working the souvenir stand smiles and Ally winks at him as we head across the street. We reach the trees by the fence. It would be easy to climb if it was chain-link, but it has the black vertical iron rods about six feet high. There is a bar running horizontal about a foot from the top and another one about a foot from the bottom.

"Look around for a tree that is close enough to the fence."

"Here Lily," Ally says as we walk a few feet to the right. "I think that branch up there is our ticket in."

"I think you're correct. Let's get up the tree."

We begin to climb and get about six feet off of the ground when I hear a familiar sound.

"Cop!"

"I see him Ally, stay behind the branches," I say as a motorcycle cop drives past the trees, but on the inside of the stadium. It looks like the Carabinieri that was on the corner. We freeze. He scans the trees and keeps going.

"Move!"

Ally keeps working her way toward the fence along a thin branch of what I think is some kind of an Italian pine tree of some kind. She reaches the edge as the branch strains under the weight of the both of us. We keep our balance holding on to an even smaller branch just above our shoulders.

"I think I can make it from here," Ally says as she jumps back in to the San Siro parking lot. She lands and falls forward in to a roll and quickly gets up. I follow. We dust the little pieces of grass and dirt off one another.

"Keep moving to a gate."

"Lily, they will probably know our tickets have been scanned."

"I know, but I don't see any other choice," I say as we reach in to our pockets and locate our game tickets. A bit wrinkled and wet from sweat, but they will have to do. We head to INGRESSO 8 and hope for the best. I approach first and hold my ticket out in front of me. The girl looks at it, sees the sweaty wrinkled mess, and waves us both in.

"Grazie," Ally says.

"Prego," the girl responds confusing me again. No time to dwell about it.

"How much time do we have?"

"Well Ally, we sort of left when there was like ten or fifteen minutes left in the first half. Then we went for that sightseeing trip. That probably took the rest of the first half and half-time. Then we went for our jog which I would say took just about the rest of the second half. Then we shopped."

"So, the game should be ending as we speak."

"Yep."

We hear the final whistle sound and start to walk as fast as we can up the ramp and back on to the concourse. Mobs of fans start to pour in to the concourse going both directions. I glance at the signs for the sections.

"Ally, we are in the red section. Go right."

"225. 223. 221. X03. X02 and X01. 112," she says calling the sections off aloud as we turn the corner. "110. Ok. I don't see our folks."

We both walk down the little tunnel that leads to our seats. I don't see our parents, but we carefully look at the scoreboard. A.C. Milan-3 Inter Milan-3. Cool. They tied. We turn back toward the concourse.

"Hey y'all. What a game!" my dad yells.

"Yeah, that was really something," I respond as I give my dad a big hug and then my mama hoping I don't smell like sweat. "Great game. Didn't expect a tie."

"Did y'all see that crazy fan run on to the field and kick the soccer ball?"

"I think it was like back home when they try to kiss one of the players," says Ally.

"Crazy everywhere!" says my mama.

"Hey y'all took your jerseys off," says Carilyn. "Good thinking. You don't want to get them ruined."

"They'll make good souvenirs," says Doc Nick. "Now let's find our way out of here. Marco Polo, lead the way."

"Hey, I like your hats," my dad says trying to figure out when the heck we bought them, I'm sure.

Nobody pays any attention to us leaving the stadium. Just two families walking with their excited daughters after a really exciting game.

The next morning we leave the hotel, take the train from Bruzzano to the station, jump on the Metro to San Babilia, a stop away from the Duomo, and then bus 73 to Linate, the airport about thirty minutes away on a good day. We do all the usual airport stuff and eventually make it to our gate which is on the same level as the tarmac where the airplanes park. Ally and I did some shopping for one last time in one of the airport stores and I bought an A.C. Milan hat. Ally picked up another Inter jersey without any numbers on it. We got our usual snacks and drinks and stuffed them in to our carry-on back packs. The lady at the gate makes a few announcements and I see a shuttle pull up in front of our gate. We pass by as they check our boarding passes and get on the shuttle. Once fully loaded, we depart the gate area and head out past a bunch of parked jets getting ready for this morning's flights. There is just a hint of a light fog in the air and it is just about daylight. The shuttle stops by one of the jets and we get off and climb up the set of air stairs and board the airplane. I walk down the aisle through the same blue interior as on the other flights and find my seat. We are in the very last row. Ally takes the window seat and I take the aisle. There are only two seats in the row next to the window. I look to my right and see five seats in the middle and then two seats on the other side next to the opposite window. Our folks are four rows in front of us in the middle section.

"I can't believe Brandon was ready to jump on a plane and come here."

"I know. Kenneth also."

"I couldn't really give him any details, but at least the bad guy is gone."

"You did good Lily and Panthera too."

"Can you imagine any other two weeks as crazy as these past two?"

"It happens every time we go on vacation together. Maybe next time we should just go to Panama City Beach and stick to harassing the cute life guards."

"Sounds good to me," I reply as I see a flight attendant making her way down the aisle handing out newspapers just before take-off. "Oh no."

"What is it Lily baby?"

"Look at the cover of that newspaper," I say as Ally stares at the cover in disbelief.

"Would you like a paper?" the flight attendant says as she reaches our seats. She speaks with just a slight accent and her dark hair makes me think that she is Italian. Of course another bi-lingual flight crew.

"Hello, I would like a paper."

She begins to hand me one in English.

"Can I get one in Italian please?"

"Si," she replies.

"Miss, what does this headline say?" I ask her while staring at a full color picture of Panthera hanging out of the Ferrari's passenger window with part of the San Siro as the backdrop.

"It says: CIRCUS TIGER MAKES DARING ESCAPE IN FERRARI." She scans the article. "Yes, Italian authorities believe it was supposed to be some kind of hoax to be part of the half-time show at the San Siro and that the Ferrari was probably driven by a former race car driver who hasn't lost their driving skills."

"Is there anything else?"

"No, not really. They don't even believe the picture is real."

"Ok. Thank you," I reply thinking maybe the authorities don't want to alarm the future tourists with tiger attacks like in India.

"Prego," she says.

"Why does everyone keep saying that? I am not pregnant."

"It means you are welcome in Italian."

"Oh," I reply sinking into my seat a little deeper feeling a little dumber now.

"Baci," she adds.

"What is that?" I ask.

"Hugs and kisses darling, hugs and kisses."

I wonder how she knows what I need.

CHAPTER XXXI

"Pass pass pass!" Everything from the eighteen yard line to the goal is mine. I own it. The goalie can't stop me.

"Kayla, I'm open!" I see only one defender near me as Kayla, playing on the left wing, crosses the ball toward me. Beautiful pass. I zero in on the ball. It looks like it is coming in slow motion. I'm in the zone. I feel it. The soccer ball bounces once to my left just in front of me. I trap it with my right foot in midair and side step the defender. Hum, don't think she ever had a chance at that one. Nope. Just me and the goalie now and no off-sides. One on one. She comes forward from the goal trying to cut off my angle. I faint left then quick to the right. She tries to react. She dives to the right. No honey, I am going the other way. I take the shot. Bam! Top left corner-G-O-A-L! Three to one is the final score as the second half ends. Game over.

"Hey Lily, nice shot." I give Kayla a big hug.

"No way. I could not have scored if you didn't have a great pass like that." We walk over to the bleachers and my mama hands me a water bottle.

"Hi Miss Abby," Kayla says as she grabs some water.

"Well hi there Miss Kayla. Great game." Mama congratulates Kayla and the rest of the team and coaches on our first victory of the season.

"That was a fine looking goal," my coach says.

"Thanks coach. Are we practicing on Saturday?" I ask.

"I think we'll be all right this season. It looks like you got some training in during the summer."

If she only knew.

"Yes mam, a little bit."

"Ok. Listen up," coach says as the team gathers around her. "No practice this weekend. Next practice will be after school on Monday."

The soccer team hoots and hollers with a few sarcastic "boos" about no practice on Saturday. Mama and I jump in the van and head home to where my dad should have just gotten there after a late day at the office. I look over at the bleachers one more time not knowing why my Aunt Bess and Uncle Jake didn't show up for my game. It is the first one that I can recall them missing.

"Mama it isn't like them to miss a game."

"I know baby."

"You talked to them and they said that they would be there, right?"

"I did, but maybe they had car trouble or something came up. I tried Aunt Bess's cell phone, but you know they can barely figure out how to turn it on."

"Did you leave a message?"

"Yes, baby, stop worrying. I am positive they are fine."

I reach up and feel for my tiger necklace under my soccer uniform jersey. It is still there. Mama continues the ten minute drive to the house. We reach the turn for our driveway. Mama pulls the mini-van into the driveway and I don't see my dad's car, so he is not home from work yet. The mini-van barely rolls to a stop. I jump out and start running across our yard to Aunt Bess's and Uncle Jake's house about one hundred yards away. Uncle Jake's pick-up truck is parked in front of their house.

"LILY!" my mama screams, but I only run faster.

My legs begin to burn as I sprint faster than I ever have. I feel like I can't get any air in to my lungs. I can swear that I hear Jax barking as I get nearer to their house. How did he get out of our yard? I think he is at their back door. I reach the front door on their house and try the door knob. It is locked. I run around to the back door. I turn the corner to find Jax on the back porch, now howling madly.

"It is ok Jax, I am here," I say almost out of breath.

I can see that the screen on the screen door is ripped. The back door is opened about a foot. The glass just above the door knob is shattered. I run into the kitchen and grab my tiger necklace giving it a yank and throw the crystal in front of me. In a flash, Panthera appears and immediately runs upstairs like she was shot out of a cannon to the second floor. I reach the top of the steps and turn left toward my Aunt and Uncle's bedroom. Panthera is sitting in the doorway. She looks at me and lets out a deafening roar. I approach slowly. I step up behind Panthera and look in to the bedroom. I can see my Uncle's tan and brown cowboy boots on his feet sticking out just past their closet lying next to their bed on the floor. They are saturated with dark red blood. My Aunt's bare legs are protruding just past the other side of the bed, on the blood soaked green carpet. I drop to my knees next to Panthera and hug her neck as I begin to cry.

"LILY!" my mama screams as she enters the house through the back door.

"I'm sorry Panthera, but you have to go."

She looks at me with her glacier blue eyes and I can swear I see a tear drop.

"Don't worry Panthera. It's not over..."

CHAPTER XXXII

"It is nice to see you again Lily," says Princess Ellora as we sit inside what must be the dining area of her castle. Simple wooden table about twenty feet long. It appears to be made from logs. The top of the table is as smooth as glass and flat. I can see my reflection. The underside is still curved like trees, but the bark has been removed. I don't know what kind of trees they were from, but appear fairly dark. There are twenty chairs surrounding the table. They look like they have been cut from the same trees. All of them with high backs and wooden arm rest. Two of the chairs are at the ends of the table. Nine are across from me and there are eight more on the side that I am sitting on plus mine. I can see four large stained glass windows in front of me and four more behind me. They appear to have multiple tigers depicted on each window. The windows are about six feet tall with an arch at the top. The floor is made from gray and white marble squares about two foot by two foot each. I see one doorway to my left and another doorway to my right. To my front and between the windows is an archway and a set of steps leading down to somewhere. There is a large unlit marble fireplace in the middle of the wall behind me. Above the mantle is a relief sculpture depicting many tigers following Kalkita and Kasara into battle. I stop looking around and stare at one of the windows that doesn't contain any tigers. They seem to be more illuminated by the oil lamps on the table.

"They are my parents. I had the window made from one of their portraits," says Princes Ellora.

"I am sorry. I didn't mean to stare." Kasara looks radiant.

"It is ok," she says in her ever comforting voice.

"They are beautiful. Your father looks like a true warrior sitting on that white horse. Your mother appears to relish being by his side."

"She never would have left him Lily if things didn't turn out the way that they did. They would have been together forever. I would like to think that they are now, somewhere, in the heavens maybe."

Princess Ellora walks over to the table from the window and sits down across from me. I thought she would be at the head of the table, but doesn't seem to care about projecting herself in a some kind of noble way.

She is as beautiful as ever. Maybe the most beautiful woman that I have ever seen. She is still wearing a red and gold sari. Her hair still seems to match the color of her skin. Her eyes are the color of the submerged part of an iceberg. A group of red and gold butterflies float around the dining room. Garutte is sitting to her left, however, his massive stature seems to make the sitting down part challenging for him. His wings are folded back behind him. His arms are resting on the table. Kalio is sitting on the floor next to me. He seems to be relaxed, but on guard at the same time. I watch his ears twitch back and forth listening for any dangers. His nose is actively sniffing the air while his black tail sways just a little. There is a blue dwarf sitting to Princess Ellora's right side. She spots me staring once again.

"He is called Zerksaba. He once controlled all the powers of the waters and oceans until King Shivalla got the advantage over us," Princess Ellora explains.

"It is nice to meet you Zerksaba," I say as I lean over the wide table to shake his hand. He stands up on the chair and leans toward me extending his small hand. It feels cool and moist.

"It is a pleasure to meet you too Lily."

We sit back down. The gold necklaces around Zerksaba's neck bang off of the edge of the table making a clanging sound. He adjust them and goes back to eating, his chin barely higher than the table.

"Is this everyone Princess? Isn't there more of your people?"

"Yes there are more. Our people are spread out watching for anything that King Shivalla's forces might do."

"When will the fighting stop? Am I traveling back in time each time I see you?"

"Lily, it is a never ending battle for balance. When one side gets the advantage the other comes back and fights harder. We would hope for an everlasting peace, but it doesn't seem to work out that way. There is usually one person, or a small group of people, who don't want peace; therefore, the fighting always continues. No you aren't going back in time. Time is continuous. You just have a gift to parallel in to different time periods as though it is happening in your present day."

"I see. I still don't understand why I was chosen. Why am I the one? People died at the clinics and I could not save them. I could not save my dad's aunt and uncle."

"It is like Brandon told you. Sometimes you have to wait for the bad things to happen before you can do good. You have been picked by all of the gods. You will get stronger. Your intuitions will get better. You will not be defeated. You are the one who will lead us to final victory over the ways of King Shivalla and the likes of him."

"I feel like the people that died were sacrificed because I could not help them..."

"Just the opposite Lily. It is because of your dad's aunt and uncle that you will find the man that you are looking for. When that time comes, you will be more prepared than ever before. Panthera will show you the way."

"Thank you Princess Ellora," I say as she stands up and comes around to my side of the table and sits down beside me. She takes both of my hands in hers. For the first time, I really stare into her eyes. They sparkle just for a split second as if plugged in to an electric outlet and then someone turns off the power. I get the feeling that I have seen them before and shake off that possibility. Princess Ellora's eyes depart from mine and focus in on the tiger crystal head dangling from my neck. I reach up and grasp the crystal between two fingers of my left hand. Princess Ellora shivers for a moment. Kalio lets out a soft moan. I don't know why, but I drop the crystal beneath my shirt and out of sight. Our eyes lock once more.

"Shouldn't I come to you; I mean you are a princess?"

"No Lily. I am not that kind of princess. We are all equal. And one more thing Lily, like Atmaja told you, wear your sari for special occasions. You will know when."

"Lily...Lily...Lily," I hear my mother calling my name as Princess Ellora's soothing voice fades away. "It is time to get ready for the funeral. Are you awake yet?" she says as she knocks softly on my bedroom door.

The funeral was peaceful. I haven't been to that many and never like going to begin with. It usually means that someone I cared for deeply has left me. Ally, Carilyn, and Doc Nick came down. Some other relatives that I haven't seen in years came. Doctor Lacefield and his wife Janelle, along with Miss Shay and Wayland from the hospital also came. Annabelle, the paramedic from the crash just before we left for India, showed up with Taylor from Rescue 5. I did not ask any questions, but they look like a couple now. Our neighbor, Darbie, the one who works at the comm center, came. Even Fire Chief Edmonds was there, but thankfully he didn't say "sheeeet" one time. Folks from the Eufaula Pilgrimage paid their respects. My friends from the soccer team and school were there, among others. I wish Brandon could have made it, but I know he just finished his first week of school back in London. I told him not to spend all that money and miss classes. He said he understood. We still keep in touch daily on the web and I can't wait until I can see him again in person.

After the funeral we returned home. I told Ally that I would see her in a little while then I convinced my parents that I needed some alone time. They were terrified to leave me out of their sight, but I managed to convince them that I wouldn't be gone long. I went out behind our house and headed in to the thick woods. It is an area I know well having played there all the time since living in Eufaula. I kept walking for several hundred yards until I reached a small open grassy area. It is just big enough to let a few rays of the sun shine through. I reached up and grabbed the tiger crystal from my neck and tossed it out in front of me. Panthera instantly appeared. She walked up to me and bowed her head down as if to pay respects to me. I reached out and put my hand on her head and rubbed gently. She lowered herself down to the ground and I followed lying down next to her with my back against her soft fur. It began to drizzle. A sun shower. Beautiful rays and cold drops of water. How appropriate, I thought. Panthera kept watch while we lay there together for hours.

CHAPTER XXXIII

ONE YEAR LATER

I head toward the exit walking past the Mini Cooper with the British flag painted on the roof. It is one of the old models, not the new modern style, but neat looking none the less. Mostly red with a couple of white racing stripes down the hood, or as they say here in England, bonnet. I'm still learning the local lingo after arriving only a week ago. I exit Cool Britain with my shopping bag full of souvenirs and turn left on Coventry Street. The shop is impressive. I don't know if there is an American souvenir shop with the U.S. flag plastered on to just about anything you can think of. Maybe in New York. Who knows? Cool Britain takes it to another level. I didn't go too crazy and just picked up some coffee mugs, t-shirts, and a tea set for my mum.

I join the crowd of tourists on the sidewalk and walk only for a minute before stopping to take a picture of the group of black horses jumping out of a fountain. At least it looks like they are trying to. Pretty cool. I make a note to myself to remember to research who designed the fountain. Piccadilly Circus comes in to full view and I keep to the left of the busy roundabout. The sights and sounds are kind of crazy. Billboards stacked on top of each other running up the sides of buildings advertising everything from beverages to electronics to current stage plays here in the West End section of London.

I stop for a few minutes and take some pictures of Eros, the statue of love. There are a few couples sitting on the steps surrounding the statue, but for the most part, the tourists keep walking heading off to the next spot on their sightseeing map. I begin walking again and take a left on to Regent Street. I see a red and white sign sticking out from one of the buildings advertising Aberdeen Steak Houses. I casually glance at the posted menu as I walk by. My stomach rumbles a little. Just past the steak house is a blue neon sign running vertical down the front of a building announcing the play *Mama Mia* is performing inside. I make a special note to check it out when I can. The twentieth London black cab passes by me since I turned on to Regent. They're kind of neat and remind me of a car from the 1940's. The roof of the cab continues all the way to the rear like a small van. There isn't any trunk, or boot, as they call it here. When I rode in one the other day, I sat in the rear seat with my back against the back of the taxi. There wasn't any other seats in front of me. Instead, the whole section of the floor by my feet was open, so that you can come in through the side door and just toss your luggage on the floor right in front of you. The driver was separated from the passenger area by a large clear Plexiglas divider and I spoke to him through an intercom system. Less muggings I suppose with that arrangement.

I continue down the hill for several more blocks until I see the street that I am looking for. I cross Regent and turn right on to Charles II Street. More buildings stuck together, but less traffic than on the backed-up Regent Street. I go straight until the green trees of St. James square come in to view. When I reach the tiny park, I keep left and follow St. James around eventually coming to Pall Mall and then turn right. I walk until I see my next street, Marlborough Road. Judging by the street names, I am expecting a cowboy wearing a blue jean jacket and tan Stetson, to come riding around the corner on a horse any minute now. I laugh to myself over that thought, turn left, and continue for several blocks. Finally the Mall comes in to view, the huge flag lined street that leads away from Buckingham Palace. I have seen it on TV before during the last royal wedding, but to be standing on the sidewalk watching the colorful flags of the Empire blow in the wind, is impressive.

I stop for a minute, pull out my camera again, and snap some pics up and down the street in both directions. There are cars on it now, but it gets shut down for all the major Royal events when needed. It feels about as wide as a six lane highway. A large patch of grass separates the wide sidewalk from the almost brown looking roadway. There must be at least one hundred white flag poles with blue bottoms lining both sides of the street.

I can see Buckingham Palace to my right and head that way. The palace looks majestic and the House of Windsor flag is flying high above the roof telling me that the Queen is home. My guide book calls it the royal standard to be more accurate, I guess. I travel the couple of hundred yards and finally reach the gold gilded gates and peek through.

There are two guards standing in front of their little shacks that kind of remind me of human cuckoo clocks. They have on the usual red coats and bushy black hats that defy gravity. I don't know how they don't fall off their heads or how the whole soldier just doesn't tip over. I smile and snap some pics. No response from their stone faces. At least last year Ally and I got a smile from the Italian Carabinieri. Oh well. I ponder for a few seconds as to what the Queen might be doing and then begin to wonder how much one of these gates actually cost? Oh well, they are beyond my salary which is nothing.

I turn back behind me and snap some pictures of a Queen Victoria monument. It is pretty impressive sitting high up on a giant kind of birthday cake structure made from concrete. The statue is trimmed with more gold. Flocks of tourists pose on the steps of the monument trying to get the best photo possible. The sky is still blue this late in the day and if they aim their cameras right, they can get the top of the London Eye, the giant wheel looking thing with the glass pods hanging off of it, in the back ground of the picture. I glance at my tourist map again and make a right as I face the statue with the palace behind me.

I cross through the traffic and head down Spur Road with Saint James Park on my left. I check out the pond with the light green weeping willow trees almost dipping their branches in to the water. I reach the edge of the park and turn left on to Birdcage looking for a hotdog stand. I see the little brown structure about thirty yards in front of me. I reach the stand and take in the aroma of the freshly cooking food and my stomach twitches again. I nod to the girl serving the single customer and she smiles back at me. I walk around the stand to the right and spot the redwood picnic table that I am looking for.

"Hey y'all. That's quite the hike."

"Lily baby, you made it," says Ally as she stands up from the table and gives me a hug.

"Kenneth, did you get Lily's order?"

"Yes Ally pumpkin," he says as he points to the white paper bag on the table. "Two small hotdogs with ketchup and mustard, no onions, extra nitrites."

"You almost remembered. Regular nitrites. Thank you," I say as I give Kenneth a big hug.

"Yes, it was Brandon who ordered the extra onions and extra nitrites only," Kenneth adds with a laugh.

"Very funny Ken," Brandon says as he keeps chewing his mouthful of hotdog while standing up, walking around the picnic table and throwing his arms around me.

"Hi baby," he says as I squeeze him as tight as I can.

"Hello darling."

"Wow, did you miss me or what?" he says trying to catch the air I squeezed out of him. "I like the new look."

"Yes I did and thank you, I needed an update."

"It's only been since this morning," he says as I release my grip, kiss his mustard covered lips, and sit down at the table with everybody.

"I know. Call me crazy, but that's what you do to me."

"Ok. Love birds...," Ally says. "Eat your food before it gets much colder.

"Thank you."

"Any problems walking down from Brandon's Bloomsbury apartment?" asks Kenneth.

"None at all. It is cool to live so close to UCL. I stopped at Cool Britain for some souvenirs to send back home."

"Yeah, I can tell by the bag. Are your parents still freaking out about living with Brandon while you study art in London?"

"No Kenneth. Not anymore. I think they are actually ok with it now. They know I am in good hands and that all my friends are here with me."

"That's good to know," says Kenneth.

"So, anyway, my hacker buddy at the college was able to track down you know who from that side profile picture of his face that Ally took of him on your Paris flight," says Brandon.

"That's confirmed?" I ask as I watch the birds on the other side of the black metal fence hoping for some hotdog handouts.

"Yes. My bud was able to hack in to all the airport security cameras at the security check points." Brandon keeps chewing and pretending to be a tourist like the rest of us. "He got a match on a flight coming out of Canada to Geneva about a month after that incident last year at your home in Alabama.

I nod and continue watching the little black bird with the red beak and yellow feet. I break off a piece of my hotdog bun and toss it to him or her.

"Where did he go from there Brandon?" asks Ally.

"Well, my buddy kept using his program and didn't get a hit until seven months later."

"Where was that?" I ask as I look back at Brandon.

"Germany."

"Did he fly in to Heathrow?" asks Kenneth.

"No. It turns out he took a ferry from France to Dover two days ago," explains Brandon. "Got a hit on another security camera boarding the boat."

"What was he doing all the time that he was off of the radar?"

"Don't know Ken. Maybe some side jobs to supplement his income."

"Where is he now?"

"Lily, he is in a hotel in Bayswater."

"Where is that?"

"On the other side of Hyde Park near Kensington palace."

"It is a good thing that I still feel like sightseeing then," I say as I toss the last of my nitrite filled hotdog to an unsuspecting pigeon. Poor guy, or gal. Can't tell.

"Brandon, how did your hacker pal find the hotel?" asks Ally.

"Our frequent flier guy slipped up and used the same passport at the hotel as he did to board the flight in Geneva."

"Do you have a room number?"

"Better than that. We have a room number and my bud made an electronic hotel key that will open up his door. It is one of those credit card looking things. Just stick it in the slot and wait for the green light."

"Wow. That's good stuff Brandon."

"I know Ally. The bad guy is good, but even though he went to that makeup school by Pittsburgh, under the assumed name of course, he still forgot to put on a fake nose. It would have changed the profile of his face and we may never have tracked him down."

"Ok then. I guess I have some more sights to see," I say as I wipe some ketchup, mustard, and nitrites from my lips. "Ally, will you hang on to my souvenirs for me?"

"Absolutely. Are you sure you don't want us to join you?"

"No Ally, I have to do this by myself, sort of."

"Brandon," I say as I stand up and meet him at the edge of the table. "Thank you so much."

We wrap our arms around one another and kiss again.

"Are you sure?"

"Yes baby. A year of on-line kalarippayat video lessons taught by you, and my— you-know-what; I think I will be fine."

"Ok. I love you," he says as he slides the hotel credit card key, a tube pass, and directions in to my back pocket.

"I love you too."

"Come here Lily," says Ally as we hug and she kisses my forehead. "We will meet you at Royal Albert Hall in two hours, if you aren't there, then we are coming to find you."

"Gotcha. That's in Kensington, right?"

"Yes, by Hyde Park before you enter it. Kensington Road. Can't miss it. The round looking place."

"Ok Kenneth," I reply as he gives me another hug.

"All right everyone," I say in my best British accent. "It is time to crack on." They laugh and smile at my humor.

I wave bye to the birds and head out past the hotdog stand making a left and continuing through Saint James park. I admire the green well-kept grass, the trees, and all the runners exercising. Seems like there are an extraordinary amount of joggers in this city. It must be a good half mile before I reach the corner of the park. I reach a sign that says Storey's Gate. I look over the map of the park mounted on the two posts and confirm my location. Yep all the buildings on my right and grass and trees on my left. I'm going the right way. I leave Saint James and head slightly right crossing Horse Guards Road on my left and continue on to Saint George Street. I can see Big Ben, the giant clock on the tower, straight up ahead. I keep walking surrounded by buildings on both sides of the street. Not real tall, but enough concrete and glass to give a boring view of just buildings, and oh, traffic. Mostly six or seven floors high, at least it seems that way. Must be the same architect, because they all look identical to me.

I finally reach Westminster Bridge. I snap some pictures of Big Ben and across the river, take some of the London Eye. Both impressive in their own way. Big Ben because of its age and the Eye because of its size which must be over two hundred feet above the ground at the top. I must look like an ant down here to those people in the wheel right now. I walk on to the bridge and peek to my left and my right to check out the Thames River. Kind of neat to see all the big passenger boats hauling tourists up and down the waterway. I think a river cruise would be in order in the near future. I can make out a World War II ship docked to my left that I think is a museum with tours now.

I look back over my right shoulder and check out Big Ben from the bridge. It looks cooler because I can see all of the Parliament building now. Huge, running down the edge of the Thames. Pretty old too, judging by the looks of it. Definitely gothic looking. I reach the middle of the bridge and stop to take a picture of Big Ben and Parliament. I then turn left and snap one of the London Eye from the side.

"Sorry! Sorry! Parden me! I was looking at the river."

I am barely able to keep from dropping my camera as a female jogger about knocks me over. She grabs onto my right shoulder and keeps me from falling down. She looks to be around my age, or maybe a year younger, with chestnut colored hair pulled into a tight long French braided pony tail hanging around the front of her left shoulder. The end is tied with a small pink ribbon. She speaks with a heavy proper British accent.

"No. It was probably my fault. I shouldn't have stopped on the bridge," I say hoping for some forgiveness.

"American?" she asks.

"Yes. Sightseeing."

"Have you checked out the Tower of London yet?"

"No."

"Well, you have to go. Take the tube to Tower Bridge. You can't miss it," she says a little out of breath as she begins to jog in place. "It is where they put all the nobles to death. You might even get to see the crown jewels."

"Thanks. I will."

The jogger continues past me heading toward where I just came from. I decide to head down the steps in front of me toward the Eye. Very cool. The guide book says it takes about thirty minutes to do a rotation. Must be excellent views from the top of the wheel. I reach a building to the right of the wheel and read over a sign that says this is where you buy the tickets and for like an extra ten pounds, you can jump to the front of the line to board the wheel. I have to remember that. I turn right walking away from the London Eye and go straight eventually crossing Belvedere. I stop for a second, look behind me, and snap a pic of the giant wheel. I take a left on to York Road and keep walking.

After another two blocks I see the round red and blue Underground sign for Waterloo station. Also, called the subway, but known here mostly as "The Tube." This is my ride to Westminster. I pull out my Underground pass and head in to the station. I make my way to the escalator and begin my decent. I reach the bottom, turn right, and descend again on another escalator. Holy crap! I must be friggin two hundred feet underground. They definitely named it correctly. Ok, I need the Jubilee, gray line. I jump onboard and enjoy the ride back to Piccadilly. I change trains and cross back over, well under, the Thames on the blue Piccadilly line. I count down my stops and get off at Gloucester. I think only about twenty minutes passes since I left the London Eye. Should be confusing enough for anyone watching this hapless tourist.

Once I reach the street surface, I pull out my idiot tourist map. I get a few looks, but nothing major. Yep, keep walking, just another sightseer. I pick up my pace a little and head up Gloucester Road about eight blocks. All the buildings look the same to me, white or brown concrete or brick. Mostly residences, I think, but I pass by one pharmacy. I turn left on to Kensington Road like my directions say. I make a note for later, so that I can get to Royal Albert Hall. I glance at Hyde Park to my right, but it isn't the entrance I am using, so I keep going down to the corner and turn right up Palace Ave. I keep on the right side of the street. The elongated brown-red brick Kensington Palace comes in to view. Very cool to see where Charles and Diana used to live together when they were married. I stop and take a picture through the iron bars of the fence and under the shade of the trees in front of the palace. I can even make out one of those Smart cars parked near the car port. It's nice to know they care about gas economy and the environment. I wonder if Prince Charles is driving it. Maybe it belongs to Harry. I take a right in to Hyde Park and keep walking maybe fifty yards and snap a picture of the side of the palace with the black and gold gates in the foreground. I love the gold decor. Nothing like it in America . I keep going after that thought and turn left on to the Broad Walk, a nice wide paved pedestrian road through Hyde Park.

Another white statue catches my eye even though I don't have time for much more sightseeing today. I stop for just a minute directly behind Kensington Palace and admire the sculpture. I am a hapless sightseer after all. Beautiful, white, wearing both a crown, and, according to the black plaque, a coronation robe. She is holding a short staff in her right hand and some sort of scroll in her left hand. Queen Victoria never looked more picturesque. It says it was presented to her after fifty years on the throne by her daughter Princess Louise, the designer of the sculpture. A couple of more pics and this stupid tourist continues on. I snap a few of the palace and palace gardens, well as much of them that I can see from the Walk, and keep going toward Bayswater. I pass by some park benches that actually have a place to park and lock your bicycle next to them. That would be good for Alabama.

As I get nearer to the other side of Broad Walk, I see a sign for the Princess Diana memorial. I wish I had time today, but will come back again to pay my respects. I see the exit up ahead and keep walking even faster now seeing as I am on a schedule. I pass by the last set of hedges, exit Hyde Park, and turn right on to Bayswater Road. The traffic is heavy. I pass by the Queensway tube entrance and the one millionth red double-decker bus passes by me followed by the ten thousandth black cab intermingled with the occasional regular car. I keep walking down the right side of Bayswater. The tall hedges from the park stay to my right and buildings and businesses stay to my left on the other side of the road. I eventually see a gas station, I mean petro as Kenneth says, and look for a place to cross over to the other side of the road.

I spot the next crosswalk and stop and wait for the four lanes of traffic to come to a halt before I cross. I look down and read the message written in white paint on the asphalt "LOOK RIGHT" before crossing. I do as I am told and look right and cross half of the road and then look left. I'll never get used to the traffic driving on the opposite side of the road in England. I wonder how many distracted tourists were hit by giant red buses before they started painting instructions on the road itself?

On the other side of Bayswater Road, I continue with Hyde Park still off to my right and more businesses and buildings off to my left. I pass by a smaller souvenir shop on the corner to my left. I remember my directions telling me that I only have another block or two before I find the street that I am looking for. I walk for another block and see the sign for Leinster Terrace. That's the street. I approach the corner, cross the one-way road with traffic coming out of Leinster and turning on to Bayswater, and begin walking up the other side of Leinster. I can make out the hotel that I am looking for further up the narrow street. I pass by a few shops off to my left. A deli, or supermarket, of some kind. Larger buildings are on my right. Maybe more apartments or offices. I keep walking a bit slower now. The smell of what I think are fish and chips catches my nose. I look over to the other side of the road and spot a kabob shop with the meat slowly turning upright on a rack in a display window. I conclude that they sell fish and chips too. Smells delicious.

The glass door to the kabob shop opens and out comes a man carrying a white take-away container. Dinner to go I guess. Oh crap. My heart races. I look closer. It has to be Mr. Handsome. I know it is. Same build and height. He is wearing brown pants with a white button down shirt. His hair is colored blond and he has on gold trimmed aviator style sunglasses. I stop and face the other way hoping he did not see me. What do I do? Did he see me? I walk back down the street from the direction that I came from. Come on Lily, you are just a dumb tourist. Think. Think. I reach the corner of Bayswater and stop. I pull out my tourist guide. I hope I look lost.

Several minutes pass by. I cautiously turn around still holding my guide book. There is no sign of him. I start breathing again. I put the book away and start walking back up Leinster again. I pass by the kabob shop. The full size of the hotel comes in to view. White and massive looking. Not very tall, six or seven floors maybe, judging by the windows on the outside, but the building itself looks like it runs continuous for a whole city block. I pass by the first couple sets of stairs until I find the main entrance with the word hotel written above it in black square letters. I cross the single lane street and head up the three concrete steps leading to the entrance door. I open the door and enter the hotel doing my best to look like a guest. I look to my left to see a small light brown wood trimmed lounge area. There are small tables and a few comfortable looking chairs. Some people are hanging out after a day of sightseeing, I guess. At the end of the lounge is a small bar. A few more people are ordering drinks. It looks like quite the variety on display behind the bartender reflecting on the racks with the mirror behind it. I look hard to my left and out on to Leinster through the large dark tinted windows. I don't see anything unusual like lookouts for Mr. Handsome.

The front desk is directly in front of me. I smile at the girl behind the counter and veer off to the right toward the elevator. She smiles back at me and doesn't ask me any questions. I hope she thinks I checked in with the day shift staff. I press the button and wait nervously for what seems like five minutes, but I am sure is only a minute and the elevator door opens. I get in and wait for the door to shut. I take a deep breath and exhale slowly. I push the button for the fifth floor. I can swear that I smell fish and chips.

As the elevator begins to rise, I reach up and rip the red, black, and white A.C. Milan hat off of my head. I take off the long black wig. I drop the tan backpack to the floor, open it, and pull out my crimson single strap pack and open that one. I stuff the hat, wig, and other backpack into it. I take off my overly large white framed sunglasses and drop them in to the pack. I check the floors. Ok, passing third. I remove the somewhat too large silicone prosthetic nose from my face and rub off the spirit gum dropping the nose into the pack. I peel off the dark mole next to the right side of my mouth and also drop it into the pack. I leave on the extra thick black Cleopatra like eyeliner extending outward from the corners of my eyes. I pull off Brandon's blue polo shirt with the British flag on the chest that I borrowed from Brandon. I hurriedly unzip the sides of my warm-up pants and remove them stuffing them into my pack. I zip it shut and throw my arm through the single strap and lift the pack on to my back with the strap resting across my right shoulder. I make sure the bottom of the black and gold sari falls all the way down to my feet. I adjust my black choli and put on the last piece across my left shoulder and pin it by my right hip with the the small tiger pin. I reach into the outside pocket of the pack and take out the gold band and slide it on to my forehead and push the ends of it under my hair. The gold tiger face on the band feels centered. The elevator beeps at the fifth floor. I look up to see the red number five lit up above the doors as they open. I glance at the permanent black henna tattoo on my left wrist and remember what it means. I had it done to honor Uncle Jake and Aunt Bess, and I will follow my calling.

I take a deep breath, run my hands through my hair one last time letting it hang down, and exit the elevator. I look left and right and don't see anyone. I reach up and touch the tiger crystal hanging on my chest under my choli. I go right and start looking at the room numbers. 508. 510. 512. 514. I see a small red and gold object hovering in front of the door for 514.

"Well hello their little butterfly," I say silently as it beats its wings faster as if to acknowledge my greeting.

That's the room I am looking for. I stop by the door and the smell of the fish and chips is stronger. I lower my pack off of my shoulder and set it on the floor next to the door. Slowly, I pull out the key card from the pack and quietly insert it in to the slot above the brass door handle. A tiny green light appears. I cautiously push the handle down.

Bam! The door opens violently. An arm reaches out and rips me in to the room throwing me on to the maroon carpeted floor. I knock over a chair with my left arm and come to rest next to a wood desk. I can see a pink backpack lying on the floor next to me and wonder for a moment whose it might be? Not Mr. Handsome's colors. For some reason, I focus on the white monogrammed initials on the front of the pack in Old English script- a large J in the middle, an S before it, and a T after it. New girlfriend, maybe.

The door shuts. Mr. Handsome is standing in front of me. He sets my pack on the floor beside him. He is only wearing blue track pants with a white stripe down the outside of each leg and no shirt. I see scars across his chest that look like he has been shot several times in the past. My heart is skipping beats. He turns and locks the door with a dead bolt. Across his back are four dark pink grotesque looking scars running from his right shoulder to his left hip. The top scar looks infected and has fresh yellow-purple scabs on it in spots. He turns back around and faces me.

"Do you think I am stupid? I am the best. I know someone has been tracking me. I followed my picture with some idiot programmer's rookie attempts to find me." He approaches closer. I rise up on to my hands, but remain sitting. I turn to my left and can see the open container of half eaten fish and chips on the desk. Not real appetizing at this moment. He sees me looking at his scars.

"If bullets didn't stop me, what did you think a cat was going to do? No Lily I am alive and very well. You must explain that cat thing to me when you have time. However, I do like what you are wearing now. Did you dress up for me? Are you reliving your time in India with what's his name? Are you supposed to be a superhero now?"

"I don't know what you are talking about."

"No time for games Lily. We have to get to know each other. I have this room for another night. Who knows, you might even like me. Despite being rude to me at the airport in Paris. What are you now? Wait, you must be eighteen or nineteen right?" he says as he takes another step toward me.

"Don't make me puke!" I begin to stand up.

"Well then we have to do it the hard way then," he says as he reaches just inside the bathroom door to his left. He brings his arm back out holding about a twelve inch long shiny silver curved knife. "Where is your help now? I know you enrolled at UCL. I didn't think you were the artsy type. Where are your friends? I've come to London for all of you." He passes the knife back and forth in front of himself. Left hand to right. To left. This is getting bad.

"I have something for you, Sapphire."

He hesitates, caught off guard by the fact that I know his name, but he can't figure out how I know.

"Good. First name basis and a gift. How thoughtful."

"Yes, but it is in the front pouch of my sari tied around my waist. I need to stand up."

"So, stand up," he says as he walks the last two steps to me. I get to my feet and start to reach in my pouch.

"Wait. I will get it," he says.

I stay standing perfectly still not taking my eyes off of the knife. He stops in front of me. I can smell vinegar on his breath. He reaches in to the small black silk pouch.

"I don't feel anything."

"It's there." He keeps talking and for the first time I realize there is no French accent like in the airport. He isn't German either like Ludwik thought. He is American.

"Wait. I feel something small and round."

"That's it."

He pulls the item out of the pouch and stares at it with a look of disbelief on his face.

"I believe that belongs to you," I say as I look at his sapphire blue left eye as it begins to twitch. His pupils begin to dilate, filled with rage, I'm sure. "You dropped it in India."

"My brown contact lens. We'll do this the hard way you b..."

As fast as I can, I take one step back, jump straight up, and bring my left knee up in front of me. While in the air I bring my right leg up past my left and extend my foot out in front of me making contact just under Mr. Handsome's chin. There is a crunching sound as his jaw shatters. I continue the bicycle kick, flipping backward, and land on my feet. He falls back toward the door as he begins to raise the knife above his head. His eyes widen with rage. I reach up and break away my tiger crystal necklace and throw it at him. A flash of gray, black, and white fur flies past my eyes in a blur as Panthera comes to life.

"Say hello to my cat, Panthera, the best defense against a knife."

THE-END?

PRESENCE

The My Tiger's Eyes Series

Book 2

CHAPTER I

"Hey, listen to this," Kenneth says as I continue to clear the table next to him. "Store robbery in Swansea foiled. Goodwill bystanders able to apprehend would-be thieves, but left the scene before authorities arrived."

I continue to gather up the dishes from the last patrons.

"Brandon, weren't you and Lily in Swansea this past weekend on a mini holiday or something?"

"Lily, were we in Swansea last weekend?" Brandon asks playfully while sipping his chai.

"I don't think so." Subconsciously, I wipe the table faster with my worn out towel. "I thought it was Cardiff."

Ally laughs as Kenneth continues to read the newspaper.

"The thieves claim that they were held at bay by a giant white tiger while a small female tied them up. Authorities added that it appears the same as similar cases in London and other parts of England. They have seventeen other criminals locked up all claiming the same thing," Kenneth puts down the newspaper and looks at me. "When do I get to see that gift that you brought back from India two years ago?"

Brandon laughs while Ally interrupts.

"Now honey you know it isn't something that Lily can just whip on out here at the curry house," says Ally trying to soothe Kenneth's disappointment. "Lily, leave a bit of that paint on the table. You are almost down to the bare wood."

Ally chuckles at her own amusement. I stop wiping.

"Lily, when is your shift over?" asks Brandon.

"Well, your aunt said I am done in about fifteen minutes."

"Are you still going with that girl from your class after work?"

I take Brandon's empty cup and put it on my tray as I make my way to the beverage cart full of dirty dishes and then return to the table, remove my apron, and sit down next to him.

"We shouldn't be long."

"It is almost eight o'clock," he says with worried concern.

"We are just going to meet some friends at the library on the other side of the city and then we'll be right back," I reply trying to reassure Brandon. "I think it is at the Metropolitan University."

"I know where it is," says Kenneth. "They have a good art section."

"That's why we're going."

"When is your classmate coming?" asks Ally.

"Any time now."

Ally Stephano is my best friend from home. Well sort of. We grew up together, but she lives in Columbus, Georgia. Our fathers met while they were both physicians in the military. Her mama and my mama are best friends. Our families would vacation together over the years and visit each other as much as possible. Ally is now twenty, a year older than me. Her straight blonde hair is about shoulder length. She must be about a half inch taller than my five foot three inches, but athletic looking probably due to her pilates obsession. That and I think all she eats is cauliflower and broccoli which would keep anybody thin.

Ally and I have been through a lot together over the past two years. She was with me on a medical trip to India where we volunteered, along with our folks, at some clinics providing medical care in the jungles of Kerala. It is where I met Brandon and Ally met Kenneth. The four of us have been more or less inseparable since then.

Kenneth Hammersmith is about twenty two years old now. Appears to be around six foot three inches tall and, if I had to guess, weighs two hundred pounds. I think that is fourteen stone in English terms. He still works as a paramedic for the ambulance service in London and attends City College part time majoring in pre-medicine. When he is not working, or going to school, he competes in triathlons. I don't know where he finds the time to train.

Brandon Karup, pronounced ka-roop, is now twenty. It was instant attraction when we first met at his parent's house. The Karup's would host the volunteers from Doctors Helping the World at their home in Kerala, India. Brandon's raven black hair is longer now than the first time that I saw him. Straight, parted in the middle, and resting just on his upper back. He usually has it pulled back into a pony tail like the way he is wearing it tonight. His golden brown eyes are highlighted even more by his natural dark tan skin. Brandon is a couple of inches under six feet tall and maybe one hundred and seventy pounds. I still can't find any fat on him anywhere. He practices kalarippayat, an ancient Indian martial art, almost every day. His ripped chest muscles are poking through the top of his shirt as if trying to get out of the button down shirt that he is dressed in. Every day I wake up amazed to be his girlfriend. He suggested that I attend University College London, so that I could go to school with him and we would be together. It took some convincing, but my parents gave in on the condition that Ally would move to London with me. Brandon has one more year left of his civil engineering program with a minor in archeology.

As for Ally and I, we are both studying art history with the hopes of working in a museum somewhere in Europe. Despite the fact that our dads are physicians, and our mamas are nurses, we needed to get jobs to help support ourselves. I was lucky that Brandon's aunt and uncle were looking for extra help at their Indian restaurant, the Kerala Curry House, here in Soho. Ally was able to land a job at a book store near Piccadilly Circus.

What I mean when I said that Ally and I had been through a lot together, well actually the four of us, is that it was two years ago during the summer just before my senior year of high school when we faced some serious drama. People died. Kenneth was badly injured. Ally and I were running for our lives in India when the gift of Panthera, a magical white tiger, was bestowed upon me. I had been having visions of Panthera and of a princess named Ellora in my dreams. The dreams came true when it was needed the most. Panthera led the way and Brandon, Ally, and I were able to rescue the people in the clinics, our folks included. Panthera and I have been kind of helping out ever since then no matter where we are. This is what Kenneth is talking about in the newspaper. If I come across something bad that is happening, I summon Panthera and we help out the good guys.

"Hey, look who it is," says Ally as the door to the restaurant opens and Gemma walks in. "Over here."

Ally waves her arm in the air to get Gemma's attention. Gemma makes her way through the dwindling crowd of customers and reaches our table.

"Hi Gemma. I think you know everyone except Kenneth."

"Hello Kenneth," Gemma says as she extends her hand.

"Nice to meet you. I am Kenneth, Kenneth Hammersmith," he reply's as he stands up to shake her hand.

"Gemma, do you have time for something to eat before y'all two go to the library? asks Ally.

"I don't think so. I believe we are a few minutes behind schedule," she answers in proper English.

"I am trying to place your accent," Kenneth says. "Manchester?"

"No. I am from Epsom."

"Right. Nice to meet some good people from Surrey." Kenneth takes a drink of his tea. "I used to play a little tennis at the lawn and tennis club in Epsom," he says with an inquisitive tone in his voice.

"I know it well. My mum works at the hospital next door," Gemma says as if defending Kenneth's inquiry. "She is a nurse."

"That's good. You two better get going," Brandon interrupts before Kenneth asks anymore questions.

I get up from my seat and put on my girlish light blue motorcycle jacket that comes down just to my waist. It has extra pads in the shoulders and elbows in case I crash. Brandon stands up, hands me my white motorcycle helmet from the table, wraps his arms around me, and plants a quick kiss on my lips.

"I will see you at home after the restaurant closes."

"Ok Brandon. I love you."

"I love you too."

"Hey love birds, break it up. Lily and Gemma have to get going," Ally chimes in. "Bye Gemma. Nice to see you again."

"Good night. I will eat with you next time."

"Right, good night then," Kenneth says.

I sense Gemma's uneasiness and whisk her out of the curry shop. She is as pretty as ever. Her hair is black as the night cut pixie style with some straight fringe for bangs. Olive tan skin. Close to my height and very fit looking although I have never asked what kind of exercise program she follows. She focuses her big brown eyes on me as we reach our scooters.

"Kenneth is quite the fella, isn't he?" asks Gemma in a sarcastic tone as we put our helmets on.

I tug on the chin strap making it snug just under my jaw.

"He is like everyone's big brother," I offer.

I sling my tan backpack over my shoulders and get on my light pink colored Vespa 150. Not Brandon's first choice of colors, but I think it has grown on him. I pull on my black riding gloves and zip up the front of my jacket to my neck.

"I guess," Gemma says as she starts her gray colored Piaggio and adjusts her matching helmet. "All set?"

"Lead the way Gemma," I say as I lower my clear face shield and start the Vespa.

"Follow me," she replies.

Gemma pulls away from the curry shop and I follow just behind her and to the right side of the lane. I first met her this past summer while taking an optional art course at the college. We immediately hit it off and I consider her a good friend. There is something about her that intrigues me; mysterious yet inviting. I look at her features and complexion and think of someone maybe of Spanish decent. I have yet to meet her folks in Epsom. Soon she tells me, but I do find it curious that she doesn't mention her father much.

It's not long until we make our way on to the A40, also called Holburn Street. Gemma leading with myself in tow. We come to a stop at a traffic light near the Chancery Lane tube entrance, or the subway as we call it back in the states. I pull up next to Gemma.

"Hey look there," she says pointing off to a store on the right side of the road.

"What is it?"

"I think we have to stop there one of these days."

I look at the brown brick building on the corner intermingled with the other stores.

"You mean the Glamour House?"

"Yes, of course."

"Sounds delightful, but I might need to work a few more shifts at the restaurant. It looks expensive."

"Green light. Let's go."

Gemma takes off again. Our little scooter's motors whining a bit until we get up to speed. The sky is just about completely dark now. The moon and stars are obscured by some thick clouds, but I don't feel any rain yet. Maybe by morning. There is enough light shining on the road from all the shops and street lamps making it easy to see on the main streets since we only have the single headlight on the scooters.

The bridge over the A201 comes into view and we cross over it. I recognize the bridge since Brandon has taken me this way before. The street name changes to Newgate and I stay about ten feet behind Gemma as she buzzes along on her scooter. We reach the split at King Edward Street and keep to the left and then I follow Gemma to the right on to Angel Street. The name of the street changes to Cheapside which a find amusing due to the cost of living in London, especially for college students. We come to a stop at another traffic light.

"If you look off to the right as we pass by the next small street, actually, it's more like an alley, you can see Saint Paul's," says Gemma as she buttons the top button on her black denim jean jacket.

I feel a nip in the cool air as well and try to zip my jacket up a little more, but realize the zipper won't go any higher. I secretly wish for a scarf. This is what happens after the sun moves out and the night time air comes in when it is September in London.

"Thanks. I will look for it. Brandon and I have yet to get there," I holler as the light turns green and we rev up the scooters and start moving.

I spot the alley that Gemma was talking about and I am able to get a partial glance of the huge old cathedral as we pass by about one block away. The scooters keep buzzing down the road like two angry mosquitoes. The Gherkin comes into view off to my left. It is one of the most unique looking buildings in London. I would describe it as a giant egg shaped two-tone glass land mark. Brandon did actually take me there for dinner on the top floor back in the spring. It was exciting to be eating that high up with all the views of London for a backdrop. I did see Saint Paul's dome from up there.

Gemma makes her way around a few curves and after another minute, or so, we end up on Witechapel Road. I remember the school that we are looking for should be near here. There isn't any signs for Metropolitan University that I can see. Gemma said that she has been there several times, and because she is more of a local than me, she continues to lead. We go left on Commercial and then take a quick right on to Wentworth. I glance at a street sign to my left as we drive by and it says Thrawl. I wonder if that means thrill in American? We continue straight and I think I spot a sign saying Old Montague, but it isn't well lit, so I'm not sure. Gemma soon slows down and I see her scooter's little left amber turn signal come to life and I follow her on to Greatorex. There is less traffic with what looks like some brick apartment buildings on the right side of the street. She slows down and signals me with a wave to pull up next to her.

"It isn't much further. Just a few more turns."

"Ok Gemma. Got cold didn't it?"

"Yes it did."

She accelerates a bit faster and pulls away from me. I feel better being reassured that we will be in the library soon. I follow Gemma around a bend to the left. I can't make out any colleges around here, but then again the large buildings in London can usually be hiding the place that you are looking for and you turn the corner and viola; there it is. I can barely see the street name, but think it said Hanbury. Gemma slows and turns again after a couple of blocks and then turns quickly on to Princelet. We cruise down the street surrounded on both sides with what I think are four or five story buildings. I can make out some store fronts on the street level. We reach the end of the street and I stare at the brick side wall of a building in front of us. Dead end. Either right or left. Gemma makes a left turn. I follow trying to peek at the street sign attached to the building. It looks like Wilkes Street, but is more like an alleyway. It is very dark with no lights that I can see except from the scooter's headlights. The alley appears to be one way and I don't see any traffic. Gemma slows down only after about thirty feet, or so, and turns right between a couple of small black metal poles protruding out of the side walk about three feet high. She comes to a stop and turns off her scooter. I pull up next to her and turn off the Vespa's motor, but leave the key in the on position so that the headlamp stays lit up casting a focused smidge of light on Gemma and I as if it were a spotlight shining on two actors of a stage play. It looks like an even smaller alley, but for pedestrians since the poles are blocking the path of any car that would try to turn into the alley. It would have to be a really small car anyway considering the alley is only about six feet wide. I can only make out light at the opposite end of the alley from what looks like a major road with the occasional traffic passing by. There are several light poles in the alley, but apparently no one paid their electric bill, because none of them are lit up.

"Well, this is the place," Gemma says as she puts the scooter up on to its kick stand and takes off her helmet.

She climbs off of her scooter and I do the same. I unfasten my chin strap, remove my helmet, and set it on the scooter seat. I look around and can't see any signs of a library just a lot of brick in front of me and behind me. The buildings look to be four stories high. There is a single door in front of us.

"Is this the back door to the college I ask?" hesitantly.

"Not at all Miss Lily, but this *is* the place."

"I am confused Gemma."

"This is the place that everyone will be talking about when they mention Miss Lily Morgan," she says as I struggle to make out her eyes staring at me in the dark.

My night vision is usually better than this since I received my gift, but seems to be failing me now. I don't understand. I feel myself starting to tense up even though when capturing the robbers I was calm as can be.

"Welcome to Puma Court Lily."

"Ok."

"You don't get it yet, do you?"

"No."

"We met several years ago. Do you remember?" Gemma says speaking in a stern lower voice.

"Now I am really confused Gemma," I say as she takes a step toward me.

"Let me explain it to you then I am going to make you very famous."

"That's nice, but I think we should get going. Brandon will be home waiting for me by the time we get back."

"Brandon will have to get along by himself from now on." Gemma unbuttons her jean jacket. "We met on the bridge. I was jogging and bumped into you. Do you remember that? Westminster? Think Lily think!"

Her raised voice alarms me as I begin to recall the incident.

"You had long hair. It was a different color. Why are you doing this?"

"Don't you want to be famous? You are going to be part of the tour," she says in an almost evil tone causing me to shiver slightly.

"What tour?" I ask as I begin to step toward my scooter.

"Wait!" Gemma says angrily as she steps closer. "The tour. Jack the Ripper. You haven't been paying attention. Whitechapel. Hanbury. Buck's Row. Mitre Square. Miller's Court. Goulston Street. And now Puma Court. The site of Lily Morgan's demise!"

"Are you ok? Let me get you some help Gemma. You're ill."

"I am fine," she says while removing her jacket exposing the top of a curved knife hanging in a black leather sheath from beneath her left arm. "A modern day victim to be added to the outdated tour."

She pulls the knife from beneath her arm. Now I realize where I have seen that knife before. She starts to toss the knife back and forth between her left hand and right hand. The blade is shiny silver and must be ten inches long. I slowly reach up to the collar of my jacket and let the fingers of my right hand search for my necklace. I make contact with the strap and walk my fingers to the front of my chest grasping the tiger crystal with my fingers and prepare to break it away from my neck.

"By the looks of it, I think you are starting to recall my father."

Gemma stops tossing the knife and holds it out in front of her toward me. I take a step back trying to give myself some room to react.

"Your father was Sapphire, but we initially referred to him as Mr. Handsome after first meeting him."

Gemma responds angrily," my father had a name Lily!"

"Your father was a sick rogue mercenary!"

"His name was Lee Jensen and you killed him in that hotel last year. You even got his blood on my backpack!"

"Um, yeah, that wasn't me."

She continues, "He was mangled. I don't know how you did it. He was the best and taught me everything that I know."

"There are better people out there to learn from Gemma."

I step back again and Gemma comes closer. I am running out of room. I swear that I can see that she has two different color eyes. Like a deja vu moment. One brown and the other blue, sapphire blue. Can't be. I blame it on the darkness and poor lighting of this badly written tragedy.

"Then there was my mother."

"Was?"

"You killed her in India," she says as I tighten the grip on my tiger crystal.

"Wait, you don't mean Mrs. Hair, do you?" I ask politely. "That wasn't me either. I didn't kill your mum."

"What is with the nicknames Lily?" she asks as her English accent fades a little.

"Well, they never properly introduced themselves when they were holding people for ransom."

"I was here in England at boarding school when my parents went to India."

"To India to make money holding hostages for cash. I guess boarding school must have been expensive, but now I see where you get the black hair from, like your mother. I like your eyes too. From daddy?"

Gemma's nostrils flare over my commentating. I don't really want to see her get hurt, but maybe we can hold her at bay when I summon Panthera. It's my preferred method. Yep, tie her up and go make a phone call.

"My mother's name was Carmina and she was from Seville, Spain," she retorts while taking a deep breath.

This is getting bad.

"Gemma stop this!"

I grab the crystal and bring it out from under my jacket, but keep my hand closed around it. I can see her try to focus on the necklace looking perplexed.

"My name is not Gemma!" she says as she grips the knife even tighter. "It is Sabine. Sabine Tatiana Jensen."

She steps toward me again. I quickly jump back and break the tiger crystal necklace away from my neck and throw it at Sabine. The crystal hits her chest and falls to the ground. Sabine looks down at it as the crystal sparkles just a bit.

"What are you doing Lily? I don't want your jewelry. I am not here to rob you. I am here to take your life the way you took my parents."

Sabine lunges at me like a cobra launching after unsuspecting prey. There is no sign of Panthera. Something is really wrong. She should have come to life when I tossed the tiger crystal. My ferocious white tiger is nowhere to be seen. Suddenly my feet feel heavy as I try to move out of the way of Sabine's knife as it makes contact with my abdomen. Sabine continues to slide the knife over my stomach from the left side to the right. I hear my motorcycle jacket rip from the sharp blade. The pressure intensifies on my stomach. I expect to feel burning pain from being sliced open, but I don't. I look down as I grasp my belly with both hands feeling for blood, but there isn't any. I can't see any blood rushing to the concrete alleyway either. The knife made contact with my stomach. I know I felt it. My hands come to rest on my black and gold sari, the Indian garment common through out all of India. The knife didn't slice through it. Now I understand why Princess Ellora told me to wear it all the time. It did protect me, but I still don't know why there is no

Panthera. Sabine is confused as to why I am still standing and not bleeding all over the place like she had hoped for.

As the stars begin to appear in my vision, I struggle to reach for my jaw which feels like it just exploded. The back of my head is erupting like a volcano from where it hit the brick building behind me. I never saw Sabine's punch from her left hand, or right, connect with my face knocking me to the ground. I lay dazed trying to focus, but my eyesight is blurred. I can make out Sabine straddled over the top of me. Her arms appear raised and I figure that she must be raising the knife above her head to finish me off. The sari stopped the slicing knife attack; however, seeing how my magic isn't too reliable this evening, I don't want to take a chance on the stabbing kind of blow from the knife ripping through the sari.